# no net

adam byfield

*For Catherine,*
*for the creatures*
*and for Mary too.*

# broken man

The pub was always quiet. A combination of dark wood panelling and small windows made to saturate the whole place, from the hard worn carpet to heavy floating rafters, with a cosy daytime gloom. Four shafts of sun pinned the building in place as they streamed in through the windows, alive with silent, glittering dust.

Down the side of the bar, beyond the last golden column and away from the doors, a wizened old man sat and stared blankly. Occasionally he would take a sip from the dark pint on the table in front of him, licking his lips thoroughly each time. Behind the bar an overweight, middle aged man in a much stained t-shirt was propped on an elbow, yawning his way through a newspaper.

There had been many Tuesday afternoons when the old man and the barman had been the only people in the building but today was not one of them. Slumped in the shadows between two glaring windows was a woman wearing a crumpled white shirt under a fitted leather jacket. Dazed and vacant she swirled her whisky in its glass, watching the honey shades shift. Seconds stumbled by in the heavy lidded silence relieved only by an occasional rustling newspaper page or the smacking of old, bitter wet lips.

Suddenly the doors burst inward and a wave of ambient street sound crashed over the bar, splashing into all corners. A skinny man in a too large, shapeless coat bustled into the pub, eyes locked onto the phone in his left hand while the right fumbled blindly with the strap of his bag.

The barman blinked and straightened until the new man arrived at the bar and gradually untangled himself to produce a battered, brown leather wallet. After mumbles and nods a pint of lager appeared and the skinny man began sipping while still turning from the bar.

He squinted past the glorious dust light and made out the female figure in the gloom. Casting pointless glances left and right he crossed the pub and fell quickly into a chair across the table from the woman.

"You're fucking late," she said flatly, still whipping

the whisky with flicks of her wrist.

"Very well thank you, and how are you?" The man's voice was sharp and nasal, the sarcasm tired and practised.

"Oh piss off," replied the woman, finally raising the glass and emptying it in one go.

"What crawled up your arse?" said the man defensively then eyed the empty glass as it returned to the table. "On duty?" he asked with barbs.

"Nope," she replied. "My shift was supposed to finish last night but I actually finished an hour and half ago. Since then I've been waiting here for you instead of going home to bed."

"Alright!" mocked the man, fumbling a notebook and pen out of his bag. He thumbed through the pages until a blank one appeared then clicked his pen, sipped his pint and settled.

"So you've got him then?" he began.

"Looks like it," she nodded.

"You charged him yet?" he asked.

"Not yet but it all fits, prints, witnesses, no alibi. Pretty straightforward in the end."

"He's confessed then?" he asked, scribbling as he spoke.

"Not yet, still claiming his innocence," she said.

"Who's leading the interview?" he asked, keeping his eyes on her while he paused briefly to take a drink.

A few seconds of pen scratching passed and then the familiar thick silence oozed back in between them.

"Come on," he drawled.

"Christ! They'll know it's me!" she hissed, her irritation crackling.

"Of course they won't, there's any number of people I could get this from," he cooed.

"Yeah? Then why don't you?" she said, jutting her chin.

"Must be because I enjoy your company so much," he said. "But if you want to end our arrangement I don't suppose there's much I can do about it." He reached for his bag and pint and began to stand.

"OK!" she hissed, "OK, sit down. It's the D.I. alright? The fucking D.I.'s doing it."

"Bronam?" he asked.

"Yes," she said, fiddling with her empty glass.

"Well that's it then isn't it?" he asked, taking another drink.

Another pause.

"Well?" he asked again.

"I don't know," she finally said, sounding genuinely unsure.

"Oh come on," he said. "Bronam's a human lie detector, every nasty bastard in the city is terrified of him. He'll grind this one down like all the rest with that stare of his. The guy'll try one lie after another and Bronam will just shake his head at each one until he cracks and spills. The man's a machine!"

"Not any more," she said, her voice quieter then before.

"Really?" he said, shifting in his seat to lean in closer.

"About a month ago," she said quickly. "His wife left him, took the kids. He's not been the same since."

"How so?" he asked, scribbling, thinking and talking all at once.

"It's like he's not entirely there now, y'know? He seems unsure, as if he's lost that ability to spot a lie, as if it's just gone." She sounded sad.

"So you don't think Bronam will be able to break the guy then?" he asked.

"Maybe not," she said, shaking her head.

"Shit," he said and they both thought about it.

"Good time to play him at poker though eh?" he attempted to joke. She stared, cold and hard.

"Still," he went on thoughtfully, changing his tone back to business. "You've got him now so that's that. I suppose if he sticks to pleading innocent there'll be a bit more of a trial but who cares about that? Shame really."

"What do you mean?" she asked.

"Well you lot aren't usually quite so on the ball with these things are you? Usually we get a good few months of drama, speculation about connections between the victims, who'll be next and all that. And this one, what a calling card! What a brand!" he said excitedly.

"You fucking parasite," she sneered leaning away from the table to fold her arms in self righteous disgust.

"Oh come on," he said, not impressed by her attempt at morality. "A potential serial killer who breaks every bone in his victim's body with a hammer, one by one and you lot go and catch him within a fortnight after just two victims? We didn't even get chance to give him a nickname! What could we have called him do you think? 'Bonecrusher' is a bit on the nose, maybe 'The Hammer'?"

"Are we done," she said coldly.

"Fine," he said, laughing without smiling. "Here."

He tossed a long brown envelope onto the table so that it slid towards her. She scooped it up and into the inside of her jacket in one fluid motion before standing.

"See you soon," he said with a grin, raising his glass to toast her as she moved past him.

"Prick," she said then shook her head and left.

—        —
—

Detective Inspector Bronam opened his front door, stepped over the threshold and sighed into the silence. Everything in the hallway was just as it had been when he left the day before. The unopened post was sitting at exactly the same angle on the side table next to the phone. His winter coat hung undisturbed on the same peg while his running shoes were still side by side, the laces hanging just the same too.

The sameness and the stillness and the silence, he felt it crushing him before he'd even got the door closed. Memories assailed him as he hung up his coat and moved deeper into the house.

Until very recently he would have arrived home from a long shift to find everything different, everything moved, knocked or spilled. Nothing would be where he left it, nothing would be where it should be. The house would be trembling with screaming and shouting or with music and television and he would hate it, despise it, find it unbearable.

The sameness and the stillness and the silence though, they were so much worse.

Entering the kitchen his stomach rumbled and he decided to eat before changing. He retrieved a plastic tray of processed food from the fridge and placed it in the microwave before looking for a fork.

The plate, knife and fork he had used last time were sitting by the sink, the remnants of the meal now crusted solid about them. He opened a drawer and cupboard in vain, already knowing that everything else was also dirty. Hanging his head he added the plate and and the knife and the fork to their filthy brethren lurking within the dishwasher. Closing the door he peered at the buttons and tried to make sense of their symbols.

"Come on Ken," he muttered to himself. "How hard can it be?"

Hours upon hours of hard and stressful work sat on his brow and clouded his thoughts as he tried to urge the dishwasher into life. Somewhere in the background, distant and faint, the microwave proudly announced its work done.

Blinking and sighing then cursing and growling, he rubbed at his face in despair and left the dishwasher resolutely lifeless. For a moment he stood and cradled his face in his hands, thinking of the years gone before.

They'd married young and enjoyed the romance of a traditional marriage or at least he'd thought they had. He'd worked and provided and made all the decisions, she'd shopped and cleaned and made all the meals. The kids had come along and he'd been promoted, he'd thought she'd be proud and then suddenly, out of nowhere and after so many years, it wasn't enough. It wasn't enough and she'd gone, they'd all gone.

His shoulders fell and he sighed deeply before opening the dishwasher and slowly moving the contents to the sink. At first the water was too hot and bit at his fingers as he washed the plates but by the time he had finished the cutlery the water was tepid and cloudy.

As he began to dry the fruits of his labours the sky over the back garden dulled and darkened. Placing the final teaspoon into the drawer, he turned and noticed the microwave. The meal within had long since cooled and congealed to a rubbery brick. He found the fridge cooling nothing but air and a jar of old mayonnaise. He closed the fridge, ignored his stomach and threw in the the tea towel, heading for the stairs in defeat.

In his bedroom he stood by his closet, looking at himself in the mirror. He removed his clothes slowly, as if his joints were aching, and dragged on a t-shirt and sweatpants. More recent memories set about him now and he felt his face warming with red.

They all knew at work, he knew they knew, he could see it glittering in their eyes. It was two parts pity, one part contempt with a splash of bitter curiosity. His edge was gone, that's what they thought, his special ability faded to nothing, that's what they saw and believed. Today had been his final test, those hours in the interview room with the suspect had been his last chance to revive his standing and avoid being written off.

He'd failed of course. The lad would never willingly confess to those murders because the lad was innocent, he knew that with absolute certainty. No-one had said as much after the interview but they'd all blamed him for not securing a confession and he knew it.

They thought he'd lost it, the strange talent he'd had since childhood to spot a lie and call it out no matter how convincingly it had been delivered. The talent had made him a celebrity on the force and the stuff of legends among crooks and killers and of course that was the final humiliation in all of this. He had to pretend that he had lost it, to let them think that they were right. If only she hadn't left, none of this would ever have happened.

Padding back downstairs he tried to ignore the still the same hallway and opened the door under the stairs to the cellar. Descending the steep, narrow steps, shoulders slumped, he bowed his head clear of the low ceiling and crossed the damp concrete floor to his workbench.

For a moment he stood, running his fingers over his tools, remembering how wonderful the partial quiet of the cellar had seemed when it lay under muffled but relentless noise from above. Now that the silence was the same, upstairs and down, it no longer seemed special, just empty.

"I'm sorry," he said quietly, emotion choking him as his hand closed on a familiar rubber grip. "But I've had a really dreadful day."

He turned and strode into the shadows at the back of cellar.

"I know I said I'd go slowly," he said, reaching up into the darkness to find and grasp the pullswitch. A bare lightbulb glared angry, revealing a struggling figure strapped firmly to a wooden bench, wide eyed, gagged and bound.

"But I think I'm going to have to do a whole hand today," he said and raised the hammer.

# seeds

*This is ridiculous.*

Clutching his knees to his chest, his mantra was all but inaudible. He, a highly respected academic, leading light in his field, was hiding in a cubicle in the ladies' toilets of the university's monolithic science library.

The sound of a door silenced the professor in a heartbeat. Clenching every muscle he managed to shrink in on himself even more, eyes tight shut. Feminine chatter washed over and under the cubicle door however and the professor relaxed.

He allowed his head to make tentative contact with the cold wall behind him and his rattled mind to run back over the last couple of hours. A perfectly ordinary, overcast morning, same stop start drive to the car park, same cross campus walk to the office.

Rounding that final corner however, the sight of two serious looking men in suits waiting outside his office had stopped him dead. He had never seen them before but was instantly certain that he must not, under any circumstances, find himself in their company.

Striding away from the office, he had ducked into the library after catching sight of the two again over his shoulder. Checking his watch, the professor noted that an hour had passed and tried to convince himself that the pair would have given up. After all, he'd been there so long that various parts of him had become numb, except for his back which was starting to ache.

Not long after hurrying into the cubicle, it had occurred to the professor that while he knew he was hiding from two dangerous men, to anyone else he was simply lurking in the ladies' toilets, spying on female students.

It was vital he wait for just the right, quiet moment to leave unseen. Otherwise, he had thought with a sardonic smile, his career would be over and the two men would have no reason to chase him. The thought of his work caused his hand to slip into his jacket pocket. The texture of a small paper package within seemed to calm him.

After fifteen minutes in the toilets the professor had read almost all of the graffiti that surrounded him and frowned his disapproval. Another thirty minutes of utter boredom punctuated by occasional terror however and the professor added a slogan of his own.

Sitting back, he eyed the brief, cryptic question he had crammed between larger, gaudier pieces and seemed very pleased with himself. Sudden silence beyond the cubicle door tore him back and he, carefully, got to his feet. Resting his hand on the lock, the professor listened hard for any sound without. Hearing only his own heartbeat, he took a breath and opened the door.

The white tiles of the deserted toilets stared back at him blindly. Repeating the procedure, the professor made it out into an empty corridor before setting off at a pace calculated to be casual and allowing himself to breath again. He made his way to the ground floor through surroundings previously familiar, now tainted by the morning's events.

Swarms of students, rows of books, buildings named after dead men. Yesterday it had all appeared so solid, a warm little world, set apart, comfortable and safe. Now everything appeared hollow and faded. No habit nor tradition could protect him from this threat that had invaded his life.

Stepping out into the half hearted glare from the grey sky above, the professor nodded to some students who appeared to know him. Making his way through a thin crowd, he cast his gaze about as discretely as possible while at the same time trying to keep his head down.

He had just begun to relax and turn back towards his office when his eyes met another pair, cold and grey, belonging to the taller of his pursuers. In that instant the professor stood alone in the shadow of the library, the two grim looking men in suits ahead of him the only other people in the universe.

Another breath and the mingled sounds about him returned and he headed for the great stone steps that led down to the bottom end of campus. Desperate to see behind him but unwilling to look back, the professor quickened his pace, weaving through knots of students.

Fighting the panic welling up from his gut, he glanced around. Although no-one seemed to be paying attention, the professor made a theatrical show of looking at his watch before cursing under his breath and breaking into a restrained jog.

The top of the steps loomed ahead while a snatched glance behind revealed the men closing the gap. Despite turning heads now, the professor sped up, darting left and right to find ways through the crowd.

*This is ridiculous.*

He heard his own words as his heart drove pure panic into every fibre of his being. Exclamations from behind pushed him over the edge and as he started down first great flight, thoughts of status were instantly forgotten.

Leaping down the broad stone steps three at a time, the professor could feel a great weight of speed on his back threatening to topple him with each stride. Crashing past people now, he thought his apologies but ploughed on regardless.

Clattering footsteps from behind chased him on, down and down, faster and faster, throwing himself forward again and again. He gave no thought to where he was going, his only destination was away.

Landing awkwardly he leapt again but this time knew immediately he was going to fall. The young female student below him froze, confusion and amazement vying for facial dominance. For a moment he hung in the air, thinking how hard the edges of the steps must be.

Then they collided.

The instant they hit the steps he knew her arm was broken. He felt it give under his weight and the sensation churned his stomach. Then he was bouncing down the stairs, unforgiving angles biting at him viciously until he came to a sudden halt and his right temple met solid stone. There was an explosion of brilliant white behind his eyes and then thundering, thundering pain.

Opening his eyes, the professor found he was on his feet, swaying slightly and pressing his right palm into the sticky wet pain. It seemed strange to him that he didn't remember getting up. He looked back up the steps and was relieved to see a crowd of people around the fallen girl.

He was aware that it was important he be on his feet and yet, at that moment, he couldn't imagine why. The sight of two men pushing their way through the crowd towards him however, was ample reminder and he set off once more.

Finally reaching the bottom of the steps the professor tore towards the lecture theatre building. A hard left took him down a concrete ramp and out of sight of his pursuers. At the bottom he doubled back along the edge of a fountain and slipped into the canteen that sat snugly below the neatly stacked lecture theatres.

The place was deserted. Glancing at his wrist the professor frowned, noticing that his face was not the only one to have been cracked. Just like him however, his watch was still running despite the injury and it told him it was half past the hour.

He nodded, satisfied that this explained why his footsteps echoed as he approached the lift. Having pressed the button, the professor found that waiting made it harder for him to ignore his throbbing head. Footsteps behind came to his aid however, as he span round in horror, instantly focused on nothing else.

The student gave him a strange look before hurrying on. Puzzled by the young man's stare, the professor put his hand to his brow only for it to come away red. Hurriedly he took a clean white handkerchief from his pocket and pressed it to his temple, before tapping the lift's call button again irritably. He cursed his own arrogance. His orders had come as usual but the content had been unexpected. Remembering, he found his hand around the small paper package again.

He had always assumed that they would take his work away from him one day but he'd never thought they'd tell him to destroy it. His fingers traced tiny hard shapes through the smooth paper. The potential within those objects, he knew, was beyond imagination. No more hunger, poverty, a new age of man.

And yet his bravado at the time, his unwavering

certainty that he must do the right thing, now seemed naive to the point of idiocy. Finally the rumble of the lift interrupted but more footsteps cut through the welcome sound. Turning he found the two men standing, looking at him.

Dropping the now gory handkerchief, the professor bolted for the stairs, his pursuers close behind. Tearing up the staircase he flashed past floor to ceiling windows, catching sight of the great stone steps he had descended just minutes earlier.

That ordeal suddenly appeared a much preferred option. Descending steps three at a time was one thing, but climbing them three at time he reflected, fighting the urge to be sick, was something else entirely.

Reaching the top of another flight he paused, doubled over and panting. There were no more stairs. Gripping the guard rail with a shaky hand, the professor peered down into the great void around which the stairs snapped back and forth as they rose.

A hand was snatching at the rails below as its owner rushed up towards him. There was nowhere left to go. The occupied lecture theatre beside him was the only other way off the landing.

The violent footsteps grew louder and he could even hear heavy breathing now. Suddenly one of the heavy lecture theatre doors swung open. The second man appeared, breathless but fully alert.

Without pausing, the professor set off back down the stairs he had just bested. They were right on him now, any second a hand would land on his shoulder. Hearing footsteps directly behind him he gripped the rail and vaulted straight over into the tall, narrow void.

As gravity took hold and his stomach lurched, it occurred to the professor that he hadn't really thought things through. Then he was falling and there was no time to think. Apparently of their own accord, his arms grabbed passing rail. Scrambling over and back onto the stairs, he tried to think about what he'd just done but the information simply wouldn't line up.

He was now officially trapped, with pursuers closing fast from above and below. Stepping onto the nearest landing he paced back and forth desperately.

The space was barren, just hard wearing carpet and harder angles of metal and stone.

And a bin.

The metal tube stood about three feet high with a gaping mouth on one side and a shiny hat. Snatching it up the professor weighed it in his arms as the footsteps grew louder. Now vibrating with panic, he stared longingly at the world beyond another huge pane of glass. The footsteps from above ceased abruptly and he turned to find the man with mean grey eyes standing a few steps above.

The other half of the grim double act clattered to a halt on the landing below before both began their wary approach. Their eyes were on him, a moment more and their heavy hands would be as well.

The professor found himself frozen still, yet something was squirming rabidly within him. He lowered his gaze to the bin, staring at it as if for the first time. A strange sound bubbled up through him before bursting forth from quivering lips. The resultant, and slightly effeminate scream, caused the two to hesitate briefly.

That split second was all it took for the professor to raise the bin and throw it harder than he would have thought he could, straight through the window. A second later and the pair lunged for him, but too late. Before the myriad shards of glass had reached the concrete below, the professor had thrown himself after them.

The ground raced up to meet him, a surreal and unintelligible vision. That was until the hard wet slap that was very real indeed. For what seemed like an age he lay perfectly still until the world crept back into his consciousness.

He'd felt his ankle bend under him hideously upon impact and, as he rolled onto his back, he became more fully aware of the consequences of leaping into a pile of broken glass. Focussing, he saw the two men staring down in disbelief. One vanished, apparently tearing back down the stairs towards him.

The second paused for a moment, eyebrows raised, before giving the professor a small nod of approval and racing after his colleague. Once more the professor found himself inexplicably upright.

His ankle screaming at him with every other step, he set off with a loping limp across an expanse of gravel towards the Physics building. Heaving the door open the professor could hear rapid crunching behind him. Gripping the rails to both sides of the stairs he dragged himself up flight after flight, yet again.

*This really is ridiculous.*

The professor hissed his disbelief as he turned yet another corner. He was increasingly aware that he could not sustain his flight much longer. Since fleeing his office he had been driven to acts he would have never dreamed possible and yet still they were almost upon him.

And then he was trapped.

The laboratories the professor had expected to cut through were locked behind a sign announcing renovations. He could hear dreadfully familiar footsteps behind him. No windows here, no unlocked doors. He realised he was gritting his teeth.

Snatching up the hefty fire extinguisher attached to the opposite wall, he leaned back and waited. Despite the urgency of the situation however, the professor found himself distracted.

Every three months for twelve years he had delivered a report to persons unknown in a restaurant toilet. Shifting the weight of the extinguisher to his left hand, the professor slipped his right into his jacket pocket.

The last report he had submitted had detailed the successful production of the dozen or so hard little round things he now held. A few days later he'd received the order to destroy his research and leave academia.

With an involuntary snarl, the professor gripped the extinguisher in two hands once more. All this time, all that effort just to be told to destroy a lifetime's work! Pain suddenly forgotten beneath outrage, the professor swung the heavy red tube. The base connected perfectly with the first man's face and actually lifted him off his feet with a sloppy thud.

Weirdly smudged face, neck hanging at a strange angle, eyes open and gleaming, all burned into the professor's mind. He didn't even hear the second man arrive, it was the motion that caught his eye and caused him to swing once more.

He stood there for a long time. First he became aware of his heart, then of his breath, emerging in gasping moans. Eventually he looked down at the gaudy red extinguisher and at the darker crimson coating both metal and skin.

The professor barely heard the gonging clang as he dropped the heavy tube and fell backwards against the wall before sliding down to the floor. A dozen years ago he had returned home to find a man like these, cold eyes, sharp suit, sitting in his front room. Ignoring all protestations, the man had explained things.

The promising academic and his research had caught the eye of certain people. From now on he would log quarterly progress reports. He would mention these reports to no-one. Failure to comply would be bad for his wife and children. Melting back into the present, the professor looked at the broken figures.

It was over.

There was no way he could explain the cross campus carnage of the morning, especially not the bodies. Everything would be brought into the light of day, the whole story. Relief flowed through him. Pushing guilt and horror temporarily to the back of his mind, the professor eased himself to his feet and descended the stairs without looking back.

Opening the door he had so recently rushed through, he welcomed the daylight onto his face. Stepping onto the gravel he sighed and was reminded of that original question from which his research had originally grown. He moved to take another step into..

..the heavy arm around his throat! Someone was dragging him back inside! Digging deep for any last reserves of energy, the professor struggled but felt a needle prick his throat. Seconds later and a third man in a suit let a body crash to the floor. He rummaged through the professor's pockets and retrieved a small paper package before striding purposefully out into the light.

An autopsy would reveal that the professor died of a heart attack. Later the press would report that this was the result fleeing money lending gangsters. The professor's computer would be found to have mysteriously died around the same time he had, taking with it a lifetime's work. For a while the whole thing would be quite the scandal before passing into campus folklore and ultimately, fading into history.

—         —
—

Emerging from the toilet cubicle the young woman placed her textbooks next to the sink and began washing her hands. Once rinsed, she allowed the water to continue to flow, lost in thought as she was.

Knocking off the tap and reaching for a paper towel, she frowned at herself in the mirror. There was something about it she couldn't shake, a feeling of something huge just beyond the horizon.

*This is ridiculous.*

She whispered before scooping up her books and walking out into the library. Settling down to study, she couldn't focus and reflected how silly it was to be so intrigued by a piece of graffiti on a toilet wall...

# you too

Riley was awake.

It took her a while to realise it but all the clues were there.

Sounds came first. Taps and clicks from pipes, a slick tyre puddle swish, anonymous pavement footsteps swelling and fading. Textures followed. A warm saliva slug trail from lip to cheek to ear. Worn smooth upholstery on a brutal wooden frame pressed too hard into her face. Frigid air biting her toes. Neck muscles screaming, some stretched, some crushed.

Her left eye ventured first. It flickered blurs into colours then colours into shapes before the right stumbled in alongside to bring depth if not recognition. For a moment Riley lay perfectly still and made no attempt to interpret the view. She breathed in and then out without thought or concern until focus kicked in the door.

A weary groan rattled out of her as she acknowledged the too familiar front room. She'd fallen asleep on the sofa again, in her clothes again, after tea again. She began to push up and away towards sitting but then stopped in pain sharp and sudden. Delicately now and in stages, she eased herself to the vertical, slow straightening her neck with winces.

Her right hand tingled through numbness. As she sat and swayed, blinked and licked lips, the hand rose clumsily to paw the warm wet from her cheek. Her fingers dragged themselves dry down her top and her skirt then groped into the coffee table clutter.

Pushing past the grimly congealed ready meal carton, she spotted the wine bottle and a second groan broke out into the room. The bottle mocked with its dregs and accused with its emptiness until her fingers closed on her phone. Sitting back she glanced down at the time and third groan completed the set.

Taking a breath, Riley made to stand quick but then the headache made itself known. Splintering out from behind her eyes, it knocked her back down onto the sofa. The impact jarred her waking stomach as the headache raced back to meet her neck and they all set about trying to make her vomit.

As ever and as always there was no time, for the bus was a merciless master. Gritting her teeth she pushed through the pain and stood to totter and stumble. She cut a clumsy path round the sofa to land against the door frame behind, each step was more effort than the last. She overcame the cumulative ordeal of the stairs and found herself swaying in the bathroom.

Her reflection judged her terribly, making no effort to hide its disgust. She rubbed at the cushion cut lines in her face, fading scars from another night on the sofa. She dragged off her clothes and cast them aside before washing briefly in the grimy old sink, gasping at cold water slaps.

Hiding her face in the least dirty towel, Riley stumbled back out onto the landing and pushed at the bedroom door. As ever it stuck, gave slightly then stopped, refusing to move any further. Naked and shivering she cursed into the towel then put her shoulder into the door.

It creaked and squeaked but refused to unjam as if knowing she didn't have the time. In the end she gave up and stumbled back down the stairs throwing the towel at the sofa and missing it.

A pile of clean laundry sat in the armchair, neat, well folded and smug amid the chaos. She dismembered it brutally, dragging out entrails of underwear and the bones of an outfit. Through hopping, leaning, pulling and cursing she finally got the cold clothes against her colder skin and set off back up the stairs. The toothbrush, the hairbrush, a brief touch of slap then back downstairs to find her purse and the truth of the bus fare.

If there was enough change within then she might make the bus but if not then she definitely wouldn't. If the coins counted short then she would have to go through the steps. Walking to the petrol station, queueing at the cash machine, praying at the cash machine, queueing in the petrol station to break the note then walking back right past her own front door to the bus stop.

The headache still raged, throbbing and growling so that she had to count out the coins  three times to be sure of the stacked up addition. She was in luck, of a sort and so snatched up her coat then grabbed her bag and her keys. Heading out of the door she locked it, fought her way into her coat and fast walked to the end of the street.

Rounding the corner she saw the bus at the stop and broke into a stomach churning sprint. The doors were closing as she reached them panting but the driver took pity and hissed them apart. Stumbling on she gave him the change then took the ticket and three more short steps. The bus was full, seats and aisle so that she could do nothing but stand and hang on.

The bad breath and body odour, the motion and noise all fanned the flames of the headache. She squeezed her eyes shut and clung to the rail, fighting the urges to vomit and cry. Then came her stop and the walk down the hill and then finally into the office.

The bland furnishings and stale light were unchanged from the day before and from all the days before that. As she walked through reception it engulfed her completely. Home was a dream, she had never really been away.

Riley spent the morning on the phone, apologising while customers screamed. Then came lunch and a terrible sandwich before an afternoon of filing in a windowless room. She was nearing the end of several weeks of work ordering paper questionnaires by surname. She hated it and hated it but was very nearly done. Surrounded by the stacks she'd painstakingly built she was just nursing her latest papercut when her manager appeared at the door.

"I'm not paying you to sit on your arse," he said with his usual lack of charm. Riley frowned but but her lip.

"I just cut myself," she said by way of an explanation, offering the bloodied digit as proof.

"Well get a fucking plaster on it then!" came the scathing response. "You can't be getting blood on these Riley, they're really important ok? Jesus!"

"There aren't any plasters in the first aid kit," said Riley, failing to keep the edge out of her voice.

"Well don't you have any with you? I thought

women had everything in their handbags. You should really plan ahead a bit more," he said and then turned to leave. Riley drew a breath under which to curse but stopped herself as he sprang back to the door.

"So this is all nearly done right?" he said, glancing doubtfully at the stacks around the room.

"Yep," replied Riley. "Last eighteen months of customer satisfaction surveys all in order by customer surname."

"What?!" he snapped, stepping into the room, wide eyed.

"Last eighteen months..." Riley began to repeat but didn't get the chance.

"In date order, right?" he said menacingly.

The silence between them was bitterly cold. Riley swallowed and licked her lips, a thrashing panic rising up through her chest.

"You specifically said customer surname..." she said, quietly, carefully.

"Fucking hell Riley! I mean, for fuck's sake! Weeks you've been at this, it should have been done ages ago and now you're telling me..." he snatched up a questionnaire from the nearest pile before throwing it back down on another.

"But you said customer..." Riley tried again, quivering with frustrated fury.

"I don't want to hear it!" he screamed. Riley could see curious colleagues gathering to watch from the corridor.

"It's just one thing after another with you, excuses, excuses!" He ploughed on, in full flow now. "This isn't a fucking game Riley! It's me who's going to have explain to the board why these aren't ready for data entry, did you ever think of that?!"

"I'm sorry," she heard herself say. It was a kneejerk response to the verbal violence but she hated herself for it anyway.

"Sorry doesn't get it done does it?!" He raged before pausing for breath and lowering his tone to a venomous hiss. "Look, I've had a complaint about you from a customer you spoke to on the phone this morning, Mr Tate? So before you start sorting out this mess I need you to go and ring him and apologise alright?"

"But..." Riley didn't even know where to begin with that one.

"Just fucking do it!" he screeched, back to full, eye bulging volume.

Riley closed her eyes and took a breath. A flash bulb image tore at her, papers flying, that vile mouth bloodied, those piggy eyes widened by shock. Then she remembered her rent, her bills, the cost of bus fares and food. Opening her eyes she walked towards him, past him and out through the door, trying to ignore the clawing tang of cologne. He followed her out into the office, haranguing her all the way to her desk while her colleagues looked on like vultures.

"And don't start fucking crying either, I don't have time for it. You've got a review coming up next month and none of this is going to reflect well on you at all. I think we might need to consider your future with us altogether..." and on and on it went.

She stayed two hours later than usual and made a start on the resorting. Every second that passed, every paper she picked up, read and put down, each required a colossal effort of focus and will to hold back the shame and fury.

Finally, long after everyone else had gone home, Riley trudged back up the hill to the bus stop. She saw the bus pulling away but had nothing left to put into a sprint and so slackened her pace instead. Reaching the stop she checked her phone and realised the buses were past the point of regular service. From now on they were hourly and so she settled against the side of the shelter to wait, pulling her coat collar up around her ears.

By the time she got home the sky was thoroughly black. Locking the door she threw her bag and her coat at the tangle of laundry and set yet another cheap bottle of wine down beside its empty twin. Stepping into the tiniest of kitchens she threw a ready meal into the microwave and slammed the door, jabbing venom at the innocent buttons.

She stood and raged at 800W for three and a half minutes exactly, seething fingers drumming the worktop. Then snatching a fork and burning her hand, she stormed back into the front room and dropped into the sofa. She opened the wine, turned on the TV and waited for the food to cool edible.

During the distractions of work she had forgotten the headache but now it began to seep back. It crept around the edges of the TV noise to niggle at her eyes and her temples. At least it was Friday, the one saving grace. She repeated the name of the day to herself, a despairing, cold comfort mantra.

Having eaten the meal and drunk half the wine she stared at the TV but saw nothing. The day began to slip away from her so that her shoulders dropped and her jaw unlocked. She began to plan, the usual stuff, squeezing as much quality as possible out of the weekend.

This time it would be different. This time she actually would go for that walk in the park, take that long bath, read that book and cook something real for her dinner. The familiar arguments rolled through once more, making time for herself, leaving work at work, there's more to life, life's too short and other empty words as well.

As the latest wine bottle began to mirror its brother Riley began to slump and doze drowsy. The effort of the week caught up and piled on. Every part of her was leaden and everything was weary, aching with hollow fatigue. She knew it was time to go up to bed but movement seemed an impossible dream. She knocked off the TV and laid on her side, just resting her eyes for a moment. The moment came and was and went and then she filled the room with snoring.

—       —
—

Riley was awake.

This was no gradual journey of discovery however, but rather a sudden brutal blast of sensation. The headache was well rested and assaulted her with renewed vigour while the sofa slept aches bit harder than ever. Rising to sit, Riley clung to her only torch, two days away from work. Seen in its protective light the morning didn't seem so bad.

Glancing at her phone she noted it was still early then dropped it back amongst the clutter. Yawning while stretching, she considered how much time she would allow herself in her actual bed before getting back up to start the well planned weekend. Each time she tried to decide however something pulled at her sleeve, an irritant felt but not seen.

She stared around the room but spotted no difference and so rose with a shrug, stepping towards the kitchen intent on water. As she rounded the sofa however a cluster of sharp, white corners drew her eyes to the floor. Before the front door lay three envelopes face down.

Riley stopped, stared and frowned. She knew they hadn't been there the night before, yet it was far too early for the Saturday post. The irritant returned. It whispered of a terrible, terrible thing but too quiet to be heard. Exploring her teeth with a fuzzy tongue she dithered a moment more. Her pounding head drove her on however, as a glass of water and a real bed trumped the mystery.

She scooped up the envelopes and stepped into the kitchen. At the sink she retrieved a half full glass from the draining board, emptied it then sat it under the tap, allowing the water to flow as she flicked through the post. The first two were junk, wastes of time both but the third was clearly financial.

Lines folded her forehead as she stopped the tap and took a sip of cool water. She stared at the last envelope as if trying to read its contents without opening it. Her heart quickened a little as she placed the glass on the counter and applied both hands to the tearing of paper.

Sliding out the folded sheet she recognised her regular savings account statement and so her stomach relaxed. Unfolding and scanning the page however caused it to bounce back and clench. Spreading the page out on the counter top she ran her hands through her hair and read it again, her heart rattling in her chest.

Riley's savings were gone.

No matter how many times she read the page, turned the page over, picked it up or put it down, the three little zeroes refused to change. Someone had withdrawn every single petty penny she had managed to save over the last year. Shaking her head Riley fought off the facts. She thought instead of all the temptations she had resisted, the urges to plunder her nest egg for a holiday or an outfit.

Closing her eyes and leaning on the counter, Riley focussed instead on her headache. It was suddenly a welcome distraction from those three dreadful little circles. A strange, cool flatness came over her so that her shoulders dropped as she reopened her eyes. She drained the glass of water slowly and methodically before refilling it and taking another sip.

It was just another thing, just stuff, just hassle. It was obviously a mistake, one that would no doubt be an absolute chore to resolve but that she would fix eventually. She shoved her scorn at the paper so that it slid across the counter and hid a corner of its shame beneath the toaster. She turned her back on it triumphant.

Sipping the water she returned to thoughts of her weekend before stepping back into the front room. For the first time she noticed that despite the headache induced nausea, she was ravenously hungry and pondered going out for breakfast. She added her glass to the table top clutter and retrieved her phone, intent on action. Checking the time again however she suddenly froze.

Her stomach plunged. Her heart broke. Her mind span away in abject horror. Stumbling against the sofa she sat heavily onto its arm, still staring slack jawed at the phone in her hand. A second more and the screen darkened and for a moment her thumb hung poised to relight it.

It couldn't be true. It mustn't be true. Part of her couldn't bear to know.

She closed her mouth and closed her eyes and swallowed. When she opened her eyes they were wet, dashing ahead of the confirmation to come. Holding her breath she depressed her thumb and let out a sob as the screen sprang back into light.

It was Sunday.

She'd slept right through. All of Friday night, all of Saturday day and all of Saturday night. Half of her priceless weekend was gone and already the working week loomed large once more. Collapsing sideways onto the sofa Riley threw her phone so that it clattered away from her and then wept.

Great sobs wracked through her as frustration and despair bled out of her in long strings of tears and spit. She cried and moaned and poured silent screams into cushions until she felt her throbbing head would burst. Eventually came a lull.

Nothing had changed. It was still Sunday, her savings were still gone, there was still no way out and no hope. For a long time she stared blankly at the ceiling, utterly vented and empty. After a while she shifted to untangle herself and lay flat out on her back, wiping the tickling strings from her face.

There were chores to be done, the tyranny of things that must happen. Work clothes to wash, food to buy and no end of things to be tidied. The horrifically bland Sunday routine, a prisoner condemned, straightening her cell in the shadow of the gallows.

And then came the noise.

She felt it before she heard it, a great throbbing roar that seemed to shake the entire house. It rolled up from beneath and rattled the bottles on the table, one pulsing surge after another. Sitting bolt upright, eyes wide with shock, Riley froze as her mind groped blindly for an explanation. Still the throbbing continued, driving her off the sofa and back to her feet.

The sound was coming from the cellar and the only thing it could be down there was the boiler. Suddenly a whole string of events ran through her mind, a clear and silver thread. It started with a broken boiler, passed through a heartless landlord to an empty savings account and ended with frost on the inside of the windows.

The throbbing grew more insistent as if the boiler

were building up to an explosion. Wiping her face and sniffing away the anguish of before, Riley dashed through the kitchen to the stiff little cellar door nestled in beside the fridge.

Wrenching it open she struggled her way through and onto the dark cellar steps, flicking the light switch as she passed. Even at the top she could smell the damp and feel the cool slime through her socks. Treading as quickly as she dare, she braced herself against the clammy walls and descended into the chaos of the cellar.

A bare light bulb swung from the low ceiling but made little effort to provide any real illumination. The cellar was full, piled chest high with boxes and suitcases, broken furniture and bicycles. The roaring of the boiler was even louder down here so that it bullied any thoughts from her mind. She skipped past the usual irritation at the junk, none of it hers, and began to pick her way through it.

The damp was bad enough to form puddles on the uneven concrete floor and she winced as her socks drank up the foul and held it against her feet. The raging boiler was not in the cellar itself but worse, in the coal cellar. This was a tiny, unlit room, fetid and black that sat directly beneath the kitchen.

When the rows upon rows of terraced house had originally been built there had been holes from the street directly into the coal cellars through which weekly supplies had been delivered. These holes had long since been bricked up however leaving an obsolete little spaces behind a solid, bolted wooden doors.

The route through the boxes meant that Riley had to cross the cellar and come back to reach the door and all the while the boiler grew louder and louder. By the time she was half way she was beginning to wonder if she shouldn't have just run out into the street rather than trap herself down here amongst the mountains of crap, directly in the firing line when the thing finally decided to blow.

Reaching the coal cellar door Riley winced at the sound and fumbled blindly with the rusted bolt for a few seconds before realising it was already open. Dragging the door outwards she was immediately struck by a wall of even louder throbbing.

Just enough of the cellar bulb's feeble light filtered through to show the boiler on the opposite wall. Stepping onto the ancient but dry cobbles, no slimy concrete in here, Riley scampered toward the boiler on the balls of her feet, cringing more with each step.

Arriving at the raging tank she clapped her hands to her ears and stared wildly at the front of the boiler. The bottom was covered by a hinged plastic cover and she pulled at this so that it swung down revealing a scattering of switches and dials. Crouching she desperately tried to read the barely lit, faded text before giving up and lashing out at what appeared to the most obvious candidate for a power switch.

With a click and groan the boiler died and the throbbing shuddered into silence. Riley took a step back and realised she was panting for breath. For the first time she glanced around the coal cellar itself and then suddenly noticed the smell.

The damp from the cellar without was fairly overpowering but in here the stench was almost unbearable. In the shadows toward the back of the room another indistinct mass of junk rose to the low ceiling, hidden by almost total darkness. It smelled like something had got trapped in there and died, mice or perhaps even a cat.

Clamping one hand over her nose and mouth Riley squinted through the stench for a moment, tilting her head to one side to scrutinise the rotting junk pile. Then she returned her attention to the boiler. Had she turned it off in time? Was it ruined? There was only one way to find out. With a slightly shaking hand she reached out and flicked the switch back on.

Immediately the tiny, cobbled room was refilled with sound, rumbling and clanking. After a few seconds of fidgeting however the boiler seemed to settle down and return to its usual low grumbling. Riley blinked her relief but waited a minute more just in case.

Nothing.

The boiler seemed fine, back to itself. Riley realised she'd forgotten just how foul the cellar was, the stench and the damp and the slime and the shadows.

She closed the panel and turned to leave, intent on getting back upstairs as quickly as possible without slipping into the grunge.

Facing the door however she noticed for the first time a cluster of cobblestones at her feet that appeared different to the rest. She still had a hand clamped to her face and was struggling against the smell. With effort she managed to overcome the urge to flee long enough to step towards the patch of cobbles and look closer.

As curiosity took hold she tipped her head to one side again, trying to understand what made these particular stones look so different. Suddenly it clicked and she realised that there was no mortar surrounding them, or whatever it was you put between cobblestones. It was as if these stones had been dug out and then carefully replaced.

Still her body was straining to leave, to get away from the smell and the gloom but her mind raced away, asking questions and guessing at answers. Why would someone take out the cobbles? To get to the ground underneath. Why would someone want to get to the ground underneath? To bury something perhaps. Why someone bury something under the floor  of the coal cellar? To hide it from other people, to keep it safe. Why would they need to keep it safe? Because it was valuable perhaps.

Acting out her indecision Riley hopped from one cold wet foot to another. It was probably nothing, it was almost certainly nothing. But what if it was something? She thought of the three little zeroes on the piece of paper sat on the counter directly above. She thought of the following morning, the wrench of leaving for work yet again.

If there was something valuable down here, something she could sell, perhaps she could replenish her savings. Perhaps she she could even live off it long enough to quit that soul crushing job and find something new instead. It was all the reason she needed.

Taking one last filtered breath through her hand Riley lowered herself to kneel and began to pull the loose stones up and out. She tried to breath through her mouth and even then only in short shallow breaths.

The first stone was the tricky one. The cobbles were slimy and closely packed making it almost impossible to get a decent grip. Eventually however she managed to tease one of the stones up out of the floor after which it was relatively easy to pull up the rest.

After removing the first couple of stones Riley could see a wooden surface below. As she pulled them up one by one a small trapdoor in the earth below was revealed. Sitting back on her heels Riley frowned and rubbed at her temples. The headache was worse than ever now so that she thought her vision might even be blurring a little.

The trap door still held her attention however. She had hoped for an old tin full of jewellery or something but the trapdoor still held the promise of riches below. Digging her nails into the edge of the wood she managed to pry the door up enough to get her fingers underneath.

The hinges were old and rusted and complained bitterly at first but then staggered open to reveal a deep, black square. Riley leaned forward a little, planted her hands on the cobbles on either side and peered down in to the void.

There was nothing.

She was becoming used to the stench from the junk at back of the room but sniffing at the hole she found she couldn't smell anything at all from below. The air wasn't stale, there was no smell of sewage or damp as she thought might come from pipes. She leaned back on her heels again and held her hand over the hole. The air felt perfectly still, nothing flowing in or out. She wondered how deep the hole went.

She went back out into the cellar and grabbed a splintered chair leg from out of the nearest box. Returning to the hole she held the chair leg above it for a second then let go, leaning forward to listen for a clattering impact. She heard none. Besides the low grumbling of the boiler the cellar was utterly silent and no sound of impact came from the hole. Riley sat back and frowned her confusion.

Suddenly a sound caught her attention, the low drone of a housefly. She looked to the door and sure enough a fly came into view, probably having left its post at the kitchen bin to come and explore the newly opened territories.

As she watched, the fly made its zigzag way into the coal cellar then spiralled down towards the hole. She froze, not wanting to distract or divert the fly, following it with her eyes, holding her breath.

Sure enough the fly swooped straight down into the darkness and the moment it did the sounds of its buzzing ceased. Riley waited and then waited some more before slowly, gingerly leaning toward the hole. Turning her head she listened intently but could hear nothing from the darkness below.

Straightening up she frowned her bafflement at the hole before starting to rise to look for something else from the cellar. Just then however two tiny objects erupted vertically from the hole causing her to fall backwards onto the floor in shock.

Both objects shot straight upwards but upon reaching their apex the one on the right began to buzz. It flew off towards the boiler before wheeling round to weave back across the hole and out of the door.

The second object fell in an arc to the left of the hole, skittering onto the cobbles before laying perfectly still. Scrabbling back onto her knees Riley leaned in and peered at the tiny thing. It was another fly, laid flat on its back and unmoving, apparently dead. Her face twisted in disgust but curiosity and confusion still held sway within.

She kept her eyes fixed on the dead still fly as she moved slowly to the door before turning to face the heaped debris of the cellar, selecting objects at random to be dropped into the hole. While rummaging in one particular box Riley caught sight of a bundle of knitting supplies, needles, patterns and several balls of wool. Snatching up one of these she returned to the coal cellar.

Sitting cross legged before the hole she arranged the objects around her and was just trying to untangle the ball of wool when a buzzing sound snapped her eyes back to the dead fly. Sure enough its legs were starting to swim sickeningly. A few seconds more and as she watched, the fly wriggled back to life, flipped onto its front then took flight and droned back out into the cellar.

The way the flies had been so forcefully ejected kept playing through her mind. Again she hovered her hand over the hole but again she felt no movement, no updraft, the air was perfectly still.

Riley dropped more things into the hole including pieces of crockery and glassware. Not a single sound emerged from the hole however, no smashing or splintering, the darkness just swallowed the objects up.

Among some mouldering camping equipment Riley had found a store of glow sticks. She bent one until she heard the crack and the gel within began to emit a thick green light. Carefully she tied a double thickness of wool around the stick and began to lower it in to the hole.

The green glow swung gently from side to side but revealed nothing, no walls, no edges, no features of any kind. Gradually she unrolled almost the entire ball of wool, peering after it down into the dark until the glow stick had become a faint and distant green smudge.

It was impossible.

The distance covered by the length of wool was too great, the hole couldn't possibly be that deep. Gently, wary of breaking the slender, fluffy strands, she began to move the wool in small circles. The motion made its way down the wool, growing as it went until she could see the glow stick far below sweeping out a great slow oval.

It struck nothing. It illuminated nothing. The green glow flew freely down below in the distant dark, cutting through a vast open space. How could such a space exist immediately  beneath rows upon rows of terraced houses? Where were the foundations, the pipes under the street?

It was impossible.

Riley sat back once more, cross legged and pondering as she idly twisted the strand of wool between finger and thumb. There were no riches down there, certainly none that she could get at anyway. She wondered if she could make money form selling the story but quickly realised that even if there was any profit to be made from publicising the impossible thing it would fall to her landlord rather than her.

She began to wrap the wool around her hand, no longer looking over the edge, no longer looking at anything but just pondering the impossible thing and what it could mean. She was racking her brains trying to think of what else she could do to explore the hole when she suddenly noticed the mouse.

At first she recoiled, scrabbling back away from the thing where it sat near the edge of the hole. It had wandered in from the cellar while she was thinking and now sat there, quite brazenly, its tiny pink nose and associated whiskers quivering as it sampled the air.

Riley's stomach turned in revulsion. Her eyes fixed on the thing and took in every detail. Its fur was a mix of grey and brown patches while its hideous little hands were sharp and pink. Its eyes were black and glistened in the gloom and she noticed that its right ear was torn, presumably from a near miss with a cat or bird.

The mouse sat the quite casually while Riley glared at it, unable to move in case she caused it to move. As vile as it was sat still, the thought of it scurrying around, too quick to see, tangling itself around her feet, perhaps climbing up her leg, that was worse.

Riley shivered, her face contorting even further as her stomach turned again. Her head felt as if it might split wide open at any moment and she desperately wanted to leave, to get upstairs and outside into the relatively fresh city air but now she couldn't take her eyes from the mouse.

Eventually, she licked her lips and began to move her free hand. Slowly, slowly, her fingers crept across the chilled, slimy cobbles until they landed on the smooth texture of an old, crumbling phone book. Never taking her eyes from the mouse, not even blinking, she curled her fingers around the heavy book until she had it in a firm grip.

Then, holding her breath so that her temples throbbed blindingly, she moved herself around so that she could put her weight behind it and began to shift the phonebook towards the mouse. As soon as she began to slide the book across the cobbles the mouse became alert and aware though it seemed only slightly curious and not at all afraid.

Finally, clenching a scream in her throat, Riley slid the phone book at the mouse with all her might and then cringed away back to the wall. The mouse turned to dash but too late. The mighty book slid over the greasy cobble and struck the mouse, taking them both over the edge and into the darkness. She heard a single, high pitched squeal from the mouse and then nothing.

Allowing herself to breath again Riley shook her head as a mix of guilt and relief washed over her. As weird as it was the whole thing had been a waste of time. There was probably a perfectly simple explanation, some ancient cavern with strange acoustics, just a dead, empty cave. There was nothing left to do but put everything back where she found it and head back upstairs, back to the Sunday chores.

She felt her chest grow heavy at the thought, the ordinary reality of the world above crowding back in. As she reeled in the glow stick however she knew she had no other options. She wound and wound the wool for what felt like a long time, growing bored and frustrated with the task and yet not wanting it to end due to what would come after.

Eventually she decided she had been too long ravelling and so looked into the hole to see how much further the glow stick had to travel. As she approached the edge however, two small objects shot up out of the blackness.

Riley screamed and fell backwards again, just as when the flies had emerged. She immediately recognised the object that landed to the right of the hole as the mouse. It hit the cobbles and bounced before scurrying away, right past her and back out into the cellar.

She watched it go in horror before turning her attention to the motionless lump that had landed to the left of the hole. It was another mouse, laid perfectly still but as she forced herself to move closer and look, she could see its chest fluttering. It wasn't dead.

Frantically she tore the coil of wool from her hand and threw it into the hole. Standing she backed away until she met clammy brick behind. Her eyes remained fixed on the prone mouse, not daring to look away. Her mind raced. How could there be nothing in the hole?

There had to be something in there, something alive. The flies and the mice had been thrown out, spat out even. What was it? What lurked in the darkness beneath.

Riley clenched and unclenched her fists compulsively, digging her nails into her palms over and over. Was she going mad? Perhaps that was it, perhaps she had lost her mind. Her head hurt so much she could barely think and when she did she realised she had no idea how long she had been down here, down in the coal cellar playing with the impossible hole.

Still she stared at the mouse, eyes horror wide and manic locked, drilling through the gloom. When the mouse began to move she clapped her palms to her mouth to stifle the scream. The pounding in her head, the twitching of those tiny, vicious pink hands, the stench from the junk in the shadows, all of it piled in on her until she felt her knees beginning to melt.

Stretching one of her hands down to her side she half fell half sat, cold cobbles pressing up beneath, cold brick pressing in behind. The mouse was awake now, its beady little black eyes were open. In a flash it righted itself and hunkered down, nose twitching, ears turning unsure.

Riley stopped. The wooziness, the terror, all of it, stopped. The mouse's right ear was torn. She looked at the pattern of its fur, the mixture of grey and brown patches.

It was the same mouse.

She had seen the other one clearly, the one that dashed away upon landing. It was identical, it was the same. The mouse finally made a break for it, dashing off out into the cellar just as its double had minutes before. Riley didn't even watch it go, instead she stared at the hole.

She'd already had the idea, it came in an instant almost as soon as she recognised the mouse. Now she was thinking it through, feeling it out, talking herself into and back out of it. It occurred to her again that she had no idea how long she had spent down here. The memory of resetting the boiler flashed back before her, hadn't there been a digital clock in the display, used for setting the timer?

Tearing her eyes from the hole she staggered dazed toward the boiler and reopened the plastic panel. Sure enough a tiny digital display was nestled among the buttons. It was late. By this time on a Sunday she would usually be attempting to sleep, tossing and turning in a tangle of anxiety, growing more tense and less likely to sleep with each moment that passed.

She hadn't washed her work clothes, she had nothing to wear in the morning. She hadn't eaten or bought any food. She hadn't got any cash out and didn't have any bus fare. She closed the plastic panel again slowly and precisely with a quivering hand. Every part of her vibrated with anguish at the thought of the morning to come.

Her teeth gritted, her fingers resumed their fist curls. It was unbearable, she couldn't bear it, it was too much to bear. Turning back to the hole she returned to the idea. Far away a distant part of her wailed terribly with cold and primal fear but in the moment she could not care.

As insane as it obviously was, in that moment it seemed infinitely preferable to a normal Monday morning. She just couldn't do it. She couldn't go through it all again, putting on dirty clothes, leaving even earlier than usual to get bus fare then spending all day with her head swimming from not eating.

And yet she knew she couldn't call in sick. After the scene on Friday that would be as good as quitting and she absolutely could not quit, she wouldn't survive without the job. The coal cellar seemed even smaller, as if the walls had shifted inwards. She was trapped, pinned, stuck. There was only one way out.

Atop trembling knees Riley took one shaking step and then another towards the hole. Before she was ready she was standing at the edge, her toes curling over the cobblestones. She stared down into the darkness.

It was so deep, so black and so cold. Her eyes told her she would just fall and fall until suddenly and without warning, she would be dashed brutally into pieces. She might not even die they warned her, she might simply end up laid there in mindbending agony with no hope of discovery or rescue.

Her mind ignored this physical wisdom however as she realised that she genuinely did not care. Anything was better than another Monday morning, anything at all. She stopped balling her hands, stopped holding her breath, allowed the pain in her head to flow all the way through her and stepped into the hole.

She fell through and down and down and down. Shock and terror seized control so that her arms flailed wildly at the nothing but it was too late. Wind rushed past her as she fell and fell but then came suddenly light, dim gloomy light with textures too. For an instant she stopped falling and hung weightless before her stomach lurched and she fell once more.

She closed her eyes and braced herself but almost immediately felt solid ground beneath her feet, slippery cobbles in fact. She opened her eyes again and lurched forwards, her hands shooting out to steady her and finding the smooth metal of the boiler.

She looked at it, ran her hands over it. She pulled open the cover and looked at the time, only a handful of minutes had passed. Had she done it? Had she jumped into the hole? She was certain she had but perhaps she hadn't. Perhaps she really had lost her mind.

Then she heard the sound.

She watched her knuckles whiten on the boiler casing. Holding her breath still she strained her ears and heard the sound again. Coming from behind, from near the hole, she could hear the sound of someone breathing.

As she began to turn she could feel her mind tearing itself in two. It wasn't possible, it could not be, there couldn't be anything there. She turned and turned, it seemed to take hours, her eyes bulging, lungs bursting all the way. And then finally she had turned and looked and seen. Next to the hole lay the crumpled body of a woman.

It was her.

—            —

—

Riley was awake.

The first she knew of it was the sensation of a warm, kitten soft cocoon. Moving her feet back and forth she consumed the gentle texture of bed sheets in lazy lust. Smiling easy she stretched a little, enjoying the feel of her loose, body warmed night clothes as they shifted beneath and about her.

It felt good to sleep in a bed.

Slender strands of soft focus light seeped morning around the curtains. The light smudged furniture edges and swelled colours but the time just couldn't reach Riley. Lost under bliss she rolled on one side, gasping her pleasure at a cool pool of pillow. It occurred to her then that her head didn't hurt and she took a while just to enjoy that.

Finally her waking came, eased in smooth and unfurled like a petal. Riley smacked her lips and pushed herself up to sit, leaning forward to stroke her palms across the bedspread. After a satisfying yawn she blinked at her alarm clock.

It was Monday morning and time to get up.

With a shrug and a sigh Riley pushed back the covers and then swung her legs out of the bed. Rubbing at her face she tried to remember the weekend which seemed far distant after such a great sleep. Images dark swelled to loom but she frowned them away with easy disdain. Crazy nonsense all of it.

Standing to stretch she wondered about clothes but didn't recall doing any laundry. She crossed her bedroom, opened her wardrobe and flicked the hangers back and forth. She had just about convinced herself that one outfit was work wearable when she heard the front door slam beneath her.

A chill ran up her spine as her awareness plunged out from its cosy local bubble to engulf the house and the street outside. Footsteps were clacking away, shrinking towards the end of the street. Riley dashed to the window and pushed back the curtains, straining to see who was walking.

She recognised the woman immediately. The hair, the clothes, the bag, but she didn't really believe it until she saw her turn the corner and pause to glance back so that she caught a glimpse of her face, her own familiar face. She walked slowly back to the bed, sitting heavy and staring at nothing. Again came the images, black and weird but this time she let them stay.

She remembered the boiler, the cellar and the many, many boxes. She remembered the coal cellar and the impossible, bottomless hole. The memories seemed like a dream, they had the same frayed edges yet what she had just seen out of the window left no room for doubt. She ploughed on to the wool and the glow stick, the fly and the mouse and then finally the panic of falling.

The slow, slow turn to the impossible sight, the gonging of madness trembling through. She remembered standing and staring and swaying and goggling until something had taken hold.

The idea that had driven her over the edge, to fall in and then out of the hole, had suddenly exploded into a plan and before she knew it she was acting it out. She had closed the trap door, replaced the cobbles, put away the junk and then come to stand over the copy where she had paused to look unsure.

Bracing herself, she taken the unconscious copy by the ankles and dragged it, slow and clumsy out into the cellar. She had paused there to close and bolt the coal cellar door then dragged the copy all the way back upstairs. By the time she had heaved it onto the sofa she was running with sweat but the copy had remained oblivious and inert throughout.

Creeping through the front room she had taken one more look at the copy but then it had started to move and groan, rolling onto its side at which point she had dashed up the stairs to her bedroom. For once the door didn't stick and allowed her straight on in. She wedged a chair under the handle and collapsed onto the bed.

For hours she had sat and paced and then paced and sat, trying to make sense of what had happened. As the adrenalin ran dry she became terrified of what she had done and of what would happen when the copy awoke. Eventually however the stress and fatigue had beaten her down so that she had changed and crawled into bed.

And now it seemed it had worked!

The copy had apparently awoken on the sofa, knew of her job and routine, had taken it for its own, believing itself to be her and then set off to start her working week for her! As far as her bastard boss was concerned she was at work, even though in truth she was still here, in her pyjamas, sat on her bed.

Riley glanced at her alarm clock as the implication began to sink in. A tremor of glee ran through her. At first she resisted it, not daring to hope for fear of disappointment but as she sat and watched the minutes tick by, a giddiness built inside her that could no longer be contained.

Grinning like a fool she sprang from the bed and leapt across the small room to the wardrobe. Dancing to the silence she cast off her pyjamas, exchanging them for underwear,  then snatched at the ordered row of clothes, gouging out a pair of jeans and a warm jumper. She dragged on the clothes then sprinted downstairs like a child on Christmas morning.

Exploding into the kitchen she rummaged through a drawer with joyous violence. Eventually she found the spare set of house keys, slammed the drawer with her hip, tuggedon her trainers and headed out of the house.

Spring had only recently stuttered to a start so that the day was summer bright but with a breeze that bit like winter. Riley plunged her hands into her pockets and drew her shoulders to her ears as she strode off towards the park.

As she stepped and stepped past concrete and brick she kept her head down, watching dull dull greys slide by beneath. Turning a corner and leaning into a hill however she began to slow, realising her rush, her habitual hurry. She allowed her shoulders to drop a little and looked about her as she climbed.

The off licence half way up the hill had closed down she noted with surprise and some time ago too by the looks of it. The windows were already clouded by a fast fading cataract of posters for gigs and clubs.

She breathed the cool air a little slower and a little deeper, surprised at how deep the breaths went.

Shoulders back she breathed deeper still as if trying it for the first time ever. As the top of the hill came into sight, crowned by the green park edge, Riley found she was smiling, walking slow and tall.

Taking her time she wandered a lazy circuit of the whole of the park. Along the way she opened her eyes as she had her lungs and breathed the colours as she had the air. She paused at the flowerbeds and then at the allotments, drinking vibrance and detail, all the while grinning.

Encountering a bench she chose to sit for a while and with stillness came sounds near and far. Birds and traffic, distant football and shouting, the lonely old wind all around. She closed her eyes and let it all pour through her, soaking up the time and the life and the real. It was as if she had awoken from a terrible dream, as if everything before had just fallen away, leaving her fresh and clean and bright brand new. Time slipped by and people walked by and Riley just sat there and smiled.

Her stomach began to grumble and shift restless. Lightheaded she thought but could not recall the last time she had eaten a meal. Blinking through fuzz she stood slightly woozy and ran her hands through all of her pockets.

She realised she didn't have her purse, of course the copy would have it. She thought about it for a moment, sat at her desk, pretending to be her but the picture seemed so distant, so unreal that it refused to come into focus.

The daydream faded as her fingers found paper, folded flat in her right hand back pocket. She bit her bottom lip and dared to hope, slipping the slip from behind to before. Sure enough, there in her hand, in the bright light of day a banknote. Unable to suppress a squeal of joy, Riley thrust the note back into her pocket and set off across the wide open green towards the distant but inviting pub.

She enjoyed the soft springing feel of the grass beneath and gulped down more of the glorious air. The pub gradually grew until the door was full size and she stepped through it licking her lips. The daylight at the windows and the space at the bar made the pub feel different and new. An air of excitement nipped at her ribs and she felt giddy as she approached the bar.

Riley ordered a pint and burger and chips and sat herself down by a window. Sipping at her lager she watched the traffic slide by and revelled in the nothing to do. The food arrived and she took a smell, teasing herself before taking a bite.

Despite the stinging hunger that flooded her mouth she forced herself to eat slow, enjoying the textures and tastes of food from a plate with no history of plastic or microwaves. She ate slow but steady, neither rushing nor pausing, draining the pint down in stages. Finishing finally she swallowed the last drop and placed her cutlery in the empty white space.

For a while she just sat, full up and floppy, letting her stomach get on with its business. A warmth spread through her and cushioned her mind, taking the weight out of the relentless wonder. Everything was easy and quiet and still and she felt herself beginning to doze.

Straightening up she rubbed at her face and yawned a smile away while rising to stand. Feeling solid and warm she stepped back through the door and wandered aimlessly on down the street. Reaching the shops she paused on occasion to gaze around decorated windows.

She bought a paper in the newsagents and ambled back to the park, sitting on a different bench to unfold it. She would glance through the pages then pause to read proper, taking just as long as she liked. The words all washed into her and around in her, the people, the places, the numbers and things. Yet more than these, it was the act of the reading, the fact of the doing, that truly held her attention. Just being there, doing that, how it felt, what it meant, what it was.

The sky was beginning to darken and the traffic beginning to thicken when she decided to head back home. Across the park and down the hill and the round the corner she went. Walking easy and feeling good until the end of her street came into view.

Then a new thought dawned and cut through the good, less a problem, more a concern. It was vital she knew, knew right the way through, that the copy must never see or know of her. She didn't know the time and so paused at the corner, leaning forward, eyebrows raised as she peeked.

Her street was empty and almost completely double parked. Whatever the time, her neighbours were home, their work over for one more day. Was the copy inbound or had it already arrived? There was no way to find out but to look.

Taking a breath, Riley stepped round the corner and moved hurriedly towards her front door. She paused at the step to look left and right then dropped to one knee smooth and silent. Gently, gently, she eased the letterbox in, peering into the dim through the slot.

It took her a moment to see it, but there was a coat on the arm of the sofa. She couldn't see the front of the sofa itself but now a noise flirted with the edge of her hearing. Holding her breath she turned her head to concentrate, groping out into the room for the sound. Sure enough there was a regular trill, the copy's small and rhythmic snore.

Standing again Riley bit at her lip and felt the spare key in her pocket. She had nowhere to go, nowhere but in, yet the choice came slow and uneasy. With cringing intensity she brought up the key, slipping it in with precision. Gripping the handle with her other hand, she turned the key slowly and pushed.

The door gave in silence at first but then sought to cry out at the opening. With teeth gritted stop starts, Riley opened the door then slipped on through and reversed the whole procedure. She fixed her eyes on the sofa as the lock clicked into place and then waited, not breathing, for motion. Nothing happened. The snoring continued and so she stood away from the door.

The path to the stairs was simple and short, a straight line along the back of the sofa. Riley fixed her gaze and took one step, then another eyes straight ahead. Half way there however she could stand it no more and paused to look down, palms all sweaty.

There lay the copy, snoring away, crumpled down into the sofa. The ready meal remnants and an empty wine bottle looked on solemn and silent in the gloom.

She stared at it and stared at it, her head shaking on its own, the disbelief refusing to budge.

She cocked her head to one side to watch its impossible face. Its closed eyes squirmed within a dream, its neck twisted ugly against the cushion. Riley wanted to touch it to prove it was there but her hand recoiled at the thought.

Instead she turned and tiptoed to the door easing it open with care. She passed through the door and closed the door and climbed the stairs so slowly, easing into every floorboard real soft.

Finally she reached her bedroom, wedged the chair against the door and sat on the bed. If the copy was truly like her, if it was her in all of her ways, then it would almost certainly sleep the night through on the sofa again.

Riley lay on her bed and took up her book, wiping dust from the long untouched cover. Opening it at the the bookmark she read a paragraph or two but could find no sense and so skipped backwards until things seemed familiar.

By the time her eyes began to close she had caught up to bookmark and passed it. The tired felt good, soft in her joints and she pulled her clothes off without opening her eyes. Rolling under the covers she wriggled into comfort then sagged strings cut dead into sleep.

—        —

—

Riley was asleep.

The bed was warm enough and sufficiently comfortable and she was dreaming with a smile on her face. Waking easy, she blinked the ceiling into view then rolled towards the bedside table, reaching for the jug of filtered water.

After sitting and stretching and yawning and pouring and drinking, Riley wiped her mouth with the back of her hand. Thinking about the day ahead, she squinted to focus on the brand new red leather satchel hanging on the back of the door. She grinned at it and then sprang out of bed.

The winter was finally over and it was just about turning to spring again though the mornings were still chilled sharp. She snatched a heavy cardigan from the back of a chair and wrapped herself in it as she approached her wardrobe. She pushed all the old crap at the front to one side, the wire hangers howling at the slide. That was just the stuff she left there for the copy, her real stuff was in the back.

Leaning in she selected her clothes for the day and dragged them back out through the castoff crowds. She shrugged the cardigan to the floor and dressed quickly in the cold, hopping from one foot to other with goosebumps.

Pulling the cardigan back on, Riley eyed the satchel again and smiled. With a few quick strides she was at the door, holding the satchel's leather strap in her hand. She took a breath and then swung it onto her shoulder. The small, firm weight settled against her side and as she turned to face the mirror she patted it lovingly.

Facing the mirror she looked at the satchel, at how it hung against her, the lines of the strap and patted it again, smiling. As she watched her fingers began to work at the buckles, sharp little flicks of well practiced motion. Lifting the flap she tilted the bag so as to be able see the inside in the mirror.

Bundles of cash, neatly bound, jostled with each other within. Her heart quickened a little at the sight of it all then she and closed the flap, feeling suddenly secretive. Flushing a little, Riley buckled up the satchel and then turned to look at the grotty little bedroom for what she hoped would be the last morning ever.

Everything she had planned over the last long year had worked out perfectly so far. The trip to the bank last week before had been the penultimate step. Leaving today, savings in hand would be the last and best of all.

Giving the satchel one last glance Riley removed the chair from under the handle of the door and went out onto the landing. She paused to listen, leaning over the stairs and straining. With a nod to herself she descended lightly, opening the door to the front room with care.

Sure enough, there was the copy, asleep on the sofa as usual. Riley padded over to the back of the sofa and leaned forward, planting her chin on her arms to look at the thing. Pale and lanky, it lay heaped in a tangle, drooling all over itself and snoring. It's head was at a ridiculous angle against the cushion and every so often one of its bare, grubby feet would twitch in the cool morning air.

Riley shook her head and felt disgust contort her face. For a long time she had been terrified of it, had spent nights cowering in fear of discovery. Over time however she had realised that the copy's habits were repetitive and predictable. As long as she avoided certain rooms at certain times she could almost guarantee never encountering it at all.

Of course this hadn't worked every time, there had been a few incidents where abrupt hiding had been required. Behind the door atop the cellar steps, laid out flat under the bed or even standing in the bath behind the shower curtain. She had always avoided detection however and after a while she had come to realise that the copy just wasn't that bright.

As she began to build a new life for herself Riley had then begun to feel sorry for it. It was so flat and dull, it didn't seem to want anything, it just went through the motions. She didn't know why, but it saddened her to think that it didn't have dreams or ambitions, that it was satisfied to just stay where it was.

The copy snorted itself into silence for a few seconds, shifting in its sleep, before resuming its gently trilling snore. Riley shook her head again. She had tried to help it, she'd left flyers for courses or activities in amongst the post, she'd ordered particular catalogues and magazines to give it hints. Nothing. Even with opportunities waved in front of its face, the stupid thing wasn't interested. It didn't see, wouldn't see, didn't care.

These days she just hated it. Despised it. Loathed it. In fact it made her angry just to think about it sometimes. The problem was, as she had realised a few months before, the thing was fundamentally flawed.

Initially she had thought it a perfect replica but now when she looked at it she could see the differences, she could see it wasn't quite right. It did look almost exactly like her only pale and sickly, too thin in the wrists and the cheeks as if the copying hadn't quite worked so that something key had been lost.

Certainly it could go through the motions, the day job, the housework but it was just a shell, there was nothing inside it. There was nothing of which to be afraid and nothing for which to feel sorry.

It didn't care about its life, it didn't care about anything, it never took any initiative. It had been she herself who had taken the time to write all those letters to the bank, insisting they correct their error with her savings and to her that proved the difference between them.

The copy knew about the disappearance of her savings from the statements it had read and it presumably believed the savings to be its own. At no point over the last year however had the copy attempted to do anything about the situation. It just kept going through the motions, soulless and senseless, unwilling to put in the requisite effort to better its own situation.

It would sleep here for a few hours more then wake and cry and probably vomit. In the meantime Riley would have moved all of her things downstairs, out onto the street and into a taxi. She was leaving the copy the house and the job, more than it would have ever found on its own and more than it deserved. The worst part was it would never even know what she'd done for it, it would think it had earned it all itself.

She straightened from the sofa, still eyeing the copy with contempt. She wandered into the kitchen, patting the satchel at her side and smiling to herself. While pouring a glass of water she felt rather than heard a strange rumble from below. Stopping the tap she stood still and listened and in a second felt the rumble come again from directly below her.

Placing the glass on the side, she stepped through the kitchen to the cellar door and headed down into the dark, pulling the door closed behind her. She hadn't returned to the cellar since the night she had made the copy and the unchanged shapes and smells turned her stomach.

She could hear the boiler rumbling away to itself, just faintly from behind the coal cellar door. She needed the copy to sleep a few hours more in order to make her escape, to wake it now would mean an agonized delay, relegated to hiding until it drank itself to sleep again later on.

Rushing between the mouldering boxes, Riley slid back the bolt on the coal cellar door, stepped through and closed it behind her and then scampered quickly over to the boiler. Stood beside it she could hear the throbbing all the time now and realised it was swelling back and forth, growing a little louder every other time.

Scooping a cigarette lighter out of a deep cardigan pocket she flicked the flint to a spark. A quivering yellow painted the boiler as she opened the casing to reveal the buttons and dials. She cast her eyes back and forth across the gauges before deciding to just turn it off and on again.

She had just swapped the lighter to her other hand and was reaching out to press the main power switch when a violent wall of sound knocked her to cobbled floor. The sound was incredible, a great throbbing roar that seemed to shake the entire house. Amplified by the crowded brick walls, it made Riley's ears ring and throb.

Falling to the cobbles had bruised her elbows and robbed her of the lighter. As the boiler continued to roar she scrabbled around for the small plastic tube, eventually finding it and panting to her feet.

Through frantic flicking she lit the lighter and looked again for the power switch. This time however, as silence fell between outbursts she heard the sound of footsteps out in the cellar.

Trapped and panicked Riley stepped quickly towards the shadowy bulk that occupied most of the coal cellar. She moved around the side of the floor to low ceiling wall of junk and into a pitch narrow space behind. The smell was utterly foul and while trying not to breath she suddenly vomited a little, immediately swallowing it back down and then shuddering in disgust.

As her eyes adjusted back to the darkness she moved carefully to peer around the edge of the junk. A thin yellow line appeared suddenly below the door to the cellar. Incoming footsteps strobed closer in between the roars from the boiler. Then they stopped, breaking the line into three. She ducked back into the safety of the stench, gagging again as she heard the little wood door swing open.

For one second and then another she cringed in the stink, trying not to breathe or touch anything around her. The roar of the boiler seemed to shake her inside, rattling her stomach and forcing the air out of her lungs. Then came the agonized pause, the empty lungs locked by reluctance, finally bursting open to gasp. Finally, the stench again, great desperate gulps of it, thick and vile.

A click pierced the din and a moment later the throbbing seemed to deflate and hiss away. Relaxing only slightly, Riley leaned out to peek again only to see the copy staring straight back at her. Standing in broad oblong of light spilling in through the door it tilted its head to one side and squinted at her. She sprang back into the shadows wide eyed, teeth clenched, every muscle balled in fear.

Riley waited for what felt like minutes before releasing herself and taking a few small, careful breaths. She couldn't hear anything from the copy but she was certain it hadn't left the room either. She began to fidget with indecision as her curiosity and fear tussled back and forth.

She shifted her frustration from one foot to another in a bitter rhythm. What was it doing? She needed it back upstairs, sleeping off its habitual hangover. She couldn't confront it however, couldn't drive it away, she could only wait for it to get bored and leave.

Relenting into a sagged stillness, she closed her eyes. She tried pulling her shirt up over her nose but the stench remained as fierce as ever. Instead she pinched her nose with one hand and then the other until pain began to seep into the stiffness in her legs and lower back.

The copy was still out there, she could hear it moving around. Meanwhile she decided she would have to sit and started to lower herself carefully to the floor, her fingers stretching out into the darkness below in search of terrible things.

Her fingers had reached ankle height when she encountered texture and froze. Setting her jaw and closing her eyes she began to explore the object at her feet. It felt like a long fabric bag containing a tent, slightly greasy with damp and wedged under something else at the far end.

Leaning forward onto one knee she reached forward into the darkness, tentative but pushing herself on. At almost arms length she encountered a pile of soft but firm objects, seemingly more tents and other camping equipment, some hard and angular, some soft and cushioned, everything wrapped in fabric. Although slimy and chilled, the texture of the junk in the dark did not seem too bad even though she knew that the source of the impossibly vile smell lay somewhere within it.

By stages and driven mainly by cramp, Riley lowered herself onto the lower slope of the stinking pile. The air felt fetid and thick and as she sat amongst it her head began to throb. A blinding band tightened across her forehead so that with her hand not holding her nose she began to massage her temples.

The time dragged on and on but the copy and the stench remained. She gave up on holding her nose and hugged the bulging leather satchel to her chest instead. As she sank deeper into the pile of junk she revised her plans. Eventually the copy would leave, go back upstairs and fall asleep, allowing her to get her things and sneak out, a few hours later than planned now but out nevertheless. She began to plan the rest of the trip in detail to pass the time.

Just as she was considering what kind of coffee she should order at the train station however she was dragged back into the filth of the coal cellar by a the sound of heavy, dull slap on the cobbles beyond. It sounded as if the copy had fallen but she couldn't hear it getting back up.

Suddenly realising just how far into the junk she

was Riley began to struggle as quickly as she dare to extract herself and stand. Wincing through the straightening of both her aching legs, she leaned cautiously toward the edge of the heap, just far enough for a one eyed peek.

She was just in time to see the copy slam the coal cellar door, plunging her back into darkness. She could hear the copy moving away through the cellar and the yellow line returned unbroken to beneath the door.

Without thinking Riley moved toward the door, away form the junk and the stink. Placing her ear against the cool, damp wood of the door she could hear slow, laboured footsteps fading before stuttering distant up the stairs to the kitchen.

As sensation settled to sense Riley blinked stunned then dashed back into the shadows behind the junk pile, her hand clasped to her face and vomited violently. The strain of each retch tightening the white hot band of pain about her temples so that her knees quivered their surrender.

Sinking to the clammy cobbles, she leaned against the rough brick wall and sagged. She glanced back at the door, mouth dripping, and saw the yellow line die with a blink. Her head pounded, gouging great troughs out of any thoughts she tried to string together. She heard more sluggish movements from directly above as the dark closed in around her.

Suddenly her previously hopeless legs propelled her to stand. An eyes flashing, stomach churning lunge took her to the door where she snatched at the handle with fuzzy, half there fingers. The door wouldn't open and as she dragged at it spastically the jagged sound of the copy closing the bolt on the door just moments before came from somewhere distant and deep in the fog of her mind.

Riley leaned against the door as a great sopping blanket of fatigue landed across her. The headache wouldn't let her think, her stomach wouldn't let her move. Licking her lips she tried to focus and suddenly remembered the lighter in her pocket. After much fumbling failure she eventually retrieved the light and lit it. The trembling yellow flame pushed back the dark but a little. The shadows beyond were nothing but brick and cobbles.

Shakily Riley approached the boiler. If she could make it make a noise again then the copy would come back down. While it attended to the boiler she could slip out behind it and make a dash for the front door. She still had the money and her non lighter hand tapped the satchel absently at the thought.

Holding the lighter to the boiler Riley squinted through the pain behind her eyes at the various switches and dials. She considered just switching the boiler off but it could take the copy time to notice the lack of heating or hot water and she needed to be outside right now.

Stepping back from the boiler she held the light higher, looking for any instructions or warnings on or around it. Immediately to the left of the boiler, up at the top, just before the low ceiling, she saw a small, white square of plastic stuck to the wall.

Riley stepped closer and craned her neck to see. There had once been writing on the square but it had long since faded. All that remained were two concentric circles at the centre. The outer ring was a lightly coloured but the central circle was a deep and solid dark.

The sight of the square and its circles baffled Riley so that she allowed the lighter to rest and simply swayed in the darkness, struggling to remain conscious let alone understand. Slowly she sat, down onto the clammy cobbles. The square was familiar, she was sure she knew what it was. It was something important, something lifesaving but easily overlooked and forgotten, like a smoke alarm.

It was a carbon monoxide detector.

As if waiting at the back door to be let in by the thought of smoke alarms, the knowledge flashed inside her. It was a disposable carbon monoxide detector with a peel off, sticky back. You stuck them near your boiler so you could tell if it was giving off potentially lethal fumes. The beige circle in the centre stayed beige if there were none but would darken if the levels became dangerous.

It took her a couple of attempts but Riley

managed to stand. Again she flicked the lighter and again she peered into the central circle of the little plastic square just to be sure. It was very, very black.

The boiler was leaking carbon monoxide and probably had been for months, years even. That was why she used to feel so groggy all those nights on the sofa above. That was why she felt so groggy now, why her head hurt, she'd been sat in a tiny enclosed space with a boiler for hours and hours.

And she was locked in.

This second piece of knowledge needed no accomplice, it kicked in the doors and laughed in her face. She could feel herself slipping but she knew that if she fell asleep she would die. Despite her fear her chin kept falling to her chest, her heavy eyes falling closed as she stumbled back towards the door. She pulled at it feebly before falling against the wood to slide splintering down to the cobbles, her fingers curled cold at the handle.

She began to wish desperately that she was asleep while frantically struggling to remain awake. If only it could be a dream, a hallucination, a terrible trip from the boiler fumes. Perhaps that was what it all had been, the copy, the plan. Perhaps she'd never gone back upstairs that night, that night she had sat next to the hole. Perhaps the fumes from the boiler had overcome her and she had dreamed the last year of freedom. But then how was she locked in, trapped and dying?

She was dying.

This third flash was cold. It washed through her, thinning the fog just a little. She pulled on the handle and dragged herself upright, back to tottering feet. Getting the lighter lit one more time she waved her glowing fist about the coal cellar, desperately searching for hope.

Towards the back the amorphous heap of vile junk still lurked. Bracing herself she stepped wobbly back toward it, determined to find tools of salvation somewhere amid it. Moving back around to her former hiding place she poured light on it for the first time, hoping see something capable of breaking a door.

Instead she saw corpses.

The greasy, vile smelling heap of rods in bags and squishy old cushions into which she had sunk while hiding from the copy was in fact a heap of decaying bodies. Riley vomited again, mostly dry heaving but didn't allow the flame to die nor her eyes to leave the pile.

The longer she looked the worse it got, the more certain it was. All of the corpses were dressed like her, they all wore her shoes and each one carried a bulging little leather pouch. In fact every single corpse was her.

Her body finally revolted to surrender. She tumbled forward into the pile and was unconscious before she hit them, slumping in and amongst and fitting perfectly where she settled.

# finding the plot

And just like that, he was awake.

He wasn't aware of having been asleep, there were no hazy recollections of fast fading dreams nor of the subtle shift from oblivion to awareness, suddenly he simply was. The abrupt inrush of sensory information tipped him back on his heels so that he realised he was standing. His body caught itself, preventing the stumble but his mind reeled on within.

While the assault of light and sound began to coalesce, the cool air on his skin told him he was outside. Shades became shapes and then colours and finally fell into familiar form. Seething greens sharpened to blades and leaves and as a hand floated up from his side to his head the park snapped firmly into focus.

The hand hovered before his face for a moment and he studied it intently. He knew it to be his own, knew it with the most absolute certainty, and yet he clung to the fleeting echoes of confusion from just moments before.

A shape moved beyond the hand, tall and dark, flitting right to left so that his awareness ballooned outwards. Suddenly anchored in context, he felt another, smaller rush as sounds and smells completed the picture. He was standing on the grass just beside one of the many grey paths that cut their many ways through the park. Across the path another strip of the ubiquitous green glowed before stark iron railings which cut the drab grey violence of the street beyond into thin vertical strips.

This was London.

He knew this with the same certainty by which he had recognised his own hand and yet driving his now steadily open eyes about the place, he could find nothing that told him so. It simply was. Another figure passed by, black shoes taking brisk, clipping steps along the path, dark trousers, grey coat. He watched them as they passed, head down, shoulders hunched, ignoring him completely. This was definitely London.

After a moment more he attempted a step forward. His legs felt hollow and stiff as if brand new, or at least very, very old. After another stiff step and then one more however his legs began to walk on their own, carrying him across the path and up to the railings.

His hands reached out and his fingers curled, embracing the chill of the metal bars and grinding ever so slightly against their rough rusted texture, relishing the solidity and presence. Beyond the railings a busy street bustled.

Both sides of the road were lined with parked cars so that those moving in between crawled and barked. Immediately beyond the railing small knots of bodies threaded through one another along the pavement while beyond the still and slow moving tops of the cars a mess of bobbing heads betrayed a similar flow over there as well.

The whole scene sat in the shade of a vast building that loomed grey on the far side of the street so that the bodies and vehicles blended into a colourless background soup. Litter rode the wind, people made their way, cars stopped and started, all just abstract motion, the animation of inanimate objects.

Suddenly, far off to the left, a pattern of motion caught his eye. Something different was coming. Even at distance the figure was distinct and obviously feminine. A discrete margin of space seemed to surround her so that the crowds eased open unconsciously, as she flowed through them. His eyes fixed upon her form, utterly confident that there was nothing else worth seeing. She was the focus of the scene, everything around her existed solely to provide emphasis and contrast.

Tall and lithe, her motion was sublime so that even from range he felt he could see her muscles working with perfect efficiency, projecting an aura of strength, confidence and ease. She wore a rich cream coloured coat that ran from a high collar all the way down to her ankles. The coat was exquisitely cut so that the lines of her body flowed through its obvious luxurious thickness.

As she came closer he felt his chest tighten, his mouth hanging open just a little as he greedily consumed the details of her face. Her skin was flawless, her eyes large and soft yet sharpened with wicked wit about the cheekbones. Her hair sat strand perfect, just an occasional wisp taking flight to add a softening air of casual ease to the otherwise sculpted precision.

She had come close enough for him to be able to pick out the strikes of her heels on the pavement, clear ringing clicks cutting sharp through the sludgy hubbub. The sound drew his eyes down so that as she closed to pass he could catch glimpses of her shoes.

A void burned white in his lungs as the moment of her passing drew close. The click of her heels held him utterly so that just as the anticipated instant arrived he found himself unable to seize the ecstasy of her proximity. Instead he was himself seized by another flash of certainty: In a few more steps she would stumble. The heel of her left shoe would snap and she would fall.

Such was the impact of this knowledge that by the time he refocused he caught only a flash of her features as she glided past, her coat billowing like gentle waves on a warm ocean. Her scent remained however and for another second or so he breathed deep the subtle, exotic aroma, applying it as a salve to the bitter disappointment he felt at missing their moment of closeness. He closed his eyes and swam in her, in the very lines and curves of her, the greatness and the power, her scent and motion, the pure white joy of her being.

As quickly as it had arrived the moment passed and his body began to gasp at the frigid air, finally released from the unbearable tension of wanting. His eyes blinked and the world about him pushed its way back into his mind. She had left his sight and try as he might he could not even discover her footsteps among the grey world beyond the railings.

Without her presence the world had slipped back into the scraping of dull, flat shadows. The sense of loss this created blended with the certainty of his premonition to spark a deep urgency within him. He turned from the railing and moved quickly to the path, following it parallel to the pavement in the direction she had been heading.

Occasionally greenery blocked his view of the

street so that as he trotted, half running, half walking, he would occasionally duck and lunge, craning his neck in an attempt to catch sight of her. Each hurried step he put down raised the level of tension within him. The moment of her stumbling was closing, the shattering of a grace too divine to be soiled and this in turn fuelled a panic that rose from the very pit of him.

Then, between the low boughs of a heavy tree, vertical strips of railing-cut cream arrested his eyes. His ears immediately found the regular clicking and his nose even reported just the faintest hint of her on the air. Staring wildly ahead he saw that the path forked off, the right hand side continued through the park while the left joined with the street via a broad open gate.

Thoughts fell away as he broke into a run. He had to be there, to reach her before she fell, this was everything that he knew and in that moment, all that he was. With long, wild strides he ate up the path, the gate growing to fill his vision a little more as each foot fell.

As the turn rushed upon him he slowed to corner, hopping and scrambling to rein in his momentum before lunging towards the street. She was there, just a few steps and closing from the gate and from him. The moment was upon him. One more heartbeat and the heel would break, gravity snatching ugly to taint her confident gait.

He paused beside a large, dense bush to take a breath, preparing himself, then stepped forward toward the street, toward her, toward his gonging moment of destiny but found the ground instead.

Heavy hands had grasped him from behind, catching him off balance and abruptly snatching him from his feet. The ground beside the bush was cold and hard and he met it with enough force to knock all of the air from his lungs. Dazed and gasping he was vaguely aware of movement behind him, of the presence of his assailant and the potential for additional violence. His eyes were locked however, on the rough, squat oblongs of light that sat between the railings beneath the bush.

Her steps landed with expected perfection so that each slender ankle and foot was framed one after the other. A great roaring wind seemed to tear through every part of him as his eyes pinned themselves to the long slender heel of her left shoe. He felt his hands groping at the hard packed dirt beneath him, as his body dumbly sought purchase to rise.

The heavy unseen hands returned however, instantly grinding him into the dirt so that he watched powerless as the world slowed to a crawl. Frame by frame her left foot rose, ready to fall into the final oblong. His mouth opened to scream but hard thick fingers appeared from behind and clasped it closed and tight.

As the foot began to fall the smooth line of the heel began to tremble until, at the last possible moment, its midsection exploded. Tiny shards formed a perfect sphere about the sudden gap in the heel and hung for an instant before scattering away. The bottom point of the heel fell away too as if felled by a sniper and all the while the foot continued its descent.

He writhed in mortal desperation as the ball of her foot made contact with the pavement, her now jagged stump of a heel following behind. He saw the moment at which her body expected the lost point of the heel to make contact with the pavement, the sudden, ugly, break in flow, the flinch of her calf surprised.

As her heel continued down into new, too low territory, he felt tears spill from his eyes. He winced at the moment of impact and cried out against the hard skinned hand as her ankle turned awkward and over. Straining with every ounce of himself he threw his arm out ahead of him, his fingertips just about breaching the railings but too late.

The world sped up again, the ugly slap of her stumbled feet quickly followed by the sudden intrusion of a new pair. Black shoes, large, heavy and perfectly shined beneath trousers sharply creased. The new feet mixed a dance among hers, shin to shin as her fall was arrested. The sound of voices but not words fell down upon him until a slender, cream cuffed hand, free of blemish or jewellery, dropped into view. Her hand slipped off and scooped up her shoes, leaving beautifully stockinged feet behind in their wake.

Then the feet, with their delicate arches and

miniature toes disappeared, moving away in step with the heavy black shoes and all sense and reason fell out of his world. The hard, heavy hand retreated from his mouth so that empty and broken, hopeless and done, he fell limp against the dirt and wept.

From somewhere beyond his pit of despair he heard a gruff voice mumbling one half of a conversation. As each moment dragged by and despite his deepest and most desperate longing, the past remained as it was. Eventually his body lost patience and shifted itself and with leaden movements he turned onto his back and raised himself onto his elbows to stare at his assailant.

A huge man, fat and shabby, was looking down at him with utter contempt in his eyes. Dirty, light brown overalls stretched across his ample middle and hung baggy about his titan limbs. The man was talking quietly into a radio which he grasped to his stubble with thick, grimy fingers. His conversation apparently at an end he lowered the radio to a clasp on his busy black belt, hung low with pouches and tools.

For a moment the pair remained silent and still, until the fat man sighed his irritation and spoke to the figure at his feet.

"You prick," he said.

—　　　—

—

Walking through the park behind the man in the overalls he felt the emotion shaking its way out of him. The trembling came from his chest, shuddering out through his jaw and limbs and feeling as if it would never stop. Head down, he followed the huge, overalled man blindly, not knowing what else to do. The horrific trauma of the broken heel already seemed distant and surreal so that within the shakes his cheeks burned red.

He didn't understand what he had done and the more cool realities washed over him, the more shamed he felt. Somewhere in the far distance lay a cold, lurking fear armed with no end of terrifying, unanswerable questions. For the moment however he was too numb, too senseless to conceive of them and looked upon his situation blankly and without feeling.

He was in a park in London.

This was the only thing he knew. He did not know how he had come to be there, where he had been before nor even who he was. He did not know where he lived, where he had been born nor even his own name, at least he hadn't until the fat man had told him. He now knew the fat man's name as well, the third piece of new information he had learned since awaking, on his feet, in a London park.

He had dragged himself to his feet to find that although he was only a couple of inches shorter than the man in the overalls, he felt small beneath his withering gaze. The man's overalls may have originally been light brown in colour all over but were now decorated with a wide array of unpleasant stains. The only intentional patterns were two strings of neatly embroidered letters that sat above his left breast pocket and spoke quietly of 'B A R R Y' and his role as 'Plot Technician'.

Barry had stared at him for at least two seconds as he had swayed slightly atop traumatised legs.

"Oh for.." Barry had groaned, cutting himself short before sighing and addressing the mess in front of him. "Pull your finger out Prot, there's work needs done," he had said.

With that he'd turned on his heel and set off down the path without ever looking back. Prot had remained for a second, reeling and confused, before recognising a dearth of other options and walking quickly to catch up.

The walking seemed to help so that after they'd made their way round what felt like half the entire park, Prot noticed that the shaking had mostly subsided. That lurking fear was beginning to loom so that a few of the more enthusiastic questions began to surface.

He trotted a couple of steps to close the gap on Barry and tried to ask him a question. At first however his mouth felt strange, his tongue felt unnaturally clean and dry and his jaw felt stiff yet there was not discomfort or pain. He licked his lips, traced out his teeth with his tongue then swallowed and coughed before trying again.

"Excuse me," he began, but stopped immediately. So unfamiliar was his own voice that for a second he thought he had been interrupted by some unseen other. He tried again, speaking slowly so as to examine the sound of each syllable as it passed his lips.

"Excuse," he said, "me."

Barry strode on, there was no indication he had heard anything.

"Hey!" tried Prot, a little louder than he had intended so that he made himself jump.

Barry continued to ignore him and turned off the main path to approach an electricity substation, a tiny squat brick building behind a high metal fence. Pausing at the gate, Barry produced from somewhere a metal ring the size of a dinner plate, half full of every kind of key.

With improbable ease he tipped the ring so that half of the keys slid away from the rest of the bunch and pinched out the single key in the middle. This slipped soundlessly into the lock on the gate and a moment later Barry was stepping through it. He stepped to the side and held the gate as he turned to face Prot, an expression of weary irritation on his bloated, sour face.

"I'm," Prot began, his voice quavering out of control. He coughed and raised his chin. "I'm not going anywhere until you tell me what's going on."

"Fine by me," said Barry flatly, letting the gate swing from his hand and turning away to approach the substation itself.

"Wait!" wailed Prot as the gate crashed shut in his face. He flinched and cringed, his nerves still jangling, before taking a breath and pushing through the gate to follow. Barry had disappeared behind the building down a narrow gap between the back wall of the substation and the vast mass of privet hedge that loomed behind it.

By the time Prot caught up with him, Barry had selected another key from the horde and was opening a small, green, metal door into the building. He disappeared inside and Prot jogged to catch up and follow him in, suddenly afraid to lose sight of his only guide.

Stepping into the gloom however, Prot found himself stunned dumb once more. The whole of the substation was a single, mostly empty room. There were no great, crackling coils or heavy cables, no gauges or dials, in fact no substationing type equipment of any kind.

Instead, to the right of the door was what looked like the oldest of all the armchairs, sitting beside a rickety little card table. Beyond the table sat a large package wrapped in so many layers of heavy plastic that the whole thing had taken on a strangely ethereal grey colour.

From behind this package large shelves ran along the rest of the right hand wall to the back of the room, overflowing with boxes and tins of wires and bales and tools and general clutter. Directly ahead of Prot, the back wall was completely covered with great mess of plans, photographs, diagrams, notes and lists. Pinned on top of and in and amongst one another these ran from the low ceiling down to the surface of a large, broad table that sat against the wall.

The flow of paper continued unhindered, spilling down to engulf the surface of the table, the tide broken here and there by occasional tools or machine parts. To the left of the table another set of bustling shelves mirrored those on the right hand wall. These shelves ran back towards the door, stopping just short to allow for a small sink and fridge.

Barry moved past Prot from the armchair to the sink, carrying a faded green mug with several chips missing from the rim. While he busied himself with the kettle he grunted over his shoulder to Prot but didn't look round.

"The stuff in plastic's yours," was all he said.

Still struggling with the sight of the secret interior, Prot stumbled towards the shimmering mass of plastic wrap. Standing over it he realised that deep within the layer upon layer of grey there appeared to be a small wooden chair. In the lap of the chair were two other parcels, also bundled in plastic.

He tore through these first, liberating a shiny new, green mug and a set of light brown overalls. He dropped the cup back onto the bundled up chair and held the overalls by the shoulders, dropping the rest to hang before him. There were identical to Barry's in style but the limbs were slender to match his own, all perfectly clean and pressed. Above the left breast pocket four simple letters whispered 'P R O T' and beneath these the more familiar 'Plot Technician'.

"Put those on," called Barry over his hulking shoulder. "And give us that mug."

Dumbly Prot complied, retrieving the mug from the chair and placing the handle over Barry's waiting fingers. He stumbled a couple of times as he pushed his legs into the overalls before slipping his arms into them too and pulling them up over his shoulders.

As Prot pulled the zip from crotch to neck, Barry turned back to face him bearing a steaming mug in each hand and moved back towards the armchair. Placing the newer mug on the table he settled into the armchair with apparent satisfaction and cradled his own upon his swollen gut.

For minute after minute Prot simply stood, arms limp, eyes dull, watching Barry as he waited for his brew to cool. The aches and pain born of their first encounter came back to haunt him so that the appeal of sitting down to a hot drink grew and grew.

Finally, he turned back to the final plastic package and began to wrestle the small wooden chair free of its wrappings. The chair freed, Prot carried it the few steps to the card table and placed it to mirror Barry's before sitting carefully and reaching out to his mug.

For a while they sat in silence until the steam from their drinks grew sufficiently thin and they began to sip at them. Barry sighed with satisfaction while Prot sipped absently, staring into nothing, defeated and hopeless.

"What..." Prot began but then faltered, unsure which of the endless questions to voice, "...was that?" he said eventually.

"That was you almost cocking up a week's hard graft," was Barry's response, though his voice was softer than before.

"Sorry," said Prot instinctively, "I didn't..." again he lapsed lost. "I mean I don't..."

"No matter," said Barry, in an easy, even conversational tone now. "No harm done."

Prot nodded his thanks at what seemed to be a kindness.

"But what..." he began again, still struggling to verbalise his panicked tangle of thoughts. Before he could get any further however Barry had draining his mug, placed it on the table and was looking at his watch.

"Right then," he said decisively, struggling up and out of the armchair before clapping his hands and rubbing them together.

"Back to it eh?" he winked at Prot and crossed to the table at the back of the room, laying his heavy fingers on the mountains of papers.

Prot rose to follow but froze beside the table.

"Back to what?" he asked again, his confusion condensing into frustration and even anger now. "What's going on? What am I doing here?!"

"Well first off," Barry called calmly without turning around. "You're going to rinse them mugs out."

Tense with frustration Prot snatched up the mugs and carried them to the sink. The simple actions of the turning the tap, moving the mugs, placing the mugs and turning the tap calmed him a little but still he felt the urgency of his ignorance.

Meanwhile, Barry was scrutinising some papers on a clipboard, occasionally referring to one of the maps on the wall. As Prot drew breath for yet another attempt Barry got in first with another instruction.

"Now, find these..." said Barry, not looking round as a faded, typewritten list of numbers appeared inches from Prot's face, thrust and held by a tree trunk arm. Prot hovered in the pause before taking the piece of paper.

"...in there," Barry finished, his thick pinching finger extending to point over Prot's shoulder.

Prot's gaze followed the finger to the overflowing shelves behind him. His body turned to follow, grudgingly, and with a couple of doubtful glances at Barry's still uninterested bulk he approached the shelves.

Raising the page with a heavy sigh he ran down

the list of a dozen three digit numbers. There was nothing else on the page, just the tall, thin stack of slightly uneven characters, clearly punched out on a typewriter many years before. Turning the sheet over, Prot checked the back but found it blank and so turned his attention to the shelves before him instead.

The shelves were deep and each was piled almost up to the one above it with the most varied and random assortment of junk yard jumble Prot had ever seen. Heavy, greasy machine parts sat among hastily rolled up pieces of fabric between boxes and tins and bags and jars.

He frowned his lack of comprehension in turn at a stained teaspoon, a torn parking ticket, a half eaten apple, a squash ball, a mobile phone, seven dead cockroaches and on it went. Everything was covered with a thick layer of dust and the whole mess appeared singular and solid as if time had gradually melded it all into one.

In amongst the dense clutter, occasional corners of transparent plastic jutted out. Upon closer inspection these were revealed to be zip-locked plastic bags of varying sizes and content. In the top right corner of each bag a small white label had been haphazardly applied to bear a handwritten three digit number.

The bags were strewn randomly throughout the clutter piles of the shelves in and no discernible sequence. Prot spent a few minutes listlessly pulling out bags at random as he spotted them but found none of them bore any of the numbers on the list.

Throwing the last of these back onto the shelves, Prot took a step back and looked again at the list of numbers in his hand. A twitching urge ran from his fingers to his brain to clench the paper into a fist, to curse and rage at the senseless world around him. As the thought bounced back down his arm however, a need to hesitate arose before his fingers could curl.

Beyond such a tantrum lay only the same unanswered questions as before, the same fear and impotence. The task at Prot's hand suddenly took on the appearance of a sanctuary of distraction, a respite from confusion and brief instance of control. Perhaps if he completed the task his new companion would furnish him with the answers he so desperately required.

Moving to the left hand end of the shelves where they met the sink, Prot started with the top shelf and worked his way to the right. Each time he encountered a bag he would remove it just far enough to read its number and then check the list.

The first match he found was about half away along the top shelf. Eagerly pulling the bag free of its cluttered home Prot stalled and stepped back to look at it. A thick slice of beetroot swung back and forth within the bag as it dangled from his outstretched hand.

The bag was tacky with grease and dust and shot through with milky lines where harsh folds had stretched the plastic over a very long time of stillness. Glistening within however, the slice of beetroot appeared perfectly fresh, vivid juice oozing slow from the flesh and spreading thin against the inside of the bag.

Keeping the impossible thing at arms length Prot moved to the back of the room and dropped it onto the paper covered table. Barry didn't appear to notice, he was engrossed in applying his thick fingers to the clasp of a small metal chest. Finally flipping the catch, Barry lifted the hinged lid with great care to reveal a rank of corked test tubes within, all held snug in a great bed of foam.

Returning to the shelves Prot couldn't help but cast a barrage of curious looks back towards Barry. He searched quickly, keen to find another bag and with it an excuse to return to the table for a closer look at what Barry's was doing.

The next bag he found contained half a dozen thickly sliced pieces of cheese. Without a thought for the old-without-but-new-within weirdness of the bag, Prot dashed back to the table, just in time to see Barry setting a microscope down in a clearing he had made amongst the papers. Lingering as long as he felt he could, Prot watched in fascination as Barry removed the first test tube from the case and pulled out its cork.

Almost rifling through the heaps now, Prot finished his search of the top shelf and moved down to the next, working quickly back to the left. It was only a matter of seconds before he had found the next bag. This one had clearly lain undisturbed for years in order to acquire a vivid ring of rusted brown from a corroded old spring pressed down upon it. Inside however lay a perfectly fresh, thick slice of white bread, free of indentations or mould.

Barely even looking at it, Prot returned to the table and paused to watch fascinated as Barry drew a tiny amount of clear fluid from on of the test tubes with a long pipette. With confident ease he deposited a single drop of the fluid onto a tiny oblong of glass, rested the pipette among the clutter and pressed a second sliver of glass over the top of the first before sliding the snug pair beneath the microscope. Leaning forward, Barry placed his eye to the eyepiece of the microscope while his thick fingers adjusted the focusing wheel to the side expertly.

"How're them bags coming?" he asked, still concentrating on the much magnified image of the slides.

"Yeah," spluttered Prot, his cheeks flushing slightly. "I'm doing it, I'm doing it."

His body turned to move back toward the shelves but his head lingered, dragged along reluctant before finally turning away.

As he collected the last few bags, Prot threw glance after glance back at Barry and saw him check samples from each test tube in turn before finally selecting two particular test tubes and mix their contents together in a third empty tube. The two clear fluids clouded slightly as they mixed. Dropping the last bag among the others Prot drew breath to ask just what it was that Barry was doing but was again beaten to it by another thrusted document.

"Right," said Barry. "Now make this."

This time the document was a large, faded, black and white photograph of a sandwich. The top slice of bread lay to the side awaiting placement so that the arrangement of contents was clearly visible.

"Just like that mind," Barry added as Prot took the photograph. "Needs to be spot on, he's very particular this one and he'll notice if it's off."

Laying the photograph down Prot shook his head

exasperated. Rubbing his eyes he sighed before pouring a venomous glare down into the photograph on the table. At the top left of the slice of bread that formed the base of the sandwich there was a small gap between the crust and the bread. Snatching up one of the two bags containing slices of bread he saw that the slice within matched exactly.

Opening the bag he was immediately aware of the soft fresh scent of the bread and enjoyed the smell despite himself as he slid the slice out onto the heap of papers. As he worked his way through the rest of the photograph and the rest of the bags his irritation began to be edged out by wonder.

The sandwich ingredients in the bags weren't just the same as those in the photograph, they were exactly the same. The shape the juice from the beetroot made as it touched the bread, the way the edges of the cheese crumbled, the jagged edge of the slice of ham.

The sandwich he was creating was the sandwich in the photograph, the exact same one and yet there was no way it could have been made, photographed and then disassembled. The beetroot juice couldn't have been sucked back out of the bread, the cheese couldn't have been uncrumbled. Equally, there was no way the ingredients or their combination could have been reproduced, not to such perfect accuracy.

It was impossible.

The sandwich he was making was just an everyday, banal and tedious thing and yet it was impossible, it could not be. The only explanation he could think of was that the old, black and white photograph, dogeared and faded, had somehow come from the future. It must have been taken at this point, just as he had finished the construction, and then allowed to age before being brought back in time to guide his hand.

Prot felt his head begin to spin again.

Shakily he reached for the second slice of bread, dumbly seeking to finish the job and put an end to the cheese and ham madness.

"Hang on," said Barry, staying Prot's hand while attaching a small spray head to the top of the cloudy test tube. Prot stood frozen, his mind reeled as he watched without question now, he was beyond questions, as Barry squeezed the head of the test tube three times over the sandwich. Three tiny clouds of the milky substance within the test tube breathed misty over the sandwich before settling and disappearing amongst the fillings.

"There you go," said Barry, apparently satisfied. Prot added the final slice of bread then stood back and watched as Barry carefully packed away the test tubes and the microscope.

"Now," Barry continued, consulting his clipboard full of papers once more. "Wrap it up just like this," he said, offering Prot a piece of tin foil and another photograph.

Barry stood and watched seriously this time as Prot pushed through the fog of his dazed mind to wrap the sandwich, carefully matching the folds of the foil to those in the photograph exactly. When he had finished he offered the shiny package to Barry for inspection. Barry held the photograph and the wrapped sandwich in opposite hands and scrutinised both.

"Yeah," he said eventually. "That's good is that, well done."

Casting the photograph into the clutter Barry pushed the sandwich back into Prot's hand and gave him a brief slap on the shoulder, returning his attention to his clipboard.

"What the..." Prot managed after a moment or two, surprised by the sound of his own voice. "What?" he tried.

Barry ignored the question and planted a thick finger in the midst of one of the street maps pinned to the wall above the table before them.

"You know this street here?" he said.

Prot squinted at the map until he recognised the lines.

"Yeah," he said, surprised at himself. "I do, I know that place."

"Right then," said Barry. "Well take this there and find this guy's house. It's number twenty-three."

The heavy finger moved from the map to a large

black and white photograph pinned next to it. The photograph showed a thin, flamboyantly dressed man with thinning hair and tight skin. It had been taken at distance but the man was clearly visible, walking briskly down a nondescript street, a long slender scarf flowing out behind him.

Prot blinked at the photograph a couple of times and swallowed. The surveillance photograph made him uneasy, especially when combined with all the maps and what appeared to be credit card bills, phone bills and minutes of meetings; personal things made sinister through their collection and arrangement on the wall of this weird little room.

Sifting through the clutter Barry produced another sheet of paper and a key, pushing them both in Prot's hands to accompany the sandwich.

"There's his schedule and his back door key." Barry explained. "He'll be upstairs in the shower and that for a good twenty minutes so all you need to do is just walk in and swap the sandwich on the counter for that one you've just made, alright?"

Prot tore his eyes from the wall and tried to focus on the unevenly typed list of times in his hand. *'Waking and ablutions'* was listed from 08:03 to 08:21. Prot looked at the door key, old and tarnished, then back at the photograph of the man. The memory of the milky substance sprayed onto the sandwich pushed it's way back to the fore of his thoughts.

"Is this all," Prot wondered how to phrase it. "I mean, is this ok? What we're doing, it seems a bit..." he trailed off doubtfully.

"We do what needs doing," was Barry's flat response. "Nothing more, nothing less. We make sure that what needs to happen, happens."

"What? But why?" Prot's questions came easier now as the fear of before returned to sharpen his wits. "What was that stuff? Are you, are you going to kill him?"

Barry didn't respond but frowned instead, looking down at his clipboard, flicking through the many sheets until apparently finding what he was looking for, stabbing at it with a finger.

"Nope," he said. "That's not what's on the ticket. Job sheet says he just needs his stomach turned, simple as that."

"But why?" pushed Prot, swallowing as his own stomach turned in sympathy. "Why do I have to do this?"

"Because I did the heel on her shoe and it took me bloody ages as well," snapped Barry. "It's about time you started pulling your weight, I'm not doing everything round here."

Prot lingered still, staring down at the assortment of items in his hands, so dull and normal and yet all three loaded with insanity.

"Well go on then," Barry added after another moment more.

As he stood unsure, Prot's hands began to act, folding the paper and placing it into one of the many pockets in his overalls. The key went into a breast pocket, the sandwich into a larger pocket at his thigh, his nimble fingers unfastening and refastening the relevant buttons as if he had been wearing the overalls all his life.

Then, as he watched, his legs carried him back across the room to the door, as if the overalls themselves were moving him. Before he could catch up with it all, he had stepped through the door into the cool outside air.

The narrow alley behind the substation was hemmed in with high brick walls now. A vague memory of greenery attempted to assert itself but was pushed back into the queue of other impossible things.

The cool breeze roused him a little as did the motion of his limbs. Making his way round the squat building he was confronted by a sleepy residential street beyond the front gate instead of the park. He briefly felt the need for surprise but finding that particular well to be dry he simply shrugged and pressed on.

Stepping out onto the street he glanced about him and was assailed simultaneously by two powerful sensations. Each was perfectly sensible in its own right yet perfectly impossible in combination.

He knew this street, the sense of recognition upon

seeing the houses, of the comfortable familiarity of the gardens was palpable. At the same time however, he knew that he had never been here before, that each step he took was his first upon each paving stone.

A whirling disorientation threatened to engulf him but amid all the other confusions and impossible things Prot chose simply to cling to the familiarity, weird as it may be, and to the hint of security that accompanied it.

The street was quiet with the anticipation of an early weekday morning. As he moved off to the right Prot could almost feel the impending flurry of activity. Over the next hour or so most of the residents of the street would emerge from their homes and leave for the day, rushing off to whatever occupied them. Then the street would settle back into mid morning stillness, waiting for the postman to disturb it's slumber.

Prot reached the house that belonged to the man in the photograph and paused to look it over. Upstairs the curtains were still drawn but, removing the long faded, carefully folded timesheet, he knew that slow stretching activity was just beginning within.

Glancing about him and finding the quiet street quite empty, Prot moved up the side of the house, past an immaculate garden, and made his way down the side, round to the back door.

By the time he reached it the tarnished old key had appeared in his hand to partner the piece of paper. Prot hesitated before inserting the key, tapping the sandwich that hung by his thigh and drawing a deep breath.

With exaggerated care and delicacy he slid the key into the lock, turned the handle and pushed the door. It gave without a sound and swung inwards to reveal a dining kitchen whose perfect order and cleanliness was obvious even beneath the curtained gloom.

Stepping inside Prot closed the door slowly, leaving it slightly ajar rather than closing it fully. Placing his weight with incredible care he held his breath as he approached the kitchen counter. Sounds of movement above froze him solid and images of discovery and capture caught his heart in his throat.

Glancing up at the clock however he noticed the

minute hand trip to the three and at that moment he heard running water from above. Releasing his long held breath Prot relaxed just a little and returned his attention to the counter.

Beneath a series of carefully placed objects the counter gleamed and the faintest smell of lemons hung in the air. All in a line, equally spaced and laid parallel, there sat a file of papers, a notebook and pen, a magazine, a banana, a yoghurt and spoon and finally, a squarish object wrapped in tin foil.

Prot licked his lips and retrieved the sandwich from his pocket. Weighing it thoughtfully he looked at its twin on the counter for a moment before quickly switching the two. Placing the freshly stolen sandwich back into his pocket he looked at its replacement on the counter, tipping his head to one side.

After another moment's consideration he moved forward to nudge the sandwich a little to the left then stepped back to look at it again. One more minor, twisting adjustment and he nodded, turning back to the door.

The sound of running water above ceased and in its absence a high, quavering singing voice became audible. Smiling for what felt like the first time ever, Prot slipped out of the door and pulled it to behind him, hearing the neat little click of the lock.

He strode confidently back down the side of the house and out onto the street. Further down, past the substation, a harried looking woman was ushering two small children into the back of a car, too busy with her shepherding to even glance in his direction. A strange feeling of satisfaction warmed Prot's bones as he slipped through the gate and around the tiny building to push open the door and enter.

Back inside he found Barry immediately to his right, fussing about the kettle by the sink. Striding past him Prot approached the paper heaped table and deposited the sandwich, paper and key onto the piles before turning back to face the room.

"How was that then?" asked Barry over his shoulder.

"Yeah," said Prot, finding his voice steady and

solid. "Alright actually. No problems."

"Good lad," said Barry, turning to face him now and offering a steaming mug. "Get on that," he said with a grin.

Barry crossed the room to his armchair and settled into it with a sigh, cupping his drink in two hands and gently blowing at it. Prot felt the warmth from his own mug and mirrored Barry's pose upon his wooden chair. For a minute and then another the pair sat in comfortable silence. With a gentle grunt Barry stretched out his legs, crossing them at the ankle, and took a deep grateful sip from his mug.

"S'pose you'll want to know what it's all about then," he said eventually in a contented tone.

"Wouldn't mind," replied Prot, matching Barry's calm but all the while having to push down hard on the eagerness in his chest.

"You're in a book lad," said Barry simply, but then thought about it and added, "kind of."

Prot furrowed his brow and opened his mouth but nothing came out. Instead he just shook his head and waited for more information.

"All of this," Barry continued, waving vaguely at the room. "You, me, all what we do and that, it's the inside, the inner gubbings, the engine if you like, of a book, a romantic novel to be precise."

Prot tried to get a grip on the words, running them over again and again but each time they just slid away without giving up their meaning.

"So," he tried. "What? We're not real? None of this is real, it's all just..." he faded away, lost and incredulous.

"Well I don't know about that," said Barry in reflective tone. "What is 'real'? What does that mean? I leave that kind of thing to the thinkers, me. All I know is that out there there's a plot to deliver and it's up to us to make it happen. Plot Technicians you see," he said, tapping the embroidered breast of his overalls before taking a deep sip of his brew.

Prot looked down at his own overalls and viewed the upside down words with suspicion.

"But," he began with scorn in his voice. "That's

not, I mean, it doesn't work like that. Fiction's just fiction, it doesn't need to be engineered, the writer just writes it, don't they?"

Barry chuckled though not unkindly.

"Oh yeah," he said, grinning. "The writer writes it and it all just happens, just like that!"

Prot felt his cheeks redden but still couldn't accept Barry's words.

"Alright look," said Barry, shifting his weight in his chair to turn and face Prot earnestly across the little table between them.

"I know it looks like that on the page lad, like someone sat at a desk somewhere has an idea, writes it down and then it all just happens like magic. But you see in order to go from their high faluting ideas to something actually happening, poor sods like you and me have to graft for it." Barry scrutinised Prot's face but could see he didn't get it.

"Take this morning for example," Barry tried again, scooping his clipboard off the table. "Now the writer, she says in here," he paused as he thumbed through the sheets. "Here we are, she says in here that the lass, the main character in the book, well she's walking down the street and the heel on her shoe breaks just at the right moment so that she stumbles into some tall, handsome gent. They have a little back and forth, sparks fly, blah blah, they go their separate ways."

Prot recalled his first moments of the day, the memory of the woman's beauty almost overshadowing his desperate confusion.

"Well now," Barry continued. "What are the chances of that happening? Of her heel breaking at just the right moment? Never going to happen is it? So that's where we come in. I spend a week building a micro explosive into a perfect replica of her shoe, make the switch and then detonate it just as she walks past him. Meanwhile you turn up, late I might add, and then try and get in the middle of them!"

"Sorry," was all Prot could think to say as he tried in vain to process Barry's words.

"Ah you're alright," said Barry kindly. "You didn't choose the job and I can't really blame you for being taken with her, after all she is literally the centre of the universe round here."

"What about the sandwich?" asked Prot though more to keep up his end of the conversation than out of any considered curiosity.

"Well," said Barry, flicking back through a few more sheets. "Here we are, in order for her to bump into the handsome gent again, just by chance of course, the lass needs to leave her office later than usual today."

Prot still didn't get it. Barry tried again.

"Now the writer's got it down here that the lass's work colleague goes home sick in the afternoon leaving her with a load of extra work to do which makes her late in leaving but again, can't very well rely on blind luck can you? What if he doesn't get ill, stays there all day, does all his work? She leaves on time and the whole thing's ruined see?" Barry placed the clipboard back on the table and returned his attention to the patiently waiting mug.

"But what about us?" cried Prot, surprising himself with his childish tone. "There's never any of this in books. I've never heard of Plot Technicians, no-one has!"

"You're right there," Barry sighed sadly. "We do all the graft, work us fingers to the bone to make it all hang together. We make them writers' dreams come true and no-one ever knows. They get all the credit, no-one even knows we exist, don't think that don't stick in my throat as well lad."

"I didn't mean that," said Prot hotly. "I meant it's ridiculous, it's not true, it can't be!"

"Oh I don't know about that," said Barry, draining his cup thoughtfully and placing it on the table between them.

"I reckon there's worse ways to spend your time. Now then, imagine you were working in one of them horror stories. All blood and guts and severed limbs, not to mention having to shepherd bloody great monsters and the like about the place.

"Just imagine it, some unnameable horror from the deep, all tentacles and evil and that and you've got to get it into just the right place at just the right time and all in the dark as well! I don't envy the lads who have to do that stuff I can tell you."

"No," said Prot quietly before suddenly slamming his mug onto the table and erupting from his chair. "No!" he roared.

"This is nonsense!" he raged as a bemused Barry looked on. "I'm not having it, I'm not! I don't know what's going on here, I can't explain all this, but I know one thing, I am real!"

"There's no point fighting it lad," Barry tried calmly. "You're born to it, you've no choice. You've just got to make your peace with it is all."

"No!" screamed Prot again, pacing back and forth. "I am here, right now, I am here, I am breathing, my heart is beating, I am thinking, I am real. I'm not a character in a book or some kind of behind the scenes plot guy."

"Plot Technician," Barry corrected.

"Whatever! I'm a real human being and I'm going to prove it to you!" Prot dashed over to the table and began scanning the pictures and maps on the wall frantically.

"Oh yeah," said Barry, gathering up the mugs and carrying them to the sink. "And how're you going to do that then?"

Prot's eyes locked on one photograph in particular showing a tall, handsome man in a suit striding down a busy street. Although he'd only seen his feet that morning, Prot knew instinctively that this was the man that the most beautiful of all women had stumbled into. The two were scheduled to meet again, by 'chance', that evening and as Prot's eyes greedily consumed the man's itinerary a plan began to form in his mind.

"Right then," he said, turning triumphant to face Barry who was washing their mugs in the sink. "I'll wait till tonight then I'll go and meet her first, I'll talk to her..."

"You can't go talking to the characters lad," Barry said, shaking his head. "Doesn't work like that."

"Well we'll see won't we?" snarled Prot. "If she speaks to me, even if it's just to tell me to get lost, then at least I'll know, at least I'll have proved it, that she's real and I'm real and all your Plot Technician stuff is just nonsense. Just have to wait until tonight that's all."

"You've no need to wait," said Barry, settling back into his armchair to examine his clipboard.

"What?" snapped Prot, faltering slightly.

"Well think about it," Barry continued without looking up. "You don't have every second of every day in a book do you? It's all split up into scenes isn't it. A load of stuff happens then time skips ahead to the next bit."

"You mean..." Prot tried, not quite getting it.

"See for yourself," Barry said, nodding towards the door.

Prot crossed the room quickly and wrenched open the door. Sure enough the pale morning air had been replaced by an early evening chill. The heavy foliage was back though now obscured by the gathering darkness.

"Right then!" said Prot, hesitating only slightly in the face of yet another impossible thing. "You'll see!" he said, ignoring the slight quaver in his voice as he pointed a righteous finger at Barry.

"Go on then," Barry sighed. "Off you go."

"I will!" snapped Prot, striding out into the darkness and slamming the door behind him.

The coming cold of the night gripped him but served only to take the edge off Prot's steaming rage. Rounding the now familiar brick wall of the sub-station he found himself back in the park.

According to the documents on the wall, the handsome man would catch a taxi on the other side of the park. From there travel across town to where he would, quite by chance, leave the taxi just as she, the almighty, wonderful she, was emerging from her office building.

Breaking into a jog, Prot focused all his energy on the task at hand. The impossible things didn't matter now, there would be some kind of explanation later. Maybe he was mentally ill, maybe he was on drugs, either way he knew he would need help, help to get back to normality. Maybe then he would remember his life, who he was.

In the meantime however all that mattered was proving Barry wrong, proving to himself that no matter what kind of crisis held him in its grip, it was a crisis born of reality, something ordinary, something explicable.

As his feet pounded the path and he closed distance on the far side of the park, Prot relished the feeling of the air tearing in and out of his lungs, the spikes of pain from his complaining muscles, the pounding of his heart in his ears. He felt solid and real and alive.

The busy street that edged the far side of the park came into view and Prot took a moment to double up and wheeze, waiting for his breathing to return to normal. Passing through the gates to the park he stepped out onto the street and squinted in the glare of the passing headlights.

People bustled all about him though no-one seemed to notice him. In his overalls he supposed he looked like a groundsman, a council employee busy with some park maintaining business in which no-one else was interested.

Scanning the street Prot's eyes locked onto a familiar shape of shoulders. There he was, the handsome man, just flagging a taxi. Exploding from his standing start, Prot dashed through the crowds, pushing and shoving and ignoring the outraged cries behind.

The handsome man was just climbing into the back of the cab as Prot skidded to halt behind him. Hesitating just for a second, Prot lunged forward, grabbed the man's perfectly sculpted shoulder through an expensive feeling coat and dragged him back out onto the street.

The man staggered a little, his mouth and eyes all three wide with surprise. Before he could react Prot lunged past him and dived into the back of the cab, slamming the door shut beside him. The man on the street banged on the window, angry and cursing now but Prot merely sneered in return, keeping a firm grip on the door handle.

"Here!" shouted the cabbie, turning in his seat to stare at Prot in disgust. "You can't do that! What do you think you're doing?!"

"It's an emergency!" panted Prot. "I can't explain how important this is, I'll pay whatever you want but please just go, go now!"

The cabbie turned back to face forward, grumbling
but pulling the cab away from the curb anyway.

"Where's this emergency then?" he called back to
Prot, still suspicious.

"Wherever he was going," said Prot, twisting in his
seat to look through the back window at the receding
figure of the handsome man.

"You what?" said the cabbie.

"Wherever that guy asked you to take him, take
me there," Prot said again, smiling as the exasperated
figure in the shrinking distance threw his hands up in the
air.

"This don't sound right to me," said the cabbie,
half to himself.

"I'll pay you double, don't worry about it," said
Prot though upon hearing his own words felt a sudden
sinking feeling in his stomach as he realised he had no
money in any of his many pockets. Swallowing he
winced a little but then nodded, reminding himself of his
priorities and resolving to deal with one thing at a time.

Still gripping the door handle Prot tapped his foot
nervously. It occurred to him for the first time that he
was about to come face to face with the woman he had
seen that morning. What would he say to her? What
would she think of his overalls?

His stomach clenched and suddenly there was cold
sweat on his skin. He'd told Barry that it didn't matter
what she said, simply meeting her would be enough to
prove the Plot Technician theory wrong. Now he thought
about it though, it began to dawn on Prot that she might
reject him, in fact she almost certainly would. The
thought was too terrible to comprehend.

"Oh god," he groaned.

"What's that?" asked the cabbie, half turning to
look back at Prot just as a van lurched wildly out of side
street directly ahead of them.

Prot barely had time to screw his face into a
terrified cringe as the cab ploughed straight into the side
of the van. The impact threw him forwards into the
plastic screen that sealed off the front of the cab and in
the moment of impact he could have sworn that all the

world was full of gongs, booming blind forever.

For some amount of time, Prot had no idea how long, he lay on the floor of the cab in a painful, crumpled heap. Then, slowly, he began to unfold himself upright, his fingers gingerly touching his face, his tongue testing his teeth.

He could hear voices on the street outside and after a series of painful blinks he managed to peer through the splintered windscreen to see the cabbie out on the street, raging  at another man, apparently the driver of the van. Prot sat back onto the rear seat of the cab and groaned to himself until the sound of distant sirens anchored him back in the world.

What about her?!

Taking a breath he dragged himself out of the cab and into a standing position. Dazed and wobbly he stared about him at the small crowd of onlookers that had gathered around the crash, hoping it was a good one.

"Here," called the cabbie, noticing him and pausing his tirade against the other driver.  "You alright mate? Probably shouldn't be moving about like, you just sit tight till the ambulance gets here."

Prot waved him away vaguely, turning from the taxi and stumbling off down the street. The crowd of onlookers parted to allow him through, all looking him up and down with gruesome interest.

Everything was a blur as the traffic honked and blared, trying to push through the crash narrowed road. Holding a clammy palm to his now aching face Prot tried not to look at the painful headlights and instinctively moved back towards the park. He needed to see the board again, the schedules and the photographs, work out how he could reach her another way.

Just then a particularly loud car horn threw shards of pain into his head so that he turned to stare at it in horror. It was another black cab, making reasonable progress down the street for all its protests but it was the sight of the passenger that stopped Prot in his tracks. Looking perfectly calm and unruffled, the handsome man sat comfortably in the back of the cab, leaning forward a little trying to see what was holding things up.

Prot watched him pass, his jaw hanging slack, his face throbbing beneath his hand. Then all of a sudden his stomach convulsed and Prot turned to grab at the railings of the park, vomiting onto the street. When he had finished he stood shaky and turned back to the road. The handsome man and his cab were nowhere to be seen.

—        —

—

"How was that then?" asked Barry as Prot stepped back into the room.

"Not great," rasped Prot as he fell onto his chair still cradling his rapidly purpling face.

"Good work that though," Barry said. "Pulled him out of that cab just in time you did. Imagine if it'd been him in that crash, that would have cocked everything right up wouldn't it."

Prot lowered his hand from his face and turned to spit venom at Barry but stopped.

The shelves down both walls were empty, as was the table at the back of the room. Above the table bare brick wall stared back at Prot while Barry stood knee deep in dozens of black bin bags. Barry winced at the sight of Prot's face and clambered over the bin bags towards the sink.

"Above and beyond that was lad, you really went the extra mile, well done," he said. "I'll put the kettle on shall I, make us one last brew."

"I thought I could," Prot began but then had to pause to wince and take a breath. "It's all true isn't it? What you said before, what we are."

Barry left the kettle to its business and crossed the floor to stand at Prot's side. He landed a heavy, fatherly hand on Prot's shoulder and spoke gently.

"Yes lad, it is," he said.

"I really thought I could do it," Prot moaned, returning his hand to his face.

"I know," said Barry, patting Prot's shoulder and moving back to kettle. "You did what needed to be done, doesn't matter why you did it, that's just what had to happen."

Prot sat and felt miserable, listening to the water pouring into the mugs. He sniffled to himself a little as Barry placed a steaming mug on the table next to him and settled into the his armchair. Eventually he took his cup and sipped at it. The hot liquid hurt his lips but it felt good and stabilising as he swallowed it down.

"What's all this then?" Prot asked, gesturing to the clear spaces and bulging bags.

"Well we're done now aren't we," said Barry with a smile.

"What do you mean?" asked Prot, clutching the heat from his mug and turning back to face Barry.

"Well that's it," Barry continued, pulling the last piece of paper from out of the back of the clipboarded pile and blinking at it.

"The two of them go off on holiday together, Caribbean somewhere says here. There'll be a team out there to deal with all that, lucky beggars. Then it skips forward a few years to them being married with a kid. There's another team for that and all and good luck to them, you don't want to work with kids lad, I can tell you." Barry dropped the sheet of paper on top of the clipboard and sipped absently at his brew.

"But what happens to us now?" asked Prot, panic rising in his voice.

"Well, nothing," said Barry, looking confused.

"Nothing happens to us now. This is the end."

# life goes on

"This is bullshit!" she snapped, fury humming in her ears.

Across the desk a large older man was busy sweating through a pinstripe suit and applying a handkerchief to his ruddy jowls. He paused at her outburst, his face appearing to melt even further with disappointment.

"Felicity," he reproached, "I hardly think that's warranted."

"It is entirely warranted, Jonathan," Felicity replied unrepentant. "Entirely."

Another rush of rage fired her out of the green leather chair and set her pacing the plush carpet. Her slender fingers tangled with one another as she pinballed between the concrete walls of the tiny, windowless room. Jonathan returned to dabbing himself but followed her with a look of concern.

"When you said you'd found a real opportunity for me I thought you meant a Deputy Advisor role or," she paused and turned to face him. "Or something, not this."

"The commemoration ceremony is vital keystone in our little corner of the world," Jonathan said, waving his handkerchief at her. "We need these moments, these milestones, to reset our compasses that we may stay the course. We need our ceremonies and our remembrances to see this house and that other place through these darkest of..."

"Oh don't give me that Jonathan," Felicity snapped, cutting him off but not unkindly. "I wrote that speech for you five years ago."

The fat man stared into the middle distance for a moment with a frown of confusion before shaking his jowls.

"So you did," he said wonderingly. "And a bloody good speech it was too," he added, returning fully to the conversation with jolly punch of the air. "Landed bang on with all sorts of chaps that one. Both sides of the house mind you."

"Jonathan," she said, dragging him back to the matter at hand.

"Forgive me my dear," he said, waving her back
into the chair. "I may have over egged it a bit I confess
but this really is an opportunity."

She looked at him.

"Of sorts," he added.

"Compiling a minute by minute timeline of the
day?" she asked hopelessly. "So that we can all relive it
one moment at a time?"

"Bit ghoulish I know," said Jonathan, his nose
wrinkling as if at an unpleasant smell. "Not my idea. All
about continuity apparently, that's the message this time
so they tell me."

"NAML," said Felicity flatly.

"That's the chap!" Jonathan snapped back, briefly
excited. "Not A Minute Lost. We know precisely what
happened during every single minute of that day and
we've recorded every single minute since. When the dust
settles and the old..."

He paused to think.

"The old Redeployment Day!" he announced,
excited again. "When it finally comes around, we will not
have lost even a single minute. All present and
accounted for."

"But it's just going through the archives Jonathan,
pulling out numbers. I might as well be here compiling
policy documents. Where's the opportunity?" Felicity's
rage had cooled and  condensed into dripping despair.

"Well, during the meeting of the cabinet last week
the chaps started talking about the commemoration,
NAML and all that. Said there was work to be done, that
they needed someone with a level head, a safe pair of
hands, someone with an eye for the details and a nose
for the truth. A good egg, someone who..."

"And?" Felicity said, nudging the old man towards
what she hoped was a point.

"Well," he said, as if his point was self
explanatory.

"Well?" she nudged him again.

"Well I said I had just the chap, signed you up for
it there and then. Of course I didn't know the precise
details at that point," Jonathan's chin sank onto his chest
and avoided her eyes.

"Jonathan," Felicity scolded him gently.

"I know," he replied, glancing at her sheepishly. "And I am sorry, really I am. I just wanted to find something new for you to do. I know how bored you are here and you really are ever so capable. Seems like such a..."

"A waste," she finished.

"Well," he replied as if unsure what the word at the end of the sentence was supposed to have been.

"Still," he brightened. "It is an opportunity for you to show the other chaps what you can do eh? Show them how it's done? Yes?"

"I know," she said, attempting to return his hopeful smile. "You're right. But ten years Jonathan! It's been ten years, I can't be a Junior Deputy Advisor forever, I just can't."

A heavy silence settled between them. The bare lightbulb hanging from the concrete ceiling cast harsh white light over the ageing furniture and mouldering books. The fat man shifted in his chair, sweating, puffing and dabbing until he could bear it no longer.

"You're a bloody good Junior Deputy Advisor..." he began.

"It's not even a real job!" Felicity snapped, exasperation relighting her spark of rage. "You made it up! I'm the sodding intern! Everybody knows I was only ever here in the first place because you knew Grandmother and even then it was only supposed to be for two weeks."

"Well just be glad that you were here my girl!" snapped Jonathan with sudden, genuine anger, his jowls flapping pale to startling effect. "Might I remind you that had you not been here, be it at the request of your grandmother, fine figure of a woman that she was, or otherwise, that you should have been condemned to suffer the same unimaginable fate as the millions of poor souls beyond these walls, desperately trying scrape a life from the ashes of a ruined world."

Jonathan's rebuke echoed around the tiny office, bouncing sharp off the smooth concrete walls. Felicity stared down at the heavy carpet between her shoes, feeling a shameful warmth in her face.

"They don't even know we're here," she said eventually, her voice smaller now.

"They know," said Jonathan, resolute still. "Some of them anyway. And even then it matters not. What matters, Felicity, is continuity of government. Our great nation may have been brought to its knees but we shall not yield!

"While the great people of this island nation fight on, we meet their contribution in kind and continue to do our duty come what may. No matter what Felicity, no matter what you see, we shall represent the common man and prepare for his future so that when the day finally arrives that some of us might leave this place, then they shall see that the enemy did not win. They did not prevail. For we remain, Felicity, Her Majesty's Government remains and will return to lead them in the rebuilding a new and ever Greater Britain."

"Who wrote that?" asked Felicity.

"One of Simon's I think," he replied absently his passion disappearing as abruptly as it had risen. "Still stands though."

"I know," she said. "But that's my point. It is important and I want to help, to contribute, to contribute more than this. I've got ideas Jonathan, things I want to do, things I want to achieve. I'm ready."

"Oh I do understand my dear," said Jonathan. "But you know how it is in here. There's simply nowhere for people to go and so everyone stays where they are."

"So I'm just stuck here, making coffee, taking minutes, compiling summaries of other people's work, forever?" she said.

"Well not indefinitely," he said. "Eventually time will begin to avail itself of some of our more senior colleagues and vacancies will arise."

"Dead man's boots," she said morosely.

"Exactly that I'm afraid," he said.

"Great," she said and slumped back between the green leather wings of the chair.

"For you, certainly," he said.

"What do you mean?" she said.

"My dear," he said with a gentle smile. "You complain because you hold the most junior post under the mountain and yet do not see that it is the most valuable post of all."

The expression on her face told him she did not. With significant effort he hoisted himself from his own green leather chair and stepped to the nearest of two floor to ceiling bookcases.

"How long do the boffins say it will be before the atmosphere outside is even remotely safe?" he said while inspecting a leather bound volume.

"Twenty-five to thirty years," she replied. Everyone knew this.

"And in twenty-five to thirty years," he continued. "How many members of the current population of this place will remain do you think?"

He left the question to hang over his shoulder as he doubled over to examine a lower shelf, wheezing a little along the way.

Felicity watched the great hulking wreck of a man strain and puff his way through standing back to straight and considered the question seriously.

"I'll certainly never see the sun again," he said, dropping back into his chair.

"Jonathan..." she began with concern.

"No no," he said, batting away her pity. "It's a simple fact my dear. By the time we can open those doors and return to our constituents, to our people, most of the people walking these corridors will be gone. As the youngest among us you will be one of the elect, one of the last representatives of Her Majesty's government. It will be you and those like you who leave this place to build a brand new world and by God girl I'd bet every penny I own that by then you'll be leading them out there as Prime Minister."

"In the meantime I spend the next three decades gradually moving from one dead man's desk to another while my hair goes grey," she said, her voice breaking slightly as the reality of it crushed her insides.

"Well," said Jonathan in lieu of anything else.

"How old were you when we came in here?" she asked.

"I, er," he began as if unsure where the question would take him.

"How old?" she repeated.

"I was fifty-six," he said, his chin and eyebrows all rising slightly in attempt to retain some dignity.

"Fifty-six," Felicity repeated. "You had half a century of the old life, of life outside, surrounded by people, free to move, to change, to be. Half a century. I was nineteen years old when the bombs dropped Jonathan, nineteen. I've been under this mountain almost my entire adult life. By the time I see the sun I'll be almost as old as you are now, my life will have been and gone." She sagged back into the chair, deflated and defeated.

Jonathan opened his mouth to speak but when no sound emerged he closed it again. His eyes searched the desktop as if inspiration might be found among the paperwork and tea cups. Finally he looked up again, eyes large and wobbling.

"Felicity," he said, quietly and with compassion. "No-one wanted the world to end."

—    —
—

She stepped from the plush carpet of the Minister's office out onto the swept smooth concrete of the corridor and became very aware of her footsteps. The corridors under the mountain all looked exactly the same. At some point in the distant past a quite insane amount of public money had been spent on secretly boring a network of perfectly tubular passages through the bedrock of one of the country's largest mountains.

The passages honeycombed the mountain's innermost guts and had been lined with concrete to provide smooth flat floors and hard edged echoes. The perfectly curving walls were interrupted periodically with small angular cut outs that framed doorways to offices and meeting rooms, stairways and store cupboards and eventually even kitchens and dormitories.

The overall effect was one of bleak, relentless claustrophobia. The unimaginable weight of the mountain above was an ever present speck in the mind's eye of all who dwelled within it. Occasionally people would succumb to the pressure and collapse into a mindbreaking panic that had come to be known as Mountain Fever. Sometimes they would recover, often they did not, it wasn't something anyone liked to talk about.

Although she'd never seen them herself, Felicity had heard rumours of grand dining halls and lush palatial suites hidden somewhere in the complex. Apparently there was even a viewing platform with special, foot thick glass, all reserved exclusively for only the most senior government figures of course.

On the one hand it seemed fanciful that even they could have an actual view of the outside world. On the other however, the idea that even the best and the brightest, the most powerful men and women in the land were equally doomed to life in the same concrete boxes as everyone else inspired a feeling of futility that threatened to overwhelm her.

For almost a decade, the largest open spaces Felicity had seen were the two parliamentary chambers far below her, set even deeper into the radiation shielding rock. Both were almost perfect replicas of their Westminster originals, so much so that when Felicity was occasionally able to watch a debate she could almost convince herself that she was back in London. In those moments she would imagine that she was sitting but a short walk from a rainswept pavement beneath a vast and beautiful slate grey sky.

Strip lights hummed a rail along the ceiling as she set off towards her next meeting. The occasionally flickering bulbs bathed everyone below in harsh, haggering tones so that most people kept their heads down when walking. She joined the knots and strings of officials all moving quietly about their business. Approaching a curve in tunnel she glanced up and groaned inwardly as a familiar figure came into view.

"Felicity," he drawled. "How's my favourite tea girl?"

He was only a couple of years older than her but dressed almost exactly like Jonathan.

"Simon," she said through a gritted smile.

Simon was a Senior Advisor in the Prime Minister's office and made a point of never letting anyone forget it. He was the living cartoon embodiment of exactly the kind of public school boy, upper class thug cliché which the party had fought so hard to combat during the last election before the bombs had dropped. Men Of The People had been the line but of course back then there had been a public and their opinion to worry about.

"Don't know why you hang around the old duffer you know," he said, full of scorn and glee. "Lovely little bit of stuff like you should be at the sharp end of the party, where the action is. You should come and join us, give you a chance to have a pop at the other lot. Believe me, you'd be made to feel very welcome at the PM's office and it'd be a much better use of your.." he paused to actually look her up and down.

"..talents," he finished, pleased with what he believed to be wit.

"Fine where I am thanks," Felicity replied and tried to step past him.

Stepping toward her he blocked the way and leaned in closer to lower his voice.

"Come on Felicity," he growled. "We both know it's going to happen eventually, why the games?"

"What?" she said, disbelief loosening the chain on her temper.

"We're all getting older darling," he said, licking his lips. "I mean Christ, you must be nearly thirty! Back in the old days I'd never have even considered it but beggars can't be choosers. You and I are all that's left of the pretty young things, it's inevitable, I mean who else is there down here that you would even look at twice?"

Her heart rattled against her ribs with furious anger. She worked hard to keep the vibration out of her voice in case his mistook the tremble for fear.

"I've made myself very clear on this point Simon. I am not interested," she said, her words clipped and sharp.

Again she made to move past him but he snatched her wrist, gripping it tightly as his nostrils flared. He took a breath and smoothed his hair with his other hand,

taking his time to composing himself, completely
oblivious of the steady flow of people moving past them.

Felicity looked down at Simon's hand open
mouthed, stunned at his brazen behaviour. She looked
at the people moving past them, making eye contact
with several. Fear rippled through their expressions as
people looked from her to Simon and then averted their
eyes, staring back to the floor or a vague middle
distance. No-one wanted any trouble.

"What are you doing?!" she hissed.

"You're a tease Felicity," he hissed back. "Just
because we're short on choice down here that doesn't
make you fucking special you know. Sooner or later I'll
have you, I'll have you and you'll love it, you'll see."

"I wouldn't sleep with you if you were the last man
on earth," she said, holding his wild eyes with grim
resolve.

"Give it time darling, that may literally become the
case." He smiled without warmth.

"I would rather see humanity extinct you utter
pig," she said, spitting the words into his face with all
the quiet venom she could find.

His cold smile fell and just for a moment Simon
stared at her with almost tangible hatred, his teeth
slightly bared, a vein throbbing in his temple. Genuinely
unsure what he might do, Felicity braced herself,
slapping a rising terror back down within her. All the
while people moved past and around them.

Then, suddenly, Simon released his grip on her
wrist and took a step back. Smoothing his hair again and
laughing, a harsh barking sound that echoed around
them.

"Well," he said in too smooth a voice. "I can't
stand here all day making small talk with the likes of you
I'm afraid. The PM has yet another summit meeting with
the leader of the opposition this afternoon and is
awaiting a full and detailed briefing from yours truly." He
strode past her and on, the traffic parting before him. As
he receded into the distance behind her she could still
hear him shouting greetings or vulgar slurs at
colleagues.

Felicity remained where she was and felt her

knees tremble. A chilled what-could-have-been type terror rushed up from the pit of her stomach and hated herself for it. Tears began to sting her eyes but this was a step too far. With grim resolve she dismissed the trauma and set off again to her meeting, grinding frustration and fury between her teeth as she went.

—     —

—

Despite walking as quickly as possible short of actually running, Felicity was almost a full ten minutes late for the meeting. Mouthing her apologies she ignored the frowns of some of her senior colleagues, took her seat and opened her file as quietly as possible.

To her surprise the meeting was being chaired not by Rachel, her Head of Section, who was nowhere to be seen, but rather by John, Rachel's boss. Arriving late had meant she missed the explanation for this however and she didn't dare invite further disapproval by interrupting to ask for a recap. Instead she focused on the discussion and on recording the notes and action points for Jonathan that justified her presence.

Very little of the content of the meeting was new and so it was not difficult for her to catch up with the conversation. Each item on the agenda was simply an update on progress, had there been any, or more often a simple reiteration that something due to happen had not happened yet but certainly should happen very soon.

It was only when they reached the final item on the agenda marked 'AOB' that Felicity disengaged her autopilot and hoped to be able to make her notes differ in some way from all those she had taken before.

"So then," began John. "Any other business from anyone?"

After receiving a complete set of shaken heads from around the table the chair nodded in return before raising his own item.

"Just to say," he began, his tone weary and disapproving. "Obviously the PM is attending this crisis summit thingy with the leader of the opposition this afternoon so don't expect much from his office today."

"For goodness sake, not this again. What on earth do they want this time?" said a sharp faced man called Andrew. He was so painfully thin he appeared to sit within his carefully tailored and yet now baggy looking suit.

"They're just trying to justify their own existence as ever," replied Margaret, an older woman on whom copious amounts of make up had failed to cover dark heavy rings below her eyes. "I mean to say, what is the point of them now? They have to do this every so often just to feel important."

"Quite," agreed John. "A total waste of valuable time as far as I can see however the PM has agreed to it so..."

"But what's on the agenda?" asked Andrew again. "What's the point of it?"

"Oh the same as always," explained John. "Lack of elections. Constitutional crisis. All of that."

"Ridiculous," snapped Andrew, shaking his head so vehemently that Felicity wondered if his neck might snap.

"They'll never get anywhere with that and they know it," added Margaret. "It's all very well complaining about the status quo but until they can come up with a viable alternative they haven't a leg to stand on."

"I know, I know," said John. "We've been through this time and again. As the PM put it himself last time, a government elected a dozen years ago may not be ideal but it's better than a government never elected at all!"

"Unless the opposition can present realistic proposals by which to canvass the electorate and conduct an election they should be barred from raising the matter," said an elderly man whom Felicity had genuinely suspected of having fallen asleep. "I don't know why the Prime Minister stands for it, bloody disgrace if you ask me."

"I agree with you completely Harold but this time they're threatening to boycott the commemoration," said the chair. "Ten years since the bombs but twelve since the election."

A stunned silence entered the room and loitered.

"Disgusting!" hissed Margaret eventually.

"Simply vile," spluttered Harold.

"How dare they.." began Andrew.

"I know, I know," said John, raising his hands to try and calm his colleagues. "It's madness obviously and nothing more than an empty threat I'm sure. Anyway, consider the PM's office out of action until tomorrow. If that's everything? Thank you for coming and I shall see you all again next week."

As people began to stand and leave the room became cosy with the murmurings of various private conversations. Felicity approached the older woman just as she reached the door and fell into step with her as they headed back out into the corridor.

"Hi Margaret," said Felicity. "How're you?"

"I'm very well thank you my dear and how are you? Jonathan keeping you busy?" replied Margaret.

"Oh yes," said Felicity. "Busy enough. Erm, Margaret, I was just wondering..."

"Mmm," said Margaret, pulling a paper from her file and scanning it as they walked.

"Well, doesn't Rachel normally chair those? I just wondered where she was today," Felicity said.

Margaret stopped and turned to face Felicity with a serious expression, the paper hanging limp and forgotten in her hand. She ushered Felicity over the one side of the corridor, standing out of the way of the main flow of people.

"Oh Felicity, didn't you hear?" Margaret asked.

Felicity shook her head as a tight feeling took root in her stomach.

"I'm sorry to have be the one to tell you this my dear but Rachel is dead," Margaret said, placing a hand on Felicity's arm.

Felicity found her own hand at her mouth as she attempted to process Margaret's words. "But.." she began. "What? How?" she tried again.

Margaret's expression darkened.

"They found her yesterday morning," she said. "Hanged herself I'm afraid."

Felicity felt a gasp escape between her fingers.

"Mountain Fever?" she asked.

Margaret nodded, but woodenly and without conviction.

"That's what they've said officially," she said knowingly.

Felicity's expression asked the question for her. Margaret sighed and leant a little closer to whisper.

"You're a very pretty girl Felicity," she said.

Felicity frowned her irritation at what appeared to be an irrelevant and unnecessary compliment.

"Take my advice," Margaret continued. "Just don't get caught alone anywhere ok? Make sure you're always around other people and be careful of the storerooms and the dormitories."

Felicity's confusion continued before suddenly crumbling away to reveal the unnamed horror. Revulsion and anger tangled inside her before erupting with violence.

"You mean?!" Felicity snapped too loud.

Margaret fixed her with a fierce expression and hissed livid.

"Keep your bloody voice down girl!" she said. "It's just a precaution, just in case. I mean it's not like it happens all the time for goodness sake. It's really very simple, you just have to avoid putting yourself at unnecessary risk that's all. That's where Rachel went wrong you see, silly bitch, brought it on herself really. If we all just took the appropriate steps then there wouldn't be a problem."

"Appropriate steps?!" hissed Felicity, physically shaking with rage.

Margaret looked up and down the corridor before juggling her various files to present her handbag to Felicity. She opened it carefully and continued to scan the corridor while Felicity peered inside. The unforgiving fluorescent light fell gleefully into the bag and then sprang back out from a blade among the shadows within.

"The girl who cleans my office got it for me from the kitchens," explained Margaret as she closed the purse or possibly handbag and rearranged her load. "I suggest you acquire something similar for yourself."

"But!" Felicity exclaimed again before forcing herself to lower her tone.          "Margaret," she continued. "How can you tolerate this? We have to tell someone, we have to do something!"

"And do what exactly?" said Margaret, irritation colouring her tone. "Tell whom exactly? Where do you think we are Felicity? Let's say we did, let's say we had evidence and we identified those responsible. Where would we put them? Where would they live? Who would put them there? Who would keep them there? And most importantly my girl, who would replace them in their work?"

Felicity felt her stomach plunge as the previously huge and terrible news of Rachel's suicide was now dwarfed by the enormity of the broader situation facing her and all the other women under the mountain. She swallowed hard but knew she was not keeping the fear from her eyes. Seeing this seemed to annoy Margaret and she continued unabated.

"We are all here my girl, here under this damn mountain, because we are indispensable to the continued functioning of Her Majesty's Government of Great Britain and Northern Ireland. Each of us is a vital cog in the machine of that government and unless this great nation of ours is to fall into absolute savagery then each of those cogs must be kept in place, no matter what." Margaret motioned for Felicity to join her in resuming their progress along the corridor.

"You mean they're untouchable," said Felicity under her breath, struggling to maintain a more socially acceptable facial expression. "They can do whatever they want?"

"More or less," Margaret shrugged. "I mean to say, this is hardly a new state of affairs now is it? This is just the way it works Felicity, the way it's always worked. It's the price we pay as women for getting a seat at the table.

"We have to be stronger than the men with their fragile little egos. If we want to get on we can't allow these things bother us and the fact is that not all women are up it. In the past I would have said if you're not tough enough then you shouldn't be here, dyke feminists and soppy little wallflowers and the like," she paused to sneer while Felicity winced.

"Now of course there is no way out. We're all stuck in here whether we like it or not so we just have to make the best of it. Of course being locked underground exacerbates all the little boys' natural instincts. I'm afraid that's just men for you my dear. They can't control themselves, that's why it's so important that you minimise their opportunities to impose themselves upon you and to find yourself a way in which to discourage them when they try. I can talk to my cleaning girl for you if you want, she won't mind."

"It's ok," said Felicity quickly and automatically while still reeling from Margaret's tirade. She slowed to stop beside an office door. "I'll sort something out myself."

"Seeing Sir Gerald are you?" asked Margaret, nodding at the door.

"What? Oh, yes. I'm working on NAML, he's going to brief me on the details," said Felicity.

"Ah yes," Margaret beamed as if the previous few minutes of conversation had never happened. "I heard you were doing that, well done! Good opportunity for you there."

"Yes," said Felicity, still distracted. Her desperate career ambitions seemed petty and insignificant now. "Thank you Margaret," she said, managing to make it sound genuine and even making eye contact.

"Not at all my dear," she replied. "Not at all," and hurried off down the corridor. Felicity took a deep breath and attempted to clear her head before turning to knock on the door.

— —

—

"So then, Freya is it?" Sir Gerald asked. From the point of waving her into his office and into a chair he had not once raised his eyes from the document in his hand.

"Felicity," said Felicity.

"Hmm," was Sir Gerald's frowned response. Felicity couldn't tell whether he disapproved of her name, her correction or the document he was reading. Whichever it was though she knew it probably wasn't good for her. They sat in silence for a minute more while he continued to read. At length he placed the paper on the desk and finally deigned to actually look at her.

"Not A Minute Lost," he said. "Well then, important stuff. I hear you're going to crunch the numbers for us, build up the timeline. One of Jonathan's aren't you?"

"That's right," said Felicity.

"Ah well, nevermind," said Sir Gerald, his eye wandering back to his desk. "I'm sure you'll do anyway. I take it you understand what's required?"

"I think so.." Felicity began.

"Oh no," Sir Gerald interrupted, suddenly completely focused on her. "No, no, this is far too important for thinking so. This needs to be done well, it needs to be done right!"

"I understand," said Felicity, carefully snatching back control of the conversation. "In fact I've had some ideas as to how this could work.."

"No, no," snapped Sir Gerald again. "We don't need ideas. For God's sake woman! We just need the numbers. We just need somebody competent to compile the data, that's all. Are you up to this? Perhaps I should give this to somebody else, someone from the PM's office."

"No!" snapped Felicity, refusing to allow even so slim a chance to be taken away. "No really," she softened. "I understand, a full timeline of the run up to the bombs dropping through to the present day demonstrating continuous control of information and thereby continuation of strong government. Just the numbers, no problem."

"Hmm," said Sir Gerald again, sitting back in his chair to eye her critically. "Perhaps. We need the dry detail but also a bit of personal interest to leaven it. We want to be able to build a picture of a hard working team, the best of the best, putting Britain first, bowed but unbroken, all of that."

He waited a few seconds more, staring at her

before appearing to come to a decision.

"Fine," he said, losing all interest in her in a heartbeat, his eyes falling back to the desk. "Have the data on my desk by 10:00am tomorrow."

"What?" asked Felicity, stunned into rudeness.

Sir Gerald caught the tone and looked up again, surprised and ready to be deeply offended.

"Ten o'clock," he repeated slowly, as if talking to a small child.

"But," Felicity began, grasping for the words. "The commemoration's not for three weeks. I assumed there'd be more time.."

"The Minister has given his word to the Prime Minister that these numbers will be with his office tomorrow. I don't how things work over there in Jonathan's office but here we are not in the habit of making liars of our Ministers!" Sir Gerald huffed. "It's vital that we're able to give the PM the opportunity to review the timeline, should he find the time and wish to do so at any point over the next few weeks."

"You mean he probably won't even look at it?" said Felicity, entirely failing to keep the edge out of her voice.

"Is there a problem young lady?" asked Sir Gerald, his voice lowered into aggressive contempt.

Felicity caught and collected herself. She pushed the violence building in her chest back down into her guts and even managed a bright smile as she tried not to vomit.

"Not at all," she said happily. "Ten o'clock tomorrow. No problem."

—  —

—

At 6:00am the strip light in Jonathan's office, just like every strip light under the mountain, began to sputter back into life. At 10:00pm every night the lights dimmed to an emergency level in an attempt to replicate the cycle of day and night. Apparently this helped with the claustrophobia and prevented Mountain Fever.

The change in lighting had made no difference to Felicity however as she had worked right through the night. It had been an intensely emotional experience but now, as the lights came back on and she sat in Jonathan's office waiting for him to arrive, she felt strangely calm.

She had seethed through the rest of her day, a string of meetings alternately interspersed with the writing up of notes from meetings past and the writing of reports to inform meetings to come.

The conversation with Margaret had been consigned to the back of her mind and categorised under too-big-to-look-at for now. The more immediate and infuriating issue was the series of minor ups and ever deepening downs that she still referred to as her career.

After the initial disappointment of finding out the true nature of the opportunity Jonathan had found her, Felicity had resolved to make the best of it by producing such a high quality piece of work that her abilities, or rather the wasting of her abilities, would finally be recognised.

Upon receiving the impossible deadline from Sir Gerald however it had become clear that it might not even be possible for her to complete the work in time, let alone to do so accurately or impressively. If the finished product was found to be lacking then not only would she have failed to establish the beginnings of a good reputation but would instead have gained one as an incompetent.

Subsequently, as soon as she had finished her daily work at around 7:00pm Felicity had skipped the evening meal and heading straight down to the archives. She was delayed at the entrance when the armed guards couldn't find her name on the list as apparently Sir Gerald's office had not sent the requisite paperwork. Eventually however one of the guards had managed to contact Sir Gerald himself and confirm that she should be allowed in.

"He wasn't too pleased mind," said the guard sympathetically as he unlocked the heavy steel doors. "Said we'd interrupted the PM's banquet. I expect you'll have to pay for that later."

Felicity had smiled her thanks grimly and entered the long, low ceilinged room. Trying to ignore yet another setback before she'd even started, Felicity had found a terminal and settled into the desk.

Glancing about her she'd noticed only a couple of other people in the archives, both spread distant amid the many empty desks and terminals and both apparently engrossed in their work. As she'd logged into the archive system in total silence, Margaret's words had elbowed their way back to the forefront of her mind.

Felicity had realised then that she hadn't acquired a deterrent, bladed or otherwise and had looked at the stationery she had brought with her instead. The cheap plastic pens were quite pointy but not particularly intimidating.

She'd looked round again at the other occupants of the room. One man, one woman. She'd glanced at her watch and felt her chest tighten as she thought of the work ahead. There was nothing for it but to take her chances she'd decided, she would be more prepared in future.

After a few random forays into the vast body of official records it had become apparent that the most efficient way to compile the minute by minute timeline required would be to start at the present day and work backwards.

A seemingly boundless volume of meeting schedules, maintenance timetables and ministerial diaries meant that it had actually been relatively easy, though somewhat laborious, to build up a picture of everything that had officially happened under the mountain since the day the bombs had fallen.

By the time the lights had dimmed into night mode she was almost six years through and into a steady rhythm. As the lights flickered down Felicity heard movement behind her and had glanced about to see the other female occupant of the room collecting her things to leave. The man at the far end of the room was still working.

The sound of the heavy steel doors being heaved open and then closed again had swept an air of finality through the room. Felicity felt the tension pressing down on her just like the mountain above but had forced it out of her chest, breathing carefully until her heart slowed a little and then returned to the task at hand.

Midnight came and went and then a couple of hours more until Felicity had finally sat back in the hard, uncomfortable chair and allowed herself a sigh. She had produced as close as was possible to a complete record of all official events that had taken place since they had arrived under the mountain.

It wasn't the record she would have liked to produce, several times an hour she had had to resist the temptation to stray into analysing the lists of dates and times more deeply when interesting patterns caught her eye. It was what they had asked for however, nothing more but nothing less either.

She'd rubbed at her tired eyes and stretched, allowing herself to relax just a little. All that remained was to review and record the events of the fateful day itself. She knew she could spend a few hours on that, perhaps even include a little added value initiative work and still get an hour or two of sleep before work.

Suddenly a strange noise had caught her ear and stiffened her body. As if muffled by the silence the sound had only just been audible so that Felicity had had to strain to be sure she'd heard it over the pounding of her own heart. A weird and rhythmic trilling had drifted over her as she'd straightening up to look around the room, her weary eyes newly alert.

Eventually her eyes had managed to follow her ears to land on a lumpen shape at a distant desk. The man in the far corner had fallen asleep slumped over the terminal and was snoring peacefully to himself. Relief had washed through her then and she had even allowed herself a small smile at the fright that had gripped her.

Returning to the terminal she had set about searching out and reading through the various sources of information relating to the day the bombs had fallen. It was a story so thoroughly etched onto the minds of all who had lived through it that she had found little need to pay any real attention, nodding to herself at each familiar fact she encountered.

Despite the ten years that passed however,

occasionally she had encountered records of incidents that still chilled her or caused her eyes to sting with tears. Their swift and complete removal from the world had made it easy to forget those left behind. The millions of ordinary people who had died in the blast, the many more who had died soon after and of course those who had survived amid what was left.

There were transcripts of radio conversations between officials under the mountain and desperate people outside. Understandably, there appeared to have been a period of absolute chaos outside in the immediate aftermath.

The transcripts recorded survivors apparently out of their minds, laughing maniacally over the radio and trying to convince the people under the mountain to leave their sanctuary and come outside. Later came the quieter messages, strangely deadened voices begging for sanctuary or food. All were denied.

Felicity had summarised the issue of the messages from outside as briefly and simply as she could, stripping out the more emotive content that she knew would be deemed inappropriate. Finishing this section of the timeline she had paused and allowed herself to think about the world outside, the unimaginable terrors and hardships, the total decay of civilisation into barbarism and obscenity. Alongside these thoughts the crushing weight of the mountain had appeared warm and embracing rather than cold and indifferent.

It was while running through the payroll records that she had encountered a number that made her pause. Of course the world's financial systems had been burned to ash along with everything else, there were no banks or currencies outside any more. Under the mountain everything was provided by the state from vast, effectively endless stockpiles. There was no need to purchase anything.

Regardless however, all staff were technically still paid for their work. Numbers on screens were added to other numbers on screens and assigned to people's names. One day, when they finally emerged from the under the mountain, back out into the sunlight to set about re-establishing the world of before, these records would be brought out with them and everyone would receive their hard earned, accumulated salaries, less food, lodgings and taxes of course.

This was well understood by everyone and yet the numbers Felicity had seen from the first days after their arrival didn't seem to make sense. She had noted the anomalies down on a fresh piece of paper and moved on, committed to returning to the issue later.

She had begun to scout around for other databases she might access and was surprised to find that the clearance granted to her by an irritated, mid-banquet Sir Gerald had included access to military computer logs.

The moment the data appeared before her Felicity had seen her opportunity. These logs detailed the performance of all the various military systems, both offensive and defensive down to the second or in some cases even to the microsecond.

Here was her chance to shine and provide the added value that she hoped would change her life. Within the NAML presentation designed to demonstrate the government's ability to regulate and control everything of value she would enable the PM to go one step further, to present the government machine as being even more impressive and precise.

Working through the logs however, more numbers had arisen that caused her to pause and frown. At first glance the records simply could not be correct which of course flew directly in the face of everything the project was aiming to achieve.

Felicity had then begun to look through earlier logs recording activity from weeks and then even months before the attack. The more she had read the more she had scribbled on her pad and the colder she had felt inside. Perhaps the logs were correct after all, perhaps the systems were accurate and precise but if that was the case then the implications were even more serious.

And so she had dug deeper and made more and more notes until she was certain. Then she had gathered up her things, left the archive and made her way to a phone. Jonathan had not been impressed by being woken at so early an hour but the tone in her voice had convinced him to agree to meet her in his office.

As she waited she flicked through the notes she had made once more, running over and over what she intended to say to Jonathan and wondering how he would react. Just as she was beginning to wonder if he was coming at all the door behind her opened and Jonathan bustled in.

She could hear him wheezing as he moved past her and then grumbling to himself as he edged around his desk and collapsed into his chair. He was dressed in just the same dapper gentlemanly manner as ever but appeared dishevelled. His eyes were puffy and bleary, his thin hair tousled, his pallor pale.

"Now Felicity," he grumbled, attempting to focus on her. "What on God's green earth is so very important that you would rouse a chap from his slumber at such an unsociable hour?"

"It's the NAML research Jonathan, I think I've found something, something bad," Felicity began. Jonathan shifted irritably in his chair and grunted for her to continue.

"Well there are two things but let's start with this. These are the staffing records from the week immediately we arrived," she placed a sheet of numbers on the desk between them.

"And these are the same records for last month," she said, placing a second piece of paper alongside the first.

"Felicity, it is six o'clock in the morning. I have no appetite for figures at the best of times and I am certainly not going to start reading them now. If you could move towards your point it would be very much appreciated," said Jonathan.

"There are more than a hundred people missing from that second list Jonathan, one hundred and seventeen to be precise," said Felicity, landing a finger on the second piece of paper. Jonathan did not look impressed.

"My dear," he began wearily, dragging his thick fingers down his jowly face. "People move between departments all the time, restructuring and whatnot and I'm afraid that even in this wonderful sanctuary of ours, people do occasionally die."

"No," replied Felicity firmly. "I've cross referenced these lists across all departments and compared them to the death register. These people are no longer under the mountain, they're no longer being paid Jonathan. They're no longer paying tax."

At this last Jonathan's eyes widened, his jaw dropping slack. A more serious expression seemed to clear his eyes.

"Well now," he began carefully. "That doesn't sound right does it."

"Every one of them was employed in some kind of service role, cleaners, cooks, guards. Not one of them is a Civil Servant or a party employee. They're all people whose disappearance might go unnoticed, has gone unnoticed," Felicity corrected herself. "Where are they Jonathan?"

She handed him a third piece of paper which he accepted, apparently now willing to consider figures after all. Frowning up and down the list Jonathan mumbled to himself, licking his lips as the piece of paper trembled slightly in his hand. Eventually he placed the paper onto the desk and clasped his hands on top of it.

"This puts us in a very difficult situation Felicity," he said, his voice quavering slightly.

"You haven't seen the half of it yet I'm afraid," said Felicity, retrieving more papers from the file on her lap while Jonathan seemed to deflate.

"These are our military computer logs, defensive and offensive systems," she placed the papers over the previous. "And these are the same from the Russian systems," she added.

"How the blazes.." Jonathan began.

"It turns out we had some kind of window into their systems, just as they probably did into ours. Sir Gerald gave me unrestricted access," Felicity explained. "Look at the times I've highlighted."

Jonathan looked at the papers doubtfully and leaned forward to read them rather than picking them up, apparently reluctant to even touch them. He peered at the rows of figures for several seconds before sitting back in his chair.

"What am I looking at?" he asked quietly.

"The times I've ringed there are the moments when the Russian's launched their missiles and when we launched ours," said Felicity.

"And?" asked Jonathan, squinting down at the figures again.

"They're the same," said Felicity.

"Well," said Jonathan in a desperately reasonable tone. "Our systems really are top drawer you know, best in the world, incredible response times and all that, diodes and electrodes and internets and things, have to be. The Russians' kit probably isn't all that bad either."

"No Jonathan," said Felicity again. "The times are identical, to the microsecond. The missiles were launched simultaneously."

What little colour remained in Jonathan's early morning face drained to grey in an instant. His jaw fell slack while his fingers pawed at the edges of the paper. He looked down at the figures again, wide eyes roaming the columns desperately.

"Now that certainly can't be right," he said shakily.

"That's what it says," said Felicity. "They didn't fire first Jonathan. It wasn't retaliation."

"Then what?" asked Jonathan, sitting back in his chair, the shock still frozen into his face.

"I don't know," Felicity admitted. "I can't work it out. I've been back through the earlier logs and there are records at both ends of attempts to break into the systems, ours and theirs, as if someone was trying to find a way in."

"Some kind of lefty terrorist hacker type?" asked Jonathan.

"Maybe," said Felicity doubtfully. "But what does some terrorist group gain by destroying the whole world? It doesn't make sense."

"They don't!" snapped Jonathan, suddenly back on firmer ground and more confidently indignant for it. "They don't make any bloody sense at all, never have done! Damned maniacs the lot of them, disgraceful behaviour."

"But the staffing lists Jonathan, think about it. Who does stand to gain? Perhaps those people for whom the apocalypse doesn't mean death and destruction but rather lifelong luxury  and indisputable power. The kind of power that after ten years makes people feel like they can do anything they please with complete impunity, free to rape and even murder." Felicity was leaning forward in her chair now, the words tumbling out breathlessly.

"Either way, I don't think the Russians are," she paused to compose and correct herself. "Were our enemy. I think the enemy is in here with us Jonathan and I don't just mean in here under the mountain, I mean within the party, within the PM's office even. Rape and murder Jonathan, right under our very noses!"

The old man stared at her open mouthed for several seconds before closing his eyes and taking a deep breath. When he opened his eyes they were hard and cold.

"Now you listen to me," he said in a stern tone Felicity had never heard before. "I appreciate that you have found yourself deeply frustrated by your limited prospects and by God I have tried my best to help you, but manufacturing a story such as this simply to raise your own profile is completely unacceptable and quite frankly beneath you."

Felicity drew breath to protest but Jonathan raised a thick finger to halt her.

"It is obvious that these records are false, that they have either been incorrectly kept or tampered with after the fact. Now obviously the poor quality of these records puts us in a difficult position given the aims of the NAML project, I presume you haven't included any of this nonsense in your work for Sir Gerald?" Jonathan paused, his face ruddy once more, eyes self righteously bright.

"No," said Felicity. "I sent an appropriately sanitised version of the records to his office before I came here."

"Good," snapped Jonathan. "I'm glad to see you had that much sense at least. Now it is vital that these.." he paused to think. "..indiscrepancies remain completely confidential. Imagine the damage that could be done if the other lot got hold of this. Could be exactly what they need to successfully challenge the legitimacy of the government and then what? Bloody anarchy that's what!"

Felicity allowed her face to twist into absolute dismay.

"You and I have a duty Felicity," Jonathan continued. He scooped up the papers she had presented into a single pile, placed them in a desk drawer and locked it. "A duty to those poor souls outside to maintain Her Majesty's Government until such time as we can return to them to restore order and civilisation.

"It is a duty to which I have devoted my life and indeed one to which I will in good time give my life. I will not see it sullied by the ambitions if a silly young girl, no matter how bored or frustrated she may be. If your Grandmother could see you now I believe she would be ashamed and it saddens me greatly that you would seek to tarnish her good name in this way.

"I will see that our colleagues at the Treasury and the Ministry of Defence are discretely informed of the inaccuracies you have uncovered here so that the record may be corrected. In the meantime I think it would be a good idea for you to take a leave of absence from the duties you perform for this office until such time as I can decide upon a more appropriate role for you." Jonathan concluded, straightening his back clasping his hands before him resolute.

"But Jonathan," Felicity tried.

"Minister," snapped Jonathan. "From now on your shall address me as Minister. Good day."

"But," Felicity tried again.

"I said good day!" Jonathan roared, now entirely red in the face.

Felicity nodded and stood to leave, feeling as if she had been kicked in the stomach. The heavy fatigue of a night without sleep piled in on top of her so that the files she carried seemed leaden. As she turned to leave she felt her eyes sting with tears again and this time allowed a couple to fall.


—        —

—

It was well into the evening when Felicity finally awoke in the dormitory. There was a general buzz of noise as her colleagues returned from their evening meals. Some were preparing to return to work for a few more hours, others discussed recreational plans for the night ahead.

Having washed her face and changed her clothes Felicity ran the gauntlet of greetings and small talk to escape the dorm and made for her office. The terrible revelations of the night before and her subsequent conversation with Jonathan had taken on the fuzzed out quality of a nightmare.

Upon checking her emails however the crushing reality of it all returned. There was but one single email waiting for her, usually unthinkable over the course of an entire working day. It seemed that the one time the wheels of government turned with real efficiency was when it came to cutting someone out of the loop.

This put an end to her innermost hope that Jonathan had rethought her dismissal and written the whole thing off as an early morning tantrum. Instead there was just a curt, two sentence message from Sir Gerald's office.

No mention was made of the NAML work she'd handed in, instead she was informed that an investigation was underway into allegations that she had unlawfully accessed classified information. She should await further communication however it was their duty to advise her that serious disciplinary action may follow.

Numb and floating she returned to the dorm and sat on her bed. A couple of days earlier she had felt as if she were at the very bottom of the pile and yet now, after a full twenty four hours of hard, dedicated work she was infinitely worse off than before.

There wasn't anywhere lower within the party's policy staff to which she could be demoted and since the bombs had denied her the chance of a university education the Civil Service was out as well. There was nowhere to go but into the ranks of the service staff.

A queasy shiver rippled through her as she imagined Simon's joyously spiteful face the first time he saw her dishing out food in the canteen or emptying the bins in the offices. She'd probably have to wear a hairnet or overalls or some such thing.

She clenched her fists and felt tears fall and her lips pout before checking herself. A fierce red heat come to her face as she viewed herself from the outside and saw the spoilt little girl Jonathan had described.

Unclenching her fists she looked down at her palms. It occurred to her that she was alive, that she was safe, warm and well fed, more than could be said of the people outside. She took a deep breath and wiped away her tears before turning to remove a file from beneath her bed.

Even while she had been doing it she hadn't been entirely sure why she'd made copies of everything before going to see Jonathan, she certainly hadn't been expecting him to react as he had. By that point however she had been so tired yet full of adrenalin that she hadn't really known what she was doing, it had just seemed important at the time.

Leafing through the tables of numbers she wasn't sure what she was looking for until she came across the transcripts of the conversations with the people outside. Before even reading them she felt the terrible sadness they inspired return. Her guilt from her moment of self indulgence pushed her to read them again, to inflict the sadness they carried upon herself as kind of penance for forgetting the people outside.

Soon her tears were flowing again as she read the pleading, desperate words and the cold, official responses. She ploughed on into the trauma, greedy for grief as she read and reread the heartbreaking words, whipping herself along. Sobs wracked her and the words blurred into nothing as her eyes refilled with fluid and pain.

Then something caught her attention, somehow slicing through all the emotion. Another part of her locked onto the words and pushed everything else to one side. The last transcribed conversation was between an official and a woman claiming to be the mother of a sick child. She was pleading with the official to take her child promising that he wouldn't eat very much and was well behaved.

It was a gut wrenching as the rest of the conversations but the dialogue wasn't what had caught Felicity's eye. The conversation had not taken place across hundreds of miles over a radio but via an intercom and recently too. The woman been physically stood outside a door leading into the mountain, Single Person Service Entrance 213 according to the transcript.

Felicity wracked her brains, recalling the events of the day they had arrived. There had been huge, impossibly thick steel doors across a vast walkway that had allowed hundreds of people at a time to walk into the mountain.

On the way in she'd also caught sight of other, even larger entrances through which great convoys of trucks had passed carrying equipment and supplies. She had never seen nor even heard of a normal sized or rather a single person door into the mountain.

She rifled through the file some more, letting sheafs of paper fall to the floor before seizing upon a particularly dull works schedule entitled, 'Hinge, Handle & Lock Maintenance'. Every single door under the mountain was listed in painfully small type over several pages.

Felicity scanned through almost the entire list before finding the entry for Single Person Service Entrance 213. Listed alongside were the dates and times of the most recent maintenance activities along with a note recommending replacement of the hinges which were apparently starting to seize. The final column of the table included a corridor reference number denoting the exact location of the door.

She paused to think, trying to place the corridor in her mind's map of the world under the mountain. For the first time it occurred to her that despite having spent a decade of her life  in this place, she had actually seen and knew very little of it. In fact the more she thought about it the more likely it seemed that no one person could know all of it.

For long seconds she stared at the corridor number until it seemed etched into her mind's eye then discarded the schedule and began searching for another. The 'Floor & Surface Cleansing' schedule was easier to find and in a few moments more she had found the relevant corridor reference number.

Working her way back up the list she found that the order in which the corridors were cleaned basically described a route through the mountain. She continued up the list, back over several pages, until she finally came across a corridor she knew.

She plucked the relevant pages from the schedule and placed them beside her on the bed before gathering up the rest and forcing it all back into a tangle of creases within the folder.

Having slept all day she was no longer tired and her suspension meant that the next few days held nothing but anxious waiting. Her stomach twisted back and forth as she interrogated herself as to the sense of the idea that beckoned.

Finding the door would mean a long, dull and ultimately pointless walk. Even if she found it she knew there was nothing beyond it but the horrors of radiation sickness and the desecrated ruins of her childhood.

Still though, the thought of the intercom intrigued her. What if there were still people outside the door? New people, different people. If they were there they would inevitably beg her to open the door, something she knew even in the midst of this desperate madness she could not do.

Even so, she could speak to them, she could refuse them gently and with compassion instead of with cold indifference. She could let them know that there were still people under the mountain who cared and who would one day return to put things right for them. It wasn't much, it was almost nothing in fact, but perhaps she could give them hope for the future.

She stood but stopped as a second voice took the lead. There almost certainly would not be anyone at the intercom, what were the chances? It would take her hours to find the door only to then turn around and walk all the way back again. That assumed she could find it at all of course.

There was a good chance that she could become completely lost in the rarely frequented bowels of the mountain, wandering hopelessly through identically blank and empty corridors.

Perhaps, the voice suggested in a more threatening tone now, that was exactly what had happened to those one hundred and seventeen missing people, perhaps they been consumed by the labyrinth, condemned to die of thirst alone and in the dark.

Paralysed and dithering Felicity weighed her options. Her quest to find the door was almost certainly pointless and potentially lethal but the alternative was to lie on her bed and stare at the ceiling while self satisfied men in pin striped suits planned out the rest of her life.

The mental image of Sir Gerald smiling to himself sadistically while writing his recommendations with a gilded fountain pen was enough to break the deadlock. Resolute and fearless she strode from the dorm and headed for the door to the nearest staircase.

Reading the cleaning schedule it had not occurred to Felicity just how much of the journey would be vertical. Upon entering the first stairwell she realised that in order to reach the first corridor on the list she would need to descend more the a dozen floors.

The stairs were the same moulded concrete as the corridors, utterly bland and relentless. As she made her way down flight after flight, turning back and forth, back and forth, the scene began to take on a surreal air. As her body carried her through the motions her mind drifted off into childhood memories of drawings of impossible, endless staircases and self feeding waterfalls.

She was so distracted by this that she actually missed her floor and had to retrace half a flight of the hard edged concrete steps. She passed through the door and out into a corridor identical to the one she had left above so that if felt as if she hadn't moved at all.

Checking the number on the tiny plastic plaque screwed into the wall against those on the schedule however she found that she was in the right place and so continued on. She hadn't encountered a single person on the stairs and she found this latest corridor to be equally deserted.

Just as she rounded another long slow curve and the door to the next stairway came into view the lights above began to flicker and dim as the officially sanctioned night time began. Shadows swelled out of the recessed doorways to lap at her feet and seemed to amplify her footsteps.

Treading more carefully she approached the door to the next stairwell and opened it as slowly and quietly as she could. More concrete stairs ran up and down before her and she resumed her descent. As she went she tried to keep her progress along the route straight in her mind to counter the feeling of endless, timeless stepping.

Her mind drifted back to the conversation with Jonathan, replaying it over and over and considering alternate approaches that might have been more effective. She wondered if she should have raised the matter with Jonathan at all or perhaps taken it to someone else. She thought that perhaps Margaret would have taken it all more seriously. Then she remembered their conversation earlier in the day and Margaret's pragmatic attitude concerning the worsening living situation for female colleagues.

So lost in these thoughts was she that she didn't notice the change in flooring until her foot almost landed upon it. The concrete stairs continued downward in exactly the same manner but from the landing below and downwards a broad red carpet ran down the centre of the floor.

Between two thin margins of the hard grey beneath, the carpet was thick and lush so that Felicity's feet seemed sink into it at every step. The contrast with the previous, countless ankle juddering footsteps was amazing so that she felt she was walking on springs.

Reaching the next landing below Felicity noticed that the doors had changed as well. Above the doors had been plain, functional steel. Here she was confronted with ornately carved and polished wood. She paused to take in the design, the jarring weirdness of luxury carpets and decorated doors against the grim concrete backdrop reminding her of Jonathan's office.

Consulting the cleaning schedule Felicity noticed that she had only one more floor to go before the next horizontal section of the journey. She trotted down a

couple more spongey flights of carpeted stair and
approached another of the spectacular wooden doors.

Felicity heaved the door open and stepped through
into a softly lit chamber. As the door swung quietly
closed behind her she took a few tentative steps
forward, squinting into the gloom. Gone was the
ubiquitous curving concrete of walls into ceiling, here the
walls were flat, vertical surfaces, exquisitely wood
panelled and dotted with ancient oil paintings. The floor
was a great wash of intricate tiling, gleaming subtly in
the dimmed lights.

The decor was familiar and yet so unexpected that
Felicity found herself tiptoeing across the tiles, the hairs
on the back of her neck standing out to see their bizarre
new surroundings. More ornate doors punctuated the
wood panelling on either side before a grander set of
double doors appeared through the gloom at the end of
the chamber.

She opened the left of these with the greatest
care, straining to hear footsteps or voices over the top of
the deep hinge creaking. Still there appeared to be no-
one around and so she stepped through into another
decorated space but this time one that she knew.

Felicity was standing in a minor lobby near the
main chamber of the House of Commons. Disorientated
she moved out into the middle of the lobby and turned
slowly, recognising the door through which she would
normally enter. Looking back at the doors through which
she had come she realised that she had walked past
them many times before but had never even thought
about what lay behind them.

The familiar waypoint brought the journey back to
the real and lessened the sense of strangeness that had
gone before. After pausing to drink in the comfort of the
familiar, Felicity consulted the cleaning schedule once
more and identified another door from the lobby which
she had seen but never recognised many times before.

This door was smaller and more discrete, tucked
away in a corner and camouflaged beneath decoration.
Felicity crossed the lobby, realising how much bigger it
seemed when empty and tried the handle. For a moment
the door resisted and for the first time it occurred to her

that any one of the many doors along her intended way could bring a premature end to her quest simply by being locked.

With a little more effort however the door yielded and swung out to meet her. She passed through and pulled it closed behind her. The corridor in which she found herself was a strange mix of the two styles through which she had come so far.

The walls and ceiling here were the same drab concrete from before but were also flat and met at right angles. The ceiling itself was much lower so that she could have reached up and touched the strip bulbs. The walls meanwhile were so close that she could easily touch them both at the same time.

The corridor ran dead straight for a few minutes walk before emptying into a vast vertical shaft. The concrete walls were perfectly smooth and featureless as they plummeted down into sheer black below. Hanging in the middle of this void a rickety looking metal staircase seemed to float, though on closer inspection Felicity could see that it was periodically attached to the concrete with worryingly small looking bolts.

Frowning her concern Felicity took the most delicate step she could manage onto the top of the structure, holding onto the thin metal handrail fiercely. As she shifted her weight onto the stairs she was sure she felt the whole thing tremor slightly, as if adjusting to the newly added load.

She took a breath and lifted her back foot off the smooth grey safety behind and moved completely onto the stairs. A faint creaking sound echoed up and down the shaft and she imagined she could hear the thousand little bolts straining in their holes.

Her hand insisted on retaining a painfully firm grip on the handrail even though she knew that it would offer her no help if the stairs decided fling themselves down into the shaft. Gradually she gained some degree of confidence and began to move down the rickety stairs with more speed, keen to reach the floor she needed and be off them as soon as was safely possible.

The doors back onto the main floors were less regular here so that she would often go down a dozen sets of stairs without encountering one. Dim round bulbs were set into the concrete every so often so that she could only ever see a few flights above or below her at any one time.

This produced the unpleasant effect that occasionally Felicity could look around her and see nothing but the walls of the great shaft and the rickety metal stairs stretching off apparently forever both above and below.

Another hole in the wall denoting a landing and a door began to appear through the gloom below. Felicity resolved that even if it wasn't the floor listed on the cleaning schedule she would go through the door regardless and then find an alternate route, anything to get off the metal staircase.

As it turned out however, the number stencilled onto the wall next to the opening was exactly the floor listed on the schedule. With a huge sigh of relief Felicity stepped off the stairs and back onto solid grey. Without even looking back she yanked the metal door open and strode through it, keen to put the experience behind her.

As she pressed on through more tight and increasingly poorly lit corridors it occurred to her that at some point she would have to retrace her steps back up the terrifying metal staircase.

She suggested to herself that ascending them might not be as bad as it wouldn't involve looking down into the seemingly bottomless depths. She also made a point however or reading any sign she encountered carefully in case it hinted towards an alternative route back up to the lobby.

According to the cleaning schedule it seemed that the vertical part of her journey was complete and that Single Person Service entrance 213 was located somewhere on the floor she was now exploring.

At most junctions corridor numbers were stencilled onto the bare concrete, only occasionally did she encounter small plastic plaques listing the name of specific areas or rooms accompanied by directing arrows.

Once, when pausing to check the corridor numbers against the schedule she noticed a plaque with an arrow

that said simply: STOREHOUSE 5. The arrow alongside it
pointed left while the schedule told her she needed to go
right. She lingered by the sign for moment however,
peering off down the left hand corridor, her curiosity
painting spectacular pictures onto the darkness ahead.

Shaking herself she resumed her progress, looking
for the next landmark corridor number and trying not to
think about how deep into the mountain she now was.
The close walls and low ceiling seemed to conspire with
the heavy shadows to pull the oxygen out of the air,
leaving nothing but a sense of breathless claustrophobia
behind.

Felicity was so focussed on controlling her
breathing and holding the panic at bay that when she
first heard the sound it didn't register at all. It was the
second sound that stopped her dead. The sound was
incredibly faint and distant, obviously distorted by the
endless corners around which it had bounced.

She closed her eyes and tilted her head to one
side, straining to hear. Was it shouting? Cheering
maybe? She licked her lips unsure and looked back down
the corridor to where she had come from. The paper
schedule felt rough between her finger and thumb and
as she gently rubbed at it she imagined she could feel
the type as if it had been subtly embossed on the page.

The memory of Margaret's biter rant washed back
over her, underlined by the memory of her encounter
with Simon. Fear began to snatch at her heart, she could
feel it trying to take hold but the thought of trekking all
the way back up to the dorm helped her keep it at bay.
Finally she resumed her pace but stepped carefully now,
keen to make no sound.

The further she went the louder the sound became
so that she began to walk close to the wall, pausing to
peer round each corner she encountered before moving
on. Soon she could make out individual voices.

It sounded like a small group of drunken men,
cheering and chanting enthusiastically. Occasionally the
voices would synchronise into a low but rising sound.
This would build agonisingly until erupting into an
explosion of cheers and applause studded with whoops
and yells and usually followed by the chanting of a man's

name, different each time.

Cautiously rounding another corner Felicity was faced with a T junction. Squinting at the faded numbers on the wall ahead she saw that her destination should be to the right. The sound of the men was incredibly close now however so that she was convinced it was just around the corner to the left.

Felicity stared down at the schedule, there were only a few more corridors to go. She forced her straining eyes down the list of numbers over and over, pushing them into her memory. She closed he eyes and recited the numbers to herself then checked the list again to be sure.

Nodding to herself she folded the paper incredibly slowly and slipped it into her pocket. Then she approached the junction, sliding her back along the left hand wall until she reached the corner.

The noise was so close that she could pick out individual conversations amid the chaos. She counted at least six different voices and though she couldn't quite place them they all sounded familiar. Crouching down Felicity turned and began to lean towards the corner to look round it while bracing herself to flee.

As she allowed just the thinnest possible slice of the right side of her face to round the corner she immediately pulled back. Further down the left hand corridor there was an open door to the right. The raucous sounds were being generated within that room and spilling out through that doorway. Leaning against the door frame was a figure.

Forcing herself to breathe slowly and deeply Felicity prepared herself for a second, longer look. Leaning out again her right eye scanned the figure up and down. It was a man wearing a black dinner suit complete with tails, a white, high collared shirt and a white bow tie. He was holding a large glass of red wine in one hand and a smouldering cigarette in the other.

It was Simon.

He was staring into the room, eyes narrowed but gleaming. Every so often as the cheers would rise a flicker would run through his expression but otherwise he was motionless, lips thin, nostrils flaring.

Pulling back around the corner Felicity cursed to herself silently. An aim that had seemed fascinating, even important, was now revealed as childish and naive. All she had really achieved through the hours of walking had been to voluntarily thrust herself into exactly the kind of situation she had been specifically warned to avoid.

Suddenly the thought of Rachel's suicide brought fresh tears to her eyes. Felicity knew that if something happened to her down here no-one, probably not even Margaret would believe that she hadn't invited it. Why else would have come all the way down here?

There would be no sympathy only a secret shame, trapped under the mountain with no choice but live side by side with Simon and his friends for the rest of her life. No wonder Rachel had hung herself. Would she really have done any different? Could she?

Part of Felicity told her to leave, to retrace her steps and not look back. She didn't know what was happening in that room but she knew being discovered here by those men could only end badly for her.

Another part of her disagreed however and clenched a fist at her side. How many more decisions would she allow men like these to make for her? How much more was she prepared to give up or accept at their say so?

Even the briefest of glances had told her that Simon was smashed, drunk and probably more, completely transfixed by whatever was happening within. All she need to do was make it around the corner and off down the corridor without being seen. A dozen or so steps, seconds at most and she would disappear into the shadows leaving him none the wiser behind.

Her heart was pounding in her ears, palms damp, mouth dry. She approached the corner once more, leaning out so slightly until Simon came into view. He was standing just as before. As she watched he took a drag on his cigarette and a sip of his wine without ever moving his eyes from the room.

Felicity began to step carefully backwards, keeping just the thinnest sliver of Simon in view until she felt the right hand wall against her back. Her fingers traced the wall behind her, reaching right until they found they corner. Slowly she slid to her right, moving out into the corridor and full view.

She took one step backwards and then another, facing Simon full on now, watching his eyes which still weren't looking as she retreated towards the shadows. Gritting her teeth she dared to turn so as to move more quickly and surely. Unable to see Simon now she held her breath, stepping as quickly as she could without sound.

Peering ahead she could see the next corner around which she would be hidden and safe. Closer it came, she tried to lengthen her stride, her arms raised on their own to reach out to it.

"Hey!" came the voice from behind.

She froze, the terror turning her to stone and stopping her heart. Somewhere inside she was screaming at herself to run but her foolish head turned her round instead. Simon had stepped out into the corridor fully and was squinting at her through the gloom. As she watched he recognised her, his eyes widening, a terrible smile spreading out across his face.

"Tea girl!" he bellowed joyous. "Come to join the party? I knew you couldn't say no! Ha!"

Finally something broke inside her and she was scrambling away down the corridor. She snatched at the corner and dragged herself round it, hammering her legs into the floor and plunging on into the shadows. Simon's voice echoed off the walls, chasing to snap at her heels.

"Come on!" he was bellowing. "It's the one I was telling you about! She's here!"

Felicity realised her face was wet but she blinked away the tears to focus on the numbers on the walls. She turned sharply again and again, sticking to the route for fear of losing herself and coming full circle.

"Just leave it!" Simon was screeching distant.

"But Eggo hasn't had his turn yet," came a second, echoing voice.

"It's not going anywhere all trussed up like that, we'll finish with it later! Come on!" Simon yelled over the sound of splintering glass so that Felicity could see him flinging his wine to the floor.

Heavy footsteps thundered up from behind now with whoops and howls in amongst. Felicity heard herself sobbing but pushed on to skid round another corner. Her lungs were burning, her heart threatening to break through her ribs but her legs ran her on regardless.

"Where is she?" came a voice.

"Can't see her," came another.

"She can't have gone far," that was Simon. "Split up. Find her."

Felicity skidded again but this time too far so that she tumbled over into the brutally solid floor. She scrambled around the corner on all fours then hugged her freshly bruised knees to her chest and listened. The footsteps and shouting continued but seemed to maintain their distance.

She thought hard and counted carefully. She had rounded five corners since Simon had seen her, at each one there had been at least one other turn she could have made instead. Unless they were lucky it would take time to find her. They didn't have her yet.

Her first attempt to stand was sabotaged by trembling legs but through silent cursing the second worked better. As she pressed her rubbery legs back into action the details of the maintenance schedule for Single Person Service Entrance 213 sprang back before her eyes.

It wasn't a single door just straight to the outside, that wouldn't meet the radiation shielding requirements. It was more of an airlock type setup with and inner and and an outer door separated by a small chamber.

If she could get through the inner door and into the chamber she could hide. Of course it would be a perfect barrel for fish, potentially the deadest of ends but as she couldn't think of anything else to do it appeared to be a gamble worth taking.

Valuing silence over speed, she opted for a quick walk over a plunging sprint and her legs and lungs agreed. At each corner she paused to compose herself then peeked before rounding it boldly.

The footsteps and voices echoed all around her, so that it became impossible to tell where the men were. They called to one another that different areas were clear and where to look next so that Felicity realised they knew the corridors much better than she did. This was where they came to have their sinister little parties, away from prying eyes where they could do as they pleased.

As she turned the penultimate corner and approached the last she heard the slap of heavy feet just behind her. She broke into a sprint and rounded the final corner to find a heavy looking door half way along the corridor ahead. The numbers 2, 1 and 3 were stencilled onto the metal in large, familiar type.

She rushed to the door and pulled violently at the handle, trying to temper her panic with silence. She could hear heavy breathing from back round the corner and slow footsteps growing louder as they ate up the distance. The door gave a little but then stopped, the hinges apparently seizing. Leaning back Felicity hung all her weight from her arms and dragged until she thought her joints would splinter.

As the footsteps came closer and then closer still she knew that at any second the guy would reach the corner. If he saw her before she made it inside and got the door closed again then it was over, she'd be trapped and they'd have her, her flight would have been for nothing.

Finally the door swung open so that she stumbled backwards while it revealed itself to be several inches thick. She sprang forth again, diving over the threshold and dragging the door behind her.

The outward swing had apparently convinced the hinges so that the return journey ran more smoothly. Though incredibly heavy the door had been hung in such a way as glide gently closed with a faint hiss as the air tried to get out out of the way.

Felicity sat down hard, her back to the door and tried to listen past her heartbeat. There was shouting outside, muffled now by the door but even so seeming more distant as each second ticked by. It appeared that she had made it through in time and that they had moved on in their search.

She found herself weeping but managed to smile a little through the tears at the thought of Simon's frustration. She vowed to herself that were he to mention their encounter at some future time she would feign ignorance so convincingly that perhaps he would come to doubt what he had seen and even begin to question his sanity.

As she fantasised about Simon's painful descent into Mountain Fever she looked around the sanctuary she had found. The walls and ceiling in the chamber were even closer than the corridors outside. The room was utterly barren apart from the identical doors at either end and a small device built into the wall next to the far one.

It was an intercom.

Felicity wiped her face and got to her feet. She crossed the chamber in three short steps and raised a hand to touch the small panel. This was the intercom through which the woman had pleaded in vain for the life of her child. The official who had refused her so coldly had stood in this exact spot when he'd done so.

She turned her attention to the door. It was identical to the other in almost every way except that this one featured a faded poster filled with warnings spelled out in red, capital letters. Some of the type had faded completely but some fairly graphic diagrams ensured that the message was still clear. She was leaning in close to try and read some of the detail when a noise made her spring back from the door.

"Is somebody there?" crackled a voice.

It had come from the intercom.

—  —

—

"Hello?" came the voice again accompanied by a little red light.

Felicity goggled at the intercom, jaw slack, eyes dull. She recalled the conversations she had imagined while sat on her bed and realised she had never seriously expected to have them.

But now here she was, listening to a voice from

the outside. There was someone on the other side of the door. She quickly wiped her face then slowly approached the intercom, her hand coming up to carry a cautious finger to single red button on the panel.

"Is there somebody there?" came the voice again, making her jump and pause. She licked her lips and took a breath then pressed the button. The light turned green.

"Hello?" she said, her voice small and unsure.

"Hello," came the reply. "Who's that?"

"Erm," said Felicity before cursing herself and shaking herself.

"My name is Felicity," she said with more confidence. "What's yours?"

"I'm Stephen," came the voice again. "Are you going to open the door?"

Her heart ached as she found herself in the footsteps of the official from the transcript now literally and figuratively.

"I'm so terribly sorry," she said as kindly as she could. "But I'm afraid I can't do that"

"Oh," said Stephen. "Well, I really wish you would but I understand. It's ok."

"Thank you," said Felicity guiltily. Wasn't she supposed to be helping them? "Are you ok out there?" she asked.

"Yeah, I'm ok," said Stephen. "Thanks for asking. Are you sure you won't open the door?"

"No," said Felicity, firmly this time. "I really can't."

"Fair enough," said Stephen. "So why are talking to me then?"

"Well," said Felicity, a little taken aback by how calm and direct the man's voice sounded. "I read about this entrance in some official records and decided to sneak down here to find it. I thought I maybe there might be someone here I could talk to and here you are!"

"Wait," said Stephen. "Do you mean you're alone in there?"

"No, no," said Felicity quickly, moving onto the motivational script she had prepared. "There are many of us in here, the government still exists. I know it must be terribly hard for you out there but I wanted to tell you, that's why I came, your elected government is still going, we're still here and we care about you all very much.

"It's going to take us a long time but eventually, when it's safe, we're going to come out again and help you rebuild. Together we'll put things back the way they were before. We haven't forgotten you and we certainly haven't abandoned you. I know it isn't much but I hope that helps. There is reason to hope you see, reason to survive, things will get better eventually, we'll make them better for you, I promise you we will."

There was a long pause. As it lengthened Felicity began to cringe. What if they felt she was patronising them? She really did want to help but there was so little she could do. Didn't they understand that these words were all she had to give them? Eventually the intercom crackled back into life.

"Ok," said Stephen slowly. "That's great thanks, not really what I meant though. I meant, are you alone in the chamber between the doors?"

Felicity's hand dropped from the intercom. There was something strange about the voice. She remembered some of the other transcribed conversations where the people outside had sounded like maniacs. They had tried all kinds of tricks and ploys to convince the officials to open the doors to let them in.

Suddenly she felt very foolish. She had no idea how she was speaking to. On the one hand it could be a terribly traumatised victim, the kind of person she had so desperately wanted to provide with even just a little piece of hope. On the other though it could be a dreadful, sadistic criminal maniac. Who knew what horrific things went on out there now? She thought hard before returning her finger to the button.

"Why do you ask?" she said, trying to keep her voice level and light.

"Well you said you'd snuck down," said Stephen. "I just wondered if that meant you were on your own in the chamber."

"And why should that matter to you?" asked Felicity, a slight edge creeping into her tone.

"It doesn't matter to me at all," came the matter of fact reply. "But you do know that the inner door can only be opened from the other side right? Unless you've got someone out in the corridor to let you back in I'm afraid you're a bit stuck."

Felicity stepped back from the intercom as a frozen finger traced her spine. She span on her heel and stared at the inner door accusingly. Stepping forward she reached out a trembling hand and gripped the handle. Sure enough it was stuck fast. For almost three minutes she wrenched at the handle, hanging from it and kicking at it until she stumbled backwards and fell to sit on the cold hard floor.

"Hello," came Stephen's voice from the intercom again. "Hello Felicity? Are you ok?"

Felicity buried her face in her hands and screamed silently. She was trapped, locked in a concrete box and not just any concrete box but a concrete box into which she had put a huge amount of effort to seek out and walk into. No-one knew she was in it either, she'd gone to great lengths to make sure of that as well. She'd killed herself, she realised. She'd basically, effectively, killed herself.

"Felicity?" said Stephen again.

Slowly Felicity pulled herself up off the floor to stand in a string cut slump. She shambled back to the intercom and lifted a heavy hand to the button.

"I'm locked in," she said, her voice flat and empty.

"Oh," said Stephen. "I'm sorry to hear that."

"No-one knows I'm in here," she continued. "By the time they even start looking it'll be too late, I'll be.." she trailed off. "I mean how long can you go without water, that's like two days or something right? I mean I'm just.. I'm.."

"Felicity," said Stephen seriously.

"Yeah," she replied absently, defeated.

"Open the door," he said.

Felicity nodded. She knew she was dead anyway, it was just a matter of how. Staying in the chamber meant certain death, slow and painful. At least if she opened the door she'd see the outside again before she died. It might be radiation sickness, maybe they'd rape, torture and eat her like the rumours said, who knew? She looked around at the barren space. The unknown was better than the definite.

She moved to the outer door, ignoring the faded but still screaming text and pictures and landed her hand on the handle. With tired resignation she pushed it down, leaning in against the resistance and leaned back to pull.

After a moment of nothing the door gave with a mighty hiss and swung in to meet her. Closing her eyes she felt her lower lip wobble but refused to cry any more. She stepped out over the threshold, her eyes still closed and heard the door swing shut and seal behind her.

It was done.

"Hi," said Stephen, his voice so much closer and clearer than through the intercom. Felicity opened her eyes to look at him but gasped instead, stumbling back against the door and collapsing to the floor.

She had emerged onto one of the lower slopes of the mountain but it still commanded a mind boggling view. The sky was impossibly huge overhead and violently blue, spotted only occasionally by a scattered white clouds. The sun was painfully bright so that she had to half close her eyes to see. Even so she could still make out great rolling fields of green, patched darker by lush forests spread out below.

In the far distance she could see towns, low clusters of buildings, windows gleaming in the blazing sunlight. Thin, tiny strings of traffic dotted distant roads, smoke rose in slender columns from occasional factory chimneys. It was a picture postcard of a peaceful, prosperous world.

"Hey," Stephen tried again, stepping in front of the view to capture her attention, his shadow relieving her stinging eyes.

"What.." Felicity tried but the words wouldn't come. "But.. I.. How.. What?"

"It's ok," Stephen said gently, squatting down in front of her. "I know this must be very difficult but I'm going to explain. First of all, you're ok, you're safe. I'm not going to try and eat you or anything."

Felicity stared at him as the attempted joke fell to the ground between them. Stephen was young, younger than her even. His skin was tanned and he wore rugged functional clothes. They appeared to have been repaired many times but were well kept. In his hands he held a folder which he opened. He offered her his hand to help her up but she just stared at it so he sat down cross legged in front of her instead.

"So you must be Felicity Daniels, is that right?" he said, consulting the file.

Felicity fought to keep her eyes from the gonging landscape over his shoulder and nodded dumbly.

"Ok," he said carefully. "Well first things first, it says here that your Grandmother was your only living relative."

She nodded again.

"Well I'm pleased to be able to tell you that she's still going in fact she doesn't live that far from here. We can take you to see her, when you're ready," he said.

"Grandmother?" Felicity managed.

"That's right," said Stephen smiling kindly. "She's fine."

"Oh," Felicity gasped, then broke down into hacking great sobs.

They sat together in the dirt for a full five minutes while Felicity sobbed her heart out and Stephen rested his hand on her shoulder.

"It's always difficult," he said gently.

"I'm sorry," said Felicity finally, wiping the strings of tears and mucus from her face, suddenly embarrassed by the state of herself. "I don't understand what's happening. It's the middle of the night, I was.. How can this be?"

"Of course,"said Stephen, closing the file and carefully placing it on the ground. "That's quite common I'm afraid. Over time your clocks in there have slipped a bit that's all. It's actually," he paused to consult his watch. "Just after eight in the morning now."

Felicity looked from his face to his watch and back again, unsure what to do with the information.

"Look," he began again. "There's going to be plenty of time for you to get to grips with this but if you like I can give you the short version right now?"

She shrugged and then nodded blankly.

"Ok," he began as if reading from a script. "So about ten years ago a hacker pulled off the most spectacular prank in history."

"A hacker?" said Felicity, remembering the military computer logs. "Yes, I saw the records. They launched all the missiles at once."

"Well," said Stephen. "No, not really."

"But," Felicity started to try but gave up again.

"The hacker, or hackers, we still don't know who they were, managed to access the security systems of every government in the world. Somehow they made it appear as if a nuclear strike was imminent. It turned out that almost all of those governments had secret bunkers like this one," said Stephen, pointed to the door at her back.

"They all evacuated, dashed off into their bunkers and locked themselves inside. The hackers had made it utterly convincing, even fooling the bunker systems that detected air quality and everything outside. At first it was funny, a global joke, seeing all those important people dashing off to hide in their holes but then when people tried to contact them to explain, well.." it was Stephen's turn to trail off.

"They didn't believe you," said Felicity, remembering the transcripts. "But what about all the people begging for food, pleading to be let in?"

Stephen nodded and looked serious.

"Once we realised that the people inside were never going to believe that it was a joke people began to try other approaches, anything at all to get you guys to open the door just so you would see that everything was ok out here but then..." he faltered.

"Then?" asked Felicity.

"Well, it was funny at first like I say, but then people began to realise." Stephen swallowed as if to prepare himself. "Their governments honestly believed that their countries had been annihilated by nuclear war and their response had been to leave us all out here to rot.

"We knew how much food was stockpiled in there,

the hackers had leaked all of that information too. As far as our leaders knew we were all starving to death while they were sitting on vast piles of clean food and yet they wouldn't share it, wouldn't help us. People became more and more angry until it was decided to just leave you in there" Stephen turned to look over his shoulder at the landscape below.

"So who runs things now?" asked Felicity, clinging to specifics so try and avoid being overwhelmed by the bigger picture. "Who's in charge?"

"Nobody, not anymore," replied Stephen absently, still staring out at the view.

"What do you mean?" Felicity scoffed. "Someone has to be in charge."

"Not really," said Stephen, turning back to face her. "It was a bit chaotic for a while to start with. Various different groups tried to establish their own new governments or set up new countries even but no-one could prove any kind of legitimate claim and there was no longer any appetite for any kind of politics among the people."

He spoke as if reading form a script and Felicity wondered how many times he had practiced the speech before.

"You have to remember," he continued. "It wasn't just governments that ran away, it was the opposition parties too, politicians of all colours, not to mention the super rich. They'd all made their own arrangements too, so the boss of every multi-national corporation, the head of every major crime family or syndicate, they all disappeared overnight as well."

"Then other people tried to take over by force. They seized what was left of the big corporations or the organised crime networks, but it didn't work. All the power they'd had before had come from having mountains of money and from exploiting the law from one side or the other.

"Suddenly there were no governments to make or enforce laws for their benefit and all currencies became worthless in a matter of weeks. They had nothing of value with which to pay people, no legal advantages by which to force people and most of all they couldn't convince anyone that the work they wanted people to do was actually worth doing.

"Of course they tried using violence but once people realised they couldn't rely on the police anymore they started banding together to defend themselves and protect one another and ultimately, they had the numbers. In the end all those old structures just fell apart.

"Eventually, after a couple of years people began to realise that while all these different groups had been fighting over who should be in charge, everyone else had just been getting on with it.

"The people who actually did all the important work just carried on doing it, in fact left to their own devices they did better if anything. The lights stayed on, food was still being grown and distributed, the schools and hospitals were still open.

"People stopped panicking and started pitching in, finding out what they were good at, finding solutions to each other's problems. It just worked and by time the third anniversary rolled around everything had pretty much settled down to how it is now."

"So there's no-one in charge?" asked Felicity, struggling to take it all in.

"Nope," said Stephen.

"No government, no big companies, no criminals?" Felicity asked.

"Nope, not really," said Stephen. "I mean it's not perfect, we still have problems but it's better than it was before. I don't think anyone would want to go back now."

"I just don't.. I can't.." Felicity shook her head and then buried it in her hands.

"I know," said Stephen. "It's too much to take in all at once. It will get easier, I promise. There's no rush."

"But what about you?" said Felicity, dropping her hands again and staring blankly at the view. "Why are you up here?"

"Oh," said Stephen. "I volunteer up here a couple of times a year, a bunch of us do."

"But why?" asked Felicity.

"You're not the first person to come out you

know," Stephen said.

Felicity started, her jaw falling slack.

"What do you mean?" she asked, suddenly alert.

"Well," he said, retrieving the file and flicking through it. "So far you are the ninety-ninth person to walk out of that door. Next one's a century!" He smiled at her for a second then thought better of it and continued. "After the first dozen or so we set up a guard station up here. Well they call it a guard station, I call it a shed!"

Stephen pointed to a small wooden shack built against the side of the mountain just a few feet away. It looked roughly made but sturdy.

"There's nearly always someone up here, we usually manage to keep it covered between us. We monitor the air lock doors and have personnel files on you all," he said, waving the file at her. "So that we can work out who you are and tell you about your families when you come out. That's usually the first thing people want to know about. You were an easy one to find by the way. You're the only Felicity in the whole facility, did you know that?"

Felicity shook her head dumbly. The sky was just all too big, to open and too bright. The rough rock and scrub all around them too full of texture, endless clanging details overloading her senses. She felt as if she were drowning. She closed her eyes for a moment and concentrated on breathing, resisting the urge to replay everything that Stephen had said, holding it at arm's length until she could think.

"What happens now," she managed to say.

"Well it's up to you," he said, standing.

He offered her his hand and she took it, wobbling all the way up to stand.

"I can take you down to the nearest town, put you in touch with your family but," Stephen paused and looked her straight in the eye. "We always ask you guys for a favour first. It's up to you of course, there's no obligation."

"What is it?" she asked wary and weary in equal measure.

"Well I've a radio in the shed. Would you mind

trying to contact the people still inside. If you can prove to them who you are they might listen to you. You could convince them to come out," Stephen said looking hopeful.

Felicity looked back at the heavy metal door and then up and up at the mountain exterior that towered off into the clouds. She thought of Jonathan and Margaret, of Simon and Sir Gerald and of ten years of her life in there with them, under them.

"Fuck them," she said finally.

Stephen smiled sadly and nodded.

"That's what everyone says," he said.

"Can you take me to my Grandmother?" she asked, turning her back on the mountain.

"Of course," replied Stephen. "Come on, I'll take you into town."

Felicity followed him down the path and didn't once look back.

# sleep to win

"He's got another one," said her father, announcing the news to the breakfast table without looking up from his Sunday paper. Kate drove her spoon through the thickening mush of her cereal in listless circles and suppressed a sigh.

"Who's got another what dear?" asked her mother, buttering a slice of toast while her keen eyes interrogated the pages of the catalogue splayed out before her.

"This Sandman guy they're all talking about," her father replied. "He's killed another one."

Kate watched as he lay down his own spoon and leaned in to focus on the paper more intently. He slid his fingers across the plastic surface of the paper so that the text of the headline story grew larger and she noticed his hair was thinner than ever on top. She wondered when he would finally admit it and start buying the spray on stuff.

"Says this one had been there for five days before they found him," he went on, shaking his head sadly. "Just sat there, slumped in a chair staring at nothing. Died of thirst apparently."

"Dreadful," said her mother absently as she took a bite of toast and tapped the catalogue twice to view the next page.

"They don't know how he does it," her father continued. "No sign of forced entry, not a mark on them, no drugs in their system, total mystery." He swiped the story away and returned to the news at large.

Kate found herself staring at the box of cereal standing in the midst of the breakfast clutter all of which was gathered around a large hole in the centre of the table. A cartoon creature, something between a fox and a bear, was dancing about and grinning inanely on the cereal packet, mouthing a silent jingle over and over. The motion hooked her gaze, dragging her eyes back and forth. She closed her eyes, trying to fend off the sense of suffocation.

"I don't know who he is," spluttered her older brother George through a mouthful of bacon. "But I can tell you what he is."

"What's that dear?" her mother asked mechanically, still lost in the catalogue. It occurred to Kate that the automated checkout machines down at the park sounded more alive than her mother when she was shopping.

"He's a Muslim," George went on, pausing only to take three great gulps of coffee before shovelling in another stack of meat.

"I guarantee it," he said, the passion building in his voice demonstrated by the spray from his lips. "It's a plot to reduce consumption and undermine the Company. I bet's it's not even just one guy, I bet it's a whole swarm of them, dirty bastards!"

"George!" snapped her mother and father together in a rare moment of focus and eye contact. Kate looked from her mother to her father and back again. Her father's eyes were blue while her mother's were brown, she'd forgotten that.

"Well it's true," mumbled George petulantly, lowering his tone so that their parents lowered their eyes. "The leader said so in his address last week."

Kate looked at her brother now, leaning into his food and taking great care not to splash or drop anything on the carefully ironed shirt and tie of his crisp new uniform. His hair was the regulation shoulder length, slicked back into the regulation ponytail, while all about his mouth, his desperate teenage attempt at the regulation goatee clung to crumbs and droplets of breakfast.

"Now George," her father said, his tone warning but gentle as he moved on to the main body of the paper, sales figures and economic performance. "You know your mother and I are proud of you for joining the union."

"Very proud dear," her mother chipped in, licking her buttery fingers before finally choosing the wood finish over the steel and placing the order.

"But we've had this conversation before haven't we," her father continued. "You can't just repeat everything the leader says. The BUC doesn't want blind slaves. The Company doesn't got to all the trouble of making the papers for nothing you know. It's important to educate yourself and make up your own mind."

Kate looked at the words scrolling across the page in front of her father and resigned herself to being washed over by the familiar tide of chatter.

"But Dad, it's so simple!" George protested. "The British Union of Capitalists exists to defend the hard working people of this country against their enemies," he said, brandishing another rasher at them all. "I don't need to read the newspaper to know who my enemy is! The Muslims hate our way of life, they want to destroy everything the Company has done for us. This is just another of their despicable tricks."

"I know son," replied her father. "And I'm not disagreeing with you about that but it says very clearly here in the paper that the Company can't find any kind of link between the victims. They come from all walks of life, from marketing strategists and logistics managers to assembly line workers and delivery drivers, the full spectrum of society.

"None of them are key Company people, they're all easily replaceable so the impact on Company infrastructure is minimal. Even the loss of their combined lifetime's consumption is tiny in the grand scheme of things, certainly not enough to hurt the Company financially. If it is a terrorist plot it's not a very effective one. No son, it's more likely the work of a single disturbed individual, someone with a very special power over people."

"Weak minded people! There've been no victims from the BUC," said George, changing the subject while glancing down at his uniform to check for crumbs.

"Not yet son," her father cautioned. "We'll see."

"There!" announced her mother, face aglow with pride and joy. "A full new kitchen and dining set, all style and colour co-ordinated in an antique wood effect style. It'll be in by the end of tomorrow, isn't that wonderful? No more of this old thing!" she added, tapping the table and looking round the table in satisfaction.

Kate reeled from the sudden attention and eye contact. She felt as if in a single moment she had been dragged from a warm burrow into cold, harsh daylight.

"We've only had this one a week," Kate said quietly, hearing her own voice. It sounded strange and flat.

"What do you mean darling?" asked her mother, confusion lining her face but not denting her happiness.

"You just got this set put in last week," Kate said, returning her attention to the mush that had been her cereal, unable to hold her mother's enthusiastic gaze. "What's wrong with it the way it is?"

"Well..." her mother began only to be immediately cut off again by George.

"Shut up, Muslim!" he snapped, genuine anger and disgust ablaze in his eyes.

"George!" her father warned.

"Come on Dad!" George whined, outraged. "You can't let her say things like that! This is how it starts, this is what they do. Oh, you don't need new stuff. Oh, you can make do with what you've got, no need to consume, to contribute. Before you know it she'll be wearing a burka, just the one burka mind, same one every day till it stinks!"

"Get bent George!" Kate screamed, suddenly kicking back against the pressure, lashing out at the closing in walls.

"Kate!" her mother exclaimed, looking genuinely shocked and upset.

"Well it's his fault!" Kate continued, feeling tears in her eyes and hating herself for them. "I was just saying. It seems stupid that someone spends all their time making all this stuff and we just throw it away. It doesn't make sense. It's greedy. And stupid."

Kate pushed her bowl of former cereal away from her so that the mush lapped lazily over the edge. She folded her arms, glaring at George. "He can't call me a Muslim just for saying that, it's not fair."

"George, apologise to your sister," said her father wearily, frowning his concern at a line graph in the paper.

"Why should I?!" snarled George. "It's that kind of nonsense puts ordinary, hard working people out of a job, takes food out of the mouths of their children..."

"George..." her father said, his eyebrows raising,

threatening to pull his eyes from the paper and back to the table.

"Fine," said George sourly. "You're not a Muslim. There."

"That's better," said her father. "Kate is entitled to her opinions son," he added so that Kate thrust a bitter smile at George before sticking out her tongue.

"But George does have a point too sweetheart," her father went on while George smirked. "I know it might seem strange at your age, but if people didn't buy new things then people wouldn't be able to get jobs making and selling those things and then how would they live?"

Kate glared at the balding top of her father's head and pouted. She could feel a deep burning sensation inside her as if all her limbs were going to explode. A swirling rage of resentment and frustration built up inside her until it reached the back of her throat.

"Now, we can all just get back to having a lovely breakfast together can't we," said her mother. "Kate dear, you've let your cereal go past its best haven't you."

Half rising from her chair her mother swept the bowl of cereal mush, spoon and all, into the gaping hole at the centre of the table. Kate watched the bowl slip over the edge before disappearing in silence to be consumed by the bowels of the house. Leaning back in her chair now her mother retrieved a brand new bowl and spoon and placed them in front of Kate, pushing the carton of milk a few inches closer as well.

"Pour yourself another bowl dear, you'll feel better once you've had something to eat," her mother said with a loving smile.

Her mother's bright, affectionate eyes cut through Kate's rising fury so that with a nod she swallowed it back down and reached obediently for the cereal box. The fox bear type thing was still dancing away, grinning and singing in silence until Kate's fingers touched the box.

At the moment of contact the moving image on the box was suddenly accompanied by sound so that the little thing's moving lips suddenly produced a shrill little voice, wavering away to the familiar jingle.

Kate groaned inwardly as she poured a fresh pile of tiny shapes into her brand new bowl as quickly as possible before setting the box back on the table and releasing it so that the sound ceased. She looked at her fingertips where they had touched the box and rubbed them together as if dirty.

Taking a breath she repeated the whole operation with the milk, cringing as the cow that strutted back and forth across the cartoon suddenly became audible. She quickly doused the little shapes in her bowl, tiny tanks, guns, helmets and boots in the self chilling, white liquid before putting the carton back and taking up her spoon.

"Mum?" she said through a crunchy mouthful.

"Yes darling," her mother replied, now engrossed in a clothing catalogue.

"Next time you go shopping can you get the ad-free stuff?" Kate asked.

Her mother was looking back and forth between two almost identical summer dresses and biting her lip. "Oh I'm not sure about that darling," she said distractedly. "Advert free packaging is ever so expensive you know and it is just exactly the same stuff inside the box. Besides, I quite like the little jingles, they brighten the place up don't you think?"

"Typical," muttered George who had finally finished eating and was now staring down into the latest edition of the BUC newsletter.

"What?" snarled Kate.

"A minute ago you wanted to ruin the economy now you're asking for the most expensive food in the shops." George glared at her with haughty contempt. "I suppose you think money just falls out of the sky like a gift from Allah or something."

"Now George," her mother attempted to intervene but Kate could stand no more. She thrust the second bowl of cereal away from her as she had the first and leapt from her chair to leave.

"And that's your solution is it?" George called gleefully after her and she fled the kitchen. "You're going to boycott food now are you? If you had your way we'd all starve!"

Erupting into the hall Kate stalled to a trembling pause. There was nowhere to go. In that moment, the thought of her room sickened her, its walls full of ever dancing pop star posters or the always-on ad screen, all vying desperately for her attention and custom.

The hallway ad screen was just restarting its perpetual loop, shapes, colours and motion designed to be irresistible to the human eye. Glancing back to the kitchen, she checked she was out of sight then moved to stand immediately next to the ad screen. She allowed herself to lean back against the cool wall and stared straight ahead.

The spot beside the hallway ad screen, which she had discovered accidentally a few months earlier, was the only place in the house where her eyes could escape the otherwise ubiquitous animated advertising. She clenched her fists, fighting the tears of rage that had returned to her eyes and was vaguely aware of her parents half heartedly chastising her brother in distracted tones behind her.

Her father was explaining reasonably that it was natural for a child of her age to wish to rebel, that teenagers like her needed to test the limits of their environment and that saying outrageous things was just a part of that. Then came the sound of the end of the meal, of everything being swept into that gaping maw at the centre of the table.

The half empty milk carton, the half full cereal box, the almost untouched tub of butter. The bowls, cups, jugs and glasses. The knives, forks and spoons. The papers, the napkins, the catalogues and just about anything else to hand. All of it went into the hole, to be disappeared, buried and forgotten and then replaced afresh the following day and every day after that.

Kate closed her eyes and let her finger tips run over the smooth wall behind her. She found its solidity comforting, a feeling of permanence in a world that seemed otherwise hollow and plastic. Her mind ran desperately through all that she knew, looking for anything that might actually mean something, for anything of non-disposable significance. She found nothing and then still nothing until the search itself began to scare her.

She had to get out.


—          —

—


Kate left the house and walked down the garden path. She ignored the miniature water features in the style of ancient Greece and the wild-look flowerbeds, carefully overflowing with lush blooms and thick vines. The whole thing was being remodelled today and would look entirely different by the time she returned.

She paused at the garden gate to rest her right palm on the gatepost. A tiny electronic sound informed her that the post had read the chip in her hand and so she opened the gate and stepped through.

From this point on, each step she took on the Company's pavement would result in a charge being made to her parents' account. For a minute or two she was consumed by spite and shortened her stride, even pausing to take an occasional backwards step just so as to clock up more charges.

Guilt soon overcame her anger however so that she returned to a normal walk. Her parents weren't bad people and she didn't really want to make their lives any more difficult. They were normal adults who did the normal adult things. Her father worked hard six days a week as a manager at a factory to earn as much money as he could. Then her mother worked even harder every single day finding ways to spend it all again.

Since the day she was born they had bought her endless numbers of things and amongst them had been almost everything she'd ever wanted. She knew she had no right to complain.

She hated George of course, his endless arrogance, the way he went out of his way to be nasty to her at every opportunity. She probably loved him as well though, at least she assumed she did, somewhere deep down. He was her brother after all so she had to really, that was how it worked apparently.

Thrusting her hands into her pockets Kate slowed

her pace and craned back her neck to look up. Through the panes of the great glass canopy far above her the sky shone a vibrant blue. She took a deep breath of the perfectly conditioned air, clean and temperate for which her parents also paid, and wondered how it would feel to be actually outside, right outside.

The thought thrilled her so that her heart quickened. Would it be colder or warmer? Would it be windy or still? How would it smell? Would it stay the same all day or change minute by minute? Such chaos! As the end of the street came into view Kate continued to fantasise, to imagine how it would feel to be at the fickle mercy of the weather, to never know what the day might bring.

Turning onto the main road she joined the crowds heading toward the park and suddenly found herself blushing. It had been fine to imagine while walking alone but now, surrounded by others, she felt self conscious as if her outrageous thoughts would show on her face and shame her before all these strangers.

Feeling heat rising behind her cheeks Kate reminded herself that that was how the Muslims wanted everyone to live. It was the one common denominator across the whole dizzying array of types of Muslim she'd been taught about at school. The anarchist ones, the communist ones, the anti-capitalist ones, the environmentalist ones, the animal rights ones and all the rest of them, they all wanted people to live out there under an open sky like animals.

She remembered the class in school where they had been shown horrible pictures, dreadful, nightmare images of people shrivelled by drought or drowned in floods, smashed to pieces by mighty winds or choked to death by toxic smog. The heat in her face was cooled by the chill in her spine and she was left with a feeling of sickness, shame and guilt.

Shaking her head Kate pressed on, determined to leave those thoughts behind her. As she stepped onto the nearest escalator and began to descend from the residential level down to the upper level of the park below, she wondered which of her friends would be out.

Arriving at their usual meeting place at the fifth

fast food outlet along from the escalators she waved to her friends before approaching the counter. While she shopped she thought about how her friends would react when she told them what she had said at the breakfast table.

She bought a full breakfast with a large drink, a couple of magazines, a hairbrush, some sweets and bracelet from the automated checkout machine then carried it all through the crowds to join her friends.

Elizabeth, Diana and Victoria were sitting on one side of the table while Phillip and Charles sat opposite. All had piles of half eaten food and forgotten trinkets spread out before them and smiled to greet Kate and she arrived.

Placing her purchases on the table Kate touched her palm to the back of the seat folded under the table. At the recognition of her chip the chair unfolded itself away from the table to allow her sit, starting an invisible meter that would charge her parents by the second.

"Hey Kay!" called Victoria in a song song voice so that everyone laughed as she sat.

"Hey guys," Kate replied. "What are we talking about?"

"I was just telling everyone about my mum," groaned Diana.

Kate tried on the bracelet she had bought, twisting her wrist back and forth to look at it.

"So like, I get home yesterday and she's got me the new shoes I was talking about, you know, not the new ones but the new, new ones?" Diana said, ignoring Charles and Philip as they rolled their eyes. "The ones with the extra strap?"

Kate decided she didn't like the bracelet after all and dropped in onto the table before starting to pick at her food.

"So she's bought them but just them and I'm like, Mum?" Diana continued. "Where're the rest of them? I mean Jesus Christ, if you're not going to get the entire range then what's the fucking point right? I just threw them in the bin and walked out, I mean it's ridiculous!"

The conversation continued in the familiar vein, each exchanging the usual stories about how disappointing and frustrating their parents were. Kate listened and laughed and smiled, pushing her almost untouched meal to one side and flicking listlessly through one of the magazines.

"I told my mum she shouldn't get a new kitchen," she said suddenly during a lull. There was a pause.

"Kate!" said Victoria wide eyed, drawing her name out into two syllables.

"No way!" Philip grinned. "What did she say? Did she go mental?"

"Wait, wait, wait," Elizabeth intervened. "What did you say, exactly."

"Well," said Kate, leaning in conspiratorially and enjoying the excitement bright in her friends' eyes. "She'd picked out the latest kitchen dining set, you know the antique wood one?" They all groaned their recognition. "And I just said, why bother? Why not just keep the one we have?"

She leaned back and let it sink in.

"Damn!" said Philip.

"That's just wild," said Diana.

"So like, what did she say? Was your Dad there? What did they do?" asked Victoria.

"Nothing really," said Kate, suddenly realising she had run out of story. For a moment she cursed her parents for being so tolerant. Why couldn't they have given her a better tale to tell? "I mean I think they were shocked but they didn't rise to it you know? George went nuts of course."

"Those BUC guys though," said Victoria. "They're always getting uptight about something."

"Why did you say that?" asked Charles suddenly. Until now he had been leaning back in his chair, watching Kate with narrowed eyes from outside the huddle. Kate thought about the question and realised she wasn't sure. The feeling of drowning, of being crushed by emptiness returned from before. She recoiled.

"I don't know," she said and heard the edge to her voice. "Just to mess with them I guess," she added, regaining her composure. "You know how it is, family breakfast, bor-ring!"

Her friends nodded their agreement and the conversation moved on. Charles remained quiet though, hanging back from the chatter and looking at her cooly.

Eventually her friend's began to drift away towards things to do until only she, Charles and Victoria remained. Kate decided to head back home and rose to leave. Once more she pressed her palm to the back of the chair and it folded away beneath the table, stopping its internal meter.

She gathered her purchases, the uneaten breakfast and the undrunk drink, the unread magazines and the unused hairbrush and the worn but now unworn bracelet and dropped them all into a nearby waste bin.

She was heading through the crowds back towards the escalators when she felt a hand on her shoulder. Charles had caught up with her, still carrying his curious expression from before. He fell into step alongside her.

"What you said before," he began. "What you said to your Mum, why did you say that?"

The hairs on the back of Kate's neck stood on end. Her flirtation with this particular taboo had seemed exciting before, she'd enjoyed shocking her friends. Now however she was beginning to wish she hadn't mentioned it. Pink guilt began to flush her cheeks.

"Like I said before," she answered defensively. "I was just messing with them because it was all so boring and that."

"Right," said Charles, clearly unconvinced. "What made you think of that though? There are plenty of things you could say to wind your parents up. Why that?"

"I don't know Charles," said Kate sourly. "It just occurred to me. What do you care anyway? Have you joined the BUC or something?"

"No!" said Charles, shocked first at her question and then again by the vigour of his own response. He looked about them as they reached the escalator. Stepping on he moved closer to her and lowered his voice.

"It's nothing like that," he said. "I just wondered if maybe you thought about things like that. Sometimes I..." he trailed off and just raised his eyebrows instead.

"Well," said Kate carefully, lowering her own voice to match his tone. "I was just thinking maybe it might seem a bit daft to spend all that time making something just to throw it away. Maybe."

Charles nodded and looked around them again.

"What're you up today?" he asked.

Kate shrugged.

"D'know. Not much. Why?" she asked, intrigued.

"Thought maybe you'd like to come and meet some people I know," said Charles.

"Some people?" Kate asked, her heart beginning to pound in her chest.

"Yeah, just some people. They sometimes talk about those kinds of things, the kind of things you said to your parents. Sometimes," he said.

Kate thought about what her parents would say, what George would say, what their friends would say. Then she thought of the cool hallway wall against her back and the terrifying search that could find no purpose. She thought about those pictures and their stark warnings of terror and death. Then of the sky through glass and the thrilled thoughts of outside. The rising frenzy of unbearable restriction, the feeling of drowning in hollow plastic nothings began to simmer within her again.

"When?" she said.

"I was going to meet them right now actually. You can come if you like," he said.

They reached the top of the escalator and stepped out onto the residential level. Kate looked around her and then shrugged as if she had neither care nor interest in anything at all.

"Yeah ok," she said.

They walked slowly side by side down the deserted, uniform streets of cookie cut detached houses, each dressed in one of three or four of the latest styles. At this time of day adults either shopped or worked while their children either sat in their rooms or frequented the park. There was no reason for anyone to be out on the street.

They chatted about who had said what to who, who had done what with who, teachers they liked, teachers they didn't. Charles didn't tell Kate anything she didn't already know and he didn't seem surprised by anything she said but it was comfortable to swap words back and forth. It distracted her from the building butterflies fluttering around the questions of what was to come.

"Have you chosen your courses for next year?" he asked at one point.

"Kind of," Kate replied. "My best grades are in Productive Sciences so mum and dad say I should do Manufacturing Techniques."

"Yeah but what do you want to do?" asked Charles, staring at the pavement.

Kate felt herself flush a little at his bold intimacy, at being asked to share her own personal desires. She swallowed and licked her lips quickly before responding, not daring to look at Charles.

"Resource Extraction," she said quietly before adding, "but I don't think they'll let me. Mum says it's a boy thing."

"Why do you want to do that?" Charles asked.

"I don't know," said Kate, her defences rising instinctively.

"Yeah you do," said Charles, still staring at the pavement.

Kate stopped and stared at Charles's back until he stopped too and turned to face her.

"Why do you want to study Resource Extraction Kate?" Charles asked again but this time looking her right in the eye. His expression gave her nothing and she suddenly felt very alone out in the street with him. She felt nervous and intimidated but this quickly condensed into irritation so that she raised her chin defiantly and met his gaze before answering.

"Because I heard if you get promoted high enough you get to go visit the other countries. You get to go outside to where they mine the raw materials," she said firmly, challenging him to judge her. "I want to go outside."

Her words hung between them for a moment as she waited to see how Charles would react. Then his stony expression folded in on itself to form a genuine smile and his eyes flashed with respect as he nodded, obviously impressed.

"Cool," he said simply then turned away and continued walking.

Kate felt relief flood through her and then a strange warm feeling, a rare and delicate sensation. She had experienced a genuine, positive connection with another human being. She caught up with Charles and fell into step beside him, riding high on confidence and comfort.

"What about you?" she asked. "Have you picked yet?"

"Ah Christ," he said, batting the question away with the back of his hand. "I don't care. Probably end up doing Market Branding or Comms Copywriting, something like that. Whatever gets them off my back you know?"

They lapsed into silence for a way and Kate realised that although they'd known each other all through school she had never spent any real time alone with Charles before. She glanced at him out of the corner of her eye and noticed for the first time that his shoulders had gained a more adult bulge to them, his jaw a firmer line.

A different breed of butterfly began to fight for space in her stomach as they turned a corner. The pavement narrowed slightly as the houses switched to a smaller design, huddled together in pairs. The fixtures and fittings of these houses lagged several weeks behind those from before. The narrowing pavement pushed them slightly closer together so that a couple of times the back of Charles' hand almost brushed against the back of hers causing her heart to beat a little harder.

Suddenly Charles stopped and looked about them. Kate followed his gaze around the street questioningly. There wasn't another person in sight and almost every one of the tiny house had it's out of date curtains drawn. Without a word he stepped off the pavement onto the tarmac of the street and then continued, following the kerb.

"What are you doing?" whispered Kate urgently.

"Walking in the road," said Charles nonchalantly

before flashing her a wicked grin.

"But we'll get in trouble!" hissed Kate, glancing up and down the street nervously.

"Nah," said Charles. "Who's going to know? Plus no-one round here cares anyway, I do it all the time."

"It's illegal!" Kate hissed again, her heart finding a third new reason to pound.

"Why?" asked Charles, moving ahead of her then turning to walk backwards and face her.

"What?" asked Kate distracted as she continued to scan from one end of the street to the other and all the windows in between.

"Why is walking on the road illegal?" Charles asked, still grinning.

"Safety," Kate said, the common knowledge leaping from her lips without her even having to think about it.

"Give over," Charles said, shaking his head. "There's no traffic here and with all the speed restrictors and safety overrides on cars these days when was the last time you heard of anyone being hit by one? Come on, why is it really illegal?"

Kate stared at him angrily but his grin and his question conspired to pull her curiosity through her fear. As he saw her expression soften slightly from worry to puzzlement he raised his right hand to show her his palm then tapped it in the centre with his left index finger.

She looked from his palm to her own and then down to her feet. It was as if a cloud that had been covering the sun had suddenly passed, bathing her in golden understanding.

"Because it's free," she said wonderingly, stopping to look back at Charles open mouthed.

"Bingo!" he said, stopping too and laughing as he curled his hand to point at her.

"The sensors in the pavement track people chips to charge them," she said, working it through.

"Yep," said Charles encouragingly.

"And the sensors in the road track vehicle chips to charge them," she continued.

"But..." Charles prompted.

"One doesn't work with the other so if you're not

on the pavement the chip doesn't charge for your movement," she said, hearing her own words while wondering how they had never occurred to her before.

"So?" asked Charles. She looked up to find that he was now offering his hand to her.

She looked up and down the road again, biting her lip as struggled with herself. Then a rush of hot blood swept through her so that she suddenly became very aware of the texture of her clothes against her skin. Before she knew it she found that Charles' grin had spread to her own face and she was reaching out to take his hand.

She stepped from the pavement onto the road and they resumed their walk hand in hand. She could feel the stupid grin on her face, unbreakable and uncontrolled so that she dare not look at Charles. His hand was warm and firm in hers and somehow the fact that she couldn't breathe properly because of it was exhilarating.

For a little while they walked on hand in hand, grinning foolishly and not looking at one another. Eventually Kate took a breath and broke the silence, a slight tremor in her voice as she attempted not to giggle.

"So where are we going?" she asked, gritting her teeth immediately afterwards to try and retain some control of her face.

Charles coughed a couple of times to clear his throat before answering.

"To a cafe in the other park," he said eventually. "Meet some people I know."

"I didn't know there was another park," said Kate, focusing hard on the conversation.

"Yeah," said Charles distractedly. "It's not like the proper one, it's much smaller, older. Doesn't have any big shops in it or anything, it's just for the people who live down there who can't afford the proper one."

They rounded another corner and Kate saw the ground ahead of them drop away in the familiar park entrance fashion. As they approached the end of the road however she was amazed to find a narrow flight of bare concrete steps instead of the usual escalators.

The stairs weren't quite wide enough for them to

descend side by side and so after a moment's touching reluctance Charles dropped her hand and lead the way. For the first few steps Kate was distracted by their novelty but soon her eyes were drawn down into the gloom of the dingy little park.

Charles had been right about the absence of familiar brands. Instead of comfortable, colourful logos all vying for her attention she found only drab, functional signage. There were butchers, grocers and bakers, dimly lit displays of sub par produce interrupted occasionally by shabby little newsagents and cafes.

Her eyes ran quickly across the shop fronts, not wanting to linger too long for fear of dirtying her gaze. As Charles stepped off the stairs and onto the plain concrete floor she gasped. Some of the shops were actually vacant with shoddily boarded frontages failing to hide their shame.

As she caught up with Charles he caught her hand. The same thrill as before ran through her again but this time a little more distant as she continued to gape at the strange little shops all around them.

"Come on," said Charles, pulling at her hand. "It's this way."

He led her on down the central walk and for the first time Kate noticed a thin scattering of shoppers ahead of them. Like the houses they had passed just before reaching the steps, the people seemed smaller, cheaper and less well dressed. They moved in and out of shops or loitered here and there. None of them seemed to be speaking to one another and all were either standing or walking.

Kate suddenly realised that there were no pay benches in the park nor audio ads piped through hidden speakers. The silence made the tiny place feel somehow cavernous so that what had been strange and exotic became eerie and threatening. As they passed the shoppers some of them looked at her listlessly as if almost curious but too tired to really care.

She brushed a strand of hair from her face self consciously and walked closer to Charles, suddenly very aware of how much her clothes had cost. He squeezed her hand, sensing her discomfort and after a few paces more he leaned in to whisper.

"This is it," he said.

They had paused before a cafe. There was a yellowed, curling menu in the window and just a couple of bulky forms hunched over tables amid the gloom within. Over the door was a large faded sign from which the paint had begun to peel as if trying to escape the decay. She just about made out the words Church Gate Independent Cafe before following Charles into the dimly lit interior.

Nobody looked up as they made their way between the tables. A large woman in an apron stood behind the counter, eyeing them coldly. Charles nodded at her as they passed and she returned the greeting though only slightly. Kate tried a brave little smile in her direction but received nothing but staring in return.

Charles led her to and then through a doorway at the back of the cafe after which she found herself following him up an incredibly narrow wooden staircase in almost total darkness. The stairs creaked underfoot and Kate marvelled at every one. It was like something out of a film.

As they reached the top Charles stopped before another door. Kate waited behind him on the top stair, glancing back down into the pitch behind her. Charles landed a strange series of knocks on the door, motioning to her to remain silent while they waited.

Suddenly a wave of fear washed cold through her. Where was she? What was she doing? Who was on the other side of the door? She turned away from Charles to hide her face and stared down into the darkness below.

In a heartbeat she knew she shouldn't have come, shouldn't have followed Charles into this cold, alien place. She turned back to Charles, drawing breath to tell him that she wanted to leave, that she was going to leave. In her mind's eye she played out the fast walk, she knew she dare not run, back down the stairs, through the cafe then across and up and out of this horrible little park.

At that moment however the door swung inwards, flooding the stairs with a feeble wash of light. A silhouetted figure murmured menacingly then stepped back out of sight. Charles turned and motioned to her to follow before stepping through into the light.

She hesitated on the stairs, frozen with indecision before swallowing hard and stepping up onto the landing and then through the door. Blinking in the new light she made out the shape of Charles and stepped close to him, then jumped as someone she hadn't realised was behind her closed the door and sealed them in.

They were stood in an attic room with a low, sloping roof. Up near the top of the slope one grimy little skylight provided thin illumination. A group of perhaps a dozen people were sitting around on occasional sticks of furniture or in some cases just on the floor, talking in groups of two or three. The hushed tones dropped off into accusatory silence and though her eyes had not yet adjusted Kate could feel theirs all over her.

"Who's she?" came a voice, hard and unkind.

"She's ok," said Charles. His voice was different, colder than before. "She's with me."

The was a pause and Kate held her breath until she thought she might faint. Then the muted conversations flowed back and the moment had passed. She realised she was gripping Charles's hand tightly as he led her over to an unoccupied corner.

A young man approached them, bone thin and bespectacled. He nodded to Kate with what appeared to be a friendly smile then he and Charles began talking, quick, quiet and serious. Kate gaped at the man, openly looking him up and down before catching herself and closing her mouth.

His clothes were literally unbelievable so that Kate could not lift her eyes from them. She recognised the style as being at least a year old, a year! The people in the park outside had been a few weeks, perhaps even a month or so behind the fashion, but to see someone shamelessly dressed in clothes so old was almost too much for her to take.

He raised his hand to adjust his glasses and Kate gasped out loud so that both the man and Charles stopped talking and turned to look at her. The elbow of the man's jacket was worn right the way through. there was an actual, ugly hole in the fabric so that she could see his shirt poking through from beneath.

"Henry, this is Kate," said Charles. "Kate, Henry."

Kate turned her head to face Henry but her eyes remained fixed on his elbow which had returned to his side. Eventually Charles nudged her and she managed to tear her gaze away and look Henry in the face.

"Hi," she said reflexively, her voice flat and stunned.

Henry twisted his arm and looked down at his elbow before looking back to Kate with a kind smile.

"Bit weird the first time isn't it? Bit of a culture shock?" he said.

Kate continued to stare at him and just nodded dumbly.

"You get used to it," Henry continued. "I was the same the first time I came here."

"Are you Muslims?!" Kate shrilled suddenly, cringing at her own words as she realised her panicked tone had been loud enough to silence the room.

She could see them now, beyond Henry's skinny frame. They were all older than her but still fairly young, late teens and early twenties and all dressed in similar shabby, ancient clothes she realised. Shamelessly comfortable with their rips and tears, ugly mixtures of styles long forgotten and thereby forbidden.

And now they were all staring right at her.

Some of the stares were mocking while others outright glared, only a couple were gentle. Kate shrank back from the scrutiny. She pressed herself against Charles's side and tried to stare at the floor but didn't quite dare to look away from the crowd.

She felt Charles draw breath to speak but then somebody laughed and suddenly the whole room was laughing. A violent heat rushed to her face and she could feel the redness burning. The laughter did not feel malicious however and in a moment she realised the tension had lifted. The other people in the room returned to their conversations again while Henry ushered them down onto some brittle looking old wooden chairs.

"That's not the word we'd use," Henry explained kindly. "But that's certainly what a lot of people would call us. I'm sure Charles will explain later but right now we're just about to get started."

By degrees the rest of the people in the room arranged themselves to face the back wall and settled into a comfortable quiet. Henry stood before them with his back to the wall and once everyone appeared to be ready he began to speak.

"First of all," he began, his voice soft, quiet and yet firm. "I'd like to thank everyone for coming. Whether it's your hundredth time here or your first," he paused to nod a smile at Kate. "You are all most welcome.

"As ever we start with a reminder that this place of ours is intended to be a safe space for debate and discussion and that we are all expected to treat one another with the respect we find so lacking outside these walls. I will be your facilitator today and by consensus agreement the topic is The Principle And Practice Of The Reuse Of Disposable Goods And The Impact Thereof On The Corporate Hegemony."

Kate listened intently as people began to debate the topic but dense nets of terminology and reference made it difficult to follow. She thought she understood the general themes, they were talking about reusing or recycling things they had bought, both serious crimes and how much harm they did to the Company. When a product was reused the Company was effectively robbed of the value of the replacement that could have been bought instead.

She had debated similar topics during Effective Negotiating classes at school but she had never heard it argued from the points of view being voiced around her. There seemed to be an unspoken consensus that being harmful to the Company was a positive thing and so the debate centred around how to make such crimes as harmful as possible.

Despite strong desires to both fit in and learn she still found herself shocked by some of the ideas being proposed and then embarrassed for feeling shocked. When one young woman started talked about making clothes and tools that could last a person a lifetime, Kate almost laughed. She caught herself just in time as the people around her nodded and murmured their approval.

The alien concepts were compounded by the

bizarre way in which the debate was conducted. Henry remained apart from the debate but chose who got to speak next, apparently based on the order in which they had put their hands up. Kate watched him watching the room, acknowledging each raised hand with a subtle nod.

At first she couldn't work out how he was keeping score. At school the teacher's always kept a written tally of the score as the debate progressed so that speakers could see how far ahead or behind they were. She wondered if Henry was keeping track in his head and if not knowing the score as they went was a conscious choice to make the debate more exciting.

As the discussion rolled on however she began to suspect that actually no score was being kept at all. Kate felt herself plunge down into even deeper confusion as she realised that debate probably wasn't going to end with the usual declarations of victory and defeat. They were just talking for the sake of it.

Occasionally someone would attempt to interrupt, apparently driven to anger by something the current speaker had said. At these points Henry would intervene and calmly ask the interrupter to wait their turn and for no reason that Kate could see, they always did.

Even more baffling to her was when people arguing one way, though she couldn't always grasp what way that was, would listen patiently to someone else who apparently disagreed with them. Then sometimes and absolutely inexplicably, they would change their minds, conceding that their previous position had been partially or entirely incorrect.

Eventually none of it made any sense. The process, the content, it was all insane. People who appeared eyes blazing furious with one another one second would be share kindly knowing smiles a moment later, even if they still didn't agree.

Kate turned to look at Charles with question marks for eyes but found him transfixed, an incredibly serious expression holding his face solid and tight. The words began to wash over and around her as frustration began to erode her interest. She looked around the room, taking the opportunity to examine the people around her while they were distracted.

Suddenly she found a dark pair of eyes looking back at her and almost jumped off her chair. Off in the corner sat a much older man, possibly even as old as thirty, whom she hadn't noticed before. He didn't seem to be paying any attention to the debate but was instead staring right at her, right into her or so it felt.

Kate thought he looked tall though it was hard to tell as he was sitting on the floor. His face was pale with high, arrogant cheekbones below a shock of messy black hair. He wore an ankle length black coat which sat on him in such a way as to suggest a firm, muscular frame beneath. His hands bore long elegant fingers that held a pen and notebook respectively.

Holding the man's gaze Kate felt the same red heat from before beginning to rise into her cheeks. One of the man's eyebrows rose slightly and he titled his head just a little to one side. Then in a single fleeting moment he scanned her up and down, appraised her in her entirety and dismissed her utterly, returning his attention to his notebook,.

Kate felt her chin jut a little at the rejection and she added a frown to her stare to display the offence she had taken. The man did not look up from his notebook however so that eventually she looked away again. She tried to return her attention to the debate but the long black shape of the man remained in the corner of her eye, a relentless, oblivious irritant.

Eventually the debate ended and everyone broke back out into small groups, excitedly discussing particular points that had been raised. Charles moved over to a couple he appeared to know well and Kate stood beside him while they chatted.

Hot drinks were made and distributed in scandalously chipped and non-matching mugs which Kate politely declined. The tall man in black was talking with Henry in hushed, serious  tones and didn't look up at her once. He was still there when she followed Charles back out onto the stairs and through the park.

"So what did you think?" asked Charles excitedly as they walked back along the road among the low rent residential blocks.

"It was," Kate struggled to think of the word. "Amazing," she settled on. "I didn't know anything like that existed, I didn't know people like that existed. I mean you hear things but..."

"I know, right?" Charles continued. "I know it all seems a bit mad at first. It takes a while to get the hang of it and kind of catch up with all the terminology and that but it's just so different to anything else, it's.." he tapered off.

Kate waited to see if he was going to continue but his gaze seemed blurred, his mind elsewhere.

"Who was that old guy?" she asked eventually, trying not to sound interested.

"Hmm?" asked Charles.

"The old guy in black," she said, squeezing his hand so that he looked at her.

"Oh," he said, suddenly back with her. "That's Uncle Jo."

"Jo?" she said slowly, rolling the strange sound around in her mouth. "What a weird name."

"I know," Charles said.

"So is he Henry's uncle?" Kate asked, maintaining a lack of enthusiasm.

"No," Charles laughed gently. "It's just a name, everyone calls him that, I don't know where it comes from. Why?"

"No reason," Kate said, suddenly defensive then checked herself and added. "I didn't like him. He seemed up himself."

"He's ok," said Charles. "He's just a bit intense, you'll get used to him. If you want to go back that is. What do you think?"

"Yeah," said Kate quickly. "Definitely. I mean I didn't really get everything they were saying but I think I'd like to hear more about it, learn to understand the ideas better. It's all just so different, it's like.." but she didn't know how to finish the sentence.

"Like going outside?" asked Charles gently. He looking at her knowingly and smiled.

Kate remembered her earlier confession and felt a swell of feeling for him, the rush of their first hand holding returning. She squeezed his hand and returned the smile.

"Yes," she said quietly as they stared into one another. "Like going outside. Thank you."

They walked along a little further until the corner that would lead them back among the more respectable homes came into view. Charles stepped up onto the pavement and Kate followed him distracted.

"So listen," he said, suddenly serious again. "You know you can't tell anyone about it right?"

"Of course," said Kate.

"Because you know what Security would do. We'd all be in a world of trouble," Charles said, straining the point.

"I know," she said reassuringly. "I won't breathe a word of it, promise. It can be our secret."

"Our secret," echoed Charles relaxing back into smiles. "I like that."

They walked on in comfortable silence for a while until she remembered Henry's response to her question before.

"Charles," she said as her house came into view up ahead. "They seemed cool and everything but..

Charles stopped and turned to face her, taking both her hands in his.

"What?" he asked.

"Well," she said. "Are they Muslims?"

"Not technically," he said, obviously thinking hard on how best to phrase it. "They explained it to me when I first went. The word Muslim actually means someone who was part of this cult from the old days called Isling."

"What like the old name for that town down South, Islington?" Kate said, searching for anything she knew that might help hide at least some of her ignorance.

"Yeah I think so," said Charles. "They all lived there and had all kinds of mad beliefs and costumes and stuff. I don't really know what that part of it was all about but later the word just ended up being used for anyone whose beliefs didn't fit in with the Company's you know? So I guess in that sense, like in the way people use the word these days, I guess they kind of are."

Kate drew breath to ask a question but Charles

beat her to it.

"All that stuff you hear about though, about bombs and fasting and not eating pork and all that stuff. It's all just made up, it's all just lies the corporations tell us to make us scared of them. You saw them today, they're not scary at all, they're just like you and me." Charles said.

"I guess so," said Kate, unsure. She didn't disagree with Charles but the weight of a lifetime's learning about the terrible evils of Muslims was hard to overcome.

"You'll see," he said and they resumed their walk to her front gate.

When they reached the gate they paused, still holding hands and unsure how to disengage. Kate looked at her feet, suddenly feeling shy and giddy all over again. When she looked up she realised Charles was looking at her mouth. She looked at his lips, thin and pale, just slightly glistening. For a moment she thought he would start to lean in, wondered if she would lean in too to meet him.

But then the moment had passed and he was looking at her eyes again. They let their hands fall apart and shuffled slightly. Kate turned to look at her house and then back to Charles not knowing what to say.

"So I guess I'll see you at school tomorrow then," said Charles.

"Yeah ok," said Kate.

"I'd best get home," said Charles.

"Yeah ok," said Kate.

They stood in silence for a few seconds more.

"Well, bye then," said Charles and finally took a step away from her.

"Bye," she said and turned to pass through the gate. She walked to the front door completely oblivious of the brand new Zen style garden, too desperate to turn and look. She resisted until her hand met the front door.

Then she glanced over her shoulder and saw him further up the street looking back. He waved. She waved back then dashed through the door and up to her room to hide the smile she couldn't turn off from her parents and from her brother.

— — —

The following Sunday morning Kate found herself back at the kitchen table making circles in her cereal again. George was away at a BUC camp for the weekend and without him to rant at her and rile her it had been a quiet breakfast.

With no need to break off and referee, her father had engrossed himself completely in the Sunday newspaper while her mother was lost as ever to the catalogues. The only sounds across the table were the tinny jingles that would briefly erupt from the various boxes and cartons when touched. Otherwise there was silence.

A week earlier Kate would have found the silence stifling and infuriating, a thick spiteful substance oozing into her to slowly drown her. Now however she welcomed the calm, the lack of parental attention. It created a space within which she could think and recall.

Memories of the previous weekend, the long walk with Charles, the touch of his hand, the secret meeting, the exciting, dangerous clothes and words. During the week at school she had seen Charles every day but only ever among friends. They had not spoken of their visit to the other park but every so often had exchanged a glance, a secret smile that lit fireworks joyous inside her.

Suddenly from a darker corner of her thoughts, the image of Uncle Jo stepped forward  casting a great shadow over everything else. The lines of his long black coat, his high cheek bones and slender hands. His careless, smirking expression as he had sized her up and dismissed her. The same strange feeling she had felt at the time begin to rise from her stomach again.

It was a twisting, maddening irritation, a sweating, heaving conflict. He repulsed her, infuriated her but no matter how hard she tried to let the memory fade, his mocking rejection of her replayed before her mind's eye over and over. She found a desperate thirst behind the images, a fevered need to make him see her, not her clothes or her ignorance, but she herself, to force him to recognise her value and worth.

The image of his hands plagued her further. His long pale fingers clasping his pen so lightly, scribbling away with such spiteful elegance. His hands looked soft and cold and the idea of their lack of warmth sent fresh heat rising to her face as she began to wonder how those hands would feel against her own skin. If he touched her arm with those long delicate fingers, would she find them cold or warm? Would she like the way they felt?

Shuddering Kate forced herself back into the room and surveyed the table in search of distraction. Gone were the clean moderns lines of the previous week, everything was now rendered in dark wooden tones and intricately fashioned metals. She paused her stirring and looked down at the spoon in her hand.

It was much heavier than last week's cutlery, a long wide handle carrying intricate patterns of dots ending in a broad, generous bowl a little too large for her mouth. The other end of the handle erupted into a great mess of twisting patterns, some kind of ancient coat of arms woven into the metal.

The same design cascaded across the gleaming new metal teapot, coffeepot, milk jug, sugar bowl, salt and pepper shakers. The dark wood of the table was reflected in the new panelling on the walls around her which ran down into a thick, heavy and dizzyingly patterned carpet beneath.

Her mother closed the catalogue she had been scrutinising, satisfied with her purchases and reached for the next. During the brief intermission she glanced over at Kate's bowl and then upwards to Kate herself.

"Was that ok darling?" she smiled. "Have you had enough?"

"Yes thanks," said Kate. She let the heavy spoon slip under cereal and and pushed the bowl away from her a little, smiling back and enjoying the rare warmth of calm, maternal contact.

"Have you got anything planned for today?" asked her mother, opening the next catalogue before her but resisting it's pull on her gaze.

"Not really," said Kate, tracing her fingertip over

the ornate end of the spoon.

"You can help me if you like," said her mother hopefully, gesturing at the catalogues. "I need to pick out a whole new kitchen and dining area before this afternoon, there's an offer on."

Kate deflated just a little and realised she had allowed some of the warmth to drain from her expression.

"Oh I know," said her mother, misunderstanding and looking at the room around them. "I've enjoyed this historical look too, it is lovely isn't it with all the little details. Very classy but it's time for something new. I'll let you choose the countertops."

Kate winced at her mother's eager tone as she offered her the countertops like a special sugary treat.

"That'd be nice wouldn't it dear?" her mother asked her father. "Kate helping me redecorate the kitchen?"

"He's killed two this week," replied her father, not looking up form the paper as he sipped his coffee. "This Sandman is getting serious now, Security need to do something!" Her mother rolled her eyes at her and smiled.

"What do you think darling?" she asked.

"No thanks!" Kate said with gentle scorn, retreating into the easy guise of moody teenager. "I'm going to the park, see who's out."

Her mother looked only slightly disappointed then smiled again.

"Oh well, fair enough then," she said. "I suppose you're not a little girl anymore are you. Have fun darling, don't stay out too long. Clear you're things away before you go won't you"

Kate watched as her mother's eyes fell back to the catalogue, widening with excitement as they rapidly scanned the latest products. She began to rise from her intricately carved, high backed chair and push her bowl and box of cereal towards the hole at the centre of the table ut then paused.

She glanced across at her father as he frowned into the paper and her mother, gaping into the catalogue, both utterly oblivious. She continued to push the items towards the hole but then slipped the spoon out of the bowl and into her mouth. Cleaning the residue of cereal from it she eyed her parents again before slipping the spoon quickly into her pocket.

The rest of her breakfast went silently into the hole and she turned and left without another word. Out in the hall she rushed past the ad screen and up to her room. As soon as she entered the various posters sprang to life, slipping through their looped movements, all clammering to catch her eye.

Ignoring them utterly Kate stood with her back to the door and scanned the room inch by inch. Almost everything in it, furniture, fixtures and fittings would be ripped out and changed during the week, updated to the latest style.

Eventually however, her gaze settled on a tiny island of permanence. On a shelf on the far wall stood a trophy that she had won at a school science fair years earlier. The trophy consisted of what appeared to be a solid gold rack of solid silver test tubes all sat on a broad, blocky base of cast iron bearing a gleaming, golden plaque.

Kate crossed the room and lifted the trophy easily with one hand. The whole thing was actually just a hollow plastic shell. With a little encouragement the bottom of the base popped off to reveal a small void within. With a slightly trembling hand she retrieved the spoon from her pocket and dropped it inside the upturned trophy before replacing the base and putting the whole thing back on the shelf.

The trophy looked exactly the same, no matter how hard she looked at it or from which angle, there was not a sign that it had even been moved. To Kate's eye however it now appeared marked, it was now somehow different, dangerous and exciting. Grinning to herself and the butterflies in her stomach she sat on her bed, no longer allowing herself to look at the trophy but feeling its presence still.

She didn't look at it as she took a brand new pair of trainers out of their box and put them on. She continued to definitely not look at it as she stripped the plastic from a newly arrived jacket and put it on and didn't even look once while applying her make up.

Finally, as she left her room she couldn't resist one last glance. In a few days the kitchen would be remodelled and the secret contents of the trophy would become technically illegal. As the weeks and months rolled by and the styles of interior design continued to shift and change, that same hidden object would become increasingly radical and dangerous, the stakes of discovery rising ever higher.

Thrilled to trembling, Kate dashed from the room and down the stairs, calling to her parents over her shoulder as she burst through the front door and sprinted down the garden spraying the carefully raked gravel everywhere. As she half walked half danced down the pavement she noticed that the carefully purified and climate controlled air tasted sweeter and fresher than usual, even though she knew it was not.

In her mind's eye the image of the spoon lurked still, ticking away on the shelf. The thrill remained but now bled into thoughts of Charles and their time together the previous weekend. She would wait as long as she could stand it, months if she could hold out that long, then retrieve the spoon from the trophy and show it to him.

As the escalators down to the park came into view she laughed out loud at the thought of his face, his dropped jaw and wide eyes. He would stare at the forbidden piece of metal in her hands and then look up at her such admiration in his eyes, he would be so impressed by her, astounded by her.

Stepping into a thin crowd on the nearest escalator Kate followed the fantasy further. She could take the spoon to the cafe, revealing it with a casual flourish that would silence the room. Cold stares of suspicion or disapproval would melt into grudging respect and in turn flow into acceptance. Even Uncle Jo would have to be impressed, she imagined the shocked expression on his face now as he reassessed his judgement of her.

So absorbed was she by the daydream that she stumbled from the foot of the escalator,  almost crashing into the back of the shoppers ahead of her. As she regained her footing she tried to compose herself shoving the images to one side to focus instead on her immediate surroundings.

Falling in step with the crowds she made her way towards the usual meeting place, scanning ahead for her friends. Meanwhile the echoes of her fantasy began to cool, whispering to her from distance. She was entering into an adult world with serious consequences, she couldn't afford to be a silly little girl. Straightening her back to walk a little taller she raised her chin and tightened her face.

Suddenly a flailing arm caught her eye and beneath it she found a group of familiar faces. They had secured a table by the railings overlooking the lower level of the park. They were all grinning and beckoning her to join them. Weaving through the crowds her stomach dropped a little when she realised that only the girls were there, or rather that Charles was not. She paused to stand by their table, swapping the usual automated greetings then headed off to the counter to make her purchases.

The disappointment at Charles' absence clouded her thoughts so that when she reached the front of the queue she barely noticed what her hands were doing. Returning to the table she placed her hand on the back of a closed up chair then waited as it read her chip and unfolded before sitting down. It took her a moment to realise that the girls had all fallen silent and were staring at her.

"Kate," said Victoria finally, intently. "What are you doing?!"

Kate looked at her friend and shook her head confused.

"Is that all you've bought?" said Elizabeth, leaning forward to hiss across the table.

Kate looked down and a heartbeat chill washed through her cold and clean. In her hand she held a large paper cup full of lemonade and ice, a thick straw protruding from the top.

And nothing else.

She had fallen at the first hurdle, betrayed herself almost instantly. The image of the spoon in the trophy crashed back into her thoughts but now accompanied by Security breaking it open while her sobbing mother looked on, helpless and ashamed.

She stared down at the drink and then up at her friends. She searched desperately for some kind of escape but her mind stalled over and over until her voice lost patience and took control of the situation.

"I forgot my tray," she heard herself lie. Snatching at the unexpected lifeline she followed it towards safety, making a show of looking over her shoulder to the counter hidden behind the queues.

"I've left it on the side," she added, rising from her seat. "Hang on."

The girls exploded into tension breaking laughter, exchanging eye rolls and calling her playful names.

"I bet I know what she was thinking about," said Diana, looking knowingly around the table.

"Char-arles," all three girls sang in unison before collapsing back into giggles.

Kate felt herself flush but was grateful for the camouflage.

"Shut up," she said, making a good show of being bashful as she hovered next to the table.

"Everyone's seen how you two have been looking at each other," Diana continued.

Kate flicked an appropriately offensive hand gesture at Diana which inspired a new wave of laughter then returned to the queue. When she reached the counter she took up a tray and began to fill it quickly with food and trinkets and magazines.

Then she began to worry about overcompensating and slowed her hands, agonising over how much to take. Finally she paid for what she thought was an acceptably busy tray and made her way back to the table.

"So have you kissed him yet?" asked Elizabeth.

"No!" snapped Kate, a kneejerk she instantly regretted. "It's not like that," she mumbled then, trying to row back from the urgency.

"It is so totally, exactly like that," said Victoria, grinning.

"You went off together last Sunday," said Diana, pushing. "Where did you go? What did you do?"

"Nowhere, nothing, y'know, nothing," said Kate, staring down into her food, suddenly terrified that her friends might see reflections of the cafe in her eyes.

"Come on!" said Elizabeth. "You can tell us. Where did you go?"

"Nowhere really," Kate struggled. "We just walked around a bit, just chatting and stuff."

"Oh yeah," said Victoria, taking her turn. "And what were you chatting about?"

"Things," said Kate defensively. "Stuff. Just about like school and stuff and what courses we're going to choose next year and that."

"And you didn't kiss him?" asked Elizabeth.

"No, we just.." said Kate, the last two words slipping out before she could stop them.

"Just what?!" asked Diana as all three girls leaned in.

"Held hands a bit that's all," said Kate, almost to herself.

More laughter, infectious now so that Kate felt a shy little smile twitch the side of her mouth.

"That was so not worth the effort," said Diana. "Holding hands, we're not in primary school!"

"Aw, I think it's sweet," said Victoria.

"Yeah, make him work for it!" said Elizabeth.

Kate was laughing with them now, the ordeal over, her secrets safe beneath the veil of generic high school gossip. The conversation moved on to other, familiar routines and Kate felt herself relax. She fell into the regular rhythms of unreasonable parents, tyrannical teachers, girls they hated and boys they liked.

"What about this Sandman then?" asked Diana eagerly. "Isn't it awful what he does to them? I bet he's a Muslim."

"My Dad keeps going on about him," said Kate.

"I heard he hypnotises them. He puts you in a trance and programs you so that when you come round you can't move or scream or anything," said Elizabeth.

"Hypnotism doesn't work like that," said Victoria. "You can't make people hurt themselves."

"How do you know?" asked Elizabeth, annoyed.

"I saw it on a commercial," replied Victoria

defensively.

"I heard he has a secret lair outside of town in one of the Restricted Areas," said Diana. "That's why they can't find him."

"Hypnotism!" scoffed Victoria.

"Shut up!" snapped Elizabeth.

"Oh my god!" gasped Diana suddenly.

She was staring, open mouthed over the railings beside her so that Kate had to clamber over her seat to follow her gaze. It took her a moment to see him but when she did her face fell shocked to match her friend's.

Down below, in front of one of the clothes shops, a shambling old man was making his way through the crowd. He was wearing layer upon layer of filthy rags and stumbling along, obviously drunk, dragging one leg behind him. His hair was wild and grey, erupting from his head and face alike to form a tangled mess. The crowds of shoppers parted around him, people pushing and shoving amongst themselves to get away from him.

The man paused beside one of the broad tables stacked with shirts that stood in front of the shop. He placed a grimy hand on the edge of the table to steady himself and Kate recoiled at the sight of his nails, long, thick talons, yellowed and black. A broad circle of space formed around the man as shoppers established a safe distance from which to gape with morbid curiosity.

"Ladies and gentlemen," the man slurred loudly, evoking gasps and grumbles from the appalled in the crowd.

"Ladies and gentlemen, I'm ever so sorry for the er.." he paused to sway and think for a moment.

"For the interruption!" he proclaimed, joyous at remembering the word. "I'm not here to ruin your lovely day with your lovely people and all your lovely shoppings, I was just wondering if any of you fine, upstanding people might see your way clear to buy an old war veteran like myself just a little bit of food."

He raised his hand and lurched forward slightly so that a couple people in the crowd actually screamed. He rubbed his blackened thumb against his first two fingers to demonstrate just how small the amount of food he required would be.

"Just a tiny bite, anything at all would be much appreciated," he continued, the words mashing into one another to form a single sloppy sound. He drove his bleary eyes across his disgusted audience, pleading and blinking alternately, swaying all the while.

"What is he wearing?!" hissed Victoria.

The girls were shoulder to shoulder in a line along the railings now.

"Oh god," said Elizabeth, briefly shielding her eyes with her hand. "I think I'm going to be sick just looking at him."

"How did he even get in here?!" asked Diana, outraged. "Where's Security?"

"Too late now," said Victoria. "Look."

Kate followed her friend's nod to a disturbance among the crowd. Three young men were pushing their way through. As the knot of shoppers cleared Kate recognised the uniforms the boys wore, they were the same as her brother's.

There was a tall one who looked to be the oldest. His long hair was perfectly straight, his goatee thick and incredibly neat. The other two appeared younger, one with brown hair the other blonde, both sporting valiant but failed attempts at beards.

"I know him," whispered Diana. "The tall one, he's called William, goes to college with my sister."

The old man was turned away from them as they stepped out into the space, pleading with people on the other side of the crowd. As he turned back he was licking his lips absently but froze upon seeing the three. All the colour drained from his face leaving a clammy grey residue behind it.

"Now lads," said the old man, backing away until hitting the table behind him. "I don't want any trouble."

Kate saw the same hideous hand land on the table edge just as before only this time it was trembling violently.

"What do you think you're doing?" asked William while the younger two stepped out on either side to flank him.

"I was just asking these good people if they might share a little food that's all," the man's voice was strained now, high and cringing. "I'm not hurting nobody. I don't want any trouble."

"You expect these people," William continued, sweeping his arm around the crowd, "to feed you? A Muslim? For free?"

"They," began the man but his voice broke and fell. He pulled in a ragged breath and tried again. "They'd just throw it away anyway."

"Parasite!" came a shout from the crowd.

"Thief!" came another. "Muslim!"

Buoyed by the building electricity of the crowd the boys moved forward, closing on the old man so that he flinched visibly.

"See?!" William shouted. "You're not welcome here. Do you understand?"

The old man nodded frantically, not daring to meet the boy's eyes.

"These people work hard all week to earn the money they spend here. Why should they just give it to you for nothing?" he roared, allowing the question to hang so that it was answered by more calls of encouragement from the crowd.

"I fought in the war," stuttering the old man, trying to pull himself upright and take back some dignity. "I fought for this.."

William slapped the old man across the face, knocking him sideways so that he fell to his knees. The sharp sound made Kate jump violently, it silenced the crowd and rang around the park before settling back down into thick, palpable tension.

"Don't you dare," William hissed, his suddenly quiet voice trembling with fury.

"Don't you dare!" he roared then, clenching his fists as he towered over the man. "Don't you dare stand there in your filth!" his voice screeched at this last word. "And tarnish the good name of our armed forces. Those brave men and women risk their lives to defend our way of life. They go out there every single day to make sure that good people like these people here have the freedom to work, the freedom to earn and the freedom to spend!

"You never fought in any war, how could you

have? Look at you, you're useless! No self respecting soldier would ever lower himself to begging in the streets. How dare you lie about that to try and con people out of their hard earned money!"

"Scum!" shouted the crowd. "Disgusting!"

The old man raised a dirty palm in submission as he struggled to get to his feet.

"You're right," he was saying desperately. "You're right, you're right. I'm sorry. I'll leave, I'll go."

"Oh no!" William shouted, grabbed at the ragged clothes around the old man's neck and hauling him up onto his toes. "You're not going anywhere."

"You see?!" he continued, shouting over his shoulder to address the crowd now. "You see how yet again he tries to escape his responsibilities? This man has committed a serious crime here today and now he wants to run away without paying his due. Oh no, he'll just leave honest, hardworking people like you to pick up the tab, just like with everything else!"

"Please," whimpered the old man, his eyes glassy with fear.

"The British Union of Capitalists exists to defend the hard working people of this country against their enemies, against Muslim scum like you!" the boy ranted.

The old man quivered, paralysed with fear. William stared at him with cold furious eyes for a few seconds more then abruptly spat in his face. Then he twisted suddenly, throwing the old man down onto the hard polished floor in the centre of the hole in the crowd.

"You are a cancer!" William continued, moving towards the old man along with the two younger boys, The crowd pressed in around them, buzzing, hysterical, fevered.

"A plague! The source of all our society's problems," he said.

For second after second the moment hung, the old man crumpled on the floor, the boys standing over him, the crowd bristling all around. Then all of a sudden the old man erupted from the floor, scrabbling onto all fours and making a break towards the crowd.

Quite calmly, William raised his right knee and then planted the flat of his brightly polished business shoe into the side of the scrambling figure. The old man crumpled and collapsed as the two younger boys set upon him, first with kicks then falling to their knees to deliver punches.

The crowd roared as one and pressed in even closer. Kate wanted to look away but her head wouldn't turn. The old man was out of her sight now, she could just see the flailing arms of the younger boys. Their fists rose up into view and then fell back down again and again.

William looked on pleased, nodding his approval but then suddenly looked off to his left as an alarm began to sound. A pre-recorded security announcement replaced the sound of audio ads beneath the shouting of the crowd.

Kate she saw him step forward quickly, crouching down beside his juniors. She saw his hand drop to his belt and then a flash of metal as he slid a blade from a sheath. Casting another gaze back over towards the sound of the alarm he passed the blade to the blonde boy and nodded to him grimly before standing up and away from the thrashing tangle.

"You all saw it," the older boy was saying to the crowd now, hooking their attention with a swinging, pointing finger.

"This rabid Muslim lunged at the crowd, he tried to assault innocent people. We had no choice but to step in to defend you. Yet again the British Union of Capitalists has foiled an unprovoked terrorist attack on the hard working families of our country."

The younger boys stood up beside him and the three huddled in rapid conference. After a few words the blonde boy nodded and moved into the crowd. From the opposite direction a gang of Security had appeared and were trying to breach the crowd. As the blonde boy turned to go Kate thought she caught a fleeting glimpse of his right hand.

It was red.

Suddenly a woman's voice cut through the chaos. A girl fought her way out of the crowd and into the space before stopping dead to stare at the old man. The crowd was pushing back now, the circle opening out. Kate could see the old man again, crumpled onto the floor. The was no motion in his body but a broad dark pool was creeping out from beneath him.

"What have you done?!" screeched the girl.

William and the brown haired boy both stared at her in confusion.

Suddenly she dashed passed them to the table of shirts, snatching one up and then rushing to the side of the old man, skidding through the blood to drop to his side. Her hands moved quickly and with skill as she checked his pulse and the pressed the crumpled shirt into his abdomen.

"Don't just stand there!" she was screeching at the crowd now. "Someone get an ambulance!"

The boys stood open mouthed, shocked an appalled while the crowd began to turn on itself, attempting to thin and disperse. As the girl threw her eyes about wildly about, still pleading for help, Kate suddenly saw her full on and gasped. She recognised the girl. She had seen her in the cafe.

The girl looked up to the balconies desperately and just for a moment her gaze met Kate's. An instant of recognition flashed across the girl's face but Kate was distracted by the movement behind the girl.

As the brown haired boy came dashing in behind the girl Kate drew breath to warn the girl and even felt her arms coming up to wave but too late. He threw all his sprinting momentum into one huge swinging kick that caught the girl in the side of the face just as she turned. An instant rag doll, the girl fell back and down to land limp, splayed across the old man's body.

William stepped in, grabbing the boy's arm and pulling him away. He was shaking his head at the boy, a serious expression on his face as the heavy black suited figures of Security finally burst into the space.

Most of the guards formed an immediate outfacing ring around the two prone figures, gesturing and shouting at the remaining crowd to move back and disperse. Within the ring two  guards crouched over the figures of the girl and the old man, checking their pulses and rifling through their pockets.

The two BUC boys were stood away from the black

ring of armour and shields. They stood with their backs straight, arms folded as they spoke to the Security Commander. The Commander was identical to the rest of the Security in every way except for the red triangle on his shoulder.

William appeared perfectly calm as he recounted what had happened, occasionally turning and pointing as the Commander nodded. Two guards emerged from the ring holding the lolling girl between them. One side of her face was grotesquely purple and swollen and she was barely conscious. The guards held her upright by her elbows so that her feet rolled and flopped against the floor.

One of the guards held the bloodied shirt in his freehand and offered it up for consideration. The Commander looked to William who nodded, pointing to the table and then nodding at the girl. The Commander then nodded to the guards so that they span the girl around, handcuffed her before and dragging her away.

Meanwhile a minor commotion had broken out within the ring of guards. The Commander and the two boys approached and the ring broke into a horseshoe. Kate could just about make out the ragged arm of the old man, reaching up from the ground to cling desperately at the leg of one of the guards.

The guard tried to brush the old man's hand away but the grimy claw persisted frantic. The Commander and the William continued their conversation, occasionally sharing a brief laugh until again the Commander signalled his men.

With rapid, fluid motion a guard dropped to one knee and thrust a small black box into the old man. There was a brief crackling sound and a faint, fading cry and the old man's arm fell limp.

Then, with well practised co-ordination the guards flipped the old man onto his front and handcuffed him before lifting him bodily between them and carrying him away at slow, deliberate march. Cleaning staff in park uniforms had appeared and now rushed in to clean the floor. A couple of them followed the departing guards to erase the dripping trail they left as they went.

Meanwhile the Commander was shaking hands

with William. They exchanged smiles and more nods then went their separate ways, the Commander following his men, the boys heading in the opposite direction.

Within minutes the strings of shoppers had returned and thickened to fill the space. They chatted and strolled, paused to examine window displays and headed in and out of stores with arms full of bags. It was as if nothing had happened at all.

The girls left the railings and clambered back into their chairs, They huddled around the table, not looking at one another in silence from behind their drinks.

"Well, thank God for the BUC that's all I can say," said Diana eventually, stoney faced and thin lipped.

"That was awful," whispered Elizabeth, grey and visibly shaken.

"Imagine what could have happened if they hadn't have been there though," pressed Diana, staring around the table at each girl in turn. "Did you see how long it took for Security to arrive? Anything could have happened!"

"Who was that girl?" Victoria asked the table. "What was she doing?"

"She was a bloody Muslim that's who!" said Diana hotly. "They're everywhere, it's disgusting."

"I want to go home," said Elizabeth in a small voice.

"Me too," said Kate, her stomach turning over.

"God!" exclaimed Diana angrily. "You two are such wimps! I'll tell you what, if the BUC let girls join I'd sign up today."

"I do like their uniforms," said Victoria thoughtfully. "And that one with the black hair, William was it? He was quite fit."

Diana and Victoria exchanged a grin and a giggle while Elizabeth tottered to her feet.

"Will you walk home with me Kate?" she asked, her eyes wet.

"Sure," said Kate, standing too.

"Come on guys, don't go," said Victoria. "That was like the most exciting thing that's ever happened!"

"Oh let them go," said Diana with open disgust.

"See you tomorrow then," said Victoria with a

shrug.

Elizabeth rounded the table and fell into step with Kate as they set off towards the escalators.

"Wimps!" Diana shouted after them.

"I'm not a wimp," Elizabeth said with a sniff as they walked through the crowds. "I know it's necessary for our safety and all that, I just don't like actually having to see that kind of thing, it really upsets me."

"I know," said Kate, slipping her arm through Elizabeth's and pulling her friend's shoulder to her own. "Me neither, I'm exactly the same."

Even as she said it however, Kate knew she didn't mean it. Some of what she had heard at the cafe was beginning to make more sense. Suddenly and for the first time she felt like she  actually understood the nature of the foundations on which her world was built and she didn't like what she saw.

As they stepped onto the escalators to be carried up and and away from the park Kate's earlier daydreams returned but now viewed from a very different angle. She thought of the spoon and the cafe and of walking on the road. Under and alongside all of it was the ugly purple face of the girl from before.

She felt herself begin to tremble.

—        —

—

The following day at school everyone Kate met wanted to talk about the foiled terrorist attack at the park. No matter how hard she tried however she couldn't engineer a moment alone with Charles and so despite recounting the incident a dozen times, she was denied the one conversation she really wanted to have.

Throughout the day she found herself distracted by flashbulb horrors, terrible moments echoing through her. The clammy grey fear of the old man's face, the bright wet red of the blonde boy's hand and the brutal broken purple of the cafe girl's jaw. No matter how hard she tried to to focus on conversation or even lessons, the images would not leave her but persisted relentless, a trauma carousel.

At the dinner table that evening she found her stomach small and restless with no inclination for filling. She pushed the pasta around in its sauce until the textured red became too uncomfortable to look at.

George was back from camp, a new badge sewn onto the breast of his BUC uniform. He ate ferociously by her side, practically inhaling his food. Kate looked across at her parents who were talking seriously in lowered tones, something to do with money. Her mother met her gaze and paused the conversation, glancing down at Kate's plate and back up again.

"Are you ok darling?" she cooed, maternal concern wrinkling the edges of her smile. "You didn't eat much this morning either. Is it what happened yesterday?"

"It's ok petal," said her father. "It must have been very upsetting to see all that. It's perfectly normal that it should stay with you for a little while."

"Why don't we book you in with the doctor tomorrow," said her mother. "See if he can't prescribe you something to help?"

"Yeah I heard about that," said George mid chew. "Lucky our lads were there."

Kate let her go of her fork, allowing it slide under the pile of uneaten pasta. The images assailed her more quickly now, the details sharper like teeth. She closed her eyes tightly, willing herself back under control.

"I heard we're going to start putting on regular patrols down at the park from now on," George announced to the table, his cutlery scraping against his finally empty plate. "That Muslim piece of trash should never have been able to get in there in the first place."

"That's nice dear," said her mother. "Very conscientious of you, I'm sure everyone will feel much safer."

"Well someone's got to do something," George said. "You eating that?"

Kate opened her eyes to find his fingers at the edge of her plate. She shook her head and sat back. Now her lungs seemed suddenly smaller so that she had to breath faster and deeper to avoid suffocating.

George snatched up her plate, tipping it over his own so that the bright red contents slopped over. Kate looked away from the colour then jumped violently as her fork slipped from her plate to hit George's.

"George!" snapped her mother. "Look at the mess you're making. The food's supposed to go in your mouth, not all over the table!"

"Just goes to show though doesn't it," George continued as if his mother hadn't spoken attacking his new portion of pasta. "You think you're safe. You think these things happen to other people and then, bang!" he slammed his fork holding fist down on the table, making Kate and her parents all jump with the crockery. "A suicide attack right on your doorstep."

Kate blinked through her trembling as irritation boiled into anger.

"What?" she said. The syllable emerged rough like a cough.

"The suicide attack at the park. You know, you were there! Some Muslim nutter tried to attack a crowd of shoppers with a knife then when the BUC lads managed to stop him he cut his own guts out." George underlined his description by lifting a forkful of pasta so that the sauce trickled thickly back down onto the plate. He grinned at Kate and winked. She turned away, her hand at her mouth as she tried not to vomit.

"George!" snapped her father. "Your sister's been through a horrible ordeal, show some sympathy for goodness sake."

George didn't look at his father but grudgingly lowered the fork again.

"This is what we're dealing with though," he continued in a more serious tone. "They're fanatics! They'll kill themselves rather than be taken alive so that they don't give anything away under questioning. The worst bit was that girl he had with him though."

Kate stared down at the table as an unbearable pressure began to build in her chest. Her head felt hot so that she couldn't think. The edges of the cutlery and crockery began to blur so that her empty stomach flipped over.

"Looked like just a normal girl they said," George

said, oblivious to her discomfort. "Turns out she was there stealing to raise funds for the terrorists. She only broke cover when our lot stopped the attack. Ran at those lads like a rabid dog apparently. Luckily they managed to take her out before she could do any harm or off herself. They'll be asking her some tough questions tonight, asking her real hard."

George nodded to himself with great satisfaction, smiling as he ate. Kate felt a rush of bubbles surge up through her body so that she thought she might fall off her chair. A moment later she realised she was screaming.

"You don't know anything!" she was shouting at George. "You weren't there! You don't know! That poor old man didn't do anything to anyone. He wasn't hurting anyone, it was those BUC bastards.."

"Kate!" her mother tried to interrupt, shocked.

"..they came along and started it all," Kate continued unabated. "And that girl, she was trying to save his life after they stabbed him. She was trying to save his life and they kicked her in the face! They did it, I saw them! They stabbed him for nothing! I saw the big one pass the blonde one the knife! I saw it, I saw it."

Tears were running down her face as the fury visibly shook her, her fists white knuckle tight in her lap. George had frozen, his fork half way between plate and mouth as he stared at her open mouthed. Finally he placed his fork carefully back down on the plate, blinking his shock as he looked his sister up and down.

"You're one of them," he whispered as if amazed at the sound of his own words. "You're a fucking Muslim!" he roared suddenly, genuine hatred in his eyes.

"Enough!" shouted their father. "Stop it, both of you. I will not have language like that used in this house, especially not at the dinner table!"

"You heard her!" George ranted. "You heard what she said. She's one of them!"

"Stop it George!" shouted their mother on the verge of tears. "Just stop it!"

"You can't defend her!" yelled George, riding high on a wave of total outrage. "That's harbouring a terrorist."

"Don't be ridiculous," snapped their father. "Now both of you calm down and apologise to one another this instant!"

"Apologise?!" screeched George, red faced and quivering now. "I will not apologise for defending my country. If you're not going to do something about this then I will. I'll take this to the local BUC Section Commander and you can explain it to him!"

Kate's mother went very pale and in the ringing silence that followed she reached across the table to grab her husband's hand. They exchanged a worried glance then Kate saw her father nod, patting her mother's hand.

"Now George," said their father in a desperately reasonable tone. "You have to remember that your sister has been through a terrible experience. What happened at the park yesterday was horrific, an absolute outrage and witnessing it has quite understandably upset Kate a great deal.

"She's not like you son, she's not used to seeing things like that, she's a civilian and a child. She doesn't understand what she saw and she doesn't know what she's saying. We have to make allowances."

"I'm not a child," snapped Kate in a particularly petulant tone. She composed herself and tried again. "I'm not a child. I know exactly what I saw."

Both her parents stared at her, their eyes pleading furious.

"Go to your room," said her father quickly.

"I know exactly.." Kate tried again but this time her father stood from his chair.

"Go to your room right now!" he barked, pointing towards the hallway.

Through scowls and slouches Kate stood and turned, meeting George's glare with with hate of her own as she left. Moving out into the hall she could hear her mother talking quickly to her brother in frantically placating tones.

"We'll take her to the doctor tomorrow darling," she was saying to him. "She's not well, she just needs a little help to understand that's all. The doctor will prescribe her something you'll see. We have to be patient with her."

Kate reached the bottom of the stairs. The images were flashing through her too quickly to see now, she could feel them though. Each time one appeared it left a dirty footprint on her heart, stamping it over and over.

She looked up the stairs while the constant motion of the hallway ad screen tickled the corner of her eye and thought of her room beyond. The thought of sitting inside those four familiar walls, walls covered with pop stars and junk food mascots dancing about and grinning down at her, the ad screen flickering without end, it was repellant. She tried to raise a foot onto the bottom stair but it refused, her body would not allow her to move any closer to her cell.

Instead she turned and snatched at the handle of the front door. As she stepped out into the cool fresh darkness she heard voices from behind but cut them short with a slam. In another moment she was sprinting to the pavement and then through the gate and away. Away from the house with it's seething walls, away from her hateful brother and her spineless parents, away from everything, from all of it.

She ran until her lungs burned and her knees wobbled then stopped to double over and pant. For a minute of two she allowed the crisp night air to flow into her and out again, waiting  for her heart to slow down. Then she began to walk, wiping the fast cooling sweat from her face and sniffing away the tears.

Looking around her she realised she was on the streets with the smaller houses down which Charles had led her a week before. As her legs carried her on an idea began to form. The thought scared her so that she looked back over her shoulder into the darkness. She was alone and she was afraid but there was nowhere else to go and nothing else to do.


—          —

—

The other park was even more intimidating at night. As she descended the concrete steps each footfall billowed out ahead of her, proclaiming her presence to the darkness. Walking as quickly and quietly as she could, Kate hunched her shoulders to her ears and hugged herself into as small a shape as possible.

All the shops were dark and closed. By daylight they had appeared to be dying but looked finally dead by night. Initially she had thought the place deserted but the further down the central walk she went there more convinced she was of subtle motion in the shadows, of being watched by silent eyes.

Squinting off ahead her eyes locked onto what she thought was the frontage of the cafe. She altered her course to move towards it, quickening her pace when she heard what sounded like footsteps behind.

As the faded old sign grew large through the gloom Kate's teeth were chattering frantic. She was convinced that there was someone behind her now but not could bring herself to look back. The cafe was dark and empty as she approached the door, desperately willing it not to be locked.

She reached the door and stopped. The metal handle chilled her hand as she gripped it until she could finally bear it no more and looked suddenly back over her shoulder. The park was empty. There was no-one there. Her eyes scanned back and forth, trying to penetrate the darkness in the corners but aside from an occasional piece of fluttering, wind driven rubbish, nothing moved.

Taking a deep breath she tried the door and felt cool relief as the handle gave. She stepped quickly inside and closed the door behind her before moving between the tables. The door at the back of the cafe was equally co-operative so that a moment later she was groping her way up the creaking wooden staircase.

Stumbling onto the landing Kate paused, listening hard. Her fingertips found the door and she stepped close to place her ear against it. She could hear low voices within, no actual words just rumbling intonation. Standing back from the door she paused, licked her lips and dithered.

She closed her eyes and tried to visualise standing behind Charles, desperately trying to recall the special series of knocks. No matter how hard she pushed however, the sequence would not come. She grimaced in the dark, shifting from one foot to the other in indecision.

Finally she calmed herself, took a breath and closing her eyes. She stepped back to the door and listened for the voices again. They were still in there, murmuring away. Taking another breath she raised her fist and landed three gentle taps on the door. The sound of voices vanished.

The dark seemed to press in around her as total silence swallowed her whole. Time seemed to melt and stretch so that she couldn't tell how long she had stood there. She placed her ear to the door again, straining to hear any sign of life. She began to wonder if she heard anything at all in the first place. Eventually she knocked again, moving her lips to the edge of the door this time to whisper unsure.

"H-hello?" she faltered.

Nothing.

"Hello," she tried again. "I'm sorry, I don't, I don't know the knock."

Still nothing. Was she whispering to an empty room?

"I was here last week with Charles?" she continued, her hope dwindling away.

"I was at the park yesterday," she tried finally, more to herself now than to the room. "I saw what happened to your friend. I thought you'd want to know."

The silence persisted brutally, seeping into her to create a crushing void in her chest. She didn't know what to do. The thought of going home to her room was still just as repellant as before but no matter how hard she tried she couldn't think of anywhere else she could go. Despondent she turned to leave, pressing her hands to the walls and tracing a toe out in front of her to find the lip of the top step.

Just as she found it however she heard motion behind her and froze. As she turned a thin vertical strip of yellow appeared from the darkness at the side of the door. Suddenly a fierce white circle appeared, stinging her eyes and stealing her balance. She raised her hands to try and block out its fury.

Squinting between her fingers she could just about make out the deep black shape of a figure framed in the doorway. The beam from the torch dropped from her face and plunged down the stairs behind her, scanning about but finding only empty space. It flicked back up to blind her again.

"Who are you?" hissed the figure. The voice was hard and cold and not at all friendly.

"I'm Kate," she whispered urgently. "I was here with Charles last week."

"What are you doing here?" asked the voice.

"I was in the park yesterday. I saw what happened to that girl. It's not what they're saying," she said. Even behind her hands her eyes were stinging and gonging with red.

"You mean Mary?" asked the voice.

"I don't know her name," said Kate, forcibly maintaining a level tone and keeping a pleading whine at bay. "I just recognised her from being here last week."

Suddenly the light was gone and the door was closed. Kate blinked in the blackness, waiting for the vicious red circles to fade and steadying herself against the wall. She could hear voices through the door again, more urgent now. A rapid, angry discussion was taking place which seemed to build before dropping suddenly back into silence. The door opened again but this time without the torch.

"Ok," said the voice as the door opened further. "You can come in."

Kate nodded and stepped through, still blinking, following the figure inside.

The loft looked different to last time. Lit by just a couple of candles on a low table the ceiling seemed lower, the walls closer. She realised that the figure at the door was Henry who now turned to face her folding his arms. Gone was the friendly smile and charming nature, his thin face was now pinched and severe.

Over by the candles sat on the floor were three other people one of whom was Uncle Jo. Beside him sat a large, jowly man and a gaunt looking woman with a great, beaklike nose. All were dressed almost completely in black and all stared at her coldly, hints of fear behind threatening armour. Kate closed the door behind her and then stood simply there clasping her hands. She looked around each of the faces and then dropped her gaze to the floor.

"Well?" asked Henry sharply.

Kate looked up again unsure.

"You said you saw what happened to Mary," he said.

Kate nodded and swallowed hard.

—    —

—

"I was there with my friends, we were watching from the upper level," she began, unsure who to look at and so focussing just on Henry. "The girl, Mary, she was just trying to help the old man after the BUC boys stabbed him."

"Wait," the woman by the candle interrupted. "The BUC stabbed the old guy? We heard he cut himself open."

Kate blinked at the woman, shaking her head.

"No," she said. "That's what they're saying but that's not what happened. The old man was asking people for food then three boys form the BUC turned up. The one in charge started shouting at the old man and people in the crowd were shouting at him too. Then he hit him and knocked him down,"

As she spoke she found the scene rose up before her eyes so that her heart began to flutter at the images to come. She could feel cold sweat running threads down her back and began to tangle her fingers together more violently.

"He just wanted to leave but they wouldn't let him go. Then he tried to run away, that's when they say he attacked the crowd but really he was just trying to get away from the BUC boys. He wasn't trying to hurt anyone, honest.

"Well that's when they jumped on him. The one in charge kicked him and the then other two jumped on him and started kicking him and punching him. They hurt him really badly I think but they wouldn't stop. It was so horrible. They wouldn't stop." Her voice broke with a sob she couldn't quite stifle.

Even looking down to her feet she could still feel the cold stares. In the silence her sniffles sounded enormous, shaming her desperately. She wiped her nose and her eyes on the back of her sleeve and went on, pulling ragged breaths through gritted teeth.

"Then the sirens went off and we knew the security guards were coming. That was when the one in charge gave the blonde one the knife and then he, well then he.." but she couldn't finish the sentence. The image of the blonde boy's hand, the flash of glistening red swayed before her, denying her speech with its horror.

"What about Mary?" said a hard voice.

Kate nodded again and wiped again, skipping past the red.

"Yeah, well then she came out running of the crowd, I recognised her from here. She was shouting at the BUC boys. They looked really shocked like they couldn't believe it, like they couldn't believe anyone would shout at them that way.

"She grabbed a shirt off the table in front of the shop and she ran over to the old man. She was pressing the shirt on his stomach where they'd.." she looked up. The stares were even more intense now, the gloom thick with tension between them.

"She was just trying to help him, trying to stop the bleeding. Then the other boy from the BUC well he ran over and kicked her right in the face. I think he must have broken her jaw because.." but again, vibrant colour flashed up and stalled her.

The stares from around the candle had fallen now. Uncle Jo and the fat man were looking at each other while the woman glared at the floor. Only Henry continued to stare at her.

"What then?" he said.

"Well then the security guards arrived and they spoke to the BUC boys. I couldn't hear what they said but after they spoke to then the guards put handcuffs on Mary and took her away. Then the old man seemed to come round, I think he wanted them to help him but they .."

"They just what?" barked Henry.

"They used their stun guns on him!" screamed Kate, meeting Henry's cold eyes with her own now blazing wild, the words tumbling out of her.

"He was bleeding to death in front of them and they electrocuted him! Then they put handcuffs on him and carried him way and it was all red and pouring out of him all over the floor but they just cleaned it up and then everyone went back to shopping and it was like it never happened but it did happen! And now they're saying that he was trying to hurt people and that he stabbed himself and that Mary attacked the BUC boy but they didn't! They didn't! They just didn't."

Finally Kate's legs gave up and she collapsed to the floor in heap, sobbing and sobbing all over herself, beyond caring about the strangers' stares. She was vaguely aware of voices but then flinched as someone touched her arm. She looked up blurry, squinting through the tears and saw Henry standing over her. His face was softer now, closer to the way it had been when she'd first met him.

"Come on," he said gently. "Come and sit down."

Kate allowed herself to be helped to her feet and then led to a broken down old sofa. She sat down gratefully, suddenly utterly exhausted and struggling to keep her eyes open. Henry has disappeared and the three people round the candle were talking urgently amongst themselves, their voices lowered so that she couldn't hear.

Henry reappeared a moment later holding a chipped white mug which he pressed into Kate's trembling hands.

"Here," he said. "Drink this."

Kate glanced into the mug and saw it was filled with water. She had never drunk water from a mug before and it tasted strangely dull but her body gulped it greedily down regardless. Henry pulled up a rickety wooden chair and sat immediately in front of Kate, a serious expression on his face.

"Thank you for that Kate," he said. "I can see that wasn't easy and we appreciate you coming to tell us. We were starting to worry about Mary when we couldn't get hold of her. Now we know know why."

"I don't understand though," said Kate, handing the empty mug back to Henry. "Why did they arrest her at all? She was only trying to help."

"For fuck's sake," muttered the woman.

"Hey," came a new voice, deep and slow. Kate glanced over and realised it was Uncle Jo. "Give her break, she didn't have to come all the way down here. If she hadn't we'd still be guessing about Mary."

"When they arrested Mary she they will have charged her with shoplifting because of the shirt," Henry was explaining. Kate turned her head away from Uncle Jo to face him then dragged her eyes along a second later. "By now though she's probably been convicted convicted of aiding and abetting a terrorist attack."

"Convicted?" said Kate, confused. "Do they hold hearings that fast?"

"If it had just been the shoplifting then no," Henry agreed. "That would be dealt with under normal Company Policy. She'd have received an initial fine then had a public Disciplinary Hearing in a few weeks. Terrorism offences though, they come under Security Policy. Immediate, private hearings. She's probably already gone."

"Gone?" asked Kate, trying to keep up.

"Factory prison overseas," Henry said grimly.

"For how long?" Kate asked.

Henry sighed, his shoulders falling.

"We won't see her again," he said finally.

"But," Kate protested, flinching as the image of the girl kneeling next to the old man flashbulbed before her. "That's not fair! How can they do that? Will they at least look after her there? Her face I mean, it looked pretty bad."

Henry winced then rubbed at his face with his hands. When he spoke Kate realised he couldn't look at her.

"It's unlikely she'll have received any medical treatment," he said hoarsely. "Once you're arrested for a terrorism offence all your funds are seized so you've no way of paying for treatment in custody. And the conditions in the factory prisons well they're.." he paused, swallowing hard and wincing again. "They're pretty grim."

"If she's lucky it'll get infected and she'll die," said the woman.

"Hey!" snapped Henry, glaring over at the candle.

"It's true," she protested. "Better that than a lifetime of slave labour."

"Why did she expose herself like that?" said the fat man.

"Compassion," said Uncle Jo simply.

"She always was too soft," said the woman, more sad than unkind. "Knew that'd do for her one day."

"And for us. We shouldn't be here," said the fat man after a pause, urgent but controlled.

"She'll have told them about this place," agreed the woman. "She'll have had to."

"Damn it," sighed Henry. He looked around the room sadly then back to the floor shaking his head. "You're right," he said. "We'll have to clear out of here and anywhere else Mary knew about. Start all over again, again."

"Are we not safe here?" asked Kate as remembered fear was shouldered aside by more immediate terrors.

"If they were really hot for us they'd have been here already, as soon as she told them," said the woman calmly.

"Yeah," agreed the fat man. "They'll assume we don't know they have Mary yet so they'll probably give it a day or so, separate the story of busting us from the original attack that way they can string out the coverage over several days. Has more impact on public opinion that way, makes the story seem bigger."

"Still though," said Henry. "We shouldn't come back here after tonight. We need to get the message out to everyone else to stay away too. Everything will just have go on hold again, until we can set up somewhere new. I know it's frustrating but we've done it before."

"What is it that you actually do?" asked Kate, surprised at hearing her own words. Thick silence swelled back into the room. As Kate looked from face to face she found them all looking at one another, tight lipped and unsure.

"We provide a safe space," began Henry.

"Hey man! What do you think you're doing?!" snapped the woman. "We don't know this girl!"

"Oh look at her," said Henry, waving a hand in Kate's direction. "She's clearly terrified and traumatised, she's no plant."

"And if it wasn't for her we'd all be getting pinched tomorrow," added Uncle Jo from the shadows.

"We provide a safe space," Henry continued. "For people to come and discuss and explore ideas, ideas that cannot be voiced in public. We reuse and recycle clothes and furniture and through that we prove to one another and to ourselves that a different way of life is possible."

"What about that old man?" asked Kate. Her curiosity was gaining pace as a welcome distraction from current fears and remembered horror. "Are there more like him?"

"There are a lot more like him I'm afraid," said Henry. "Not two miles from where we're sat there are thousands of people like him, victims of our corporate social structure."

"Living proof that the status quo is an offence to humanity that cannot be allowed to continue," said the fat man. Henry and the woman nodded and murmured their agreement, Uncle Jo remained silent.

"So do you help them?" Kate asked. "Do you help feed them and stuff?"

"Well," said Henry, shifting a little on his chair. "You've got to understand that sourcing food outside of standard retail channels is incredibly difficult."

"And dangerous," added the fat man.

"Exactly," said Henry. "The waste disposal infrastructure is all maintained under maximum security and even petty theft is treated as a serious crime. Stealing any significant amount of food from the

Company would be almost a capital offence."

"There's nothing we can do for those people until the corporate social structure is broken down. Once the suits are no longer in charge then we can set about raising those people up out of the shackles of their poverty," droned the fat man.

"Bullshit!" snapped the woman. "It's time for real action!"

"Not this again," sighed the fat man.

"That food came out of the ground, out of the Earth, our Earth" the woman continued undeterred. "It belongs to everyone. If they won't share it we should take it by force!"

"Yeah we've had this discussion," said Henry firmly. "If you want to go and get yourself knocked out and arrested by Security then you're welcome to, see how far it gets you."

"We could do it if we all stood together!" she snapped back.

"So make the argument!" shouted Henry, his temper finally spilling over. "Make your case! Show us a plan that can work. Explain to us how we can do that and stand a even a small chance of success. If you can't convince people that your approach is right then you either go it alone or shut up about it!"

The room lapsed back into silence for a while.

"Doesn't have to be an outright fight," said the woman eventually, sulky and quiet. "Just a bit of direct action to show people we're here, even just a small thing."

"You mean like Mary did?" said the fat man, his voice dripping with contempt.

The silence returned, mournful and cold. The ceiling seemed to press down even lower as the activists sagged in on themselves, lost to bleak introspection. Kate still felt that she was missing something key however. She knew she was an outsider, ignorant and naive but she couldn't see how it made sense.

"So," she began tentatively. "You just sit around in old, empty buildings, wearing old raggedy clothes and talk about ideas."

Henry looked to the faces around the candle. No-one replied but there appeared to be a consensus.

"But how does that change anything?" asked Kate, genuinely confused.

"Exactly," said the woman bitterly.

"Fuck this!" snapped the fat man. "I'm off."

"We should all go," said Henry, rising from his chair.

Kate stood too but as soon as she did she realised she didn't know where she was going.

"Are you going to be ok getting home Kate?" asked Henry.

"I, erm," Kate twisted her fingers together, unsure how to reply.

"I'll take her," said Uncle Jo. Kate just about managed not to gasp as she watched him unfurl himself upwards from the floor to standing. He was even taller than she had thought and his long black coat seemed to melt into the shadows at his feet.

"Ok?" asked Henry.

"Y-yeah," Kate stammered. "Ok. Fine."

—        —
—

Back outside Henry and the others slipped away into the shadows without saying goodbye, each leaving quickly and quietly in a different direction. Kate was left in front of the cafe with Uncle Jo. His black coat and hair made him all but invisible in the gloom. All she could make out of his face was a pale, hovering smudge.

"So where do you live?" he asked, his deep voice swelling out of the dark.

Kate turned away from the smudge and peered into the black in the direction the concrete steps. The unconditioned air of the small park had fallen into a deep chill so that she had to hug herself tightly to prevent her teeth form chattering.

"Erm," she said, buying time while she tried to think of an actual answer.

"Don't want to go home eh?" asked Uncle Jo.

A sudden yellow flared and trembled before the blur of his face. For a second his high cheekbones and dark eyes came into blazing focus as he lit a cigarette. The yellow vanished as abruptly as it had appeared, leaving behind an afterimage that glowed and swayed red wherever Kate looked.

A tiny orange spot floated within the blur of his face now, an occasionally brightening firefly that danced to the sound of his deep exhalations. Kate nodded her answer to his question but as the smell of the cigarette washed over her she realised she couldn't see her agreement.

"Not really," she said, shivering. "No."

"You want to go somewhere and talk?" he asked. "Somewhere warm?"

Kate tried to picture Uncle Jo as she had first seen him, the tall condescending figure who had dismissed her utterly from across the room. No matter how she tried she couldn't connect that image to the friendly disembodied voice that was with her now.

"Ok," she said.

Somewhere in her stomach a distance echo of excitement tried to fly but fell. A day earlier the thought of being alone in the dark with this infuriating yet mysterious man would have made her feel hot and dizzy, confused and conflicted. In the moment however, the brutal cold of the night crushed all such thoughts underfoot, dominating her thoughts as it seeped into her bones.

"Come on then," he said simply, turning away so that the pale blur and the fiery dot disappeared from view. He set off walking deeper into the park and as Kate trotted after him she could almost see the concrete steps that led back to the streets receding far behind her.

She caught up and fell into step alongside him. The darkness was such that she could see almost nothing in front of her and so had to concentrate hard on where to put her feet. Uncle Jo seemed to move with blind yet absolute confidence however so that she had to work hard to keep up with his long strides. After a while she found the exertion provided a little welcome warmth so that her teeth gave up on their threats to chatter.

"You smoke?" he asked as a packet of cigarettes held in long slender fingers appeared before her.

Again she shook her head and again realised he couldn't see her.

"No thanks," she said. The fingers and cigarettes disappeared.

"So that must have been a pretty shitty thing to see yesterday," he said quietly.

For a moment the colours and images threatened to swell up into the darkness before her but she managed to push them away.

"Uh-huh," she managed, reluctant to be drawn into further recollections.

"Then to come all the way down here on your own and put yourself through it again for our benefit, that must have been tough too," he said.

"Mm-hmm," she said.

"That was pretty cool," he said simply.

Kate opened her mouth to deliver another non-committal sound but found herself unable to speak. From seemingly trying to steer her towards an unpleasant place he had suddenly veered off into somewhere altogether more pleasant.

The sound of his voice, genuinely impressed and respectful, had somehow relaxed her shoulders and caused a tiny ball of warmth to appear in her chest. Despite the circumstances she found herself smiling and was glad he couldn't see her in the dark.

"It seemed important," she said finally, managing to keep her voice casually flat and indifferent.

"It was," he agreed. Sudden motion caught her eye as the orange spot shot away from them into the dark, tracing a thin line to the ground.

"It's a rare quality these days," he continued. "The willingness to put yourself out for the benefit of others. Not many people have it anymore, just a few very special people, people like you."

The ball of warmth in her chest swelled so that she was suddenly very aware of her heart and despite the bitter chill all around she could feel a sudden heat on her face. Their footsteps ticked by for a while, rolling out into the apparently endless dark. Eventually she managed to speak.

"Y'know," she said but then realised she had no idea how to continue the sentence. "Thanks," she said instead, cursing herself silently for the clumsy response.

They walked in silence for a few minutes more. Kate's eyes finally began to adjust to the gloom so that glancing about her she realised they had left the park behind. They were now walking down a narrow street, flanked on both sides by long continuous buildings.

Kate squinted at the closest of these and began to pick out a regular pattern of windows and doors. It was as if the long brick structure had been carefully and regularly sliced internally to form a series of tall narrow buildings all huddling together in a line.

"Are these," she whispered, frowning her confusion. "Are these houses?"

She heard Uncle Jo laugh to himself but it didn't feel unkind.

"Yes," he said gently. "These are houses."

Kate began to peer more closely at the doors and windows. Some were boarded up while others hung open, gaping black.

"I've never seen houses like these before, they look so small. Why are they all crammed in together like this?" she asked.

"They're called terraces," he explained. "I suppose by today's standards they are tiny. They were built a long time ago to house workers from the local factories. The aim was to fit as many people as possible into the smallest space they could."

Kate looked at the distance between the doors and windows, trying to gauge the size of the rooms inside. The width of one whole house seemed less than that of her bedroom. She tried to imagine all the houses filled with people but in her mind's eye they couldn't fit and so spilled out onto the street instead.

"Who lives here now?" she asked.

"No-one really," he said. "Just me. They've been empty for decades. Sometimes you see other people about, people with nowhere else to go."

An image of the old man, grey faced and glassy

eyed loomed up before Kate. She winced at it and tried to wish it away.

"Here we are," said Uncle Jo stopping suddenly before one particular door.

Grateful of the distraction Kate looked at the door. She compared it to others either side and around but could see no difference whatsoever. Uncle Jo moved up onto the doorstep and put his shoulder to the door, grunting a little as he shoved it inwards and disappeared inside after it. Kate threw one last glance around the dark, deserted street and then stepped up and in after him.

Inside a thin veil of grey drifted through window and hinted at details of the room. The floor was bare, just rows of wooden boards, some broken, some stained. The walls were equally barren, crumbling plaster revealing large patches of bare brick. Off to her right there was a large hole in the wall that she thought could once have been an open fireplace like those she'd seen in History lessons at school.

To her left a doorway shaped hole led into what she initially assumed to be a large cupboard. Poking her head through however she was shocked to realise that the tiny space had once been a kitchen. Archaic looking appliances sagged and rusted among broken tiles and exposed piping.

"You live here?" she said doubtfully.

"Yep," said Uncle Jo. She realised he was across the room now, apparently waiting for her. "Not down here though," he added. "I'm upstairs."

He opened another door and moved through it leaving her briefly alone in the ruined space. The desolation of the place was overwhelming, she could almost feel the rot creeping up against her, trying to find a way inside to infect her with decay.

She hurried across the room and found that the door led to a narrow staircase. She could hear Uncle Jo moving through the darkness above and followed him up. The stairs twisted round to the left taking her up over the tiny kitchen and onto a landing just big enough for the two of them.

"In here," said Uncle Jo, opening another door.

Kate followed him into the room. At first glance it appeared to be a copy of the barren void immediately below it. Through the gloom however she could make out the lines of possible furniture, space filling shapes of a deeper black.

"Hang on," he said, moving across the blackened room with swift certainty.

The same yellow flare from before erupted, this time leaving behind soft flickering copies as he moved from one point to another. As the candles took and their flames grew tall the contents of the room solidified into view.

The floor at her feet was occupied by a large mattress, smothered beneath a heap of tangled blankets. Off to her right she noticed a small, square wooden desk with folding metal legs accompanied by a rickety looking wooden chair. On the desk sat a small stack of paper, a couple of notebooks and a scattering of pens.

Books were stacked waist high all around the edges of the floor, some of the piles apparently frozen, caught in the act of slipping into jumbled heaps. A tall, lop sided wardrobe slouched against where she thought the window should be. A thick nest of rags and blankets spilled out all around the upper sides of the wardrobe and over its top.

She suddenly realised Uncle Jo was just standing there, watching her, a strange look in his eyes. He smiled warmly and she felt herself return the expression almost without realising it. Her eyes flicked away from him and back to the wardrobe so that he followed her gaze.

"Black out," he said, apparently explaining. "Stops and light being visible from the street. From the outside this place still looks dead and empty, even when I have the candles lit. As long as we're quiet, someone could walk right past the front door and never know we were in here. Keeps the cold out too."

Kate nodded and looked around the room again. Despite the same bare floorboards and crumbling plaster as downstairs, the soft focus light of the candles somehow made the room feel cosy and welcoming.

"Is that important?" she asked. "For people not to know you're here?"

"Yeah, kind of," he said. "Have a seat." He motioned to the mattress on the floor then moved to the wardrobe.

"This is all Company property," he said over his shoulder as he opened the wardrobe doors and began to fiddle around with something inside. "Sometimes Security come down to check no-one's living here."

Kate eased herself carefully down onto the mattress finding it surprisingly firm and comfortable. She hugged her knees to her chest and tipped her head to one side as she tried to read the spines of the many stacked books. Many of the titles had faded to nothing and of those could read she didn't recognise one.

"Here," said Uncle Jo, striding back across the room carrying a tall glass in each hand containing a honey coloured liquid.

"Drink this," he said, offering her one of the glasses. "It'll warm you up."

Kate accepted the glass and then held it carefully as Uncle Jo sat down on the mattress just beside her. He took a long deep drink from his glass then smacked his lips, satisfied. She looked at the liquid in her glass and then sniffed at it tentatively. She flinched away again almost immediately, the smell was pungent and harsh but with a faint sweetness underneath.

She looked at Uncle Jo to find him watching her intently. She turned back to the glass and hesitantly took a small sip. Whatever it was it tasted better than it smelled but burnt her throat when she swallowed.

Her stomach turned over and for a moment she thought she would vomit. The feeling passed quickly however and was replaced with a deep, gentle warmth that seemed to spread out through her limbs. Uncle Jo leaned back onto the mattress behind her, propping himself up on his elbows.

"So you seemed unimpressed with our comrades at the cafe," he said, staring into the middle distance.

Kate licked her lips, unsure how to respond. She took another drink, winced through the aftertaste and thought about it.

"Not really," she began carefully. "I just kind of assumed a group of people like that must be doing something really serious, something that would change things."

Uncle Jo laughed to himself, sitting back up again to take another long drink, all but emptying his glass.

"That was very funny," he said turning to look at her, grinning. "When you said, 'how does that change anything?' Did you see their faces?" He laughed again, draining his drink and placing the empty glass on the floor.

Kate smiled shyly and fidgeted with her glass.

"I wasn't trying to be funny," she said. "I was genuinely asking, I thought maybe there was something I'd missed."

"Nope," said Uncle Jo. He turned to face her and then lay down across the mattress on his side, propped up on one elbow, resting his face on his hand. "You didn't miss anything. They're useless, pointless, utterly ineffectual."

Kate frowned her surprise as she took another sip. He had been right about the drink, she no longer felt the biting cold at all. She felt her shoulders relax and her neck lengthen as she turned fully onto the mattress to face him, crossing her legs beneath her.

"I thought they were your friends?" she said.

"Oh they are," he replied lazily. "It's not their fault they're useless, everybody is really."

"What do you mean?" she asked, draining her glass and placing it on the floor.

"Well it's the Company isn't it?" he said meeting her gaze and holding it. "They've long since monetarised all forms of dissent."

"I don't.." she began, trying not to sway amid the shared eye contact. She felt like he was looking through her eyes and inside her as if he could see every part of her.

"Think about it," he said in low, slow voice that seemed to reverberate through her. "As long as they profit, they thrive. If you protest in public or steal from them, bang! Off you go to the factory prisons, a lifetime of free labour for them. Profit. Let's say you go a bit more radical, try your hand at a little property damage perhaps?"

He raised an eyebrow and for some reason Kate giggled though as she heard herself she wasn't sure why. The candle light seemed to be growing thicker around them, smudging already fuzzed out edges even further.

"Let's say you get away with it even, then what? The Company uses public money to pay itself to repair the damage you've done. Profit. Then there're the reused clothes our friends wear with such defiance. Reusing goods only has an impact if it means you don't buy replacement goods.

"Those guys can't get away with that. The decline in their spending would be spotted straight away. So sure, they might be wearing an outfit to the cafe that they bought a year ago but to maintain their cover they have to buy and dispose of just as many clothes as anyone else. Profit. The clothes are a statement but they have no real impact on the Company, they don't give a shit why you're buying stuff, just as long as you keep spending."

"So you're saying there's no way to stop them or change things. It's impossible to fight them?" the thought was dark enough and cold enough to cut through a little of the fuzz thickening around her.

"Oh it's far worse than that," he said, pushing himself up and swinging his legs under him to mirror her pose. He leaned towards her conspiratorially and she saw that his skin was perfectly smooth, stretched firm over those high, graceful cheekbones. His eyes were dark and brooding with sparks deep inside that hinted of hidden but furious fire.

"It's been impossible to fight them for generations," he growled, tilting his head to one side as he considered her face. "The chance to do that passed long ago. The problem now is that it's impossible not to help them."

"What do you mean," she whispered thickly, mesmerised by his gaze now. Everything felt heavy from her eyelids to her limbs. A strand of hair fell across her face, it tickled at her nose but she couldn't find the strength to raise her hand.

Uncle Jo raised his hand instead and she held her breath as his slender fingers delicately brushed the hair from her face, a single fingertip brushing her cheek. His touch was electrifying sending a strange tingling sensation from her face down through the rest of her body. Kate heard a satisfied little sound slip from her lips before she could catch it. He smiled.

"Everything you do Kate," he was saying. "Every single thing you do all day long generates profit for the Company. When you walk down the pavement. When you breathe the air. When you eat or dress, perhaps even when you undress."

He left this last to hang between them so that a giddiness began to rise up inside her, mixing with the fuzz. Her eyes closed for a moment and she felt herself begin to fall forwards but managed to stop herself and force open her eyes, swaying a little before settling back upright to listen.

"There are no conscientious objectors in this war of ours, remaining neutral just isn't an option. We are conscripted at birth to work for their cause and our choice is a very simple one. We either devote every intimate moment of our lives to increasing their power or we simply.."

His hand was near his mouth as he spoke, fingers curled as he considered her thoughtfully. She leaned forward, literally hanging on his final word.

"..disappear," he sighed finally, rolling his wrist forward and flicking out his fingers to mime a tiny explosion.

Kate felt a thrill run through her at the eloquence of his finale. The fuzz became thicker and heavier so that her eyes closed again no matter how hard she tried. She felt herself falling forwards again but this time couldn't not halt her descent. She felt his hands on her shoulders, propping her up, then those fingers again on her face, stroking gently at her cheek.

For a while there was nothing, then she heard a voice, one of her friends from days earlier at the park. They'd said something, just before the horrible thing. What had they said? Did it mean something here?

"Are you the Sandman?" she heard herself ask, her words thick and fumbling. Uncle Jo laughed like distant thunder.

"Would you like to find out? You see there really is only one thing we can do now," he was saying, his voice somehow far away and yet incredibly intimate. "One thing they cannot take away from us, an act from which they cannot profit, a declaration no, a celebration of our humanity. The most natural thing of all."

"I don't think I feel very.." she heard herself slurring. She still felt as if she was falling, her stomach plunging down and down. She tried to rase her arms but they were even heavier than before and suddenly the fuzz seemed too thick to be friendly. A vague idea of alarm whispered off to one side and made her think about drowning.

"Shh," he was saying. "It's ok, it's ok. It's the most natural thing in the world. It's an act of resistance, the only true act of resistance that remains."

She could feel movement at her chest now but still couldn't open her eyes. He was unbuttoning the front of her shirt. She tried to speak but her tongue was too thick and too lazy to work. Instead the world seemed to twist to one side until she felt the mattress pressing in against her arm and rolled flat onto her back.

"I don't.." said someone again, she thought it might have been her. She could feel his hands moving over her, tugging at the zip on her jeans. One of her hands managed to take flight, landing heavily on his. He took hold of her wrist very gently, and laid her hand back at her side.

"You're very beautiful Kate, do you realise that?" he was saying, closer now so that she could feel his breath on her face.

She frowned and tried to turn her head but then his mouth was on hers, pressing her down into the mattress. A hollow scream stumbled in her throat as she tried to force her body back in motion. His mouth tasted sour, an acrid mix of the honey coloured drink he'd given her and cigarette tar.

He was kissing her neck now, leaving saliva all over her as he moved himself on top of her, crushing her whole body down through the blankets and against the springs. She managed to raise both her hands to her shoulders and tried to push against him but she may as well have been trying to lift the house itself.

"No," whispered a ragged voice which she thought was probably related to movement in her throat. "I don't want.." said the voice but trailed off, exhausted.

"It's ok, it's ok," he kept saying, grinding himself against her now. His hands became less gentle as he pulled more urgently at her clothes. She felt the fingers of his left hand snake under her vest top and slide up over her ribs. He cupped her breast through her bra and began to squeeze it so that it hurt. The pain triggered something inside her so that suddenly a strange feeling of cold washed through her, thinning but not quite lifting the fuzz.

"Stop," she said, trying to twist out of from under him. "Stop it!"

He placed his free hand over her mouth and began trying to get his fingers inside her bra. Her arm flailed floppy beside them off the edge of the mattress. She drove her wrist across the bare boards, dragging limp fingers along behind it, hooking splinters into her skin. Finally the back of her hand encountered something cold and smooth.

Clumsily, gradually her fingers arranged themselves around the glass. He was pulling at her jeans again now, one hand still clamped over her mouth. She shook her head violently under his hand, her clearing eyes now wide. His face was twisted, ugly and flushed, his eyes fevered with hunger.

"It's coming baby," he was panting now. "Here it comes, yeah! You want the Sandman? I'll give you the fucking Sandman!"

He lunged down at her, forcing his mouth on to hers again. The moment seemed to stretch out and hang. All the little pockets of strength throughout her body coalesced into a line and the line ran down her arm.

She managed to turn her face away to the side so that he slobbered over her ear and neck while she screwed her eyes up tight. Then, clenching everything she had and gritting her teeth until she thought they might crack she drove the glass into the side of his face with all the force she could summon.

The expected sound of breaking glass did not come. Instead there was only a muffled, wet crunching sound. Uncle Jo reared up like a startled horse, roaring as he tumbled backwards and off her. Her body lumbered into action of its own accord while her mind reeled away from the horror.

Flipping over onto her stomach she managed to get her knees up under her chest. Scrambling onto all fours then careered towards the door and was just about upright by the time she hit the landing to throw herself at the stairs. She could hear Uncle Jo back in the bedroom, moaning and sobbing. Suddenly he began to scream.

"You fucking bitch!" he yowled with tearful fury. "My face! What have done to my face! Oh god!"

Kate tried to run down the stairs but quickly lost track of her legs and overbalanced, tumbling forward. Vicious step corners bit at her arms and sides until she landed heavily back in the sitting room. Still swaying and clumsy she tried to get to her feet but collapsed back into a heap. More noise from above drove her on however so that on her third attempt she managed to stand.

As heavy footsteps thundered above her she slid her way along the fetid wall towards the front door, insisting that her legs sustain her. He was on the stairs as she dragged the door open and stumbled out onto the street.

The frigid night air slapped her full in the face so that she collapsed gasping against the wall of the house. Still she he could hear him coming, dashing through the house towards her. She lunged on down the pavement into the pitch blackness, flailing her arms in front of her as she went.

She heard him clatter down the step and out onto the street, heard him panting and wincing and cursing behind her. The street was so dark that the tiny part of her that could think was sure he couldn't see her. He would hear her if she ran but would quickly stumble into her if she stayed where she was.

A flash of desperation drove her in through the nearest open doorway. The room was almost identical to Uncle Jo's house, utterly barren and ruined. She squatted down and pressed her back to the wall just inside the doorway.

Her flight from the house had seared her lungs and even now they continued to burn. She denied them however, holding her breath as she heard footsteps out on the street. The sound came closer and closer until she saw movement in the corner of her eye.

Uncle Jo was right outside, if he happened to pause and stick his head through the door he would see her and have her for sure. The explosion of lifesaving energy from before was beginning to ebb away and she knew she would not be able to summon a second wind were he to catch her. The footsteps paused. She cringed so hard she saw flashes before her eyes. She could hear him panting his pain and his rage out in dark, hissing and spitting.

"Where are you?" he was whispering. "Where are you? Where are you? I'm going to find you, you bitch, you stupid little bitch."

Finally he moved off, his footsteps receding up the street. Kate didn't dare venture back outside but the bare room didn't feel safe either. Moving carefully, silently she crossed the room and considered the staircase. Several stairs were missing and the whole thing appeared damp and crumbling.

Gradually, she managed to climb the stairs, placing each foot with cringing care and testing her weight each time. The landing felt firmer underfoot and as she crossed quickly to the bedroom she began to feel a little safer. Even if Uncle Jo began checking inside the houses it seemed unlikely he would attempt to tackle the stairs in this one.

The room was almost as empty and bare as the rest, swept clean by the wind that poured through the gaping hole that had once held a window. The only object in the room was a large armchair. The upholstery had worn through in several places so that stuffing spilled out here and there.

Kate staggered to the chair and lowered herself into it, drawing her legs up under her. She hugged herself tightly, trying to ignore the cold and listening hard for footsteps outside. Seconds ticked by in the blackness, stretching to minutes and perhaps even hours until she lost track of the time altogether.

Her body felt empty and leaden, her temples pounded. By stages she sank deeper into the chair and then into herself. First the street outside, then the house around her and finally the chair beneath, it all melted into nothing and she slept.

—    —
—

Kate woke abruptly, eyes stinging in the morning light, hands snatching out in panic. As she blinked and breathed and tried to remember however, she realised that she was at home, safe in her own bed. It had been two days earlier when she had awoken curled up in the broken down old armchair in the derelict house, body stiff, head splitting.

She took a moment to feel the reassuring softness of the sheets against her skin. She remembered creeping back down the broken staircase and out of the front door before sprinting up the street, not pausing to rest until she had reached the small park where tired looking people were just starting to open the shops.

From there she had staggered up and out of the park. She remembered feeling that the concrete steps must have multiplied and that they would go on forever. Then on through the waking streets until finally she had reached the front door.

Her parents had been waiting for her, her mother's face pale and puffy from crying. Her father had drawn breath to rage at her until she had stepped into the light of the of the front room. The sight of her, dishevelled, shaking and weeping had been enough to silence him. Her mother had swept upon her then, feeling for injuries down her arms and legs and stroking her face over and over.

Since then she'd feigned illness and rarely left her bed, pretending to be asleep whenever either of them came to check on her. So far they hadn't asked her about what had happened but she knew the conversation was coming.

She sat up and elbowed her pillows back against the wall irritably until she could lean comfortably back against them. It seemed unlikely that she would be able to avoid the conversation if she stayed at home from school again, the pretence of endless sleep was becoming harder and harder to sustain.

Nodding to herself as she made the decision she swung her legs out of the bed and stood. The trophy on the shelf caught her eye and her stomach twisted to cringe as Uncle Jo's words rose up and around her. She closed her eyes as she crossed the room, unable to bear looking at the grinning figures dancing in her posters.

She entered her bathroom and stepped into the shower. After she had washed herself thoroughly several times over she felt just a little bit better and stepped out again to dry herself. As she dressed for school and gathered up her things she fought hard to keep her mind calm and blank, not allowing herself to remember. After taking a deep breath and descending the stairs she met her mother in the hall.

"Good morning darling," said her mother, looking her up and down. "Are you going to go to school today?"

Kate just nodded, trying to hide her irritation at the constant motion of the ad screen just over her mother's shoulder.

"Do you want to come and have some breakfast before you go?" her mother asked, half turning towards the kitchen.

Kate shook her head firmly and took a step towards the front door. Her mother caught up with her and planted a soft, cool palm on her forehead.

"Hmm," she said with concern. "You still feel a little warm. Are you sure you want go? You don't have to."

Kate gently pushed her mother's hand away and pulled together a fragile smile.

"It's fine Mum," she said softly. "I'm fine."

"Well just see how you get on," her mother said. "If you don't feel well just tell the teacher I said you can come home."

"Ok," said Kate, opening the door.

"Tell them to ring me and I'll come and get you," her mother called after her.

Kate closed the door behind her and walked to school. The familiar route, the sights and sounds, all swam about her like a dream. No matter how hard she tried she just couldn't keep the endless stream of terrible thoughts at bay. If it wasn't images from the park or the tastes and smells of Uncle Jo it was his words.

She dozed through the day, paying little attention in lessons, allowing herself to be carried on the tide of the corridor crowds in between. At lunchtime she sat quietly with the girls, listening to them chatter. It all seemed fake to her now, as if the whole place were just a film set, the students and teachers just actors. Every word she heard seemed scripted, old, tired and predictable.

It wasn't until the end of the day that she actually felt fully awake. Making her way out of school among the throngs of students she caught sight of Charles in the distance. With some difficulty she made her way through the crowds to catch up with him, touching his arm to make him turn.

She managed a real, genuine smile for him knowing that if there was anyone who could find something to say to make her feel better it was him. As he turned however his face fell at the sight of her. His brow furrowed and his jaw set, his eyes cooling contemptuous as she watched.

"Hey," she said as brightly as she could. "I haven't heard from you for a few days. You ok?"

Charles eyed her angrily, looking about as if for an escape.

"Don't talk to me," he hissed and then tried to move away.

"What?" said Kate, skipping forward to keep up with him. "Why?"

He stopped and turned to face her again, now with

genuine hurt in his eyes.

"I know what you did with Uncle Jo," he hissed.

Kate's stomach imploded, she felt her knees weaken.

"What, what do you mean?" she asked thickly.

"I know you fu.." Charles caught himself and took a deep breath. "I know you spent the night with him. He told me everything, all the gory details. I didn't think you were like that. I thought we were.." he shook his head in disgust.

"We were!" she cried. "I mean, we are! At least I thought we were, I mean I want us to be. I don't know what he said to you but it's not true."

"So you didn't go home with him the other night?" asked Charles.

"Well..." Kate began, the words crowding to stick in her throat.

"Forget it," said Charles. "Just stay away from me!"

Kate realised she was crying and that people were starting to pay attention to them. Suddenly she felt angry. She wiped the tears savagely from her face and stormed away from Charles and through the crowd, pushing and shoving and ignoring cries of complaint.

All the way home her chest burned with unbearable frustration, her mind racing in furious circles. It was as if at some point a secret trial had been held at which she had been condemned in her absence to spend her life as a small and helpless creature.

There was no right of appeal, no way for her to find and face her judges to make her case or complain. Her whole world, every single thing about and around her, just happened to her, not through or with or because of her but to her, one way traffic. She was a passive consumer and nothing more, forever, whether she liked it or not.

Hot and panting, she stormed along her street, fists clenched and trembling but the sight of Security car parked outside her parent's house stopped her dead. The sweat on her back ran cold as the broad sweeping strokes of her raging thoughts abruptly thinned down to single, terrible thread.

She scanned the street around her guiltily, looking over both shoulders, half expecting to spot heavily armoured Security hiding among the perfectly manicured bushes, waiting to pounce. One tentative step led to another and she resumed her approach but cautiously now, faltering and unsure. Meanwhile her mind raced ahead, asking and answering questions, trying to guess what was about to happen.

Were they waiting for her? Did they know about the cafe? It seemed unlikely, she'd only been there a couple of times and she hadn't actually done anything. How would they know? Why would they care? If they weren't here for her however then why? Had something terrible happened? Her initial reactive questions seemed sickeningly selfish now.

What if something had happened to her father? Her mother? Were Security in there right now breaking the news of a terrible accident? What about George? When it came to violence the BUC had a knack for being in the wrong place at the right time. They were usually hailed as heroes, defenders of national commerce and so on but occasionally they did take casualties.

She reached the front gate and found her mouth was dry. She hated her brother in an everyday sense, more than ever in fact since he had joined the BUC but she didn't really, actually hate him, she realised. She certainly didn't want anything bad to happen to him.

Approaching the front door slowly she jumped as it opened just before she touched the handle. Her mother was stood in the hallway grey faced and shrunken, a blank look on her face. She waved Kate inside but didn't meet her eyes. Kate's stomach thrashed unbearably.

She walked into the front room to find her father sat at the far end of the large sofa. He bore an almost identical expression to her mother and was staring grimly at nothing. He glanced up at her as she entered but then looked away again almost immediately.

Opposite him, across the lush new carpet and a coffee table in the latest style, two huge Security Guards were struggling to fit alongside one another on the smaller matching sofa. As she entered they came to life, like machines roused from an energy saving stasis. One of them stood up.

"Kate?" he asked flatly.

She nodded, her voice lost deep inside her trembling chest.

"Take a seat please," he said, his body armour creaking as he waved her towards her father.

Kate sat down beside her father, planting her schoolbag at her feet. Her mother followed her in and sat down on the other side of her, clutching a handkerchief. The guard sat back down while his colleague produced a small, flat device from a pocket on his thigh and brought the screen to life with a touch.

"What's going on?" she finally managed to ask. "Dad?"

She turned to her father but he was still staring straight ahead. She turned to her mother but she just shook her head and buried her face in her handkerchief.

"Kate Elizabeth Margaret Johnson," said the guard with the device. His eyes were cold and grey, his voice robotic. "You have been convicted of three violations of Company Policy and are hereby charged with four violations of Security Policy."

"What? How? What do you mean? I don't understand. I.." Kate tried to protest but the guard continued, speaking over her as if she hadn't said a word.

"You have been convicted of jaywalking, two counts, wherein you denied the Company the revenue owed for use of a pavement and or road surface and put at risk your own life and thereby risked the cumulative consumption undertaken throughout the rest of your life and the revenue that would generate for the Company.

"An invoice for a fine equalling the total revenue lost to the Company plus compensation to the Company for the risk of future loss of earnings has been now been raised. As you are currently a minor this invoice has been made out to your parents as they are liable for any costs you incur the Company until you achieve the legal age of liability."

"But I was just.." Kate tried again, finding her voice firmer this time but again the guard cut across her.

"In addition, you have also been convicted of

reuse and or recycling of produce, one count, wherein you denied the Company the revenue owed for the purchase of new produce by the retention and reuse and or recycling of a previously purchased produce.

"An invoice for a fine equalling the total revenue lost to the Company plus compensation to the Company for the risk of future loss of earnings has been now been raised. As you are currently a minor this invoice has been made out to your parents as they are liable for any costs you incur the Company until you achieve the legal age of liability.

"You have now been informed of the details of your convictions, it is assumed that you understand these details and the consequences thereof." The guard flicked a thickly gloved finger across the screen of his device.

"Wait," snapped Kate, raising her voice to a challenge so that her mother gasped beside her. "I don't understand at all! What reuse? What did I do? And what do you mean convictions? I get a public disciplinary hearing, you can't just convict me without any evidence. Dad, tell them, I get a hearing."

She looked to her father outraged and hopeful but his expression was so sad that she faltered and stalled. He shook his head just a little and nodded back to the guards. The first guard, the one who had stood when she entered the room, was holding up a large, transparent evidence bag.

Inside the bag, swinging back and forth was a large, ornately decorated table spoon. Kate's jaw dropped at the sight of it and she sat back against the sofa, feeling herself crumble against the high quality soft furnishing.

"We found this hidden in your room, clearly stolen and concealed with the express intent of denying the Company revenue through reuse and or recycling," said the guard with the device flatly. The first guard folded the evidence bag carefully around the spoon and slipped it back into a pocket on his chestplate.

"We also reviewed the movement data from your hand chip over the last few weeks," he continued. "It provides absolute proof of your jaywalking on two separate occasions on the same day. With such evidence to support both violations a public disciplinary hearing would result in the Company incurring an unnecessary and thereby illegal expense.

"In addition to this your violations of Company Policy are superseded by the charges of violation of Security Policy. A public disciplinary hearing would delay proceedings concerning these charges and so in accordance with Security Policy no such hearing will be held.

"Said charges are as follows. Number one, membership of a dangerous Muslim organisation. Number two, associating with known Muslim terrorists against the interests of the Company. Number three, trespass on restricted Company property. And number four, aiding and abetting a terrorist attack.

"You have now been informed of the charges made against you and it is assumed that understand these charges and the potential consequences thereof. You will now be transported to a Security Office wherein an immediate private hearing will be held to confirm your guilt and pass sentence." The guard tapped the screen of the device so that it blackened and slipped it back into his pocket.

"But it isn't true," moaned Kate, terror building towards tears as the guards stood from the sofa. "It isn't true! Dad, tell them. They're going to send me to a factory prison. Don't let them take me away. Daddy please!"

"Look," said her father desperately, standing to face the guards across the coffee table. "Isn't there anything we can do here. She understands what she's done, can't we just pay a fine or something." The guards both sprang to their feet.

"Sit down!" they barked in stereo, both reaching for the stun guns on their belts in perfect unison.

"Sir," said the first guard, raising his free hand to show Kate's father a heavily armoured palm. "I'm asking you to take your seat. If you do not comply my colleague and I will have no choice but to interpret your behaviour as an attempted assault after which point we will be duty bound to disable you and take you into custody."

Slowly Kate's father lowered himself back down onto the sofa, both his hands raised before him in submission.

"Ok, ok," he was saying. "I'm not trying to cause any trouble. I'm just trying to ascertain if there's any other way we can deal with this situation. My daughter..."

"She's just a child!" screeched Kate's mother through tears and sobs. "She's just a child, you can't take her away, you can't!"

The guards turned as one to face Kate's mother, looming over her, their hands still resting on their stun guns.

"Mrs Johnson," said the second guard. "Mr Johnson, it's very important that you both comply fully with all our instructions. The evidence against your daughter is overwhelming and her crimes are serious. While she is a minor she is still old enough to understand both the nature and consequences of her actions ."

"What actions?!" screamed Kate, her parents fear flowing into and amplifying her own. "I haven't done anything!"

The second guard turned to face Kate, taking a step towards her so that the gleaming kneecaps of his armour touched the edge of the coffee table. The first guard swung slowly back and forth, watching first her father and the mother. Both were poised, ready for immediate violence.

"We know you've attended and taken part in meetings at the Church Gate Independent Cafe with a dangerous Muslim group. We know that at least one of those meetings was a smaller gathering of the executive council of that group. Your presence at those meetings demonstrates your membership of the group and association with its members.

"We know from your hand chip that just a few days ago you entered a Company development area, clearly signposted as being restricted and spent several hours therein. Those areas are restricted as they contain dangerous derelict buildings which could collapse at any moment.

"By going there you risked your own life and the cumulative consumption you would have undertaken throughout the rest of your life and the revenue to the Company that would have generated. We know you spent the night in that restricted area and that you had sexual relations with a Muslim, a senior member of the group thereby further evidencing your association."

Kate saw her father's knuckles whiten in his lap while another low moan emerged from her mother.

"That isn't true," she said quietly. "I didn't sleep with him. I didn't."

"Finally," continued the guard. "We know that the Muslim group that used to meet at the Church Gate Independent Cafe, of which you have been proven to be a member, were behind the attempted terrorist attack at your local park last week.

"We even have a sworn statement from your own brother, a highly respected member of the BUC. In his statement he details your account of the attack and your outspoken empathy with and sympathy for the terrorists, one of whom it is believed you knew by name through your membership of and association with the group. Subsequently you will now be taken into custody and processed according to policy."

The guards moved around either side of the coffee table to loom over Kate, their heavy black forms blocking out all light. The first guard took a pair of handcuffs from his belt while the second reached down for her wrists.

"Leave her alone!" screeched Kate's mother, suddenly erupting from the sofa to lunge at the second guard. Without a moment's hesitation the first guard backhanded Kate's mother with the handcuffs with force enough to lift her from her feet and throw her backwards. She crashed against and then over the back of the sofa, landing bloodied and dazed on the thick carpet behind.

"Hey!" roared Kate's father, throwing himself bodily across the second guard in order to get at the first so that all three of them tumbled backwards, smashing down onto and through the coffee table.

Kate herd herself screaming as she sat frozen, watching her father grapple with the guards on the floor at her feet. Then she was moving, scrambling over the back of the sofa to her mother's side.

"I'm sorry Mum," she was whispering into her dazed mother's ear. "I'm so sorry. I love you both, I love you."

She heard a yell cut short by stun gun crackling behind her and raced from the room. As she exploded through the front door and then vaulted the front gate she could hear the sound of furniture breaking inside.

Dashing out into the middle of the road to avoid a scattering of stunned pedestrians, Kate sprinted everything she had into the black at her feet. She rounded the first corner she came to and then the next, desperate to escape the feeling of the guards' eyes on her back.

Ducking and weaving she turned and ran and turned and ran at random until she had to stop to breath. Crouching against a garden fence she stared around her, listening hard. This street was deserted and silent though if she closed her eyes and tilted her head she thought she could hear sirens in the far distance.

She stood on shaky legs and hugged herself, trying to decide what to do. For the first time she realised she was among the smaller houses and not far from the other park. Her fingers tangled with each other as she tried to think of a way out. Suddenly she realised the fingers of her left hand were tracing little circles in the palm of her right.

She held her right hand up before her face, staring angrily at her palm. No matter how far or how fast she ran the little chip in her hand would allow them to trace her. Even if it didn't trigger the payment systems on the road as Charles had said, she knew they still had satellites that could track its overall movement.

She pushed the offending hand deep into the pocket of her jeans, wondering if doing so would in anyway muffle its signal. She stared about the empty street and gardens, noting that the sirens were becoming more audible now, swelling just a little each second.

The garden she was standing in was decorated in a historic period style that had been fashionable a few weeks before. There was a carefully trimmed lawn with old fashioned flowers in the borders around it that almost looked real. There was a strange wooden structure in the middle of the lawn that they had been told in school was called a 'bird table'.

Apparently, in the old days, instead of being kept in modern, productive farm factories, birds had been allowed to just fly about all over the place. People had used structures such as these to try and entice birds into their gardens and yet they weren't for trapping the birds so that they could be harvested and processed.

Kate hadn't understood the idea at the time and it made no more sense to her now. She prowled across the lawn, desperately looking for an idea, a solution, anything that might help her escape. As she approached the front door of the house her eyes were drawn down the front step.

Upon the step sat two glass bottles, strangely shaped and empty. These were another historical decoration whose meaning had been blurred by time. Kate remembered a teacher explaining that a long time ago dairy produce had been packaged in bottles like these and then delivered to people's doors.

When people were finished with the bottles they left them outside to be collected and reused. No-one in class had been able to understand how the company that made the glass bottles could stay in business if people reused the bottles instead of buying new ones. The teacher had not been able to explain this either and had become annoyed, saying only that the world had been a very different place in the past.

Kate looked at her hand again and then at the bottles. The sirens were clearly audible now, eating up smaller sounds in their way. She snatched up one of the bottles and ran from the garden, covering a few more streets before spotting a garden with large, sculpted bushes behind which she could hide.

Crouching behind a bush in the shape of a giant teardrop she smashed the bottle against a stone and gingerly picked up the largest resultant shard with her trembling left hand. She placed the tip of the shard between the base of the thumb and first finger on her right hand and then blinked at it, licking her lips.

She looked away, out across the garden at the other shaped bushes. She traced the outline of one bush cut into the shape of a cube with her eyes and then suddenly, brutally, twisted her right hand to drag its palm along the edge of the glass.

Her whole body lit up with pain. She screwed her eyes tight shut and dropped the shard to the ground, shattering it further. Eventually she pried her eyes open again and looked down at her hand.

It was red.

A long thin mouth smirked across her palm, the lips curling out in the middle. A steady flow of blood eased over the lips, snaking out into separate streams to pour down her wrist or between her fingers. Shaking violently Kate lowered her left finger and thumb slowly towards the bleeding mouth but then suddenly vomited violently.

She wiped her left hand, now dirty from where she had steadied herself in the dirt, across and down her jeans and then resumed the pose. Holding her breath she drove her finger into the sticky mouth, pain flashing through her again.

Under and amongst the dazzling pain her fingertip spoke of something hard and smooth. Gritting her teeth and closing her eyes she drove her finger deeper down one side of the object and forced and thumb in down the other.

Her fingers were slick with blood and the pea size chip was perfectly smooth so that for several stomach churning seconds her fingers slipped about hopelessly. Finally however she got a good hold of it and pulled. It resisted as first but through whimpers and squeals she managed to pull hard enough to tear it free.

Kate held the chip carefully as she vomited again then placed it on the ground beside her. With difficulty she managed to tear a long, uneven strip of fabric from her shirt, cursing herself for not thinking to do so in advance. Then she wrapped the strip tightly around her hand, picked up the chip and stood tall on wobbling legs.

Moving back out onto the street she approached the nearest drain cover and dropped the chip into the dark. She could here fast flowing water below and hoped desperately that the chip would be swept along with it, confusing Security at least for a little while.

She resumed her sprint through the streets to the familiar concrete steps. Down these she clattered, ignoring the morbid stares of a thin crowd of shoppers. She ran through the park without even a glance at the cafe and out of the exit at the other end.

Soon she found herself among the terraced streets but in daylight this time so that they looked utterly different. In the night each street had felt like a forbidding narrow canyon with insurmountable walls at either side. Now, with a vast grey sky looming above the houses, they each appeared sickly and small. The daylight had washed out the shadows so that their interiors previously made menacing and mysterious by the dark now appeared just empty and bleak.

She walked now, letting her feet guide her through the almost identical rows. At one corner she felt compelled to turn and so moved down the street. This was Uncle Jo's street, she was sure of it, which meant that the doorway now coming up on the left was that of the house in which she had hidden.

She slipped inside and crossed the bare ruin of the front room to check the stairs. Sure enough she found the same broken down stack, rickety and gapped. The climb was easier in the daylight, the damp and the rot clear to see and soon she found herself back in the bedroom with the big old chair.

She sat in the chair, her feet planted on the floor, her hands in her lap. The sharpness of the pain from her right hand had now thickened into a heavy ache and spread right up to her elbow. The pain seemed somehow distant however as her mind flickered back and forth over recent events.

There was no way out, she knew that. There was nowhere she could go now and nothing she could do. Her nice warm life, school, home, her parents, her brother, that was all finished. Any attempt to return to that could now only mean a lifetime of backbreaking slave labour in the dreaded factory prisons.

What did that leave instead? Another life sentence,

hiding among the ruins, dodging patrols and begging for food. The image of the old man swam before her briefly. She wondered if his route to the bottom had been very different from hers.

Her life was over and she had barely begun living it. A spark of anger attempted to flare but fizzled quickly under the weight of her sadness. She was so sad that it hurt, an excruciating hollow that ached in her chest.

She wondered if she could kill herself. The pain would end and at least she would have taken some kind of action, some kind of control. But then she remembered the talk they'd had at school. Suicide was illegal. Technically it was a type of theft because it meant all the things you would have bought had you remained alive would go unpurchased.

When people killed themselves the Company automatically sued their family for loss of earnings. They would calculate how much they thought the dead person would have spent over their lifetime and then charged the family that amount plus compensation. It was usually enough to clean people out and the younger the person who killed themselves the bigger the bill.

For a young teenager like herself the invoice would be astronomical, certainly big enough to ruin her parents. At the thought of her parents she began to cry. She wondered what had happened to them. They had both assaulted Security and would no doubt now be in custody. George would probably testify against them for harbouring her, his BUC credentials insulating him from the family taint.

She continued to sit in the chair, staring at nothing as an endless series of horrible things occurred to her. Uncle Jo's words echoed around her again. She couldn't fight, not for herself, not for her parents, it was not possible to fight.

And worse, just as he had said, it was not even possible not to help them, not to help the Company grow bigger and stronger. Even if she chose the shambling, derelict life, every piece food or clothing someone bought for her would be profit for the Company.

Every meagre scrap of effort she could summon to survive would translate into money in their coffers.

Money for more armour and more stun guns for more
guards. Money for more ad screens in more homes,
more sophisticated sensors in the pavements and roads,
more ways of squeezing profit our of every day life.

Suddenly she felt something break and crack open
inside her. Through the crack flowed a strange, calming
cool. It washed over and through her and her body
relaxed back into the uneven embrace of the chair just a
little.

Everything seemed abruptly clearer, easy to
understand and stripped back to the obvious. Sitting in
the chair doing nothing at all, not moving, barely even
breathing, that wasn't helping the Company. They
couldn't profit from her total inaction. She couldn't make
things better but she realised she had at least found a
way to not make things any worse.

All she had to do was never move again.

# box pusher

My first box of the shift was a fat twenty two. It was a neat and tidy little thing headed east and down, way down. As I turned to look, the inbound chute nudged the box halfway through the heavy rubber flaps of hatch one where it stalled. For a moment it just sat there among the thick black stripes, daggers of colour sudden but shy. Then belt one finally caught hold of it and the fat twenty two emerged, full sides and corners, trundling towards me.

It was a nice clean wrap, smooth plain surfaces, straight edges. If only all boxes could be as neat as that cute little fat twenty two, my life would be a lot easier. Belt one delivered the box onto the landing plate right in front of me. A dull metal square at waist height, the landing plate was the right angle corner that joined belts one and two. I stood at the corner inside the belts, stretching but not yawning, fully waking at last. I stared down at the box and smiled.

This fat twenty two was wrapped in heavy brown paper with glued tight folds. It was almost a perfect cube, six smooth, dry sides, one of which carried just two destination labels, white and typed, simple and plain. The labels were even legally placed so that the entire box model ID was visible instead of just the last four digits like usual.

You ask any pusher you like anywhere in the levels, they'll tell you the same: more than three quarters of all boxes carry at least one illegally positioned destination label. You throw in illegal decoration, vandalism and transit damage and you're down to something like one to two per cent of boxes showing a complete and legible box model ID. Usually all you can see are just those last four digits peeking out at the end.

It's madness of course and nobody cares but for any pusher worth their daily bump, those four digits are enough. You tell the trackers at interview and they say they care, but they don't care. They don't care about the boxes, they don't even care about what's in the boxes. They just want the boxes moving, as many as possible as far as possible but then that's the box transit department for you.

Leaning forward, I eased the palm of my hand flat against the side of the fat twenty two. I appreciated the coolness and lack of texture for a moment then slid the box smoothly onto belt two and let it glide out of the corner of my eye to disappear behind me.

I heard it making its way out through the heavy rubber flaps of the hatch two but didn't turn to watch. Already another box was peering in through hatch one and I knew straight away it was a heavy. I groaned.

Heavies are long and low, medium width, think two short planks of wood stacked and wrapped. They have these ridiculous ends that are hinged on the thin edge instead of the broad edge. It's supposed to look distinctive, iconic even but in practical terms it's insane. I mean who in the levels could have designed such a thing?

So of course the ends get torn off all the time because of their stupid shape and because the people who use them never use enough glue. Also, because heavies are so long, they get stuck in the box transit chutes much more often than any other model of box.

They get wedged in chute corners then battered in the midsection by bigger boxes, lazy eights, fat thirty sixes, even the occasional wet one and those really leave a mark I can tell you. Heavies get bent and they break then they shudder through hatch one, all torn wrap and too many corners. All you can do is hope it's not leaking and cross your fingers that it won't get tangled up going out of hatch two. You know what they say: if you want it late and in pieces, ship it in a heavy.

Everyone knows they're awful, that's why they're so cheap. The original idea of the heavy was to offer a cheaper alternative to using two browns. Browns are basically flat oblong shaped boxes. They're not very deep which makes them good for paperwork regardless of papersize or papershape.

Browns are also one of the least cost effective boxes around. You get a lot of wasted space in brown, your paying to move air as much as anything. They're status symbols really, legal firms and record companies ship contracts in them, that sort of thing. If you're getting paperwork delivered in a brown you know you've arrived.

Then along comes the heavy saying look at me, I'm just like a brown except I can hold twice as much and I'm half the price. Problem was of course they designed the heavy so badly that no-one who shipped in browns would be seen dead using one and anyone who couldn't afford to ship in browns had plenty of better alternatives for only slightly more money.

I mean you'd ship in an easy forty four or even in a two in ten before you'd ship in a heavy. Hell, even a nine less six would be better and they're basically just jumped up envelopes. So the only people who ship in heavies these days are those who are either too poor or too tightfisted to ship in anything else and that's why they don't use enough glue, which is why the stupid end flaps rip off all the time. It's ironic really.

Of course when they're really wrecked and this goes for any box at all, if they're really ruined then instead of pushing them on, sliding it to the side and behind on its merry way to hatch two, you push them off, directly ahead. The box drops off the landing plate and through hatch three into the incinerator. Gone.

The heavy that came through that morning didn't actually look too bad to be fair. It had some dings and a couple of tears but overall seemed structurally sound. It was on its way south and down and the destination labels were actually legally placed but it didn't matter. Before the labels had been applied, the entire box had been blast coated with powder tone, a violent blue, which obscured the model ID completely.

I shook my head at that and gave the heavy a shove, sliding it onto belt two without even looking. It weighed almost nothing and rattled as it moved. Despite everything else, that was far and away the worst thing about heavies. Being so very cheap they're regularly used to ship tiny objects entirely inappropriate to their size without so much as a single sheet of padding.

People will take something that would be loose even in an easy twelve and ship it in a heavy. A heavy is at least ten times the volume of an easy twelve and these people use no padding either. So whatever little trinket it is that they're shipping rattles around in there getting all dinged and then they get upset with us pushers for the transit damage.

Alternatively of course, their almost entirely empty and unnecessarily long box blocks a chute somewhere and delays hundreds of other boxes. It shouldn't be allowed. Oversized, underoccupied boxes should go straight into hatch three as far as I'm concerned but these are the levels we live in.

I got a couple of browns later on in the shift actually, those were going west and up obviously, way way up. They were both very neat, though one had taken a fairly serious knock at some point. Both had illegally positioned destination labels and as they were clearly from very expensive law firms, as in from people who should know better, I struggled to care too much about their transit damage.

Besides the browns I got something like five wet ones over the course of the shift, all going east and down except for one which was headed north and on. Never seen anything like it. You always wonder if they're going to fit through the hatches they're so big. None of them were particularly heavy though so I had no problems pushing and they were all clean and dry so there was no clean up either which was nice.

Wet ones used to be really quite rare but these days they're becoming more and more common. They're the biggest boxes available, the biggest the chutes and hatches can handle, too big if you listen to some pushers. They're solid too, I've never seen a ding actually penetrate the side of a wet one. They'll dent, they'll scratch but you'll never break one open.

A lot of people don't realise but they're actually built around a thin metal frame, then the sides are built up sheet on sheet to make them strong but flexible. The corners and edges are all reinforced and they only open at the top, the bottoms are double sealed. They're indestructible works of art really, a beautiful example of what a box can be.

All of the wet ones I pushed during that shift had been completely blast coated, not a single model ID in sight. Blast coating used to be just a single colour but the powder tones they can apply these days are amazing. One of the wet ones had a detailed landscape scene that wrapped unbroken around all four of its sides. It was spectacular, completely illegal obviously, but spectacular never the less.

Other than those it was just the usual stuff, lots of lazy eights and fat twenty twos all on their way east and down as well as some easy forty fours and every so often the odd nine less six or two in ten.

I did get a bit worried around midshift. I didn't get a box for almost twenty minutes and I was convinced there must have been a blockage somewhere. Blockages mean waiting. Hours upon hours of standing at your plate, no idea what's happening but knowing that every minute you wait is another minute of pushing you'll have to make up. You wait and wait then suddenly the avalanche, all the shift's boxes at once, churning through, the crumpled offender somewhere in and amongst just looking to block one of your hatches.

If you're really unlucky you end up waiting past shiftend, into offshift and then the backlog comes through so late that by the time you've finished pushing it's time for your next interview. Then of course, unless you want to skip a shift and lose all your bumps it's straight to shiftstart and you have to work right through. Nightmare.

Anyway, I don't know if there had been a blockage or not but the boxes started coming through again, usual number, usual speed. I assumed they'd run past shiftend to make up the difference but they didn't. Got my last box twenty minutes earlier than shiftend the previous day and clocked off with a smile on my face.

Standing at the landing plate inside the belts means you're boxed in of course, oldest pusher joke in the levels that. Seriously though, you've the belts to either side of you and the walls containing the hatches joining in another right angle immediately behind you so that you're stood in the corner of a closed square.

Your belt two is supposed to be hinged at that landing plate so that once the both belts have sighed to a stop you just tickle it underneath and up it pops so you can walk out nice and easy. My belt two hasn't popped up since the hinge seized a couple of years back though so whenever I get to shiftend I have to get down on my hands and knees and crawl out under it.

Every morning I report it during my interview and every morning my tracker Ste makes sympathetic noises but it never gets fixed. I'm used to it now though and as I say I was pretty chuffed to be off earlier than usual.

The floor beneath the belts is hard and dull and always cold to the touch. As I crawled quickly under belt two then sprang to straight standing however I barely even noticed. I wiped my hands down my skirt without even thinking about it and took a couple of clacking steps across the hard workspace floor then heard no more as the thick carpet of the livingspace ate up the rest. I dropped onto the sofa and kicked off my shoes, slow motion writhing my shoulder blades back into the cushions to soothe my stiffened back.

For a moment I just enjoyed the quiet and the stillness of offshift. I closed my eyes and let my mind wander off and out, drifting through the endless walls and picturing the countless millions of other workspaces and livingspaces and corridors and offices that made up the levels. Up and down, north and south, east and west, the levels went on and on all around me as if forever and here I was, sat deep in its midst. Cosy and safe, anonymous and warm.

A gentle peace settled over me, softening the fatigue so that my shoulders dropped and  my lungs felt larger. Opening my eyes I nodded to the great broad screen that dominated the wall before me, causing it to throb quickly to glowing life.

Moving as little as possible I continued to float in warm relaxation, flicking my fingers in my lap to cycle through the various onscreen menus. I ordered a viscously unhealthy treat of a meal then flicked over to the news while I waited for it to arrive.

Reports of events from all across the levels sprang to life before me. The stories and images were all up to the minute and completely brand new and yet all so familiar that they blurred together into a kind of multicoloured static.

In the lowest levels of the distant eastern stacks the war raged on, horrific and inhuman. Religious fanatics of one kind clashed with religious fanatics of another while our troops pushed their way in between, trying to help but just making it worse.

Entire stacks were being rendered uninhabitable as one group of lunatics used incendiary weapons against another, burning out all the normal people in between. Even though it was nothing new the reports of blazes made me shudder. There was nothing quite so appalling, so overwhelmingly terrifying as the thought of fire.

I was just on the verge of losing my bubble of calm completely when the light over the catering hatch shone green and snatched my attention from the news. Glad of the distraction I stepped past the wallscreen to the hatch and retrieved my gleefully sinful supper.

Lowering myself back onto the sofa, I carefully placed the tray across my knees and lifted the lid. The steaming smell engulfed me, filled my nostrils and set my mouth to watering. I flicked my index finger from right to left to remove the news and replace it with something, anything else.

The images of flames and smoke and women screaming over their dead children disappeared to be replaced by a grinning young man in sleeveless jacket with many pockets. He was babbling on about his recent voyage through the levels wherein he claimed he had travelled so far east that he had eventually found himself in the far west.

Along the way, or so he claimed, he had visited the very bottoms of the deepest stacks and the very tops of the highest. This was apparently the start of a six episode travelogue he had recorded along the way which would enable me to experience the exotic and mysterious heights and depths of the levels from the safety of my own sofa. My fingers twitched him away.

Next was an episode of a long running drama series following a feisty young woman from the mean halls of the lower south as she fought to overcome prejudice and build a career as a landings lawyer in the well-to-do social circles of the upper north. Not only did I hate that show, I'd also seen every episode at least twice. I flicked it away.

There was a documentary about the box transit system but at first I didn't pay too much attention and concentrated instead on forcing my hand to slow shovel the food. Part of me wanted to just scoop the whole meal into my belly in one go but I managed to insist on more moderate, thoughtful mouthfuls, savouring the glorious flavours.

About five minutes into the documentary the low, calm voiceover started talking about the nicknames which box pushers gave to different boxes.

"The names the box pushing operatives gave to different types of box depended on the year the boxes were first produced and how busy the box transit system had been in the year. So for example the so called 'Easy-44' was so named because it was first produced in 5144 which was a particularly quiet or 'easy' year for the box pushing operatives..."

I froze frowning, my full mouth hanging open in amazed disgust at the absolute nonsense I was hearing. Box model names had nothing whatsoever to do with the year they were released. If they did then an easy forty four would actually be an easy seventy three for a start. And when had there ever been a 'particularly quiet' year in the box transit system?!

I closed my mouth and chomped angrily, flicking the channel on again, this time with my middle finger. There were a couple of home improvement shows, the first focusing on how to make your apartment feel bigger, the second on how to soundproof it. Next was a series of adverts for walking holidays in the historical halls and corridors of the mid north.

I was about half way through my meal and ready to flick the wallscreen off altogether when I came across a debate show. An older man, a highly respected structural tech was debating the Theory of Renovation with a charismatic young Constructionist preacher.

They were going through the motions of the same old debate which, for most of my life, had always been relatively good sport. Of course such debates hadn't yielded anything new for several generations and these days the subject seemed to become more inflammatory by the day.

"But how can humans have built the levels? The levels are infinite." the preacher was saying.

"The levels are most certainly not infinite!" insisted the tech wearily. "Lieberwitz and Walsh proved seventy years ago that if they were they would collapse under their own weight. Eventually there must be a bottom floor, a ground level upon which all the stacks are resting.."

"Oh yes," said the preacher, taking his turn to scoff. "The Ground, which no-one has ever seen of course."

"The fact that humanity has yet to rediscover the ground is in no way proof that it does not exist," explained the tech through gritted teeth.

"Fanciful nonsense," said the preacher, shaking his head and now appealing to the audience. "Just look around you sir, endless stacks of rooms and corridors, side by side, linked by an infinite complexity of bridges and mezzanines. A system of rooms so complex that no-one has ever been able to produce an accurate map of them. How then can we believe that human beings designed the levels in the first place?!"

"It's really very simple.." the tech attempted to interrupt but was immediately cut off as the preacher wrestled back control of the debate.

"Too simple by far!" he said, building towards a triumphant climax. "Your theories are nothing but arrogance and wishful thinking. You are so ashamed of yourself that you cannot face our lord God and so instead you try to explain away his greatest creation. The more you try to fill that hole in your soul, the more convinced you become that it cannot be filled. It's madness, self perpetuating madness!"

"What's madness," the tech retorted, "is to believe, without a single shred of empirical evidence by the way, that an invisible, all seeing, all knowing constructor god took the time to build these structures just so that we could live in them and argue about where they came from!"

I savoured the last mouthful of my meal then

moved the tray onto the sofa beside me. My stomach felt pleasantly full and a thickening fog rolled over me as blood abandoned my brain in favour of my stomach. The familiar argument rumbled on between crashes of applause and shouting like a comforting tune from childhood.

"Our lord God the Constructor has a plan for us, for all of us, even you sir," said the preacher, briefly lowering his voice to demonstrate his composure and compassion. "His plan lies all about us in the endless complexity of the levels. It is the only explanation that makes any sense. Let me ask you professor, let me ask you two very simple questions."

"Please do," said the tech, crossing his arms defensively.

"If humanity constructed the levels then why are there no maps? As I said before, how can it be that we could have created a structure so complex as to be beyond our own understanding?" The preacher looked again to the audience with a knowing smile.

"The levels were not built as a single structure," sighed the tech. "Thousands of years ago the original stacks were actually separate buildings, built by different people with different floor heights and layouts. This is why the levels appear so chaotic and complex.

"Over time the stacks were extended higher and higher as more floors were added. Then more and more stacks were added in the spaces between. As the ground.." he paused while the audience reacted to the preacher rolling his eyes.

"As the ground became more and more crowded and individual stacks changed hands between the people of the time, some stacks began to be joined together via bridges. Those bridges in turn became more and more common and crowded and they almost became new stacks in of themselves. This is how the mezzanines came to be."

Just for a moment my chin touched my chest and I wondered if I had been asleep. I tried to shake myself awake and squinted to focus on the screen.

"Finally," the tech was continuing. "Many of the stacks were owned by people in direct competition with one another who in some cases went out of their way to block the development of stacks belonging to rivals. This is why we encounter dead ends and other inconveniences. Of course over time all of this complexity has been compounded as subsequent generations have modified the structures further, all in isolation from one another and without co-ordination so that we end up with a system so vast and complex that we cannot yet fully map it."

"Words sir," said the preacher shaking his head sadly. "Just words, theories. Again you retreat from the truth, making up wilder and wilder stories to reverse engineer your refusal to face up to the obvious. Our lord God has a plan..."

"You said you had two questions," interrupted the tech.

"I did," said the preacher, not quite concealing his irritation. "If as you say, the infinite majesty and complexity of the levels is nothing more than the result of competitive tower building between different factions of our distant ancestors," again he paused to raise an eyebrow at the audience.

"Where then did the material to build the levels come from? Before the levels was a time of absolute nothingness from which our lord God the Constructor called both us and the levels into being as a physical manifestation of his great plan. You and your kind on the other hand would have us believe that humanity somehow created itself from nothing and then turned that same nothing into something to build the levels brick by brick."

"Humanity existed long before the levels," said the scientist wearily. "Perhaps even for hundreds of thousands of years. They must have lived on the ground surrounded by vast open spaces, quite unimaginable today. We believe they actually dug into the ground itself and removed materials from within it, using those to construct small, isolated buildings of just one or two floors."

"And there we have it!" exclaimed the preacher, leaping from his chair to address the audience triumphant. "In one breath we are told that the stacks of the levels are not infinite but rest on some mythical 'ground' and in the next we are told that these ancient people dug that very same ground out from under themselves and used it to build the stacks!"

The debate descended into microphone fuzzing shouts and a scuffle broke out in the audience. The venom and pride were beginning to pick away at the edges of my postshift high so I nodded the wallscreen off. Even though the Theory of Renovation had been widely accepted among most people in the western stacks for over a century, Constructionism persisted and if anything was now gaining ground again.

Far off in the east where the religious fanatics reigned, Constructionism was the norm. Even just talking about the Theory of Renovation could get you killed over there. To one extent or another it was a sticking point throughout the levels, a question that could seemingly never be answered.

Thinking about the current and future states of the levels depressed and scared me in equal measure so I tried not to. Dragging myself from the sofa, I scooped up the tray and padded over towards the waste hatch, dropping the tray through as I passed without even breaking stride. I pushed through the curtain beside it and into the compact washarea. I removed my clothes as quickly as possible and then stepped into the shower and toilet cubicle.

My ablutions complete I dried off, dressed for bed, stepped through into the sleeparea and slipped between the covers. As my mind began to drift towards sleep I tried to steer away from the vibrant images on the wallscreen and focus on positive things instead.

I thought how nice it had been to finish work twenty minutes early and smiled. The covers and the darkness became increasingly soft and as they blurred together I felt myself sinking happily into sleep.

Then the thought occurred, sudden and ominous like a cough in the dark. How could I have forgotten?! All of that time had fallen into my lap, a whole long evening plus a gift of an extra twenty minutes and I'd just pissed it all away in front of the wallscreen without even thinking, again.

A clammy sickness crawled all over me, waking me thoroughly as I groaned in silent self loathing. Nothing was ever going to change until I began seizing these chances to make progress instead of just sitting, passive and useless. My stomach clutched at itself as I fell into the familiar hole of self hatred. Yet another golden opportunity to work on my time machine wasted!

—        —

—

I woke as usual the next day, a little thick headed but feeling ok. I showered and dressed then pushed past the curtain and crossed the livingspace to stand before the wallscreen. The screen was blank except for a small cluster of subtly glowing figures in one corner which gently pulsed the time.

A nine faded slowly to be replaced by a zero as one more minute ticked by. I began to fidget, pushing air around my mouth to make my cheeks bulge in turn or smoothing down my already immaculate skirt. My eyes strayed from the screen and began to trace the hairline cracks in the plaster just above it in the shadows where the wall met the ceiling.

Gradually I became still and felt even the bored expression slip from my face, leaving nothing but a neutral blankness behind. Tentatively, cautiously, a politely radical thought stepped into the space. The thought whispered of an alternative way to spend the day. It spoke in low tones, hushed for fear that habit and common sense might hear and sweep it aside with brutal derision.

How many more interviews would I attend it was asking. When would it stop? Where would it end? I could always opt not to proceed it said, take a day, perhaps even two and make a real investment, a genuine commitment to what was supposed to be my true life's work.

I shifted a little as the screen remained dark and the idea pushed on. I began to bite at my thumb nail as it continued, my heart quickening as the temptation began to build. Tiny scraps of time, stolen here and there between shifts and pasted clumsily together. That was all I had been able to give to my time machine and yet even then I had still made progress.

What could I achieve in an entire, dedicated day? In two? Could I finish it? Could I change everything forever and ultimately bring peace to all the levels? The idea ballooned out suddenly, bloating to fill everything everywhere and suddenly I realised its weight.

Perhaps I didn't want to finish it. This was a second idea, the cold and familiar voice of grey reason. What if I did turn take a break from pushing, dropped all my bumps and invested the time? What if I did all that and it didn't work? Where would I be then?

Or worse, what if I did it and it worked but it made things worse? Better just to dream of it, said the second idea, better to keep the dream perfectly unreal than to realise it ugly and face total disaster. The first idea began to push back then, railing against the settling urge and citing all the highest motivations of humankind.

Just then an almost inaudible pop sounded from the wallscreen and it began to fizz into life. I shook both ideas from my shoulders and returned my focus to the wallscreen as an image faded toward crisp, edges sharpening before me.

"Morning Ba," said Ste, his waist up image now fully formed.

"Morning Ste," I said, rolling out the work smile and forcing enthusiasm into all my features. "How are you?"

"Busy," he replied, returning my smile with one of his own that very nearly masked a bitter weariness beneath. He looked down at his desk, scribbling on various pieces of paper as he spoke.

"Sorry I'm a bit late today. The nightshift guys over at south and down had a blockage at the end of their shift and left it for us. I got called in early and I've spent the last three hours sorting that out just so you guys can get started."

"Sorry to hear that," I said, feeling almost sympathetic. Ste was my tracker. He was an ok guy on a personal level, outside of work I might even have liked him, but his path-of-least-resistance approach to management regularly frustrated me. From somewhere came an unkind thought comparing our salaries and daily bumps, noting how much larger his were than mine but I batted it away.

"Anyway," said Ste, placing a new form in front of him and looking up to meet my eyes. "You ready?"

"Yep," I said. I pushed my shoulders back and took a deep breath as Ste began.

"Ok then," he said then dropped into the formal, sing-song voice of the interview.        "State your name," he sang so that each word was twice as long as when spoken normally.

"My name is Ba Adebo," I called back, bowing my head in the traditional greeting nod.

"Agreed," came the response.

"With thanks," I heard myself sing automatically.

"And so Ba Adebo, do you wish to apply for a contract of employment with the box transit department." There was no question in his tone.

"Yes," I replied automatically. "I wish to apply for a contract of employment with the box transit department."

The first idea from before called distant and desperate but the rhythm of the ritual rolled straight on over it.

"Agreed," he sang.

"With thanks," I returned.

"And so for which position within the box transit department do you wish to apply," he continued, stretching out the final word into several additional syllables.

"I wish to apply for the position of box pusher," I responded, matching his rhythm by rattling through the sounds in quick fire succession and then drawing out the last.

"Agreed," he sang.

"With thanks," I returned.

"And so, the position of box pusher is an essential one and requires candidates to hold at least two higher level degrees in disciplines scientific or technical. Please demonstrate that you meet these requirements or declare yourself unfit," Ste droned.

"I acknowledge the essential nature of the position of box pusher and hereby declare that.." I sang then paused to draw breath before firing off an unbroken string of sounds.

"..I Ba Adebo hold a higher degree in Crystal Engineering a higher degree in Transit Infrastructure Design and a doctorate in Temporal Physics which I believe meets the requirements of the contract of employment of the position of box pusher within the box transit department for which I wish to apply," I sang, my lungs burning as I stretched the final sound.

"Agreed," he sang.

"With thanks," I returned.

"And so, the position of box pusher exists within the framework of the box transit department wherein it is vital that colleagues are able to work effectively together. Please demonstrate that you have a proven ability to work well as a member of a team or declare yourself unfit," Ste continued, stifling a yawn as he glanced through some more papers.

"I acknowledge that the position of box pusher requires such experience and hereby declare that I Ba Adebo have significant experience of working well as a member of a team such as being an active member of various research and sporting teams at several universities and working as part of the interstack network of box transit department box pushers for several years." The familiar string of empty sounds led me into a brief pause for breath before continuing.

"I have developed a good ability to identify and understand colleagues' strengths and weaknesses and thereby tailor my own approach to pieces of work and provide effective support where appropriate in order to maximise the productivity of the team."

"Agreed," he sang.

"With thanks," I returned.

"And so, the position of box pusher exists within an environment of the highest service delivery standards and often challenging circumstance. Please demonstrate that you have a proven ability to deal effectively and constructively with difficult situations of declare yourself unfit." Ste was adding notes to a document in front of him now so that I was faced with the top of his head. I noticed he was starting to go bald.

"I acknowledge that the position of box pusher is held to the highest standards and can be challenging and hereby declare that I Ba Adebo have significant experience of working to and exceeding the highest standards of service delivery under difficult circumstances such as throughout my time working as a box pusher for the box transit department wherein I have on numerous occasions shown appropriate levels of initiative in order to avoid service interruptions and regularly go the extra mile by working unsociable hours in order to ensure that deliveries are made." These words were equally empty but grated against the first idea from before so much that I felt it twist the corners of my mouth and was glad that Ste wasn't looking at me.

"And so, the position of box pusher is remunerated on a sliding scale according to the accumulated amount of continual and uninterrupted service. If you should hold such experience please declare it now or permanently forfeit your entitlement to a higher starting level of remuneration," he sang, expertly restraining a cough that had caught in his throat.

"I acknowledge the manner in which remuneration for the position is defined and hereby declare that I Ba Adebo have a total of one thousand, one hundred and eighty-eight days of continual and uninterrupted experience in the position of box pusher," I returned, feeling heat rise to my face.

This was the only part of the interview that changed day to day and despite having done it one thousand, one hundred and eighty-eight times in a row before, I always felt a faint sense of panic that I might get the number wrong. I hadn't however and so the heat in my face cooled as quickly as it had come as Ste continued.

"Agreed," he sang.

"With thanks," I returned.

"And so, Ba Adebo I hereby appoint you to the

position of box pusher and acknowledge your employment from shiftstart today until shiftend or until the end of any box transit department business started today, whichever is the later. In light of your experience you will be remunerated at the basic rate plus one thousand, one hundred and eighty-eight cumulative, compound increments. Agreed," he sang.

"With thanks," I returned and we both relaxed.

"So, everything ok yesterday then?" Ste asked, visibly sagging back into only semi formal conversation.

"Yeah fine," I said. "There was a bit of a pause in the afternoon. I was expecting to go overshift but the backlog never seemed to come through."

"Oh that," said Ste, rolling his eyes and shaking his head. He leaned closer to the screen, lowering his voice conspiratorially. "That was those guys over at FFD. They got themselves into a right mess, managed to accidentally set a load of boxes addressed to east and down off to north and up instead. Had to recall the lot. You can expect some fall out from that today as they try to catch up by the way."

"Unbelievable," I said, mirroring his shaking head. Frustration at the antics of the Final Forward Distribution section was one thing we genuinely shared. "I don't suppose there'll be any come back on them for that either."

"You know how it is," said Ste suddenly weary and disgusted. "They're completely unaccountable. They waste time faffing about and messing it up then expect us to shift the boxes through the system quicker to make up the difference! It's not like normally we're sat on our hands and have loads of extra capacity to roll out is it?! And when the customers kick off about their boxes being late who has to deal with it? They fuck it up we clean it up."

"Yeah," I said flatly. I did share both his frustration and resignation but also felt some resentment towards Ste for not seeking to tackle the problem. He had a reputation for being 'uncomfortable with confrontation' which basically meant he bitched and whined when other teams let us down but never challenged them about it.

"Still," said Ste, forcing a smile as he changed the subject. "You're closing in on twelve hundred bumps there Ba, that's damn good going. Not a single day away from the belts in over three years now. Would have been.." he flicked through some papers, "..wow, five years if not for that one day you took that broke your chain. What was that again?"

I felt my jaw tighten, stretching the skin taught across my forehead but worked hard to keep the irritation from showing.

"That was my mother's funeral," I said carefully.

"Oh that's right," said Ste conversationally, stabbing at the papers with his finger. "I have it here. Ah well, at least that can only happen once right? And your father's already..."

"Yes," I said, swallowing hard. "A long time ago."

"Cool," said Ste absently, finally looking up to face me. "Well, no reason you shouldn't be able to keep your unbroken streak going indefinitely then eh? Bet you couldn't live back on basic now though eh?" Ste grinned.

Something grabbed my stomach, turned it over and chilled me through. For a moment I thought the idea from before was written all over my face, that he knew what I'd been thinking. Was it a threat, a gentle reminder? No, it was just conversation. I swallowed guilty and licked my lips.

"Yeah," I said non-committally "That would be tough."

"Anyway," said Ste, returning to the papers in front of him. "Everything ok, any equipment problems?"

"Well, my belt two hinge is still seized," I said without hope.

Ste consulted the paper in front of him, scribbling for a moment then looking back up.

"Noted," he said simply so that I knew the conversation with maintenance about my belt was obviously another confrontation with which he wouldn't feel comfortable. "See you tomorrow Ba."

"See you tomorrow Ste," I replied as the wallscreen began to fade.

Just before the wallscreen snapped back to its usual deep, gloss black a great white square flashed into life. It was only visible for a second or so, just long enough to make out a great crowded mass of text, strings of characters to small as to be barely legible. My contract of employment for the day hung there for another second or so, allowing me to technically have sight of it, before snapping to black.

And that was that, I was employed for one more day. I crossed the room, lowered myself to my knees in front of belt two and crawled underneath. As I clambered back to my feet I tried to ignore a painful twinge in my back and then stepped up to my landing plate.

Ste hadn't been wrong about the guys over at FFD playing catchup. From shiftstart onwards I had an almost constant stream of boxes coming thick and fast so that almost as soon as I had pushed one from the plate onto belt two, belt one would deposit another in front of me.

To start with the boxes were the usual fodder. There was a long run of easy forty fours, all powder toned with the same artwork and going all over the place. Looked like a special limited edition release of either a wallscreen game or music album to me, it was hard to tell which.

This was a big thing with kids these days though. You couldn't just buy the game or the album or whatever, you had to buy the special limited edition version. It was exactly the same thing but came in a bigger, powder toned box and was accompanied by a load of other novelty, branded junk. And it was ten times the price of course.

You can think of an easy forty four as looking like a fat twenty two cut lengthways in half. From above it's a square but from the side you can see it's only about half as tall as it wide. Even that was bigger than these things really needed though.

In another few days I'd no doubt be seeing a whole string of nine less sixes shipping the exact same game or album just without all the nonsense. A nine less six is a neat little square box, barely thicker than your finger and just right to hold an efficiently padded disc.

Having said that, if you looked close enough you'd probably notice a few of those nine less sixes going to the some of the same addresses listed on these easy forty fours. Those would be people for whom the special limited edition wasn't enough, they had to have all the different editions.

That was even worse. It was bad enough that they insisted shipping in easy forty fours, filling them up with crap just for the sake of it and so adding extra volume to the overall transit traffic. If people were then also going to buy the normal version in the nice little nine less sixes anyway then the big old easy forty fours shouldn't even exist in the first place!

The steady stream continued, halted only once by a damned heavy that got caught coming through hatch one so that I had to walk over and drag it through the flaps. I walked alongside it as belt one carried it to the landing plate and noticed that one corner was darkened and misshapen where liquid had seeped through.

Belt one nudged the heavy up onto my plate and I took a moment to look at it with complete disgust. It had clearly been reused several times before and was now more wrapping tape than box. So many destination labels had been stuck over the top of one another that they bulged away from the surface, completely covering the model ID of course.

I shoved the heavy roughly away from me so that it teetered on the edge of the plate for a second before gravity snatched at it and it flipped over, falling down into hatch three. There was a brief metallic chomping sound and a wave of heat as hatch three automatically opened to receive the heavy into its blazing gullet and then immediately snapped shut again.

After that the flow continued unabated so that midshift came and went before I knew it. I wondered if FFD were taking the opportunity to clear out their backlog, which of course didn't exist. Once you put a box into the system it never sat still until it reached its destination, everyone knew that. There were definitely no bottlenecks and no unprincipled staff who allowed your box to gather dust in a pile for days on end, any pusher or tracker in the levels will tell you that. Yeah right.

If they were in crisis while dealing with the recall then the audit trails would all be messed up and you just knew that some of the guys over there would take advantage of the chaos to slip in boxes they'd forgotten about or just hadn't got to yet so as to up their performance stats.

At one point I glanced over my shoulder and was absolutely stunned to see a screamer coming through the flaps. They'd finally stopped making those almost two years ago for goodness sake so how long it had been sat over at FFD was anybody's guess.

A screamer is basically a poor man's lucky eight. Screamers were one of the earliest ever designs, based on an archaic historical box form known cryptically as the 'shoo' box. No-one really knows what those were used for but the screamer was just a rehash of the same ancient design.

They were somewhere between a couple of fat twenty twos sat side by side and maybe two thirds of a heavy if you chopped one of the ends off. Low, broad and medium depth they were just single thickness sides and had a simple lid that just sat on the top, no hinges, nothing. As a consequence they always had to be tied up to make sure the lids didn't fall off and were easily penetrated by transit damage.

Eventually somebody brought the design into this century, making the sides double thickness and re-enforcing the edges. Instead of having a lift off lid, they ran a simple metal rim around the top edges so that the lid was gripped in place and had to be slid off sideways. And lo, the lucky eight was born.

Lucky eights weren't just better than the screamers, they started out at almost the same price and once they got going were actually cheaper. There were some people at the time who said lucky eights were no good because if the rims around the top got bent in transit then you couldn't get the lid off. Screamers just got outright ruined so much more often than lucky eights got bent however that in a mater of months screamers had all but disappeared.

I shook my head in disbelief as I watched the screamer slip through hatch two. I was approaching what would normally be shiftend but the incident over at FFD had thrown everything out of normal timescales. Ste had said the problem at FFD had been with a large consignment headed to east and down but so far everything I'd pushed had been to a wide array of different locations.

Then, just as I'd had this thought, the boxes began to come thicker and faster than I had seen for a long time. Suddenly there was no more variation, no more exotic power toning, no more antique models, every single box that appeared through hatch one was wrapped and addressed exactly the same.

To start with it was an unbroken line of fat twenty twos, identical in fact to the first box of my shift on the previous day. All were perfectly neatly wrapped in plain brown paper with simple, legally placed destination labels. Even the stamping on the destination labels was perfectly uniform and legible.

Then the wet ones started coming, more and more of them, probably more than I had ever seen before put together. The procession switched back and forth between fat twenty twos and wet ones until every so often the line would be punctuated by a lone brown or easy forty four.

Every single box was wrapped and addressed in perfect uniform. It was the weirdest thing I had ever seen. Most of them weighed so much that both my belts wheezed and slowed a little. In fact I actually had to lean away from the wet ones and use all my weight to drag them off the plate and onto belt two.

Shiftend came and went but still the procession of perfectly wrapped boxes came. At one point a wet one came through hatch one at a bit of an angle and got stuck. I had to wrestle with it for the best part of a minute before I could get it through. When I finally managed to shift it loose the broad base slapped down onto belt one and I heard a metallic jangle from within.

Eventually the boxes of lead weights or machine parts or whatever the hell they were stopped coming and a few ordinary boxes of various sizes, colours and styles trickled through behind. Once again I had worked past shiftend to pull FFD out of the shit. The deliveries would now be made and any delays would be blamed on the inefficiencies of the pushers while the trackers and FFD came out of it looking consummate professionals.

The last few ordinary boxes felt lighter than air as I shoved them along, already imagining the feel of the sofa at my back. To be honest I was barely paying any attention at all when the last box of the shift nosed its way through hatch one. I didn't even look at it until it landed on the plate in front of me but when I finally did I actually laughed out loud. It was a heavily damaged green.

That was just the icing on the cake. I hadn't seen a green since my first month of pushing and had assumed that they had become obsolete. Greens are not even really boxes, they're just roughly made tubes.

They're made by mashing up other boxes into pulp and then making incredibly long pipes out of the resulting goo. These pipes dry hard and are then cut into sections a little bit shorter than a heavy. Then, one end of the section is just twisted off and taped over and around to form a kind of mangled fist of card and glue. Ugly as sin.

People lob in whatever's being shipped inside then bung the open end with anything to hand and tape that over too. You end up with possibly the nastiest looking box, if you can even call it that, you've ever seen in all the levels.

Pushers hate them, ask any pusher you like, anywhere in the levels, they'll tell you they hate them. Officially we hate them because they're not really boxes, they're a cheat and an affront to serious box design. Truth be told however, it's mainly because greens just won't sit still on the belts and have a tendency to roll off the side before they reach the plate which means you have to walk round and pick them up.

Having said that, not that I'd ever admit this to anyone else, I secretly have a kind of grudging affection for greens. They are phenomenally cheap to produce and their tubular structure is incredibly strong and efficient. While their length means they sometimes get stuck and bent in corners just like heavies do, I've never ever heard of one actually breaking or even being penetrated.

Also, while the ends are incredibly untidy and an insult to skilled box makers and packers everywhere, all that bundled up tape, card and glue actually makes for a pair of incredibly effective shock absorbers.

The only real reason greens are so rare these days is snobbery. They look so untidy and irregular that no respectable company will to ship to a paying customer in a green and anyone else is too ashamed to show how little they've spent on shipping to use them either. I'd heard from pushers in the east and south that they still see greens all the time but things are different there.

This green hadn't rolled off my belt but that was because it had been folded awkwardly almost to a right angle. Belt one nudged it onto the plate and it wobbled slightly for moment while I frowned at it.

It was going into hatch three, that much was obvious, but that wasn't what had caught my eye. The green had been powder toned a pale blue all over but in the elbow of the fold half way up it the wrap looked discoloured. I frowned at at the box for a moment more then nudged it away from me just a little, the first step on its way to the furnace.

Sure enough the discolouration left a trail on the plate. It looked like turquoise sand but I recognised it immediately as glass. Specifically it was a kind of very cheap, badly made glass that shattered easily into an incredibly fine and vicious dust.

I lifted the green from the plate, tilting it carefully to keep the newly discovered hole on top while looking at it from every side. It was clear to me immediately, the fold that had broken this notoriously hardy box was too sharp and too deep to be transit damage.

Most of each half of the green looked in perfect condition, as long as you ignored that they were at a right angle to one another. This box hadn't been jammed in a corner getting battered by an endless stream of bigger, heavier boxes. It would have had to have taken a perfect hit from the corner of an overloaded wet one to be bent like that but there weren't even any scuff marks on it.

This box had been broken by human hands before it had entered the box transit system. Those guys over at FFD are such cowboys! If they didn't do it themselves they must have seen it and yet put it into the system anyway. Unbelievable!

As I lowered the green back to the plate I looked for the first time at the actual letters of the product branding, wispy white words on the pale blue background. It was a replacement part for an air conditioner, a cheap one from a company that I thought had gone bust ages ago.

I dropped the green as if it was red hot, my hands racing to my mouth but too late to catch the gasp. This was what I'd been waiting for! After a couple of false starts I stepped back to the plate and slowly picked up the box.

There was no log of which boxes went into hatch three, there was no need. Boxes got pushed, on into hatch two or off into hatch three, that was it. Pushing is a professional public service built on dedication and integrity.

The box transit system is the very lifeblood of the levels, it keeps food and medicine, goods and parts, gifts and supplies flowing. It enables people to eat, live and connect with one another through the vast and dense networks of the levels all round and between them.

Our operation and stewardship of the system is vital work which would be immediately jeopardised were even one pusher to fall. Stealing a box rather than pushing it on or maliciously destroying a perfectly sound box, these are anathema to us, unforgivable sins.

Boxes that were going to push into hatch three anyway though, well that's a bit more of a grey area. There was definitely no way I would have pushed this green on, regardless of what it contained. The box was clearly, blatantly, obviously ruined but I still hesitated before removing it from the plate again.

It would have made perfect sense to open the box on the plate and simply take what I wanted, then I could have pushed the box itself and everything else into hatch three. That might even have felt like less of a theft too.

Somehow I couldn't do it though, couldn't even really consider doing it. Taking a broken box was one thing but to rifle through it actually on the landing plate, that was just outright sacrilege.

I'd done this before of course, eight times to be

exact with this ninth hopefully the last. Holding the green to my side I crawled under belt two and headed home. As I crossed the threshold onto the carpet, officially taking the box out of my work space, I felt a cold tingle run through me.

I put the box on the floor in front of the sofa and tried not to stare at it as I retrieved a towel from the washarea. I spread the towel out on the sofa then put the box on the towel and began to open it.

I managed to avoid getting too much of the powered glass on my fingers and hopefully didn't breath too much of it in either. Inside the box were the remains of what had been a slender glass tube with large metal caps at either end.

With careful effort I managed to lever the casing off the top half of the tube without slashing my hands to pieces. Once the casing was off the crystal inside was immediately visible. It was sat snug in its housing, glinting at me but slightly.

Finally, after all this time.

It was a 3'-6!0 and I took a moment to appreciate it. I hadn't seen one since my uni days. A crowd of slender prongs held the crystal in place  and so, with infinite care, I prised each of them back with my thumb nail. I'd had to switch thumbs by the time I'd folded them all outward, forming a sharp little metal flower.

I tipped the tube over my hand and felt the crystal fall into my palm. It was smooth and heavy and just vaguely warm. I closed my eyes for a moment, savouring the feel of it and the memories it brought.

We'd had buckets of every kind of crystal you could think of at uni. They'd made them by the vat load just for us to muck about with in those days. A lot of students used to fill their pockets with them but I never did, it had just seemed a bit shabby at the time.

Then I'd graduated for the third and final time and stepped out into the real levels. I got myself a real job with a real salary and discovered just how much these things actually cost to the average citizen. Even if I could work every day for ten years straight, the cumulative bumps wouldn't get me anywhere near what I needed to buy the crystals legitimately.

I'd considered buying them black market from a student but apparently things had changed since my day. The crystals were much more strictly controlled now but it didn't really matter. The more I'd thought about it, the more the idea of entering into some kind of criminal enterprise with a total stranger had put me off the idea entirely.

I slipped the 3'-6!0 into my pocket and bundled up the towel, gathering all the debris and packaging inside it. The whole bundle went into the rubbish hatch before I went over to the sleepingarea. I lifted the mattress and reached under it to retrieve a slender grey folder. Back on the sofa I nodded on the wallscreen and ordered a few bits to eat. Then flicked over to the news and lowered the volume.

I sat for a moment with the folder on my lap but my eyes still on the screen. The pictures were from east and down again and were terrible, terrible, terrible again. A woman on her knees, pounding her hysterical grief and sadness into the corridor floor. Burned out living spaces, charred hallways, lumps of black no longer people.

Apparently our security forces were gearing up for a big push. The Constructionist zealots couldn't hold out much longer a low voice was insisting from behind the images, their supplies were running low. Meanwhile the rate of supply to our own troops was being dramatically increased with a steady flow of arms and equipment being established across the levels.

Eventually I managed to tear my eyes away from the screen and refocus them on the folder in my lap. This was my chance, my one opportunity to make a real difference and perhaps help remove these terrible sights from my wallscreen forever.

I opened out all the flaps of the folder across my legs to reveal eight more crystals, each fixed in a very specific place to form a very specific pattern. The distances between and relative positions of all the crystals were vitally important.

I retrieved the 3'-6!0 from my pocket and placed it carefully into a space in the formation. Held within a clip on the side of the folder was a long thin stylus. I removed this and held it above the crystal, biting my lip and waiting though I didn't know what for.

The stylus was an incredibly delicate and sophisticated tool which vibrated at an almost impossibly high and specific frequency. Once I touched it to the surface of the 3'-6!0 it would meld the crystal to the folder so that it would begin to interact with the rest of the circuit. This would complete and thereby activate the system. Still I held back.

It wasn't a time machine. Not really.

I'd had the idea years before, it had just popped into my head. I realised later it was what an old professor of mine had called a little bird moment, that instant when an idea just drops into your mind, perfect and fully formed, as if a little bird had landed on your shoulder and whispered it to you.

A particular combination of crystals, I'd realised, should in theory create a subquantum effect which, if it could be stabilised and amplified, could feasibly enable objects or even people to travel back in time.

Now I knew nowhere near enough about stabilisation or amplification to be able to build an actual time machine. What I thought I might be able to do however was build a small experimental circuit which could create the subquantum effect just for a moment or two, long enough to prove that it could be done.

The plan was simple. Prove the concept, write it up then sell it to the highest bidder. I didn't want millions for it, just enough so that I'd never have to push another box as long as I lived. My price would include one other condition as well of course, namely a return ticket back in time to the period of my choice.

I felt my heart quicken a little more just thinking about it. First stop, the origins of the levels. Constructionist god or human endeavour? I would return with absolute proof and the whole issue could be definitively resolved once and for all. No more riots and bigotry in the halls outside, no more charred children and weeping mothers in the east.

I took a breath and centred myself, steadying my hand and lowering the stylus. I leaned over to watch closely as the vibrating tip touched the surface. At the moment of contact I heard an impossibly distant popping sound and felt my jittering heart skip a beat.

The connection had been made, it had started. As I waited for the crystals to charge and connect, I ran my eyes over each in turn and smiled. They were like old friends to me, their shapes, shades and characters all etched into my mind.

The selfless little 7'-3!4 for example, this one a thick, squat oblong, perfectly clear like a tiny block of glass. It's linearly terminus which means once it warms up it creates and arranges meta data vital to the main flow of data around the circuit.

The data flowing around the circuit builds up as incredibly slender trails of the deepest black that twist and grow, gradually filling the crystal with endless lines. Meanwhile the meta data builds up as countless little grey dashes, racing ahead of the black lines to lead them in a particular pattern.

Then, at the moment the whole circuit is fully up and running, all the grey dashes vanish in an instant leaving the crystal decorated with just the perfectly plotted black lines. When you turn the circuit off the crystal resets to clear, ready to start the process all over again.

Next to the 7'-3!4 was the smooth white egg shape of the 12'-0!0. This is a cyclically asynchronous crystal which means that when data begins to flow around the circuit it slowly becomes more and more out of step with all the other crystals until it reached a crisis point.

If you look at it very closely you can see tiny red specks here and there on the surface. They are almost invisible to start with but as the pressure arising from being out of sync with the other crystals builds, the specks grow and brighten into vivid splatters of scarlet. Then, at the last possible moment before shattering into pieces, the crystal suddenly resets again and the red colouring fades back to its calm white beginnings.

I realised I was grinning. I'd forgotten just how much I loved working with crystals, the endless detail and variety of types and their the infinite combinations. It's so completely different to pushing I felt like a whole other side of me, my long neglected secret self was coming back to life.

Across from the 12'-0!0 was the 5'-0!0, mad little thing that it is. It's cyclically catastrophic which makes it sound a lot more exciting than it is. For a start it just looks like a pebble, small, smooth and grey.

When placed in a circuit it attempts to cross reference every individual piece of data flowing against every other piece of data. It then uses these comparisons to create new data that helps make the circuit more efficient. As that data accumulates the heart of the crystal begins to glow green, just a little at first but then brighter and brighter.

It compares and creates so much data however that very quickly it fills itself up. Once it breaches the limit of how much data it can hold it loses its ability to hold any more data and so the vibrant little green light and all the data it represents are snuffed out in an instant. There always remains just one tiny speck of green however, a fragment of a fragment which then forms the first building block of the next cycle.

I just was about to turn my attention to the good old 8'-8!0 when something caught the corner of my eye. I glanced up to my right and just about jumped out of my skin, my clenching, cringing hands holding the folder firm in lap.

To my left, hanging in mid air before my gaping eyes and mouth was a floating head, a woman's head. I sat there as if carved out of stone, staring into the woman's eyes just as she stared back at me.

I felt myself exhale and lean back a little, still goldfishing soundlessly. I couldn't look away from the woman's eyes but in my peripheral vision I could make out a weird, quivering oval framing her face.

Finally I managed to closed my mouth. Licking my lips nervously I managed to look beyond the woman who now seemed to be squinting past me as well. I could see now that she wasn't a floating head but rather that we were looking at each other as if through some kind of small window.

She was sitting in a small room, an incredibly familiar looking room in fact. The sofa she was sat on, the walls and the rubbish hatch behind her, in every way they were the same as mine. They were mine. It was as if a small oval shaped mirror were floating in front of me but instead of my reflection it was this startled looking white woman, blonde hair, tired eyes, about the same age as me.

We ceased our head tilting and squinting at the same time and returned to looking at one another. I drew breath to speak, even though I had no idea what I was about to say when my negative reflection suddenly looked away from me, off to my right and gasped.

My head was turning before I knew what was happening and then I jumped again, even more than the first time in fact. To my right was a second oval mirror only here my reflection was that of a man. He was black, also about my age and appeared equally baffled.

The three of us each turned back and forth for a few seconds, taking in turns to stare at, past and around one another in awe. Again I felt myself drawing breath and again I had no idea what I was about to say.

Just before I did however, I heard an almost imperceptible pinging sound and the ovals wobbled, twisted and faded. My gaze fell into my lap and I noticed that the crystals were all discharging, the circuit had broken.

I rubbed my eyes and sat back then let my head loll against the sofa and stared at the wall were it met the ceiling above the wallscreen. My body was shaking, my heart was pounding, my knuckles were white on the folder. Somewhere deep inside my skull however, a different part of me was working frantically.

My evening meal had long since arrived and begun to cool in the dining hatch. I could smell it distantly but my appetite was long gone. Tucked away in a corner, oblivious to the shock and the fear all around it, a part of me was piecing something together. This circuit I'd made, this experiment, it wasn't a time machine.

It wasn't a time machine at all.


—       —

—

The next morning I was so tired I even considered
not applying for work even though it would mean the
loss of all those hard earned bumps and a return to the
starting salary. I'd stayed up into the early hours of the
morning running painstaking diagnostic tests to try and
find the problem with the circuit.

I'd felt like I was just beginning to narrow it down
but as the next day's interview and shiftstart loomed
ever larger, I'd given up and forced myself to get into
bed. I lay there for what felt like hours, my mind buzzing
away planning out the rest of the diagnostics, my fingers
twitching away under the covers.

By the time my alarm sounded I didn't feel like I'd
slept at all but I knew I must have done because I
remembered dreaming. I'd dreamed about riding the
belts through the box transit chutes, clambering past
boxes jammed in corners and others wedged into nooks
and crannies and left to rot, never to emerge through a
hatch again.

I stood before the wallscreen bleary eyed and ran
through the interview on autopilot, hearing myself return
the responses. Ste asked if I was ok but I fobbed him off
with some story about noisy neighbours keeping me up.
No idea where that came from. Just before he signed off
he said something about some priority shipping causing
increased volume but I wasn't really listening.

As the wallscreen darkened I rubbed my face and
felt my legs carry me across the room to belt two.
Getting down on my hands and knees and crawling
under the belt felt like a incredible ordeal and by the
time I'd straightened up to stand at the landing plate I
was feeling particularly grumpy.

The boxes started to flow, coming thick and fast
which was just typical. For the first time in months, or
years when I actually thought about it, I hadn't put
pushing first. I'd done something else, something for
myself and allowed myself a late night. I could have
really done with an easy day, after more than three
years without a break wasn't I owed an easy day?

But no, the flow was steady and thickening, I
mean I got it all. A bunch of wet ones and fat thirty
sixes, all weighing a ton. An easy forty four that was so

soaked through with something, I dread to think what, that one panel had started to collapse in on itself so that it leaned drunkenly to one side.

There were more fat twenty twos and lazy eights than I could count and then a fragment of a box, just a flat wedge that had been part of a side. The end of the model ID poking out from behind the destination label said it had been a red fifteen and I wondered what state the rest of it would be in if it eventually turned up.

I pushed them on or off, not even turning to see what was coming just waiting for belt one to dump whatever it was in front of me. My head was pounding and my back began to ache something fierce, the whole thing seemed intolerable.

Then a seventy five safe appeared in front of me, badly scorched and looking very sorry for itself. The whole point of those was supposed to be that they were fire proof which is why they were used to ship hazardous materials.

To be fair any other box would have probably been rapidly consumed by the fire and then crumbled to ashes, allowing the flames to spread through the chutes. The thought of a serpent of flame winding its way through the box transit system, growing and unstoppable as it consumed and consumed before erupting out of hatches to consume the halls, corridors and apartments, it actually made me physically shudder.

It didn't bear thinking about. In fact the very thought of it caused me pain, dull but insistent right behind my eyes. I pushed the seventy five safe off the plate and wiped the soot from my hands, then I made a mistake.

I'd been pushing for hours and it felt like I'd been holding my breath the whole time. I just needed to to get through to shiftend so that I could get out from behind the belts and back into bed. My mistake was glancing over at the clock on the wallscreen.

I hadn't been pushing for hours, in fact I was barely even half way to midshift. My chin dropped to my chest and I felt my nose began to sting as if I might cry. I felt a trembling inside, a kind of claustrophobia as I stood there hemmed in by the belts.

My body was desperate to flee, away from the belts, away from pushing, out of the apartment but even as these thoughts screamed through me I knew it was all just bluster. With a sigh I took a steely hold of myself and forced a couple of deep breathes in and then out.

A sixty two low hopped up onto the plate, it's little protuberance pointing off towards hatch two as if keen to move on. I sighed and nodded to myself before pushing carefully it on. Sixty two lows look like two boxes stuck together. Basically they're just a three eyed nine but with a little miniature fat twenty two poking out of one corner of one side.

They look ridiculous but they're actually relatively clever. Let's say you're shipping something that would otherwise fit into a normal three eyed nine except that there's one bit of it that's just too long. Whichever way you pack it you always end up with one bit poking out the top so that you can't close the lid.

In the past you would have had to use a loud instead of a three eyed nine, which would cost you significantly more and then on top of that you'd have had to pay for a load of extra packaging to fill up all the dead space.

A sixty two low accommodates your sticky outy bit with a tiny little extra compartment. To be fair they're not a lot cheaper than a loud but what you save on packaging makes them the more economic choice. They still look weird though.

Purist pushers, usually older guys who inherited their belts from their parents and have been pushing all their lives, they'll tell you that a real box has six sides, no more, no less. A sixty two low is anathema to them. Eleven sides? They'd tell you it was madness and don't even get them started on the greens.

Not a lot of people know this but when the sixty two low was first introduced some of those old guys refused to push them. Every single one that landed on their plate went into hatch three, no matter what the condition.

Clearly they were crazy. After all as the saying the goes: pushers are people who push. There was something intriguing, something dangerously exciting about that kind of determined stance though and every time I saw a sixty two low it made me think of those guys.

These days of course it's specifically mentioned in the daily contract that you'll push any and every undamaged box that lands on your plate no matter what model or your personal feelings about it. We are public servants after all.

The flow of boxes continued, never letting up for a moment. Then, just after midshift, there was another weird procession of fat twenty twos and wet ones. Again they were all perfectly wrapped in plain brown paper, all going east and down and again they were all incredibly heavy.

It didn't matter though. Pushing so many so heavy didn't help my back but the smooth dry sides made them easy to push so I wasn't complaining. The procession went on and on, significantly longer than the day before even but each neat, sharp cornered box that came and went was one box closer to shiftend.

Eventually a brown trundled in through hatch one and ended the string. I pushed it on and rolled my head around and around, pulling at the aching stiffness in my neck with a grubby, soot stained hand. Surely this was shiftend now, it had to be, I was just about dead on my feet. But no.

Suddenly a more normally, as in illegally, wrapped two in ten shouldered its way through the flaps of hatch one, all eye watering powder tones and attitude. My mouth had opened to curse but instead just fell open further as a lazy eight came through immediately behind it, almost touching. Sure enough, immediately behind that was a fat twenty two, then a fat thirty six and another two in ten.

It was a cluster.

What the hell were those guys at FFD playing at? Clusters weren't illegal, though pushers all across the levels had been saying they should be for years. We could only do our work properly and efficiently if a decent amount of space was left between each box.

The belts in the transit system were designed specifically to prevent clusters from forming accidentally, even in the event of a blockage. That meant the only way a cluster like this could form was if the boxes had been loaded into the system all at once by FFD in the first place.

I began to tremble again but this time it wasn't fear so much as rage that rattled through me. The cluster hit my plate and for a moment I just glared at it and seethed. Obviously the whole thing wouldn't fit and so belt one continued to run against the underside of the boxes that couldn't crowd on.

I pulled the first two in ten from the cluster and examined it. It was pretty beaten up, they all were, which was another problem with clusters, but it was good enough to be pushed on. Of course I couldn't actually push it on because of all the other boxes in the way and so I had to lift it and then place it directly down onto belt two.

To a none pusher that might not seem like a big deal but quite honestly it made me feel dirty. Like I said before, pushers are people who push. We're not pickers, we're not lifters or movers, we're pushers. We do things in a very particular way for a reason and we take in pride in that.

All we need is for the boxes to arrive in a sensible, orderly fashion with a decent space between each. That allows us to give each box individual attention and then push it either on or off as we judge appropriate. This is what keeps the box transit system flowing and prevents damaged boxes from causing blockages.

I can't describe to you just how insanely frustrating it is to be forced to compromise yourself and step outside the hallowed practices to which you've dedicated yourself just because someone else doesn't care enough to respect the art of pushing.

It doesn't make any difference at their end of course. FFD just get the boxes in and whack them out into the system again, they don't care what happens down the chute, they're not the ones who get it in the neck when boxes are late or damaged.

I picked my way through the rest of the cluster, gritting my teeth and pushing through it, already practicing what I was going to say to Ste at tomorrow's interview. Then something caught my eye, the destination label on the fat thirty six.

It was going south and on, no big deal there, but destination labels also carry a timestamp showing when the box first entered the box transit system. Now I know for a fact, no matter what they're projection managers would tell you, that it takes a box, any box, at least two days to get from FFD to my plate and so the timestamps always show the date of two or more days ago.

The date on this fat thirty six however was the best part of a week ago. Those cheeky bastards had obviously fallen behind and then rather than tell anyone so that we could plan out a way to catch up, they'd just rammed the whole backlog in at the last minute and then left it all for the pushers to sort out.

Suddenly, the quiet period and subsequent early finish of a couple of days before presented itself at the front of my mind. That must have been it. That must have been when something had come up that had delayed them putting the boxes into the chutes. Then of course, rather than work past shiftend to catch up like we pushers had to, they'd just sacked it off, gone home and then later dumped it all on us in clusters.

I'd just about reached the end of my rope. I was so tired and angry and hopelessly frustrated that I was ready to just throw it all in the air walk away. Normally this would be unthinkable, to abandon my plate and just let the boxes pile up would be a dereliction of my sacred duty tantamount to blasphemy but in that moment my head was filled with hot, breathless buzzing through which I couldn't see further than returning to my bed.

I held my breath and clenched my stomach. I gripped the edges of my landing plate to hold me steady, as a strange and maddening fear rippled through me. I felt like the next box that came through hatch one would be the final straw, that I would explode at the very sight of it.

As it happened however that was the end of the day's boxes. I prised my fingers from the landing plate and turned unsteadily to lean against belt two instead. I felt strangely ashamed and unsatisfied. I been pushed all the way to my breaking point but instead of a glorious, self destructive eruption the day had just faded and fallen into a dull grey nothing.

My legs shook beneath me as I clambered down onto the floor and crawled under belt two. I paused for moment, down there on the hard and dirty floor, looking at my hands as if I'd never seen them before. It was late, very late. Just a handful of tiny hours sat between me and the morning's interview and shiftstart.

I took a moment and a breath then pushed myself back up to my feet, tottering towards away from my workspace and then stumbling over the threshold into my livingspace. No sofa for me, no TV and no food. Closing my eyes I pressed on past the wallscreen, fell onto my bed then dragged off my clothes. Rolling onto my side I yanked my covers out from under and then over me and let my body sag down into the mattress.

I felt hollow, as if there was spaces where my muscles used to be and those spaces were all filled with aching. My body desperately wanted to shutdown, to rest but the the fears and furies from throughout the day all crowded around the dread countdown in my mind's eye and held the cool peace of sleep at bay.

The thoughts that assailed me were all washed out, shadows and grey yet relentless. Somewhere distant, beneath the rage that would not quit and the aching that would not yield there was a distant, echoing fear.

I was so tired, so incredibly broken down tired that the thought of getting up again in just a few short hours to stand another interview and work through another shift, the thought of it scared me. It felt beyond my physical ability to survive it and though I couldn't look it in the face something was telling me it would break me.

I rolled onto my back allowing my limbs to stretch and trying to breathe more deeply. My only hope of sleep was to find some way to escape the panic and the rage and the dread. I began to think of the crystals.

They were supposed to be the most important thing in my life, my escape from pushing, my contribution to the levels but I had no hope nor chance of putting any work into them now.

Yet again they would have to wait until I could

carve out a hole between shifts at some point. I pictured the circuit, running over all its familiar details. Perhaps it would calm me, distract me from everything else long enough for sleep to take me. Alternatively, if I was going to lay awake all night before starting the shift that would finally kill me, at least I would spend the time constructively.

My mind's eye settled on the 5'-2!3 which I'd inserted into the circuit half way up on the left so many months before. They're pretty crystals anyway but I'd been lucky enough to get hold of an especially beautiful one, perfectly flat too which is very rare.

They usually come as long, broad oblongs, incredibly thin and fragile almost like a slip of paper which is why getting a flat one is so important. Sometimes they have little ripples or kinks in them which make them difficult to fit into circuits and vulnerable to being cracked or even broken.

Unlike most crystals, which have fixed, set colours, the 5'-2!3 has this kind of rainbow pattern to it which shifts constantly as you watch. Incredibly vibrant and intense shades of every colour swirl and twist into one another, darkening and lightening and mixing with one another endlessly.

Then within this, if you look closely enough you can usually make out a single point of white light buried right in the centre. It's usually tiny and weak, throbbing feebly as if just clinging on to itself, desperately trying not to drown in the endless colours around it.

It's linearly self-isolating so when you connect it up it attempts to sync with each of the other crystals in the circuit but fails every time. Each time it attempts to link up with another crystal the white light at the centre briefly steadies and glows brighter. Then the connection breaks down as the other crystals effectively reject it and the light fades tiny again.

These brief connections with the other crystals have almost no impact on the circuit as a whole and eventually, once it has tried and failed to sync with every other crystal in the circuit at least once, the 5'-2!3 appears to give up.

It stops trying to make any connections and then

powers down so that the white light fades almost to nothing. The gap it leaves in the circuit by doing this however then drives all the other crystals to change their behaviour.

At this point I realised that I was starting to doze. The aching in my limbs had melted into a more comfortable heaviness. The very recognition of this seemed to pull me back towards waking however, as if noticing that the distant voices were no longer there was enough to start summoning them back again.

I forced myself not to check the time and followed the circuit upwards the next crystal along instead. Visualising the 6'-3!0 I flinched a little as always which is just plain stupid. Crystals are just naturally occurring data processors. They come in an almost infinite variety and are incredibly useful and powerful, but they're still just inanimate objects. Why then do I have favourites and least favourites? How then can it be that every time I think of a 6'-3!0 I recoil as if from an ugly and dangerous insect?

The 6'-3!0 I'd managed to scavenge was thankfully small though classically shaped, a rough disc with regular triangular projections around the edge. They're always a solid, uniform dark blue with yellow trim but every so often you can catch a glimpse of a violent red glow deep within the very heart of them.

It's a linearly deceptive destructive crystal and that might be what I don't like about it,  but I couldn't tell you for sure. Basically, when you hook it up initially it appears to perform one very specific task, namely to enforce data quality rules throughout the circuit.

If another crystal in the circuit is not processing data correctly the 6'-3!0 forces the offending crystal to change its behaviour by either withholding power from it or overloading it with too much power.

At the same time however, despite ostensibly acting to strictly maintain the quality of data flowing through the circuit, the 6'-3!0 will also sometimes actively destroy valid data. Every so often it will cut a piece of data out of the circuit and hold it within so that the red light glows even more fiercely. It then dismantles the data bit by bit and deletes each bit in turn.

On reflection I think this is why I dislike the 6'-3!0 so much. It would be one thing if it just randomly deleted pieces of data, it's the fact that it does it in a such an unnecessarily long winded, almost sadistic way that I don't like.

All of this can sometimes result in other crystals being irreparably damaged and the whole circuit subsequently breaking down which means that using a 6'-3!0 is risky and to be avoided wherever possible. Unfortunately I hadn't had the luxury of being able to be too picky about which crystals I used.

Suddenly I was aware of the texture of the covers against my skin and realised that I hadn't been a moment before. I'd been asleep but couldn't tell for how long. Vague pictures moved slow behind my eyes, vagaries of dreams now sliding away.

I held still, trying allow myself to fall back under, knowing it wasn't something I could do but only something I could let happen. I quickly returned to the circuit moving, on past the hated 6'-3!0 to the 4'-4!2 above it.

If a 6'-3!0 is spiteful and unpleasant then a 4'-4!2 is almost comedically proud and pretentious. It's triangular with smooth rounded edges and starts off with a beautiful mottled green texture throughout. If you look very closely at it while it's at rest though you can just about see a tiny speck of perfect black deep in its centre.

It's linearly self-confining so as soon as it's connected to a circuit it immediately starts attempting to centralise all the data in the circuit and co-ordinate its flow and as it does this the black speck at its centre grows larger and larger. Then, as it gathers more and more data,  its connection to the rest of the circuit begins to break down.

What's really fascinating is that if you look at the data it holds as it becomes more and more isolated, you find that it is describing itself as being a more and more complete picture of the circuit.

The more data it holds the less new data it can take in but as it can't measure its own limitations it instead assumes that the reduced flow of inward data simply means there is less new data to be received. Basically it thinks it must have collected everything.

You end up with the 4'-4!2 looking almost completely jet black apart from a fine green trim around its very edge. If you then run a simple diagnostic test on it to check how many other crystals it thinks there are in the rest of the circuit, it will tell you that there aren't any. More than that though, it will also tell you that no other crystals are necessary as it has successfully replaced them all.

I think I smiled then, funny little crystals. Imagine if they could really speak, what would they say? Then I was having conversations with all my favourite crystals while trying to tactfully avoid speaking to those I didn't like. I was dreaming. I was asleep.

—     —<br>—

When I woke the next morning I was tired, but it was a normal kind of tired, just weary from not enough sleep. The trembling hysterical fatigue of the previous night was gone. As I stumbled out of bed to mechanically dress and eat absently, the rage and terror from the night before appeared strange and distant. I didn't feel great but it was nowhere near the harrowing premonitions of physical collapse and psychic apocalypse I'd felt the night before.

I stumbled through another interview and while I did mention the long shift and the cluster I found it hard to summon the venom I'd felt for the FFD guys on the previous day. That also seemed far distant and even a little embarrassing.

To be fair, their projection managers were absolute pricks and their job was as tough as mine. So while it was quite right for us to raise concerns over the appearance of clusters, there was no real need to turn it into a fight. Of course it wouldn't have really mattered if I had. When I raised it with Ste, calmly and constructively, he just just made sympathetic sounds while reading some papers on his desk.

"Mmmm," he said without looking up. "Yeah, no that shouldn't be happening but you know.."

I cringed, awaiting the deployment of Ste's favourite cop out phrase.

"..we are where we are," he said.

I managed to restrain the frown I felt tugging at my face until after the wallscreen darkened. Crawling under belt two I pondered which was the more irritating, having to unpick clusters that should never arise or the abject lack of interest of the trackers in doing anything about them.

For the first time it occurred to me that the guys over at FFD might have had very similar conversations. Perhaps they'd had equally frustrating one sided conversations with their projection managers where they tried to point out to their that lack of resource or poor organisation was forcing them into sending out boxes in clusters. Perhaps they didn't like creating them any more than I liked having to deal with them.

I was so lost in this daydream that I didn't even hear the first box come through hatch one and when it hopped up on my landing plate I physically jumped. It was another incredibly heavy wet one, neatly wrapped in smooth brown paper and going east and down. As I pushed it on I glance dover to hatch one and sure enough there was another coming straight in after it.

These processions were becoming a daily event but I didn't think much of it. I was too tired to be particular excited or even interested in these unusual packages and apart from their weight, the boxes were actually really easy to push. They were all dry, neat and smooth and all in incredibly good condition so that they barely needed checking at all.

My hands, arms and back did the work while my mind wandered, lolling from absently pondering the logistical challenges of the great box transit system across to reminiscing about  this or that crystal and some of the circuits I'd built at university.

Every so often thoughts of my not-a-time-machine would tug at my sleeve, the floating heads with surprised expressions. I batted these away without even thinking however. Whatever that circuit really was, whoever those people had really been, it was all far bigger than I could cope with. I'd get back to it soon and then everything would change, suddenly and amazingly but later, when I had the energy, later.

It occurred to me that I had no idea how long I'd been pushing. The neat brown boxes were still coming and I was in the middle of an apparently endless flow of fat twenty twos when I realised it was well after midshift.

A gentle warmth flowed through me and eased a small smile onto my face. The shift was passing quickly as if taking pity on me in my weary state. I kept on pushing, trying not to check the time, trying not to think about the not-a-time-machine, just focussing on pushing one box after another and making it through to shiftend.

The fat twenty twos dried up after a while and there was a pause in the flow. After a couple of minutes I gave in and checked the time. It was only half way between midshift and shiftend and while a tiny part of me sprang forth hoping for an incredibly early finish I slapped it back down again. There was no way I was going to get that lucky.

Sure enough after another minute or two I saw something begin to nudge its way through the flaps on hatch one though it seemed to be struggling. As the end of the box began to appear it hooked my eyes and drew them wide. I didn't recognise it at all.

I am an excellent and exceedingly experienced pusher, I mean what I don't know about boxes and pushing isn't worth knowing. The sight of a type of box I'd never seen before then was enough to push all thoughts of weariness and logistics and not-time-machines immediately from my mind.

Whatever it was, the box was still struggling to make it through the flaps and before I knew it I found myself walking away from my plate and over to the hatch to get a better look at it. It was long and relatively thin, a bit like two lucky eights stuck together end to end but when its front end finally made it through the flaps and and hit belt one it sounded like it was made of rock.

Belt one actually groaned under the weight as it

dragged the rest of the box through the flaps and then began to wheeze it along, slower than I'd ever seen a box move. This was another in the procession of neat brown boxes, same destination labels, neat and straight and legally placed. Luckily the box had come out with the destination label side on top and so the box model ID was visible.

I wouldn't want to admit it to too many people seeing as how it's possibly the saddest, geekiest thing that's ever happened to me, but when I read the last four digits of that box model ID the hairs on the back of my neck stood up.

It was an eyes and ears.

I'd read about them in box pushing trade journals but had never for a moment thought I would actually see one. Eyes and ears are just about the pinnacle of box technology, phenomenally expensive and used almost exclusively in private, closed loop, industrial box transit systems.

When this one had hit belt one I had thought it sounded like it was made of rock and that was because effectively it was. Eyes and ears don't use paper or card or anything so fragile. They are built on frames made of a top secret, patented metal alloy which is incredibly strong yet incredibly light. The sides are then panels of an impossible dense stone which are effectively welded onto the frames at unimaginably high temperatures.

As result they are virtually indestructible. I mean you think of a seventy five safe as being a sturdy box, it's fire proof and everything, or even a wet one, with its reinforced frame. Eyes and ears though, they make those other boxes look like soap bubbles.

I'd read articles about when they'd first been designed and gone through the usual destruction testing phase of box development. Those guys threw everything they could think of at it.

Shove it in a standard hatch three incinerator and leave it in there overnight?

Comes out without a mark on it, barely even warm.

Chuck it down a maintenance shaft a hundred floors deep?

Punches a hole through the next ten floors below and still looks brand new.

Stick it in an industrial compaction press?

Busts the hydraulics.

Run it against a giant circular saw?

Breaks the blade.

You could ship anything in an eyes and ears and as long as you packed it properly you could be one hundred per cent guaranteed that it would come out the other end in perfect condition.

Of course they're so insanely expensive that no-one actually uses them. Their reserved for transporting materials that other boxes can't handle. Got something face meltingly radioactive? Something bone dissolvingly toxic? You chuck it in an eyes and ears, seal it up and it might as well be marshmellows. That stone plating just stops everything dead, absolutely, no exceptions.

As belt one struggled to force the eyes and ears up onto my landing plate I realised my mouth was hanging open. I genuinely can't describe how excited I was. My heart was pounding, my palms were sweating.

Finally it settled onto the plate, looking for all the levels as if it had been there forever and everything else had been built around it while belt one whimpered to rest. I stood before it for at least thirty seconds, feeling the weight of a once in a lifetime happening pressing down on me. As I reached out to push it I noticed my hand was actually trembling a little.

At first I couldn't push it at all. I mean it was like trying to push a solid wall. Eventually however I managed to overcome my awe of the thing and really put my back into it. I found that if I grabbed it with both hands and leaned away from it, hanging all my weight off it and pulling as hard as I could it would actually shift a little.

Over the next five minutes I dragged and dragged at it, shifting it by degrees onto belt two. By the time it landed and belt two wheezed into life my arms and back were on fire and I was sweating. I barely noticed however and still couldn't take my eyes off it. I walked alongside it as it crawled towards hatch two and then stood silent, awestruck once more as it was slowly consumed by the thick rubber flaps.

The moment it disappeared from view I began to picture it mentally, desperate to keep hold of the image. Then I heard a familiar heavy thud from behind me. I turned slowly, unbelievingly and sure enough, there it was, a second eyes and ears in perfectly neat brown paper packaging, going east and down.

All in all there were five of them and while my back and my arms and my belts all complained bitterly that they simply were not built to handle such things, I could not get past the novelty of it. I panted through the pause that followed them, wiping the sweat from my brow and shaking my head in disbelief.

It was just past shiftend when the boxes began to flow again. I realised that during the course of the entire shift every single box I had pushed had been one of the neatly wrapped, brown paper jobs.

The next thing to come through hatch one however was a cluster of brightly coloured, normal boxes. I frowned at the cluster and felt the indignation of the previous day begin to rise again only to be abruptly shoved aside by a chilled and terrible thought.

If the brown papered boxes were in addition to the usual flow of boxes did that then mean that from this point on, as in just after shiftend, did that mean that I would now have an entire day's worth of normal traffic to push before I could stop?

Apparently it did.

Compared to the eyes and ears, pushing the normal boxes felt like pushing balloons. For the rest of the evening I didn't receive a single lone box, everything came in great tangled clusters. While these were still an insult to my professional dignity I couldn't help but think as I picked through them that if the guys at FFD had released all of these boxes correctly with at least the standard minimum space between them then the last one wouldn't have reached me until well after shiftstart the following day.

On the outskirts of my mind I could just about hear the wailing, furious despair of the previous day take up its song once more. The fear dressed as anger at being forced to work beyond my physical limits. This time however I simply didn't have the energy to feel so upset.

I unpicked and lifted and placed and occasionally even pushed, on and on, no longer thinking of anything at all. Grey and empty and mechanical, I worked until there was no more work to be done. The last cluster of boxes appeared about two hours before shiftstart. I picked through it, pushed most of them on, a couple of them off, then stood and swayed for a few minutes.

Finally I got down onto my hands and knees, crawled under belt two, across the workspace floor, across the living space floor and pulled myself up onto the sofa. Without opening my eyes I sent a message to Ste through the wallscreen letting him know that I would not be applying for work for that day.

It meant losing my bumps. It meant that the next day I applied for work my pay would be back down to that of a brand new, first time pusher but there was nothing I could do about it. It wasn't a dilemma or even a choice, I simply knew for a fact that I wouldn't be capable of pushing. That done, I laid down on my side and curled into a ball on the sofa and fell immediately into a black and silent sleep.

—          —

—

I woke around midshift but dozed on the sofa for another hour or so before waving on the wallscreen and sitting up bleary. I switched to the news but more for background noise than out of any real interest. Something was happening on the upper levels, anti-war protestors were blockading the corridors into the department of conflict.

There'd been sit ins like this before but apparently this time things had turned violent. I rubbed my face and yawned, vaguely aware of scraps and details. More protestors than ever before. Something about an escalation of the conflict east and down. Our troops accused of using banned radioactive ammunition. More civilians killed. On and on.

Just as I'd sharpened my eyes and begun to really listen I noticed there was a message waiting for me from Ste. I nodded it on and listened as my stomach rumbled. Apparently he was disappointed in me for choosing not to apply for work today.

Apparently I wasn't as dedicated as he'd believed me to be. Apparently my absence would cause significant damage to the performance of the box transit system at a time of higher than usual demand. Apparently if I came to my sense and wanted to work a half shift I should contact him before midshift and if I did so then perhaps I could restart a couple of bumps higher than the very bottom.

"Well apparently you're a prick Ste," I said to myself, waving the message away and flicking over the catering menu. I ordered up some hot food and wandered over to the washarea. By the time I'd showered and dressed the food had arrived so I retrieved it from the hatch and returned to the sofa, my watering mouth reminding me how little I'd eaten over the last couple of days.

The food was ok, not great but good enough to sting my aching tastebuds at the first bite. I wolfed the whole lot down and then just sat for a while, still feeling sleepy but now warmer and more content with it.

After a little while thoughts of the not-a-time-machine coughed politely having waited patiently, suggesting that perhaps now was the time to go back to it. I couldn't think of a reason not to. I finally had a break from the relentless shifts, some free time with which I could do just as I pleased. Why wouldn't I now race back to it? What could possibly be more important?

I stood and stretched and gathered up the food tray and the cutlery. I walked over to the waste hatch and dropped them in then collected my clothes from the previous day from where I'd left them in a heap near the washarea.

I put those into the laundry hatch then decide to strip my bed. I threw the sheets in the laundry hatch too and then put new sheets on the bed and had a tidy round the livingspace. I cleaned the washarea, scrubbing out the shower and the toilet then sat back down on the sofa for a little rest and watched the wallscreen some more.

Eventually I forced myself to go and collect the circuit from under my bed then returned to sit on the sofa, placing the circuit on my lap and staring at it. I wanted to build crystal circuits that could change the world. That was what I wanted to do with my life, it was what I was meant to do, it was what I was good at, it was what made me feel alive and satisfied.

So why couldn't I start?

I stared and stared at the circuit in my lap as a great trembling pressure built up around and then inside me, like a thick invisible sludge. I could just put it away again I knew, it would be so easy to put it away back under the mattress then just relax and watch the wallscreen for a bit before getting and early night.

That would be fine, no-one would judge me, no-one would even know, except me. I'd know and very quietly, just a little bit more in the far deep background, I would hate myself for it. Even hating myself would be easier though, like serving a penance or paying a fine so as not to have to actually do it.

I growled exasperated with myself and forced my reluctant hands to pick up the circuit. I was fairly sure I knew what had gone wrong with it now. Some part of my brain, somewhere towards the back had been quietly working away on the problem beneath and behind everything else.

Somehow I just knew now that the circuit had failed due to a failure of one of two connections going into the new 3'-6!0 I'd added in the other day. Below it sat the 8'-8!0, a blocky little grey oblong with rounded corners and a little lump rising out of one of the long edges. No matter how new it is, somehow an 8'-8!0 will always looked aged and battered. You can buff them for weeks at a time but it'll still come out looking scuffed and faded.

The connection to this crystal was less likely to be the problem. Although its lifespan is shorter than a lot of crystals, for as long as it lasts an 8'-8!0 is one of the most relentlessly reliable crystals there is.

It's cyclically singular which means that it tailors its output to the circuit perfectly and then, no matter how much data flows through it, produces the exact same output over and over until it burns itself out. It's a great starting point from which to build a circuit and a good safeguard against negative feedback loops.

If you're not careful a circuit that looks perfectly sound can sometimes degenerate into a downward spiral wherein it loses the ability to store any new data, then begins to lose data already stored until eventually it completely collapses. An 8'-8!0 is great for stabilising a circuit and keeping it happy.

I picked up my probe and applied it carefully to the connection between the 3'-6!0 and the 8'-8!0. Sure enough the connection appeared solid and sound. This just left the connection to the 3'-3!0. This crystal looks very similar to a 3'-6!0, it's also a kind of flattened cube. It has more rounded corners however and always come in a kind of sandy yellow brown type colour.

It's a cyclically substituting crystal which means if t encounters data of failing quality it makes a perfect copy of the original data then retires the failing version. It's a weird little thing though and no-one quite understands how it works. Any test you could think of to check would tell you that the copied data it had created was actually the original data.

Anyway, I applied the probe to that connection and immediately saw the problem. The connection had broken down due to a slight kink in the receiving surface of the 3'-6!0. In my excited haste to install it I hadn't noticed the uneven surface and so hadn't accounted for it when making the connection.

It was a matter of seconds to correct and restore the connection after which I could see and almost hear the nine crystals begin to charge as the circuit began to form. This time I didn't look at the circuit but rather began to look back and forth between two areas of empty space at head height to my left and right. I suddenly became very anxious and started to smooth my hair and straighten my back, composing myself.

Sure enough a clump of air to my left seemed to tremble as if heated from below. I blinked at it, my brain unable to make sense of what my eyes were seeing. Then suddenly the woman's face was just there, looking back at me through the small oval window as if it had always been there. I turned to my right and there was the man.

They both look as startled and as unsure as I felt and we all flicked our eyes back and forth between the other two. Several times we drew breath to speak but always at exactly the same moment so that we all started together and then immediately stopped in order to hear one another. Eventually I managed to break the deadlock.

"Hello," I said, my voice wavering just a little so that I swallowed and took a firmer grip of myself. "My name is Ba Adebo."

The woman replied first. Her voice was a little higher than mine but with a similar accent. She sounded confused.

"Erm, hey," she began. "Yeah, I'm Da Adebo."

"Me too," interjected the man as if not believing his own words. His accent was also familiar. "Well, sorry, no. What I mean is, my name is Adebo too. I'm Ta Adebo."

We all lapsed back into silence, our confusion and bewilderment reflected three ways. It was Da who spoke first this time.

"I'm sorry," she said. "I don't understand what's happening. This happened before and then it stopped. Who are you? How can I see you?"

"I built.." both Ta and I replied in perfect unison and then stopped again, staring at one another.

"You go," he said eventually and I turned back to face Da.

"All I was going to say," I began, trying to stop my mind from racing off ahead and focus instead on the words. "Was just that well, I built a crystal circuit. It's a hobby of mine and it was meant to be.." I trailed off, suddenly realising that I knew nothing about these people.

"Well it doesn't matter what it was meant to be," I continued. "It didn't work, or at least it didn't do what I'd thought it might do. Basically I turned it on and then this happened. I don't know how or why."

"I thought it was me," said Ta.

Da and I both turned our attention to him.

"I build circuits as a hobby too," he said. "I mean I've built hundreds of them, all trying to, well trying to do something anyway. But this one, I connected it up the other day then suddenly you guys appeared then it broke down again. I've literally just finished fixing it and was trying it out again."

"What were your circuits supposed to do Ta?" I asked, holding my breath for his answer.

At first he didn't speak, his eyes dropping down as if looking for something on the floor. Then he sighed.

"Ahh," he said, visibly cringing. "I know it's stupid but I had this idea years ago. I thought I could maybe build a kind of, I mean not a real one but just a kind of demo version of a, well. It was supposed to be a time machine."

A chill ran through me so that I actually shuddered. I licked my lips and took a deep breath.

"Mine too," I said simply.

"Really?!" exclaimed Ta.

"To demonstrate a particular sub quantum effect as a proof of concept?" I asked flatly.   Ta just nodded dumbly then started shaking his head instead.

"What the fuck?" he whispered to himself.

"What about you Da?" I asked, turning back to the confused looking woman only to find her blushing.

"Yeah," she said cautiously. "I built a circuit out of crystals as well."

"For the same reason?" asked Ta.

Da bit her lip and the red in her cheeks grew darker. She shook her head and wouldn't meet our eyes.

"What is it?" I asked.

"It feels kind of stupid now," she said.

"I don't think any of us are in a position to be judgmental here," I said.

"Agreed," said Ta. "I have no clue what is happening here."

"I put the crystals on the board and connected them up, but I don't know what any of them do," Da began to explain but then closed her eyes, apparently ashamed. "I just like the colours and the shapes."

"Wait a minute," I said as an idea suddenly occurred to me. As gently as I could I moved the circuit off my lap and noticed that the ovals moved with it as if fixed to it by invisible rods. I stepped across the livingspace to my bed and grabbed a notepad and pen from the bedside table.

Returning to the sofa I scribbled furiously, shapes connected by lines and moved the circuit back into position and tore off the sheet of paper to hold it up.

"Is this the circuit?" I asked, turned the sheet back and forth so that Ta and Da could squint at it.

"Yep," said Ta, nodding. "That's attempt number six hundred and thirteen."

"It looks like it," said Da uncertainly. "But this is the first one I've ever built, at least since university anyway."

I placed the paper on the sofa beside me and turned back to face Da.

"This is my first since uni too. So you studied crystal engineering?" I asked.

"Just for a year," she replied. "I couldn't get into it. I loved how they looked and working with them but I could never understand how they functioned. I changed to an Art degree instead in the end and now I create small pieces of work in my free time."

"Hang on," Ta interjected. "So you two both created the same number of circuits but for completely different reasons. But Ba, you and I created a different number of circuits for exactly the same reason."

Da and I both nodded.

"Also, I never studied crystal engineering at uni at all. So that means you guys both have the same academic background in crystal engineering but completely different interests in it. But again, Ba you and I have the same interest in it but a completely different academic background."

We nodded again as he screwed up his face with the effort of thought.

"And not to put too fine a point on it but you guys are both women, one black one white  while Ba and I are both black, one man, one woman," he said.

"That's right," said Da, amazed as if only just noticing these facts. "Does that mean something? What does it mean?"

"Not a clue," said Ta, slumping back defeated against his sofa. His incredibly familiar sofa.

"Have you guys noticed how similar our rooms are by the way?" I asked, groping out down a different line of enquiry.

Ta sprang forward again, peering through his little oval window to look past me and then Da while she did the same.

"Christ," he said. "It's like it's the same room." He actually sounded scared.

"I don't like this," said Da. "I don't understand."

"Me neither," I replied, feeling a cold clenching in the pit of my stomach.

For a while none of us spoke or even looked at one another. Instead we sat in silence thinking furiously. Again it was Da who eventually broke the silence.

"You both said you made the circuits in your spare time right?" she asked.

"Mm hmm," agreed Ta while I just nodded.

"Well it's a hobby for me too," she said. "So what do you both do for a living? I'm a..."

"Box pusher," we all said together.

That's when things got really weird.

—        —
—

The next day I was stood at my plate feeling strangely numb. Somewhere in the far distance, in the corner of my mind's eye, the mushroom cloud of an impending an emotional apocalypse loomed, but just then all I felt was numb.

I'd kept a tight lid on myself through my morning interview, not reacting even when Ste lectured me on the impact of my absence the previous day. Now though, I knew I couldn't hold it back any longer. It was coming.

Just like the previous day I'd pushed nothing but

neatly wrapped brown packages, all heavy, all headed east and down but I barely even saw them. I felt empty again but this wasn't like before. Before I had felt drained, emptiness only powerful because it defined a space usually filled. Today was different, today I felt a permanent hollow, a realisation that I had always been empty, that the substance I had felt before had never actually been anything but illusion.

I had talked with Da and Ta for hours, comparing every facet of ourselves and of our lives we could think of, desperately trying to make to make sense of what was happening. The answers were not what we had expected. They were not what any of us had wanted.

Ta and I had discussed the theory at length, trying to explain it to Da in simple terms as we went but also to one another as we tried to understand just what it was we had done. Between us Ta and I realised that we had both made the same flawed assumption when designing our circuits.

The subquantum effect we had both imagined seemed to act upon an extra dimension. We had both assumed that the additional dimension would be time but in fact it wasn't. We hadn't built time machines, we'd built windows to other worlds, to parallel universes and apparently there were just three.

As far as we could tell our circuits had opened up a channel across all possible universes. If there were any more universes in existence then there was no reason we could see why there shouldn't be additional oval windows linking us into them as well.

Of course the idea of parallel universes was nothing new, it had been around since before our recorded history even began and I remembered reading tech fantasy stories about it as a child.

It felt intuitively right that such other places should exist, even if we couldn't see or reach them. There was a strange kind of comfort to the thought that every time a decision was made the whole universe split into two wherein both possible outcomes were played out.

Every what might have been was played out somewhere, every mistake was corrected, every tearful ending rerun happy and every loved one passed still alive in a far and distant realm. Even the thought of it, just the hope of it, somehow helped take the edge off our lives.

Except that as it turned out, that wasn't how it worked at all. There were just three universes and the differences between them were nowhere near as significant as we might have hoped.

Da and Ta and I had all be born at the exact same time in the exact same room in the exact same stack. Our childhoods had been the same, we'd played the same games in the same halls with the same friends.

Our best friends had looked different, been different genders, different races, had slightly different names even, but they'd all been the same. We'd all had a best friend who was fat and sickly. Mine had a rare blood disorder which had sapped his energy so that he never exercised and put on weight. Ta's had lost her parents as a child and filled the gap with food. Da's had just been naturally heavy.

We'd all defended that friend against a group of bullies, again different but the same. The tall one with spots, the mean one from a wealthy family, the quiet one who always took it too far. We all had the same scar from one of those fights, a neat little line on our forearm. Mine was from a knife they'd waved around, Ta's from a bottle that one of them threw and Da's from falling against a nail sticking out of a wall during the scuffle.

Later we'd all mourned the death of that friend. Mine had finally succumbed to to his illness, Ta's had killed herself and the bullies had killed Da's by accident. None of us had ever really recovered from losing that friend.

We'd all gone to the same universities and got the same grades, though each in different subjects. We'd all had our hearts broken just before our first set of finals but had struggled through it and come out stronger in the end.

We'd all wanted children but had none. For me it had just never happened, I'd never met the right person and time had slipped by. Ta had been married but his wife hadn't wanted children and eventually that had driven them apart. Da had been pregnant but then miscarried, the resulting complications leaving her barren.

On and on it had gone, always different and yet always the same and the more we talked to worse it got. Our lives had played out in parallel as if drawn on overlaid sheets of plastic. The outlines didn't always match perfectly, but the motion was always consistent.

We each began to realise that while the details may differ, our reasons for doing something or the road we took, everything always came out the same. What we had thought of as crossroads in our lives were now revealed to have been only high walled alleys.

There was no choice, no free will, no control. Every single thing I had ever done was the only thing I could have done, the only thing that could ever have happened. Even when played out over and over across whole other universes, there was only one way anything could go and now I knew it I could never go back.

When I ate I knew that Da and Ta would be eating. Perhaps different food, perhaps eating for comfort rather than hunger but they'd be eating because that was the point in time at which we ate. There was no escaping it.

The circuits didn't work on their own, they only worked because we'd all switched them on at the exact same moment. I'd connected mine as an excited first attempt, Ta's had been just another routine test and Da's had been unwitting aesthetic adjustment.

When I'd broken my circuit in horror and the oval windows had disappeared I knew that the others had broken theirs too. Ta had probably calmly decided to switch it off while Da might have done it by accident.

I sat there and stared at my hands trying to tell if it was really me controlling them but all I could think of was Ta and Da sitting on their identical sofas and staring at their hands too. I closed my eyes but then thought of them closing their eyes as well.

I felt like I was drowning. If I stood from the sofa and fled the livingspace howling, out into the halls, that would just be another part of the sequence with all three of us doing the same. If I stayed perfectly still and kept the screams inside that would be all that could happen.

It was unbearable and for about an hour or so I honestly thought I would lose my mind. Eventually I waved the wallscreen on, desperate for any kind of distraction. The news was showing footage of our troops queuing up to receive yet more new equipment.

The department of conflict insisted that it was our logistical might that would win the war in the lowest levels of the east. Our ability to continually supply and resupply our troops was what would make the difference they said. Pictures like these were shown regularly to underline the point. That was when it hit me, that was the moment I realised I was hollow and had never been anything else.

The war in the east could not have been prevented, it had to happen just like everything else. Across all three universes those people died, different names and faces, perhaps a bayonet or a blaze instead of bullet but they all died just the same.

When I had started designing my time machine I had honestly believed I could help to end that war, that I could kick start the healing of our deepest rift. I could go back to the beginning and show them how the levels came to be then everyone would know and we could all just get on with our lives. What I'd actually built would help no-one however, if anything it would just make things worse.

The techs would find it all fascinating, different particles all following the same paths in three different universes. They'd probably say it was down to the existence of a sixth fundamental force. For generations all of tech had been trying to unify the five known forces into a single grand theory. Perhaps there'd been a sixth force all along they'd say, we just couldn't see it without these other universes to compare ours to, no wonder we couldn't unify the five!

Meanwhile the constructionists would claim it as absolute proof of the existence of structured plan, of the guiding hand of a higher intelligence. Submission to the will of god was no longer a choice they would say, but in fact an immutable law of nature.

They'd probably find a way to develop the circuit further so they could cross between the three universes and fight their war on inter-dimensional scale. The techs might take one, the constructionists the other and then each would have an entire level's worth of resources with which to tear apart the third.

I was supposed to be more than just a box pusher. That was the day job, I lived with it because it never felt real, the plan felt real. The secret plan to do something special and unique while no-one was looking that might just change the levels forever, that was who I was supposed to be, a creator of something special.

After meeting Da and Ta however, I had finally realised that a box pusher was all I was, all I had ever been and all I could ever be. Another perfectly wrapped fat twenty two hopped up onto the landing plate in front of me. I pushed it onto belt two knowing that as I did so Da and Ta were doing the same.

The calm sounds and motion around me had become utterly detached and remote from the world and worlds I now knew lay outside my apartment. A total disconnect bridged only by my tortured mind.

Another fat twenty two appeared on the plate, going east and down with the rest. I pushed it on blindly, thinking not of the box but of those far distant screaming mothers. As a secret crystal engineer I'd thought I could help them, save them, but as a box pusher? What could I do for them as a box pusher?

As more and more boxes arrived in front of me one after the other, I began to notice small dark shapes appearing on their surfaces. I realised I was crying. A wet one came next and I pushed it on, their children were limp in their arms and there was nothing I could do about it. A fat thirty six appeared and I just pushed it on, their tears were falling onto cold grey skin and there was nothing I could do about it.

I pushed and I wept while they wept and they bled and finally I knew it for sure. I am not special. There is no secret heroic me just waiting for the day on which I swoop in and save them all.

I'm just me, I'm just a box pusher. A heavy, clinking fat twenty two hopped keen onto the plate and waited ready, expectant. I pushed it on. They're dying over there and there is literally nothing at all I can do about it.

*PLEASE NOTE:*

*The account above is entirely fictional and is not intended to be an accurate portrayal of the practices nor performance of the box transit department.*

*Any similarities between characters and actual employees are purely coincidental and any descriptions of poor performance are for dramatic effect only.*

*All box model names cited above are informal box pusher colloquialisms and in no way represent official box transit department box model nomenclature.*

*For reference and clarity the full, official box transit department box model IDs of all boxes referred to above are listed below:*

**7MZJ-OD670-5H17**
*{ "brown" }*

**6OZ7-0L1XM-EC44**
*{ "easy forty four" }*

**78RO-270E5-EC12**
*{ "easy twelve" }*

**OMPB-9K7IT-EOO3**
*{ "eyes and ears" }*

**349A-LH31I-FT36**
*{ "fat thirty six" }*

**S990-RO8BK-FT22**
*{ "fat twenty two" }*

**B5Q5-O619A-L34F**
*{ "green" }*

**8QRZ-IIFJH-99KG**
*{ "heavy" }*

**WQTF-DX761-1ZY8**
*{ "lazy eight" }*
**D27E-IF3A5-99DB**
*{ "loud" }*

**12W8-1V008-9L56**
*{ "nine less six" }*

63ZA-4O43L-RD15
*{ "red fifteen" }*

G6S0-I6G2V-A44H
*{ "screamer" }*

8X7I-6R913-75SF
*{ "seventy five safe" }*

E17A-SHO49-62LW
*{ "sixty two low" }*

42PZ-QIFEK-I1I9
*{ "three eyed nine" }*

0DD6-10392-1TO0
*{ "two in ten" }*

L781-O51RL-H201
*{ "wet one" }*

# insufficient

"Are you ready?"

"What?" he said, staring blankly into the mirror.

"Come on!" the voice from downstairs was gleeful and impatient.

He looked at the man in the mirror. Tall and pasty, hunched over the bathroom sink, the man stared back at him with empty eyes. He narrowed those eyes and interrogated the face, searching for any hint of emotion. He found none.

More seconds ticked by as he tried to make sense of it. How could that face appear so bland, so flat and utterly neutral? Between the skinny arms, within the birdcage chest, the night's torment continued to thrash, anguish and terror, grief and despair yet not a hint of it showed on that face.

The previous hours had dragged beyond reason, endless, paralysed time spent staring up towards a ceiling hidden in black. Yet even as time had seemed to stand still, it was the certainty of the coming dawn that had buried him in soul crushing anxiety.

Then, in but a moment of flickering eyelids, the room had flashed to grey. Suddenly he was alone in the bed, a subtle, fast cooling depression all that remained of his wife. The dreaded day had arrived.

"Simon!" the voice had an edge now, a slight souring of the former giddy sweetness.

"Ok," he mumbled to himself. "Ok," he repeated, now loud enough to be heard. "Down in a sec."

He broke eye contact with the man in the mirror, then pulled the plug and found a towel. As he padded blindly back to the bedroom he noticed how good the soft fabric felt against his face. It was dark and warm within the depths of the towel, the world was removed and stayed distant. He wished he could stay there all day.

Dropping the towel he snatched up his robe and wrapped himself snug before sighing. Out onto the landing and then down the stairs, he practised the various smilings he would need for the day.

In the living room Laura was practically trembling.

She sat cross legged on the sofa holding a tall thin glass of orange juice and champagne and only vaguely watching the muted TV. He noticed the presents had already been sorted, two little piles of his and hers.

"Look darling!" she said as she saw him, springing across the room to land in his arms. "It snowed! They said it wouldn't but it has! Look!"

He let Laura drag him over to the window and accepted the glass she put in his hand.

"Isn't it beautiful?" she asked, squeezing against him.

"It is, love," he said warmly, his anxiety abating slightly in the light of her annual childlike joy. He returned the squeezing and took in the scene.

The street beyond their window, the homes, gardens and cars, had been all but drowned under a heavy blanket of snow. Crisp white edges formed smooth blunted outlines of the world that lay beneath.

Dragged back to the sofa he ignored the TV and the terrible portents of what was to come. Laura thrust a present into his hands and snatched one up for herself, grinning all the while, eyes asparkle.

"You start," she said, downright giddy.

—     —
—

"...but then of course Daniel said he didn't think she could be, so we'll have to see if she's drinking today. Can you imagine though if she is? What will Dad say? You know what he's like."

"Mm hmm," he said, a well honed kneejerk response. His fingers were buttoning his shirt but his attention was fixed on his stomach. The churning had started just after the presents, when Laura had turned up the volume on the TV.

His licked his lips and took a deep careful breath, aware all the time of his wife's position in the room. Laura had her back to him however and was comparing a dress to some trousers, talking all the while.

"So I really don't know if he'll be there or not.
Mum said he told her he would be but he's said that
before. I know it's difficult being so far away and what
with his job and that but he really shouldn't get her
hopes up if he doesn't know for sure. She was so
disappointed last year. Oh I'm so glad you're wearing it,
I knew it'd look good on you."

This last was directed at the jumper he had just
pulled over his head, one of the morning's presents.

"What's the matter darling? Don't you like it?" She
sounded concerned but also ready to be offended.

He shook himself back under control, pushing the
terror aside and rolling out one of the smiles.

"No darling," he said as warmly as he could. "It's
lovely, really. Thank you."

The taste of the kiss and the warmth of of the hug
took the edge off some of the anxiety but introduced a
new thread of guilt.

Despite the struggle to appear pleased with the
gift, he genuinely did love the jumper. It was warm,
comfortable and made him look a little broader in the
shoulders than he actually was, adding a little confidence
boost to the bargain. She had bought it he knew, for
that very reason, as insightful and loving as ever.

And yet the fact that she knew him so well only
made him feel worse about hiding his shameful fear. The
concealment was a betrayal, the preprepared smiling a
lie, fine for others but not for her.

She deserved better, better than him.


—     —

—


"Are you sure you don't mind not drinking?"

Half an hour of mid morning drizzle had converted
much of the snow on the road into slush. As her question
broke through his distraction he felt the back end of the
car slip and begin to drift.

A chilled wash of panic flowed through him as he
white knuckled the steering wheel to bring the car back

into line. Swallowing hard he focused on the road and prepared his voice to respond.

"No that's fine darling," he managed, she didn't seem to have noticed the near miss. "You enjoy yourself, perhaps I'll catch up when we get home."

Another string of guilt threaded right on through him as he realised he welcomed the excuse to refuse drinks. The thought of alcohol made his stomach thrash even harder, there was no way he could keep booze down today.

"Greg told me he and Susan are going to let little Carl watch it with us this year," Laura continued, looking out at the white and black landscape.

"Apparently Greg wasn't sure he was old enough but Susan insisted, said she thought it was very important that he understand. You know what she's like."

Out of the corner of his eye he saw Laura push her chin into her chest and gather her sternest frown to form of the familiar impersonation of his sister-in-law.

"Every year on this special day," she began in a low and intentionally droning voice. "People across the world gather to celebrate a child, a child whose sacrifice would save us all, blah blah blah."

Laura giggled and having known what was coming he managed to deliver the appropriate smiling almost immediately.

—        —

—

The smilings began in earnest with the opening of the front door.

Incoming eye contact. Eye contact check. Go eyebrows for pleased recognition sparkle and go appropriately affectionate smiling during handshake. New eye contact incoming. Eye contact check. Repeat pleased recognition and maintain pleased smiling during hug even while over shoulder in case anyone else is watching. Prepare standard snow and travel related smalltalk. Incoming set up line, set up line received. Go stock response, go smiling with hint of chuckle.

Having made it through the removing of coats and initial welcomes he followed Laura deeper into the house, deploying the smilings for each person they met, tailoring the sequence as appropriate. They stepped into the lounge, long, soft furnished and lit and then placed drink orders with their eager host.

A real fire crackled away at the far end of the room and soft, nondescript music seemed to seep from the walls. As they settled into a spot to stand and catch up with yet more relatives, he noticed his bored looking nephew approaching.

"Hey Carl," he said, deploying the particularly difficult trying-too-hard-to-be-the-cool-uncle smiling.

"Hi." Carl was not impressed but this was just as it should be.

Children were by far the most difficult, they could sense the fakery and deceit. The trick with kids was not to convince them of the smiling but to convince them of the reason for the fakery.

They were used to being patronised by adults who didn't know how to act around them. The simulation of this awkwardness as a mask to the real pain within had been one of the hardest smilings to master. He was almost proud of it.

"Oh hello Carl darling," cooed Laura. Carl tried but failed to restrain a genuine grin even as she tousled his hair.

He realised that just as the kid had sensed his deceit he also sensed the absolutely certainly of Laura's love and respect and couldn't help but respond in kind. He marvelled at the pair as they chatted away, the bond almost glowing between them. It was amazing and beautiful and utterly alien. He ached to know how it felt.

"So I hear you're going to stay up and watch with us this year, that's exciting isn't it?" Laura said.

"I guess," Carl shrugged. "Mum said I had to."

The mention of what was to come reweighted the anchor within and dragged him back into the dark. This was why he'd never feel that bond, this part of him that kept him always half in the shadows. Unable to watch he turned away but caught sight of the TV instead so that his gaze bounced on to settle on the sideboard. Time was shortening, the situation pressed in, his heart began to pound.

His brother-in-law appeared bearing drinks and he greeted his glass of lemonade with a rare genuine smile. Finally, a prop to fiddle with, to occupy the hands and periodically the mouth, cool fluids to offset fevered sweating. He took a sip of icy sweetness and welcomed the feeling of cool.

Suddenly he saw Carl's mother, his zealot of a sister-in-law bearing down on their group with a typically intense expression. He prepared himself for another particularly demanding smiling.

Eye contact incoming, eye contact check. Go half strength recognition sparkle and restrained, reverent smile. Prepare travel related opening dialogue minus chuckle culmination. Opening dialogue go, knowing nod of agreement.

Prepare for incoming diatribe, fix concerned expression and brace self to maintain control. Expression fixed, diatribe underway, maintaining control. Breathe in, not too deeply, breathe out, careful to avoid appearance of a sigh, continue.

"...of course these days people just see it as time off work. It's just about the presents and the drinking. They've lost sight of what today really means, the significance of the child, the pain of the sacrifice. And where would we be without that sacrifice? Back in the dark ages that's where. They don't know how lucky they are. That's why I insisted that Carl join us this year. Greg said he didn't think he was ready but I said it was time..."

— —

—

"It's about to start darling. Are you ok? You seem miles away."

"Yep, yep," he said. Forcing down the trembles

and pulling himself back under control. He quickly hid behind his glass, taking a huge heavy gulp of lemonade and melted ice that hit his stomach like a permafrost fist.

It was harder when he thought no-one was watching. When someone was in front of him, looking at him and talking to him the smilings kicked in almost of their own accord, an instinctive defence.

As soon as he felt free from contact however the feelings began to spill forth onto his face. With no distraction it took a far greater effort of will to maintain, to stay focussed on holding everything inside. These were the times of greatest risk, where the chances of shameful discovery ran highest.

He followed her over to the small crowd that had gathered around the TV. It was dark outside now and the lights had been turned down so that beyond the overlapping glows of fire and TV the room smudged away into grey shadows.

As Laura grasped his hand he hoped she wouldn't notice the sweat. He swallowed hard and blinked his traitorous eyes that had started to sting and blur. His heart was really pounding now as if in his throat and he felt his knees being to soften and quiver. He perched on the arm of the sofa, slipping his own arm around Laura's waist.

All eyes were fixed on the screen, no-one was looking at him. As long as he remained quiet and still and then recovered before the lights came back on, he could get through it, he could, he was sure.

Carl had been placed front and centre of the group by his mother and sat patiently in the glow of the TV while thinking all the while of his new toys. It was his mother who now turned up the volume so that the sound of drums quickly filled the room.

In the foreground of the picture a familiar news anchor held a microphone but still struggled to be heard over the crowds in the background. The capital was in darkness, the central square filled solid with people as far as the camera allowed the eye to see. The traditional burning torches dotted the endless crowd throughout adding up to a low level quivering yellow light which seemed to twitch and squirm in time with the rising hysteria.

The drums could not be seen on screen but seemed to fill the world with their maddening rhythm, infecting all with a building frenzy. The pounding seemed to reach into his chest and stamp that rhythm onto his out of sync heart so that it stuttered, hopeless and weak.

The news anchor had disappeared from the screen now though his voice remained. An involuntary gasp came from those around him as the ceremonial pathway came into view. The voice continued to describe the scene, explaining the historical significance of the decorations and noting the minor modern changes made. No-one really listened to the words but the they filled the time and provided a traditional and comforting background noise.

Cutting through the swell of the now frantic hordes a perfectly straight avenue of remained clear. A red carpet ten feet wide and infeasibly long struck straight down the line, flanked by more blazing torches until ceasing at the first broad stone step. The familiar sights and sounds triggered memories that quickly began to overwhelm him, the anxiety doubling upon doublings so that he began to silently drown.

The cameras returned to the news anchor, the crowds rippling and roaring behind and beneath him. The ceremony would be a few moments yet. His family all about him relaxed just a little and began to talk quietly amongst themselves.

He quickly established the keen smiling, the fierce grin of expectation and wide eyes of happy excitement. He met a couple of glances successfully, the smilings almost deploying themselves while inside he wept and screeched.

Now the camera cut back to a side on view of the avenue and the room hushed as the ecstasy of the crowd reached fever pitch. The drums upped their pace, pushing far beyond the bearable and a moment later the procession came into view.

He noticed his sister-in-law place a loving hand on her son's small shoulder, tears in her transfixed eyes.

First came the Acolytes appearing from the left of screen, their ankle length robes a plain and simple cream save for the complex insignia of their rank borne proudly on their chests. Heads shaven and bare, they moved as if gliding through long deliberate strides, holding their ornate ceremonial torches high in defiance of the blackened night sky above.

Next came the Priests, their robes just as long but two tone, their insignia larger and more imposing. They bore small, simple decorations upon their brows, covering their shaven heads. Their torches were larger and even more ornate and as they followed the Acolytes towards that first broad stone step they stared fiercely ahead. There could be no doubt as to the gravity of the situation.

The sound of the drums and the crowd had become a feeling, a raging sea all about them that heaved without mercy or design. He was clenching his teeth now, breathing hard through his nose and sweating as he refused and refused to vomit. All about him his family were leaning forward. Mouths hung open, hands were held with knuckles white, eyes were wide and goggling.

Finally the middle of the procession came into shot and there was the High Priest himself. Everyone gasped and cooed. The High Priest's robes were resplendent with every colour they could think of. His headdress was huge and magnificent, his insignia complex to the point of eyestrain while hanging huge from a heavy gold chain. The High Priest carried no torch.

As the procession continued more Priests and then Acolytes came into view to complete the processional party and all closed the distance on the end of the carpet one agonising pace after another.

In the bottom corner of the screen he noticed a flash of florescence as medical personnel tried to extract a limp body from the crowd. Every year dozens of people were overcome by the intensity of the ceremony such was the frenzied crush. He closed his eyes, inspired by the fallen to hope that anyone noticing would take it as a sign of intense engagement and not as the shameful escape that it was.

He took a deep breath and open his eyes. Returning to the room he saw that the procession had now reached the first step. The Acolytes moved in a perfectly choreographed flow to form lines either side while the Priests moved on and through them. The camera angle switched provoking yet another gasp as the whole of the vast stone step pyramid that dominated the centre of the capital came into view.

As the Priests began to ascend the stairs they began to peel off to the sides in pairs, forming a line on either side and leaving a central path clear for the High Priest himself. As the High Priest's foot landed on the first step the crowd erupted into a manic applause that rolled back and forth across the square before clattering up into the sky.

Somewhere amid the painful chaos he detected that the drums had quickened again, overtaking the throbbing in his temples. His head began to swim but at that moment Laura's fingers dug deep into his shoulder with rabid excitement and he managed to steady himself.

The High Priest was almost at the top now so that the camera angle shifted again, this time a closer view that included the huge stone altar that crowned the pyramid. The priest paused and turned, raising both arms to the sky.

The drums stopped.

An incredible, echoing hush settled across the crowd, the room and the world. Not a breath could be heard, all were held fast, awaiting the climax of the ceremony. He was transfixed, though desperate not to watch, not to see it all over again, not to be poisoned and violated by these same old images yet again.

He could not look away.

The High Priest stood as a giant atop the pyramid. There was movement behind him as two Priests prepared the altar but all eyes were fixed inescapably on the High Priest. A third Priest appeared now at his side to present the great ceremonial blade. The High Priest raised the blade to the sky. Huge, broad, flawless, it glimmered among the torches as if made of light. He lowered the blade to his side and turned slowly to face the altar.

This was it.

It was now.


*The High Priest stands before the altar.*
*Upon the altar lies a tiny, naked child.*
*The child's eyes are wide with fear, their body is*
*numb with cold.*
*The blade is raised to the sky.*
*There is a pause as long as a life.*
*A pale and fragile hand reaches out.*
*Little fingers cling desperately to the High*
*Priest's robes.*
*The blade falls from the sky.*
*The tiny form falls open and red.*
*The little hand falls away from the robes.*
*The skinny arm swings limp above the red that*
*now running down the stairs.*
*There is an explosion.*


Fireworks, cheering, music and drums. The world erupted into a orgy of celebration. All around him his family hugged one another and wiped away tears of joy. His sister-in-law clutched Carl to her bosom and whispered into his hair. The boy looked pale and confused. Laura was wrapped all about him but while his arms returned the embrace, his mind reeled and sobbed with despair.

As quickly as he could manage he slipped away form the group to the bathroom. Locking the door he dashed to the toilet, the vomit erupting from his throat before he could even drop to his knees. Tears and mucous and saliva and vomit poured from his face with abandon. The noise of the celebration outside probably was loud enough to drown him out but this was by luck not design. He had finally lost control.

His body shook violently and he had to cling furiously to the edges of the toilet bowl to keep himself upright. Great keening sobs racked through him, moans of sorrow and rage and despair.

It had all happened again.

For several minutes his body expelled fluids,

sounds and motion violently and without restraint.
Eventually this began to ebb so that he could sit back
against the bath and pant. Waiting in the wings, a
seething self loathing saw its opportunity and beset him.

He clambered to his feet and stumbled to the
basin. Grasping each side of the sink he steadied himself
before looking at the man in the mirror and recalling his
earlier reflections. The impossible mask of neutrality
from the morning had been shattered beyond repair. In
it's wake was a collection of features that was barely a
face at all.

The cheeks appeared sunken as if aged by many
years while the wetness of the eyes made them wobble.
The skin was grey with purple blotches, the jaw slack,
tongue lolling. Strings of fluid glistened from eyes and
nose while textured trail of vomit ran from the lips to
hang from the chin. This was the face of a broken
person, someone empty with nothing to give.

"What is wrong with you?" he asked the man in
the mirror.

He began to weep again silently, his eyes and jaw
straining to the point of pain. There was something
wrong with him, something fundamental and evil. The
great dark weight within him, that which must always,
always be kept from sight, felt heavier than ever before.
He glanced blurry through the tears, the man in the
mirror was swaying.

He fell to his knees again, still gripping the sink,
mouth wide in a silent howl. That terrible weight was not
an object, he knew that, it was not a part of him. It was
a hole. It was the absence of something vital, something
that allowed all of those around him to live and to be
happy.

He understood the sacrifices, he had known them
all his life. He knew the sacrifices kept the world safe,
that they protected the people he loved, so why couldn't
he enjoy them? Why couldn't he feel the joy and relief,
the spectacular catharsis that bound his society
together? Instead he felt sickened, repelled and
appalled. He had never felt that thing they felt and he
knew he never would because there was something
missing inside him.

There was knocking at bathroom the door. Laura's words were buried under celebratory sounds but the tone was one of concern. He washed his face quickly, not daring to meet the eye of the man in the mirror. He had to erase all signs of the loss of control, maintain the facade and continue to deceive the love of his life at all costs.

He didn't know what else to do.

—        —
—

"Back in a second darling."

He watched Laura's naked back and hips as she walked slinky out of the bedroom.

Hearing the bathroom door open and close he pulled the sheets across his naked, still sticky body. A deep and woozy relaxation seeped through every part of him so that he could actually feel individual joints and muscles go slack. His eyes closed themselves and he submitted to the glow, surrounded by peace and by warmth.

In this moment, all was well. The horror had come and been and passed and was now as far away as ever it got. The dying of the echoes, the fading of the images, both were processes familiar and reassuring signalling the end of his annual ordeal. The bed was warm and soft and soon his wife would return and they would fall asleep in each others arms.

Life was not so bad.

# surprise surprise

The house is old, stifled by the weight of years. Every room is busy in stillness, packed with ordered clutter, decades of family life, long ago vibrant but now untouched. The dawn creeps in like a burglar, trails soft fingers over every surface but finds only obsolete shapes and faded shades.

It touches his face and his eyelids flutter, he begins the process of waking. At first all is fuzz, awareness blunted as a dream slips below the black waters. A world that was all just a moment before now crumbles and powders to nothing.

Now there is waking, he has a body again, it is warm and perfectly still. All the shapes around him are blurred and bleeding but familiar just the same. She is breathing beside him, fragile little breaths, he can feel her warmth and is grateful.

And now he is awake, moving and blinking as his body remembers to ache. Slowly through winces he pushes himself up to sit and then rest for a moment. He looks at his hands, they're close enough to see but look like somebody else's.

Where did these hands come from? Thin papery skin hanging tired in wrinkles from slender fragile bones. Blue veins and liver spots, the hands of a dead man. How did this happen and when?

He turns slowly, ignoring the twinge in his back and throws a quivering hand at his glasses. His fingers fumble stiffly but find the frames and grasp them, dragging them back and up to his face.

The room slides into focus, edges sharpen, objects appear. The room is the same, the same old room, the same room every day after day. He twists again, his still trembling hand better aimed this time as he retrieves his teeth and consumes them.

The taste of the cleaning fluid is sour, the same sour as always before. He frowns and swallows and licks his lips just like he always does. He takes his old man's hands and presses them into his old man's face.

It is time to begin again.

He turns to her and watches. Her hair is a thin

shock white, her face sags slack and hollow. Her mouth is open just a little and a tiny string shines wet from the corner as she breathes shallow, desperate breaths like a child.

A smile arrives, small but warm, he feels it on his face. She's still in there that girl he knew, that girl he met and married. Under it all, buried deep, she's still there, he can see her within.

The sharp high cheekbones, the delicate eyes, the little chin the juts out defiant. If he could just dig through the clay, the clag of the years, drag it all off and away, she'd be there beneath that girl he once knew, shining and sparkling her love. He strokes her hair tenderly as the usual pain begins to burn in his chest.

"Winnie," he whispers, dry tongue rasping. "Come on my love, time to wake up."

At first she does not react but as he continues to stroke and whisper she lets out a little moan and begins to shift. Her eyes flutter open and widen but are cloudy and do not see.

"What?" she mumbles, confused. "Where?' she says and notices him, starting a little then staring.

"It's ok Winnie, it's ok. It's just me lass. Time to get up," he says, staring down at her eyes too blurred to respond.

Gradually she returns, her eyes clear and her face tightens bright.

"Ooh," she says, slowly moving herself upwards to sit. "I didn't know where I was for a moment then. I must have been having a dream but I don't remember it, I don't remember it at all."

"Shall we go down for some breakfast then?" he says, slowly rising from the bed and struggling into a robe.


—        —

—


"Martin! Martin! Come and look at this," she says. She is standing at the kitchen sink, staring out through the window at the back garden beyond. A squirrel is assaulting the bird feeder that hangs from the washing line pole.

He is buttering some toast behind her but puts the knife down and turns to join her at the sink.

"Look at him!" she says. "He's a cheeky little bugger that one isn't he? Greg and Philip would love him. Do you think Deborah will bring them today?"

"I don't think so, it's Tuesday, she'll be at work," he says as the squirrel flips upside down to try and gain a better grip on the feeder.

"Oh and they'll be at school won't they? And then they'll have one of their clubs or some other thing after school. She keeps them ever so busy you know. It's all well and good but when do they have time to just be little boys that's what I want to know," she said, still staring.

He grunts non-committally and returns to the toast. The kettle boils and he fills the teapot adding it to the tray along side cups and plates. He moves behind her to open the fridge then peers inside and blinks.

"Did you want an egg?" he calls as reaches for the box.

"Oh yes please," she replies. "I do love an egg at breakfast."

He retrieves the egg box and moves back to the counter, placing it in front of him as she chatters away behind him.

As he opens the egg box his hands are trembling again. He sees one lonely egg and five empty spaces and now his eyes are stinging with tears. He closes his eyes and forces the tears away then breathes deeply until the trembles subside.

"There's only the one left love," he says, keeping his voice almost steady.

"Oh dear," she says seriously, turning to join him in looking down at the egg. "Oh well then, you have it darling," she says cheerily, patting him on the arm. "I don't mind."

"No you're alright," he replies, not looking at her. "You can have it."

"I couldn't, it wouldn't be fair," she says, leaning

in to peer at it more closely. "Why don't we scramble it, that way we can share?"

"No no," he says, glancing at her profile as she examines the egg and swallowing. "I don't fancy eggs today. I'll fry it up and you can have it on toast."

"You're too good to me!" she scolds him kindly, straightening up and gently swatting at his arm.

"You go through and sit yourself down," he says. "I'll bring the tray through in a moment."

She moves past him to the door but then stops and turns.

"It's why I married you you know," she says.

He braces himself then looks up to meet her gaze.

"You were always so kind to me, such a gentleman," she says, beaming at him with bright and loving eyes.

And for a instant, just a fraction of fraction, it is her. He feels his knees tremble beneath him as that girl in her late teens, that girl who took his heart in the very first moment he saw her, stands in front of him once more.

Then she turns and leaves and he's alone in the kitchen. His fingertips touch the cool smooth egg just as the pain in his chest flares out. Frozen to the spot but thrashing within he forces himself to breathe.

He lifts his hand from the unsuspecting egg and curls it into an old man's fist. He lays the fist on the counter and watches it tremble. He knows it's wrong but he has chosen this path and now he has to see it through.

—　　　　—

—

It's midmorning and they're sat in the dining room. He has the paper spread out on the table in front of him and is pretending to read it intently. She is staring out of the window, watching heavy clouds slide over the hills.

The silence is thick and heavy so that every time

he turns a page the rustling paper seems to roar. Suddenly a squealing hinge, a flat floor slap and a metallic clang. The sounds chase one another down the hallway and burst into the room, filling the vast absence of sound.

"That'll be the post then," he says, rising.

She turns from the window and leans to squint across the room to the clock on the mantle.

"He's very late today," she says disapprovingly.

As he moves away from the table he grimaces to straighten his back. He tries to swing his legs further but can only summon a shuffle as he moves out into the hallway. A great fallen pillar of dusty light ploughs through the glass in the door and down the hall. He moves through it slowly, eyeing the small pile of letters sat on the floor.

Halfway down the hall he pauses beside a small table. On the table sits the telephone alongside a small notebook and elderly pencil. He is tempted by the lonely chair but stays standing and bends instead.

As his hand lands on the drawer handle he pauses to glance back down the hall. She is not there. She is not watching. She doesn't know or even suspect. He opens the drawer slowly and carefully, determined to make no sound.

The drawer is half filled with papers and pens, bits of string and unspendable coins. With great precision he shifts the detritus and retrieves an envelope buried beneath. Straightening slow he closes the drawer and holds the envelope close to his chest.

Reaching the door he bends again and retrieves the pile of post. Returning along the hallway he shuffles the letter from the drawer in with the rest and then steps back into the front room. Settling back into his chair he lays the post on the paper and begins to slowly sort through it.

"Is that the post?" she asks, turning away from the view. "Is it anything important? Maybe Deborah sent us a postcard."

He responds with a grunt as he checks each item in turn.

"It's all bills and rubbish I'm afraid," he says.

"Except for this."

He holds up the letter that came from the drawer until she notices and focuses on it.

"What is it?" she asks as she frowns at it.

"No idea," he says, his mouth suddenly dry. "But it's addressed to you so..." he offers her the letter. Her eyes sparkle with excitement and she smiles broadly as she takes the envelope from his hand.

She reaches over and takes the letter opening knife from the sideboard then turns back to the table. With great care she slides the blade under the flap of the envelope and then pushes it along the fold in series of small violent jerks.

As he watches he tries to ignore his chest and his stomach and the sweat on his palms. Finished with the knife she lays it down then teases a folded sheet of paper out of the envelope. She places the gutted envelope on the table with equal care and then begins to unfold the letter.

He watches, forgetting to breathe as she her eyes flicker back and forth along the lines of text. The further down the page she goes the closer her eyebrows huddle as confusion squeezes her features. Finally she shakes her head and offers him the letter.

"You read it Martin," she says, annoyed, "I never understand what they're saying these days. What is it? What does it mean?"

He takes the secretly familiar sheet and pretends to read it through. He swallows and takes a breath then constructs a shocked smile and attaches it to his face.

"Good lord!" he exclaims, managing to sound almost convincing. "You've won a competition Winnie!"

"Have I?" she exclaims as all her confusing and irritation evaporates in an instant.

"You have," he says, pushing on. "It says here you've won first prize which is a holiday to Paris."

"Paris?!" she squeals, clenching her fists to her chest with glee.

"All expenses paid, luxury hotels, chauffeur driven cars the whole lot," he says, pretending to scan through the letter again.

"Oh Martin!" she says, closing her eyes as if she

can't believe it's all real. "I've always wanted to go to
Paris! When is it? When is it?"

He pretends to frown at the piece of paper so that
she stops.

"What is it?" she asks.

"Well it says here the it's tomorrow," he says.

"Tomorrow?" she says, surprised and concerned.
"Oh now then," she says, her fingers at her lips, her
brow clenched again. "Well that's very short notice isn't
it. Can we... Do you think we can still go? I mean there
are so many things to do. I don't know..."

"No lass," he says, placing the later on the
newspaper in front of him and reaching out to take her
hand even though it makes him feel sick right through to
his bones. "We're not going to turn down a free holiday
are we? Especially not to Paris!"

"So," she says breathlessly, her eyes huge and
innocent saucers. "So shall we go then? Shall we go to
Paris? Tomorrow?"

"Aye," he says, patting her hand. "Aye, let's."

"Oooooh!" she squeals again. "What shall we do?
What shall we do then?"

"Well," he says, releasing her hand to tap the
letter with a crooked finger. "Says here that they're
going to send a car for us in the morning, nine o'clock
sharp to take us to the airport."

"Nine o'clock?" she says, still giddy. "Well we'll
have to make sure we're up in time to have our
breakfast and get everything ready won't we."

"We will," he says. "In fact we should probably
start packing now."

"But what about a suitcase?" she says, suddenly
worried again, staring all over the dining table as if she
might find one there. "Do we have a suitcase, I don't
remember..."

"We've got one," he says, keen to nudge her back
onto the distracted happy track. "Why don't you clear
the breakfast things off the table while I go and get it."

Again he rises and moves slowly from the room.
As he approaches the bottom of the stairs he can hear
her moving about in the dining room, singing her joy to
herself quietly. It's a tune from their youth that makes

his mouth smile even as the rest of him is screaming.

He takes a firm hold of the bannister and begins to climb the stairs. He has never felt so tired in all of his life. That cross country run, schoolboy competition, county level, ran himself empty to win it, gave every last shred of himself. He thought he'd never be that tired ever again. He'd been wrong.

Those nights without sleep when Deborah was a baby, so sickly and fragile and weak. Night after night of pacing and cooing and mopping that tiny little brow then back to work all day in between. He thought he'd never feel that empty and flat ever again. He'd been wrong.

Halfway up the stairs the pain in his chest becomes unbearable so that he has to stop. Suddenly his body feels far too heavy and has to lower his right knee to the stair. His knee won't have it however and sends spikes of pain up into his thigh so that he has to twist himself round awkwardly to sit on the stairs instead.

He looks at his old man's hands again and curses his old man's knees. He is trapped. He hates it and hates it but knows it is true. Forty years ago he would have just got on with it, taken care of everything without even breaking stride. Even twenty years ago, even ten, he could have coped with this, he could have managed. But now?

There just isn't enough of him left. He knows it and it scares him. There isn't enough of him left and so he's going to let her down. Again his eyes begin to sting and again he forces them closed, tight enough to crush the tears.

There's nothing to be gained from dwelling on it. It is what it is and now he has to see it through for as long as he can. His various pains are fading, slipping back down to their normal background state. He stands slow and turns easy before climbing the rest of the stairs.

Into the second bedroom and over to the wardrobe he stops to take a breath. Above him the suitcase reigns, perched imperious up on top. He reaches up and grasps the handle and then begins to pull, trying to get away with as little effort as possible.

At first the suitcase doesn't move but as he begins to lean back it starts to shift. He puffs and strains but eventually has it hanging off the top of the wardrobe and resting on his upstretched hands.

His joints complain but he drags it a little further and suddenly bears the whole weight. It threatens to crash down, to crush him beneath it but he manages to control the fall into painful stages. Eventually it hits the floor with a violent but not dangerous impact. He pants for a few seconds, waiting for his body to recover.

"Martin?" her voice comes up the stairs to find him, small and unsure. "Martin? Is that you dear? Are you all right?"

He swallows hard and lets out a deep breath before calling back. "It's alright love, it's just me. I'll be down in moment."

He drags the suitcase to the top of the stairs and then drags it all the way down. At each step he moves slow and careful, keeping the sound of the step landing case to a minimum.

Finally back in the hallway he drags the case to the door of the front room then braces himself to lift it. With a wheeze and a groan his hoists the case to his side and steps into the front room.

She's back at the now cleared dining table, watching the clouds again then turns as if surprised to see him. He strides purposefully across the room, desperate to reach her before he loses his grip on the case and lands it heavily on the table.

"You're still my big strong Martin," she says, grinning up at him with nothing but love. "Even after all these years."

He actually feels himself blush which in turn threatens to bring back the tears.

"Well," he says gruffly, savagely knocking the feelings away. "You'd best get that emptied."

She stares at him, still smiling, as if waiting for an explanation. Then, keeping her eyes on him, she turns her head unsure to face the suitcase in front of her. Her eyes follow on a second later.

"Ok then," she says in a small voice.

Resolving herself to this new task at hand, she opens the suitcase and her face lights up. The suitcase is packed with bags and boxes, tiny faded clothes and dented wooden toys and countless other remnants of their long life together.

He lowers himself back into his chair, watching her carefully to be certain she is distracted enough not to notice his pain. As she begins to unpack the case onto the dining table she pauses at every object, every old photograph, cinema ticket, trinket, postcard, school report.

Every single item is just the tiny tip of anecdotal iceberg. As she recounts to him in incredible, unabridged detail things that happened decades before he suddenly catches himself wishing she were dead and then hates himself for it so much it hurts.

—          —

—

It's early evening. She's still at the dining table working through the suitcase. Occasionally she calls through to him to report yet another find but mostly she chatters way to herself, giggling and sighing at the memories. Most of the bottom of the case is now visible, while its former contents are now doing a good job of obscuring most of the tabletop.

"Do you fancy a little treat darling?" he says suddenly.

Her mouth forms into a tiny o and she looks at him with a mischievous expression that lights up her face. Another time travel flash of their youth that almost knocks him from his chair.

"Like what?" she says quietly.

He gets up and crosses to the sideboard before lowering bending stiffly and rooting about in the cupboard below. Finally he straightens, prize in hand, a small cardboard box wrapped up tight in plastic.

"How about a chocolate?" he says.

"You devil!" she cries, clapping her hands and grinning. "Oh and they're my favourite too. I didn't know we had these."

"I was saving them," he says. "Saving them for a

special occasion but then I forgot all about them. Just remembered now."

She briefly forgets the scatted timeline of the their life before her and takes the offered box. She carefully rips through the plastic by running her thumb nail down one of the seams and then opens the box like a chest of buried treasure.

"They all look delicious!" she says, her wide eyes scanning over the contents. "Which one would you like darling?" she asks without looking up.

"You're alright," he says, watching her sadly. "You have them."

"No, no," she says, pretending to chastise. "I couldn't possibly eat all of these myself. Here, you have the coffee one. You like the coffee ones and I can't stand them."

He takes the offered chocolate and slips it into his mouth. She picks one for herself and does the same, sitting back in her chair and closing her eyes to savour the flavour.

"Mmmmmm," she says through a mouthful. "They're so lovely."

The coffee chocolate sits in on his tongue while his stomach turns over below. He bites into it and tries not to gag as his mood makes the sugar taste foul. He leaves her to her rummaging which is now punctuated by occasional cries of joy as she takes another chocolate. He goes through to the kitchen.

He opens the cutlery drawer. The knives and forks they used for breakfast are there, filthy, covered in dried egg and saliva. He takes them out of drawer drops them into the sink, already filled with bubbles. He moves to the cupboard and opens it, retrieves the dirty plates from in there and adds them to the sink as well. In the oven a steak and kidney pie is cooking and there's veg boiling away on the hob.

Suddenly there's a knock at the back door, quiet but firm and insistent. He freezes wrist deep in soapy water, listening hard to see if she's noticed. There's silence from the front room and for a moment he fears she may have come to answer the door but then he hears her chuckle and mutter at yet another remembered joy.

The knock comes again, harder this time. Quickly he dries his hand and moves to the back door, glancing over his shoulder before opening it. Stood at the back step are two very large men with very grim faces.

"Did you get it?" he asks the taller one quietly, throwing another compulsive glance over his shoulder and down the hall.

"Here," says the man flatly, raising a white plastic carrier bag from his side but not handing it over.

"You know what I'm going to say," says the man. "You know what has to happen."

"I'm not having this conversation with you again," he says hotly, trying to make his voice sound hard like it used to.

"She's got to go," says the man, a hard ook on his face. "There's no other choice, it has to happen and this.." the man raises the plastic bag further and shakes it for emphasis. "This is not going to work."

"Just give it here!" he snaps reaching out for the bag. The man refuses to let go and they stare at one another for a moment. He pushes his shoulders back and juts out his chin a little, bluffing that there's still something hard an vicious inside him. Eventually the man shakes his head and releases the bag in disgust.

"I've spoken to someone," the man says. "A professional."

"What?!" he hisses. "You had no right to do that!"

"We have every right!" snaps the shorter-but-still-huge other man in return. "This can't go on. It's not her fault or anything but it's too late now, there's nothing else for it. She has to go."

"How dare you!" he hisses again, trying to maintain his anger that it might drown his fear. He feels the world shifting under him, feels the control slipping out of his hands. He's back on the stairs again, there isn't enough of him left to protect her.

"This person we've spoken to," the taller man continues. "They deal with this kind of thing all the time. They know how to do it..." he pauses, searching for the word. "Kindly," he settles on. "It has to happen, you know we're right. You can't deal with this yourself. She has to go."

"My wife is not going anywhere," he says quietly, as firmly as he can. "She's staying here with me and I will take care of it in my own way."

"Gave her the letter did you?" says the taller man with just a hint of scorn. "Luxury, all inclusive trip to Paris?"

"You what?!" says the shorter man, almost shouting his outrage.

"Will you keep you voice down!" he seethes at the shorter man, looking over his shoulder again before moving out onto the step and pulling the door to behind him. "She'll hear you!"

"This needs dealing with, now!" says the shorter man. "You can't be going on holiday! You can't run away from this!"

"They're not going anywhere," says the taller man calmly. "It's a con. He's tricking her, isn't that right? It's all part of it."

For the second time he feels heat burning in his cheeks but hopes desperately that they won't see the red in the dying light of the evening. He clings to his dignity and thinks of her as he pushes out his chest and grits his teeth.

"Thank you for this," he says coldly, referring to the plastic bag. "You can tell your professional that their services will not be required. I know you think I'm just a broken down old man but I assure you both, there is no power on god's green earth that could compel me to hand my wife over to a total stranger. I understand exactly what needs to be done, I am not in denial about this. I will take care of it in my own way, is that understood?"

The men look at one another then look at him. They shake their heads and leave without saying another word. He closes the door as quietly as he can then leans his head against it. He shakes all over until he thinks he may fall but grips the door handle until his knuckles turn white and the shaking passes.

His legs feel empty as he dodders back into the kitchen and hides the plastic bag under the sink. Straightening up he turns down the heat on the hobs and the oven then makes his way through to the dining room. She looks up as he enters, still smiling, eyes bright.

"Come and look at this!" she exclaims.

He lowers himself into his seat then sags like a string cut puppet. Her words wash over him distantly. He can feel his face making the appropriate expressions, even feel his throat squeezing out the right encouraging words but inside he feels dead. Done, finished and dead.

Amid the chaotic clutter that she has slow motion exploded out of the case, a single Yale lock key sits before him. His hand reaches out and picks it up absently, turning it back and forth slowly.

At one time the key had probably been vitally important, kept close on a keyring and the subject of incredible panic if lost. But now? Now he couldn't even remember what it had been for. It was not only useless now but he couldn't even provide evidence that it had ever been of use, that it had ever been anything but an irrelevant and pointless thing.

"Now look at this," she says, thrusting a faded, blurry photograph under his nose. "Do you remember?"

The photograph was her, a much younger her, beautiful and vibrant, bursting with life. She was sat on an old fashioned deck chair on a beach under a grey looking sky, holding a chubby toddler and pointing it towards the camera.

"That was when we took Deborah down to the seaside for the first time," she says. "It was three weeks after her second birthday. The weather was terrible but we didn't mind."

His hands fall into his lap, key and all. He feels his shoulders slump but she doesn't notice, doesn't stop.

"You drove us down there in that great big red car we had, do you remember? What kind of car was that?" she asks.

"That was the Ford," he hears himself reply.

"Thats right," she continues. "Deborah wore that little blue and white outfit my Auntie Marjorie got her on the journey down but of course she was sick all over it and we had to stop. That's why she's wearing the red outfit on the photo. Do you remember she was obsessed with the stuffed animal heads on the wall in the dining room at the hotel, kept asking about them. And the owners, his father used to be a gamekeeper for the local lord didn't he and he was the oldest of his four brothers so his father taught him to hunt when he was a boy and then..."

Her gentle, loving words wash over him like acid, each sentence stripping him down, closer and closer to his dry old bones. As he nods and grunts along with her he's driving the point of the key into his palm under the table and twisting it back and forth. A little secret white light of penitent pain, soaking up all the rest that he has to keep from her.

—    —

—

It's the middle of the night and she's sleeping soundly. He rises in silence, retrieves his glasses but not his teeth and slips from the room to the landing. He creeps down the stairs in the darkness, he doesn't need the lights on after all these years.

A cold and clammy sickness is biting at his gut as he heads straight through into the kitchen and takes the plastic bag out from under the sink. It rustles noisily as he frees the the first of its contents, laying it gingerly on the kitchen worktop.

It's a box of eggs which he opens, removes five and puts them into the bin. He places the almost empty egg box into the fridge then gathers up the bag and carries it through to the dining room.

Amid the gloom the clutter of the dining table melts into a single, ruffled grey mass. He sits down in her chair, locates the letter from this morning and pulls it out from under some photos.

Carefully he folds it then lays it to one side and takes a pen and a packet of new, white envelopes out of the plastic bag. He breaks the plastic and removes an envelope before carefully writing her name and their address on the front of it. He takes the folded letter, slips it into the envelope then spends almost two minutes summoning up the saliva to seal it.

He fishes back into the bag and comes up with a book of stamps. With great care he places a stamp on the front of the envelope and then stands. For a moment his heart races, his head feels so light it might float away.

After a moment more however he comes back to himself, gathers up the various postal items and the bag and crosses the room to the sideboard. He takes a small box of chocolates from the bag and hides it at the back of the cupboard. Finally he walks out into the hallway and up to the table. He places the envelopes and the stamps in the drawer then buries the letter underneath them all.

He disposes of the empty bag in the kitchen bin and then returns to the dining room. Over the next forty minutes he painstakingly packs all the clutter from the table back into the suitcase until finally closing it with a click. It takes him another twenty minutes to drag the suitcase all the way back upstairs to the second bedroom and heave it up onto the wardrobe.

His work complete he returns to their bedroom and slips back into bed beside her. He doesn't remove his glasses but instead takes a moment to watch her. In the heavy grey gloom he can see her there, perfectly still but snoring ever slightly just like she always did.

"I do miss you lass," he whispers, reaching out to touch her cheek but not daring to make contact for fear of disturbing her.

"Greg and Phil were round earlier you know," he continues. "They're good boys really. They're just doing what they think is best but don't you worry, I'm not going to let them take you. I won't let them put you in one of those places.

"You're going to stay right here with me lass, here where I can take care of you. And even though you don't know it, even though you're not there anymore, I promise.." he feels a tear running down his dry old cheek. "I promise that every single day will be filled with all your favourite surprises."

www.ingramcontent.com/pod-product-compliance
Lightning Source LLC
Chambersburg PA
CBHW051458030726

47592CB00006B/1993